Madeleine and Therese

HAZEL WARLAUMONT

Madeleine and Therese is a work of historical fiction. Apart from the well-known actual people, events, and locales that figure in the narrative, all names, characters, places, and incidents are the product of the author's imagination or are used fictitiously. Any resemblance to current events or locales, or to living persons, is entirely coincidental.

Cover photograph of Vionnet evening gowns by George Hoyningen-Heune. *Harper's Bazaar, 1936. Courtesy of R. J. Horst.*

A wingless horse heard a story one day
About a horse with wings
And flew away.

Charles Henri Ford
Ballade for Baudaire

One

SHE REMEMBERED IT well, the rain-splattered cobblestone street rue Montaigne just minutes from the home of Madeleine Vionnet, once the most celebrated yet reclusive fashion designer in Paris.

Stepping quickly and dodging puddles, she ran for cover under the awning of Café du Marché and watched the rain fall harder, beating like drums on the slanted metal roof and dripping onto the street below - and then it stopped and she waited, almost hesitant. She took a labored breath before looking up the street squinting to see as far as she could and then started on her journey, but then paused again to reconsider. Slim and imposing with square shoulders, wistful and dignified she stood there alone, her large brimmed hat pulled down over one eye, her coat buttoned at the top. Passersby took note.

Abruptly, she clutched her umbrella and dashed into the street braving the inclement weather. "Oh gads!" she whispered as she quickened her pace and swatted the last drops of rain from her face, half laughing at being caught in the rain, of all days. Lifting her hat just long enough to arrange her hair now streaked with steel gray, she took a long, silent breath of resolve. Up ahead the group huddled together, barely visible under the spectacle of colorful umbrellas as they waited for her in silence.

An open shutter banged against a window but otherwise the street was quiet unlike the way she remembered it between the wars - yet nothing in Paris was quite the way it was. Two world wars and cultural upheavals added some patina – although in a good way she thought, like everything else worth having or like a beauty that grows if allowed to age gracefully.

Fidgeting with her leather gloves, she walked slowly toward the group touching each finger like notes on a piano. The reporters looked impatient while standing on the corner like a group of school children waiting for a bus. *Hmm, is it too late to turn back?* She decided it was as a young man from the group looked up and glanced her way, the collar of his tawny raincoat pulled up. He tilted his umbrella to one side as he walked cautiously toward her.

"Are you Miss Bonney? We weren't sure who we'd be meeting, only that we should be here at three." She noticed the errant rain drops slide down his large plastic-rimmed glasses as he reached inside his raincoat for a notepad and pencil. He added quickly, "How long have you known her?" She stared for a moment and then raised her hand to motion the others to follow, and they dodged puddles together while walking toward Vionnet's elegant town house in the exclusive 16th arrondissement in Paris.

"A very long time," she said finally. "And yes, I'm Therese Bonney. Madeleine Vionnet and I met in 1919 and this is 1974, so 55 years I guess." She smiled cautiously as she shook the rain from her umbrella and led the group up the marbled stone steps. She was tall and her slender legs were all that was visible as her rain coat billowed behind her.

A young woman drenched from the rain caught up with her on the top step. "We heard you were lifelong confidants so I guess that's why we're meeting with you first," she said flapping the rain from her coat. "Would you mind if we asked you some questions?"

Therese avoided her stare. "I think Madame Vionnet will be the one answering the questions today," she said in a hushed voice as she stopped near the doorway to wait for the snapping and closing of umbrellas. She stepped to the front.

"Good afternoon, my name is Therese Bonney and I'll be introducing you to Madame Vionnet today." Her voice was soft, almost apologetic. "I'd like to ask you to please keep your questions brief and not too detailed; she's ninety-eight as you know, and you'll certainly find her full of spirit but she does tire easily." She made a point to look at each reporter. "Madame Vionnet rarely gives interviews; she . . . well, she seldom did in her life. We're here today because she wants to show her gratitude to the press for all the wonderful coverage your publications have given her fashions over the years. She smiled hoping to put herself and the reporters at ease. "So, come in please and you may leave your coats and umbrellas on the table by the door."

Once inside, her eyes followed the curvature of the room to the opening leading into Vionnet's private boudoir. The sight of Solange, Vionnet's nurse, was a relief and she relaxed her shoulders and sighed. The reporters stood speechless when they saw the art deco interior inside the belle époque mansion - a glorious reminder of Vionnet's era. The high walls were guardians of an impressive collection of art by Picasso, Dufy, Matisse, Lautrec, and other great artists of her time. Three lacquered bookcases and a grand piano filled part of the spacious room beyond where they stood, and the reporters jotted notes before Therese hesitantly led them into Vionnet's drawing room.

Unlike her robust image during the past century she now appeared frail at ninety-eight and looking lost in her comfortable day bed of fine French linens and soft fluffy pillows - yet still beautiful with her finely defined cheek bones and eyes the color of dark chestnuts now watery with age. Still, with all the softness in the room she still had the unmistakable aura of Vionnet, the steel-hard recluse who would stare you away if you got too close or scold if you asked too many questions. Even though the reporters were invited, a rare gesture on her part, she still radiated the stigma of unyielding strength; a sentry standing over her feelings and guarding her privacy.

"We won't get much from her today, no one has," a seasoned journalist from the *Paris Guardian* whispered to another. "It is amazing though to be here in her home and see her in person." The other reporter from the French newspaper *Le Figaro* nodded and leaned closer. "Maybe she's mellowed or has something to say at this point in her life. She might even mention the Nazi thing."

"Hmm . . . do you think?"

Motioning with her hand, bird-like and spotted with age, Vionnet invited the reporters into the room while asking Solange to bring a little vodka or water for them while they stood awkwardly at the foot of her day bed.

"Please, be comfortable, all of you. Sit if you like," Vionnet coaxed by pointing to the chairs lined up near the bed. One by one they sat, shuffling their feet or adjusting their notebooks, uncomfortably aware they were in the boudoir of the legendary Vionnet. "Surely you didn't come all this way without questions," she teased. Therese watched from across the room where she stood thumbing a button religiously on her coat. Solange whispered to her on the way to the kitchen, "Don't worry, she can take care of herself."

A few reporters ask about the items in her apartment, especially the original art and furniture from the 1920s and 1930s by some of the most famous early-century Parisian artists. Although frail, her voice had an uncanny strength. "You know, we bought art from Picasso and the others for just a few francs because it was our way of offering support and encouragement to the young artists who flocked to Paris in those days."

She paused to take a breath and then smiled. "Of course the artists didn't buy my gowns because unlike art in those days, the dresses were expensive and most artists were poor. I gave away some of my gowns and bartered with a few of the artists whose work I admired because their wives liked my dresses, so it seemed an even exchange." Her small shoulders rose while she took a labored breath but she seemed eager to go on. "I didn't promote my work as much as Therese and the others always wanted me to." She glanced coyly across the room. "I let people come to me if they wanted my designs. I didn't need the money. You know, the artists desperately needed money for food so they had to sell their work on the street and to friends. Therese knew them all, I didn't. I was more interested in making beautiful gowns than friends," she said with a mischievous grin.

A young reporter from the *New York Times* raised his finger to get her attention. "Your fame comes from the way you cut luxurious fabrics, your yards of silks and chiffons. It was the bias cut, I think it's called and was just the opposite of what other couturiers were doing. I read that you cut fabric not on the grain but at a forty-five-degree angle. So what was the purpose of the bias cut?"

"Ah, so you do know something about my work." She raised both arms half way in celebration and looked pleased. "Well, everyone made dresses that flowed in the same direction. I saw that if I turned the fabric at an angle, it gained elasticity that caused the fabric to hug the body and to follow the natural curves. It literally changes the silhouette of women's figures and reveals what's natural." She used her frail hands to illustrate the effect. "It was sexier and that look liberated women at a time when they wanted to be liberated, not just in fashion but in life." That brought a brief chuckle from the group.

"Was it as important to be sexy then as it is now?" one reporter asked.

"Oh my, what a question! When is it not important to be sexy and to be beautiful?" she said, her eyes lighting up. "And what is more sexy and beautiful than to show off a woman's body if tastefully done?" She paused and Solange handed her a small cup of water. She drank it slowly and then went on. "You know, clothes should be designed for the body as a sensuous structure, and draping fabric on it to enhance that structure is part of the look I gave to my fashions so that the body and the dress can become one."

"Why didn't all designers use the bias cut if it complemented the woman's body so much?" the woman from the *Paris Examiner* asked

"Well, you see they sketched their designs and you can't really rely on a sketch to predict the fall of fabric on the curves of the body. I've never drawn a dress design. Ever! I've always draped fabric onto the body to see where it falls. It's a beautiful experience to see how fabric and a woman's body embrace each other. And I should add that many designers did use the bias cut once they figured out how to do it, but most couldn't get the hang of it," she said with some measure of delight before continuing.

"Most designers were not interested in making women look sexy; they were out of touch with the free spirit of the times, especially Paris in the 1920s." She paused to catch her breath again. "It was a time to take chances and feel free. That's why wealthy rulers, and barons, and moguls brought their wives and mistresses to be fitted with my fashions. They couldn't find that sexy look from other designers who at the time were still using those awful bustles and frills to completely cover the body."

"Wow, you are ninety-eight, Madame Vionnet, yet you speak so knowledgeably and eloquently about this past century," a young woman in front acknowledged. "How do you keep your mind so sharp? Can you share your secrets?"

"Well, my dear, one must never share secrets," she said with a chuckle. "But fashion has been my life since I was a child working in an *atelier de misère* or sweatshop. It's always been a French woman's duty to uphold fashion in France so it's what I know and still love. The memories stay close so the mind stays clear." She catches Therese's eye and smiles.

"Getting back to your technique, isn't the bias cut the infamous body-clinging style worn by Hollywood starlets like Greta Garbo and Joan Crawford, and I think Jean Harlow?" a young woman from *Vogue* asked.

"Yes, they all wore my designs, even queens and countesses because they were very flattering. I worked to free the female body from the constrictions of those uncomfortable corsets, the brassiere, the puffy underskirts, and those dreaded metal supports! Can you imagine wearing those? The best support is the natural one – the muscle corset – which practically any woman can have by exercising. I don't mean some burdensome exercise like lifting weights, but something you like to do that makes you healthy and happy. It's important to be happy no matter what you're doing – or wearing."

An older reporter in the back rose slightly from his seat, "Have you been happy, Madame Vionnet, and exactly what is the nature of your relationship with Therese Bonney?"

Madeleine glanced at Therese who had been standing against the wall but at that moment stepped quickly into the middle of the room. "I think Madame Vionnet might be getting tired so we will stop. I hope you've all enjoyed this experience. We have a press kit . . ."

"Did you collaborate with the Nazis, Madame Vionnet?" The question came from the same reporter in the back.

The silence pierced the jovial decorum and everyone stretched to peek in back. Madeleine looked down and put her hand on the front of her pink robe pulling it tighter around her small shoulders before reaching for her glass of water. Therese stood in the middle of the room, the softness now gone from her face, her posture rigid. She whispered to Solange who was standing with her. "I was afraid of this. In the past Madeleine would have lashed out putting that reporter in his place." She moved closer to the bed and faced the reporters.

"As I was saying," she said with a sharp brittleness in her voice, "we have a press kit with photos and specific information about Madame Vionnet's career, along with some important dates that should help round out your notes." She shifted her weight and glanced toward the back of the room. The sound of the door closing caused everyone to look to the rear once more. "Solange will have the kits for you when you leave." She stood staring blankly at the group.

A few gathered their belongings while still straining toward the back. Some stood up and stretched on their gloves while others awkwardly rearranged their notebooks as if there was something yet to come. It was clear they wanted more from Vionnet, reclusive all her life, probably the single most important fashion designer in France whose life was shrouded in mystery and whose story would probably never be told. Before leaving, most took a moment to say something generous, some taking her hand, others bowing politely. As usual, she showed little emotion but thanked them for coming and for their interest in her work.

The reporters walked out onto the street, some rushing to get taxis. The two journalists who chatted earlier lingered. "Well, was she confused at the end or reluctant to answer the questions?"

"I suppose we'll never know, will we? Did we really expect more?" They shrugged before following the others toward the taxi queue.

Solange straightened up the room and put the chairs back in place, and Therese filled the water pitcher on the table near the bed. When the room was quiet, Madeleine motioned Therese to sit next to her on the bed. "Did I answer all their questions, Therese? Did I give them enough?"

Therese took Madeleine's hand. "You had a chance to talk about the past," Therese whispered. "Isn't that why you invited them here?"

Madeleine stared into the empty room. They sat quietly while Therese studied her face seeing only a door opening into darkness. Therese knew that Madeleine's thoughts were often private. It was a lesson she'd learned long ago.

"Well, you were perfect, Madeleine," Therese said squeezing her hand gently. "As always, you were just perfect." They sat in silence but Therese continued to study her face.

TWO

PARIS DURING THE turn of the century was still unknown to a young child living just outside the city in the small community of Chileurs-aux-Bois. The child's father, Abel Vionnet, was a toll collector originally from the rugged Jura mountain area near Switzerland and her mother, a homemaker. Young Madeleine loved to hear her robust father tell stories about the Jura region and the hard working but proud lifestyle of the people, and he clearly took great pride in his ancestry, making the stories particularly adventurous to please his young daughter. At age three she didn't understand the stories although she did love watching her father bellow and gesture nevertheless.

One day he told her a different type of story about a mother who left her family. Madeleine was too young to understand why this story was different or why her father looked so melancholy. She never saw her mother after that so she supposed the story was true. Every morning though she would look into her mother and father's bedroom. The only nice thing they ever owned was a bedspread of soft and shiny material that her mother always arranged meticulously neat, smoothing it like a fine handkerchief while spreading it over the cheap lumpy mattress. Madeleine remembered how her mother tucked in the edges, making sure they were straight and how she'd stuff the pillows underneath to give it a plush look, then a little pull or tug here and there to make it perfect.

After her mother left, her father tossed the spread haphazardly over the lumpy bed leaving it to fall uneven with portions of the flannel sheets carelessly showing at one end or the other. Like a religious ritual, Madeleine went to the bedroom several times a day to look at the spread to see if it had been neatened. If so, she knew her mother had returned.

But sadly, all she ever saw much to her disappointment was the spread in a disheveled heap.

"How would you like to go live with Grandma in the mountains?" her father asked her one day. "You'd like it there and you can play outdoors."

"No Papa, I want to stay here with you."

"I have to work, Madeleine, and there's no one to take care of you." So against his daughter's wishes he sent Madeleine anyway only to find that her grandmother took little interest and Madeleine suffered from an assortment of maladies and sickly spells. Every week her grandmother sent the same note to Abel:

Come get Madeleine, I can no longer keep her well. I have her bag packed. Come soon!

Finally her father fetched her back and did the best he could to manage his job and his daughter.

"What's the matter Papa?" she would ask when he was exhausted from worry. Normally a hearty man, he had not only lost weight but the spark she remembered seeing in his eyes.

"How'd you like to start school early, Madeleine? I know you're not old enough but the school said you were curious and can probably do the work."

"I want to stay here with you, Papa."

"I have to work, Madeleine. You'll like school and we can talk about it every day when I get home."

"Will I have to go away again?"

"No, no, the school is here. Near our house."

"Oh, okay, but I don't want to go away like before."

So, Madeleine started school early and even though the curriculum was rigorous, she advanced and excelled over the years, eventually telling her father she wanted to become a teacher someday.

But the wife of Abel Vionnet's groundskeeper, a long-time dressmaker named Mme. Broussard, convinced Abel that Madeleine would never earn a living as a teacher and would continue to be a financial burden.

"I'll take her off your hands as a favor to you, Abel. She can work in my dress shop. She'll have to stay at the shop with the others though to be available when I need her."

When Madeleine heard the news that she would be sent away once again, leaving both school and her father, she was inconsolable.

"You promised," she said in between heart-wrenching sobs. "You said you wouldn't send me away again. Please Papa, I'll do everything you say. I'll work hard and make money soon, you'll see. Please, Papa, please let me stay."

Abel Vionnet just shrugged his shoulders saying it would be a good opportunity for her to work in a dressmaker's shop. So at the age of ten her father obtained permission for her to leave school at midterm to become an apprentice to the dressmaker, Mme. Broussard.

The term *atelier de misère* or "sweatshop" was often used to describe the negative aspects of the tailoring trade and Abel Vionnet had read about such establishments but didn't fully understand what they were, only that they were something to avoid. He read that women and children who were forced into needlework were pressured to work as fast as they could, often ending up with deformed hands and fingers.

"No, no, Abel, that will not be the case with Madeleine," Mme. Broussard assured him. "She will advance very quickly. She can start out as a needleworker stitching simple work like trim and fringe, and soon a seamstress where she can work on entire garments and be paid by the piece. She will make a good living, Able, I assure you. It's possible to advance to a dressmaker and a premier after that, almost at the top of the profession. Of course, she will never be a designer or couturier since only men advance to those positions - but don't worry Able, she will make a very good living."

Madeleine worked sixteen hours a day in a hot and cramped room often by candlelight, and at night she slept on a cot in a crowded hallway with the others laborers. In spite of Mme. Broussard's promises, she refused to advance Madeleine beyond an *arpette* or pin-picker, crawling about on the floor picking up dropped pins. Mme. Broussard was a stout woman with her hair wrapped in a tight bun and a perpetual scowl on her face. But nevertheless, Abel Vionnet gathered up his courage and complained, standing as firm as he could for a man weakened and overburdened. After some thought, she agreed to elevate Madeleine to a

Madeleine and Therese

needleworker and paid her one-half franc a day or the equivalent of seven cents. It was hard work and her hands cramped up after several hours of stitching, but if she stopped or her work was not perfect, Mme. Broussard whacked her hands with a long wooden stick.

"*Maintenir à la vertical*," Mme. Broussard would yell. "Keep it straight." Madeleine tried to hold back the tears but they flowed anyway, and she took advantage of those whacks to stop for a few minutes, shaking and stretching her arms and hands while sobbing.

In spite of her incarceration, Madeleine was surprisingly good at what she did. She liked working with fabric and turning it into something practical, especially when she could work on dresses and not just hand-sew fringe.

"I'd like to use the stitching machine, Madame Broussard. Can I please? I know I can learn it." After asking several times she was allowed but she struggled. The bulky dresses of the era with yards of heavy material and bustles and frills were a challenge to lift, especially for a small child.

In the evenings by a dim light she continued to study everything she could. Her father often arrived for visits carrying armloads of books, old newspapers and magazines probably to ease his guilt, and even at this young age she was learning about the world as it approached the turn of the century. She especially liked reading that women were finding a voice and becoming politically, professionally, and emotionally aware, although she didn't quite know what all that meant. *I wonder if Mama left home to become a "new women," or was it something I did?*

Every day she methodically recounted everything she could remember about the days leading up the bumpy spread to see if she had done something so wrong as to make her mother leave. Then she would go through the same process again to see if she could figure out why her father kept sending her away.

The years passed and still she found no answers.

Three

ON THE OTHER side of the Atlantic in Syracuse, New York, two young children scurried about the yard laughing and chasing a rubber ball, kicking it high over the wobbly wooden fence much to their delight. They'd run beyond the gate to find it, teasing each other before retrieving the ball and racing back before they got caught – since they weren't supposed to leave the yard but that made the game more exciting. When Louise, the older child, found the ball she always ran back into the yard to avoid trouble, fearing her grandmother might be watching from the kitchen window. The younger child, Therese, was insatiably curious at the age of six and couldn't wait to see what was on the other side of the fence. At Louise's urging she would usually come back, although sometimes reluctantly. That afternoon, an object in the street caught her attention and her focus shifted to the new-found treasure. It was nothing but a small piece of metal from a horse and buggy rig but its shape and shiny finish fascinated her.

"Hurry Therese, before Grandma catches you. Run fast, really fast." Louise held the gate open but Therese sat near the street in her little pinafore and high stockings looking at the object.

Their paternal grandmother cared for them during the day since Addie and Anthony Bonney both worked, Anthony as an electrician and Addie as a bank clerk and bookkeeper in downtown Syracuse. When the grandmother was short of patience she expressed her frustration in French, her own native language before coming to America. It fell on deaf ears because no one in the family understood French, least of all the children.

"Therese, come through the gate," Louise yelled from the yard that afternoon. "Quick, before Grandma comes out. Come now, hurry." But when the screen door creaked and flew open, Louise fell silent. Their grandmother stormed from the yard switch in hand. Still sitting on the curb, Therese first felt the swift sting on her back and then on her bare legs as she ran for the house. Her grandmother soon followed, yelling in French all the way back through the open gate. Therese didn't like the punishment, but she did like hearing the sound of her grandmother speaking French and she too wanted to speak French one day too, but without screaming it.

The punishment usually didn't end with the grandmother. When the children's father arrived home, always in a bad mood or it seemed to Therese, he would ask about the day as usual. Upon hearing of the girls' misdeeds, as innocent as they were, there was more whipping, yelling, and haranguing into the night. Therese took the brunt of his anger. Her mother and even her grandmother tried to intervene in the beatings but his fanatical rampages apparently had to run their course at Therese's expense. Her mother stood by helpless, wiping her hands on her apron and bunching it up in her hands with the look of horror on her face.

Therese said to Louise late one night, "Why does he get so mad? We were just playing a game. I can see why Grandma got mad and whipped me, but why does he have to whip me all over again? I don't think he likes me." Louise held her and they huddled close together in the room they shared.

"Shush, he's just mean, Therese."

Her father's behavior continued to confuse her and it seemed she could do nothing right as far as he was concerned. The beatings continued even when she didn't leave the yard.

"This has to stop," she remembered her mother saying one night to her father. "You need to deal with your own inadequacies instead of taking them out on the family." Therese didn't understand what that meant but she did remember that was night he turned on her mother, grabbing her by the throat until her face changed color.

The year that followed and after she had put aside enough left-over grocery money, Addie Bonney bought an old brown cardboard suitcase covered with travel stickers and took the girls by train from Syracuse to Oakland, California - the end of the line - to live without the father. In 1901 work was scarce, especially for a woman, so she took in ironing, cleaned houses, and did whatever she could to get by; still, food was often milk toast and scraps from the previous day. The girls, ages seven and nine, were enrolled in school immediately not only so they could learn but because school lunches were free.

"Eat everything, don't throw away any food," Addie would say each day as she braided their hair and smoothed their dresses. After school they stayed alone in the boarding house where they lived, wondering when their mother would be home or if their father might arrive soon, but he never did.

Therese jumped with joy when her mother took in ironing or worked from home, and she followed her at every step. When her mother had a job sewing sequins on women's blouses, Therese watched her mother separate the tiny orbs by color putting them into tea cups. The small shiny ornamental discs sparkled in luminous colors of reds, purples, and greens and her mother, sensing Therese's interest, let her help.

"Okay, now a blue one," her mother would say and Therese would delve her small plucky fingers into the appropriate cup and retrieve a shiny blue sequin. Unfortunately, most of her mother's work was not that pleasant or from home, so when her mother reached for her coat in the morning, Therese knew it would be another long day.

"Where's Papa?" the girls asked regularly, but Addie just hugged them, saying something vague that neither understood and he was never mentioned or seen. Therese thought about it even when she was a little older and tried to talk to her mother on several occasions, but there was never an answer that seemed clear. Therese always thought it was something she had done that separated them, like kicking the ball over the fence.

"It's my fault. He didn't like me," she would tell Louise on occasion.

"No, Therese, he was just mean."

Therese's intense curiosity earned her high marks throughout her school years in California and her list of accomplishments was long, even though her list of friends was not. With no money for college Therese took on janitorial work, sweeping and scrubbing the school stairs to pay the tuition at a small Catholic college near home before going on to the University of California, Berkeley to study languages and French theater.

Her wary approach to adulthood was defined by her studies and work, and not much else.

"Therese, find some friends and go out and have fun," her mother would urge. "I don't know what's the matter with you. Why not do things like other girls your age?"

Therese just rolled her eyes. "I don't know how to be like them. Besides, they tease me because I get A's on my papers and they just laugh when I try to join in."

So while her classmates planned weddings and careers, Therese had already decided to pursue a master's degree at Harvard and then doctoral studies at Columbia University in New York, a very unusual move for a young woman in 1918. Her mother tried to dissuade her but to no avail. Even her sister was puzzled.

"Don't you want to get married?" Louise asked repeatedly. "That's better than sitting in dull classes every day. I want to get married and be happy."

"I just don't find the classes dull, Louise. Really, I don't. They're interesting to me. Besides, I don't know how to do anything else. The other students never talk about anything interesting, just parties and clothes. I guess I'm just an odd ball."

"Well, you were always more curious, and braver too," Louise said.

Therese laughed. "You don't have to be brave to like college, Louise, really you don't."

Attending Columbia University in New York City was an awakening of her senses long dulled from endless nights of studies and a rigorous schedule of classes. So, at twenty-four she found the excitement and urban energy a welcome break. Generally, she refused invitations from classmates to go out. She felt self-conscious around other people her age, or around anyone for that matter. *I find the other students boring*, she wrote her mother. *I'm not like them and I have different interests; and, I don't mind being alone. There's so much to learn.*

Several young men pursued her. She was tall and slim with dark wavy hair and sensuous green eyes that seemed effervescent against her pale skin. One young man in particular, Jacob, waited each day after their philosophy class.

"Hey, Therese, time for a coffee break?"

She didn't like making excuses but she did. "Oh, sorry, Jacob, I have something I need to do, but thanks." She rushed off to explore the wonderful libraries in Manhattan although she didn't tell him that.

She often walked through the colorful New York neighborhoods when she had the time, and liked hearing the cadence of horse-drawn carriages and young boys shouting the latest news on busy street corners. Seeing an occasional motor car was also an exciting sight although the horses whinnied with displeasure at having to share the road with something so noisy. One October afternoon while walking on the upper west side, she noticed a flyer announcing a new French theater company, *Theatre du Vieux Colombier*, opening in the neighborhood. She stopped by that day and could hear the company rehearsing.

"Do you mind if I watch?" she said to the young man at the door. When he shrugged she eased into the second row and sat down in the dimly-lit theater. A few glanced her way but no one protested so she settled in.

Stopping by rehearsals became part of her regular routine and in time she got to know the director and actors, even chatting with them during their break about French playwrights.

"How do you know so much about French theater," the director asked her one afternoon.

"It's my area of study, along with languages," she said shrugging. "Besides I like anything French."

He turned to the others. "Did you hear that? Here we are struggling with translations and interpreting set designs and we have an expert in our midst. I'm Carl, by the way," and he put out his hand. "Can you help us?" he asked.

She blushed. "Oh, well of course."

She threw herself into the small theater company's routine with a passion, and wrote to her mother:

I'm helping with French translations, interpretations, and sometimes even stage design, and I've also taken on the job of promoting the productions, teaching myself how to write press releases and having them published! I think I've finally found people I enjoy.

The company often met in cafes after performances and insisted she join in, and she was eager to do so. She felt comfortable with them since they had a shared interest in French theater.

"So Therese, why all this passion for French theater?" Albert was one of the actors in the current play but his interests went beyond acting. He engaged Therese in conversations about the ironies of translations and anything else to get her attention. He confided to Carl that he found her fabulously attractive but elusive, and invited her out on several occasions but her usual reply was that she was busy with her classes.

"Do you always have to be learning something?"

Anna, one of the founders of the group, overheard the conversation. "Oh, stop it, Albert. She's not going out with you so leave her alone." The others cheered, playfully teasing Albert who didn't seemed to mind.

Therese helped Anna with costumes, rummaging around the city soliciting clothes for the productions and they regularly sorted through the clothes and kept what couldn't be used. They struggled financially so were always thrilled to have clothes of any kind even if none of them matched. They laughed at each other as they wore mismatched outfits without feeling self-conscious, wrapping scarves around their skirts for added warmth and wearing neck ties instead of necklaces. When Therese came in one afternoon wearing a pair of loose-fitting men's trousers, Alec, one of the actors, lamented, "Attractive girls can get away with anything."

Later that year, at the urging of her new friends and because of her expertise in French theater, Therese compiled a list of important French playwrights and their work which she annotated and published under the name of T. Bonney, knowing the stigma of trying to get published as a woman. On the set one afternoon during rehearsals, a stage hand brought a telegram addressed to her.

"Oh, for me? I don't know anyone who sends telegrams."

"Well, you do now. It says T. Bonney. See, right here."

She slipped the tissue-thin paper message from the yellow envelope. In neatly pasted strips of type it read:

Familiar with your annotation and work in New York. Would you come to Paris to work as a translator for the Sarah Bernhardt French Repertory? S.B.
April 20, 1918, Paris.

She sat down on the stage steps and put her hand over her mouth, her eyes wide and her heart beating wildly.

"Bad news?" one of the actors said, walking over and putting his hand on her shoulder.

"They want me to go to Paris to translate for Sarah Bernhardt's theater," she said looking up at him. "Look, this came from Sarah Bernhardt herself! To Paris, can you imagine that?" She read the telegram word for word again, out loud this time while standing up on the stage. The actors applauded, and teasingly asked her to read it louder. They gathered around her, some coming over to look at the telegram, but all to share her excitement.

When the lights went out after rehearsals that afternoon, she sat in the darkened theater holding the short telegram trying to imagine what it meant. *Can I really do this? I don't know what they'll expect of me; after all, I'm just a student. But Paris!* She was eager to tell her mother and vowed to call her immediately when she got home. Her first stop however, was to meet with her doctoral adviser at Columbia University and she practically ran there after leaving the theater.

Sitting across from Professor Agasty at his large desk, she rambled incoherently about her plans and that she wanted to finish her doctorate at the Sorbonne in Paris since she would be living there and asked for his help in applying. She could barely get the words out in any order. He sat listening and first lowered his spectacles further down his nose to look at her, then took them off.

"My dear, the Sorbonne is for renowned male scholars seeking doctorates, not for women." He waited for her to leave and then put his glasses on and busied himself at his desk.

With her hand on the doorknob, she paused and turned, "Is that really true? Just for men?"

Before leaving for Paris the following month she wrote to her mother, "Expect to like Paris – do already." While she didn't know it at the time, Paris would become her home for the next fifty-five years, and it began by being accepted into the doctoral program at the Sorbonne.

Four

THE YEARS PASSED slowly for Madeleine as she continued the brutal sixteen-hour days in Mme. Broussard's sweat shop at one-half franc a day. The hand-whacking didn't stop even though she mastered the work and in spite of her father's protests to Mme. Broussard. He felt Madeleine's frustration but could be of little help.

One day Abel Vionnet overheard someone at work talking about a friend who had been looking for a wife. He thought about it and decided he wanted to meet the man. He discovered to his pleasure that the man worked for the city and therefore probably made a reasonable salary. He was ten years older than Madeleine, who at sixteen had made no mention of boys but probably because she hadn't had time to meet any, her father surmised. So one evening he talked to her about marriage as a solution to her dilemma.

"You'll be taken care of and can stay home, Madeleine. You'll be rid of the sweatshop forever."

"But Papa I'm only sixteen and I don't want to be married," she protested. "Besides, I don't even know this man."

Nevertheless, at her father's urging she ultimately married the stranger in an arranged civil ceremony without ever having met him. Marrying off a daughter was not unheard of; in fact, it was often part of a parent's responsibility to find a suitable husband for a daughter. To her father's disappointment however, the city worker couldn't support Madeleine after all and insisted she continue working. Mme. Broussard would only agree if Madeleine continued to live on the premises as was the custom, and be available when needed.

"Please, Madame Broussard, be reasonable. How can my Madeleine participate in a marriage if she's not there? Don't you see?" But Mme. Broussard stomped her foot and folded her arms and he knew the matter was settled.

Madeleine's new husband picked her up after her sixteen-hour shifts and took her to his rooming house. When he was finished with her he took her back, sometimes with bruises. She felt sick and trapped, even more so than before. She was plagued with panic attacks and lost weight until the last vestiges of color faded from her cheeks. The sudden horror of her life, her mistreatment caused her to withdraw, to disconnect, and fall into depression. For her father, he could only bury his face in his hands and say it could be worse.

At her father's insistence with Mme. Broussard, Madeleine was allowed a half day off each week to spend time with him. On those days he took her to Paris by carriage and urged her to walk around the city, look in store windows, and breathe in the fresh air while he did errands. But mostly she sat in a daze, sometimes in a park or on a bench, unresponsive to life around her.

During a rain storm one afternoon, she took shelter against a store front on rue de la Paix, a busy shopping street in the fashionable 2nd arrondissement. Huddled against the building with her shawl pulled tight, she peered in the shop window. The room inside was spacious and much to her surprise several women sat sewing dresses at large tables. In the back, rolls of luxurious fabric in beautiful colors and silky textures were lined up against the walls. She leaned in closer and put both hands on the glass feeling the coolness against her fingers. She pushed her face close almost touching the window. Bobbins of thread the colors of rainbows were stacked neatly three deep on shelves, and the entire room was clean. She could almost smell the fabric, unlike the stinking drudge of Mme Broussard's sweatshop.

As she stepped back she saw the sign on the door: *House of Vincent, Maison de Couture*. She'd heard there were places where fine women went to be fitted with dresses made especially for them but she'd never seen one. *This is not a sweatshop, it's a real house of fashion!* She put her hands to her cheeks in disbelief. The seamstresses sat in chairs with plush cushions, working at tables where they could spread the fabric rather than lifting it from the floor. *Chairs with cushions!* She could hardly imagine working in such comfort. When the rain stopped she walked down the

Madeleine and Therese

street and then back. Spreading her fingers wide on the window glass again she pressed her face so close she could see the residue of her breath on the pane. She watched the women work, laughing and talking at times, and hanging up beautifully-made dresses on cloth-lined hangers. She turned and walked up rue de la Paix again and then sat on the curb. A passing carriage driver glanced at her curiously. A moment later she rushed back to look one more time.

She took a long breath and knocked quickly, pressing her dress flat with her hands and tossing her hair away from her face. A tall man with slate-gray hair and soft eyes appeared when the door opened. She gulped. He wore a velvet pin cushion over the cuff of his crisp white shirt and a measuring tape draped over his arm. He held a piece of ivory-colored satin in his hand. She looked past him to see if he was fitting someone. "Can we help you, mademoiselle?" he said looking down at her. She stood motionless, speechless. He waited and then asked again.

She blinked several times and sucked in a breath, actually a gasp. "I'd like . . . I would like to work here as a seamstress. You see, I've been an apprentice needleworker and I know I'm ready to advance. I know I am, really." Her small voice trembled and she talked faster than usual. "I've been a needleworker since I was eleven."

At her age she was still petite, so she added quickly, "Now that I'm older, well sixteen, I'm ready for more challenging work." She felt her legs go weak but stood erect, keeping her gaze steady. She blinked quickly to hold back the tears.

The proprietor, Vincent, had seen dozens of waifs from the sweatshops begging for work but this one seemed different, he thought. She stood on the walkway outside the door, her back straight, her chin rigid, her arms pulled tight against her sides like a small soldier. He wanted to chuckle but instead focused on her unwavering stare in spite of her obvious fright. A minute passed. "I see," he said easing into a smile. "Well, come in and let us talk about this . . . this advancement, as you put it."

"Papa, Papa, I'm a seamstress, a real seamstress and the chairs have cushions and there's lots of room and I will be paid enough to get a room in Paris and I won't have to sleep in the hall or work for Madame Broussard or be married anymore." Her father, stunned, stood on the corner and listened to every word as she ran toward him out of breath.

"But Madeleine, we need to talk to Madame Broussard about this. After all, she's been doing us a favor by taking you in, and you can't just leave without making sure she doesn't need you. I mean, what if this doesn't work out. And what about your husband? He might be able to support you one day."

Madeleine looked away and felt the life leaving her small frame as she stood on the corner with her father. The clamber of horse-drawn carriages in the street became faint and she watched several children playing on a grassy knoll in a park until they became blurry. She wiped her eyes with her palms before turning toward her father. "No, I don't need to talk to Madame Broussard or that man first. I am leaving, Papa, I'm a seamstress now." She felt the cobblestones solid beneath her feet.

In just two short years she advanced to a première at the House of Vincent under the tutelage and kindness of Vincent himself, and reached the top in the salon second in hierarchy only to him. As a première she specialized in the physics of clothing – the pull of gravity, the resistance of cloth, the friction, the cut, and Vincent watched her flourish. Her insatiable curiosity brought him pleasure as a teacher and a mentor. Word soon spread of this new ingénue with a flair for fabrics and design, and already she was getting offers from some of the most prestigious houses in Paris.

Her one disadvantage was working with the English-speaking clientele, of which there were many, because she only spoke French. With Vincent's blessing she accepted a temporary position in London for two months in order to learn the language and get more experience.

"Are you certain it's alright, Vincent? I don't want to leave if you need me. You've been everything to me. You've taught me skills, advanced me to the top . . ."

"Hush, you need to move on Madeleine, learn some English and work with another house of fashion to see what that's like. You work hard and your ideas are revolutionary in fashion, and you'll soon see that you won't be happy until you can design your own clothes. You've brought in the customers and I'm so grateful. Look up Kate Riley, a London fashion house on Dover Street. I have a letter of introduction that should get you a position in her salon if you decide to stay in London. It could be a stepping stone for you."

And, it was. Her five years in London was a growing-up experience that polished her skills and cemented her resolve to be a designer, a real couturier. But she wrote to Vincent:

I want to come back to Paris, the center of fashion, and plan to return in time for the 1900 Exposition Universelle where all the major fashion houses will be displaying their work.

And when she did, she was most impressed when she saw the fashions from the *House of Callot Soeurs* and the four Callot sisters. It was uncommon to have female fashion designers, so she sought out a job with the Callot sisters knowing she could learn something from them not only about fashion - but how to succeed as a woman in a man's profession.

She found the Callot sisters to be exceptional designers but not dressmakers. She had the advantage of working as a seamstress and dressmaker so she understood about design and fabric and how the two worked together. One of the sisters, Marie Gerber, was a perfectionist and she and Madeleine worked well together and became friends. Madeleine translated Marie's ideas into patterns and supervised the seamstresses, but her goal was still to design. So when she received an offer from Jacques Doucet to create her own designs in his salon, it was the opportunity she had been waiting for.

"Madeleine, you're already known for being fabric-savvy," Marie told her. "Doucet wants to capitalize on your reputation to build his own business while giving you a chance to design your own line of fashions. You couldn't ask for a better offer!"

Madeleine's first designs with the House of Doucet eliminated the yards of heavy fabric, tight corsets, and wire undergarments, replacing them all with silky, sexy gowns exposing every nook and curve on a woman's body. The employees in Doucet's salon were appalled. "Blasphemous!" one associate complained. Another threatened to call the authorities. The vendeuses, or sales women, refused to show her gowns to clients and at her first public showing, protesters and pickets lined the street and people demanded she be arrested for public lewdness. "It's disgusting to expose the body like that," one lamented. Jacques Doucet reluctantly complained, "Your designs are not helping my business, Madeleine, or my reputation!"

Madeleine could only shake her head. "I need my own shop," she confided to Marie Gerber over lunch. "I'll never get anywhere working for others. They say my designs are scandalous but I see them as liberating. Isn't it time for a change, for something new and exciting?"

"The new and exciting part, yes. Is it time for a change? I don't know," Marie said. "I think we make change by creating it rather than waiting for the need. That's what *haute couture* or high fashion should be doing. It's breaking through the ordinary for something extraordinary. Sometimes we have to push hard to do that. You have the courage, Madeleine, whereas the rest of us don't. We care about sales but you care about creating beauty and liberating women."

"Well, I also have to be mindful of sales. I worked too long in a sweatshop to want to go back if I fail."

Marie took her hand. "We'd never let that happen. You can work for us any time you want. But I do think Jacques Doucet's salon is not progressive enough for you. Open your own salon, Madeleine. You'll never know if your designs will be a success unless you try."

With money she'd saved, Madeleine soon opened the modest *House of Vionnet*, a small boutique salon at 222 rue de Rivoli so she could be "shocking without losing my job," as she put it. The year was 1912; unfortunately not a good time for opening a new business. By the time it was stocked with fabric and thread, and she was turning out beautiful gowns selling faster than she could make them, World War I or the "Great War" as it came to be called, forced small businesses in Paris to close as people fled the city. She had no choice but to wait out the war in Rome, building her courage and her arsenal of designs. She came back even more committed to freeing women through fashion, even if it meant shocking her critics all over again.

Five

PARIS REJOICED WITH excitement and energy after World War I and like everyone else, Madeleine was relieved to find the city had been saved during the war except for minor shelling. Once more, the curious flocked to the city finding it more compelling than ever. For Therese Bonney, being in Paris for the first time excited her beyond her wildest expectations. Her entry into the Sorbonne completed the picture. She was one of the few Americans ever to attend, and certainly one of the first American women to enter the doctoral program at the prestigious university. She sent a note to her advisor, Professor Agasty, at Columbia University.

You must have been ill-advised since I was indeed accepted for graduate studies at the Sorbonne. Therese Bonney

She couldn't wait to send it. *For male scholars only? That pompous ass!*

Aside from her studies at the Sorbonne, her work as a translator for the Sarah Bernhardt Theater fulfilled a dream of hers. She worked with translations and French theater under the guidance of Sarah Bernhardt herself. But more than that, she discovered opportunities galore for a young ambitious American woman in Paris by doing volunteer work for the National Catholic War Council and the International Red Cross, since both worked to expand relations between France and America. She even wrote a few articles on the Parisian lifestyle and had them published under the name of T. Bonney in American magazines. To help pay for her tuition and rent, she translated the captions of the first American movies to be shown in Paris and tutored undergraduate students at the Sorbonne. Hardly a day passed that she didn't look for odd jobs to pay for expenses.

The large study halls at the Sorbonne harbored the noisy masses of students so if the weather was nice she read in the park. On dark gloomy days she studied in cafes rather than in her cramped living quarters – a tiny studio apartment with only one window and no closet in Saint Germain des Prés. Quite often she walked to the Café Les Deux Magots since it was nearby and the aroma of coffee offset the chill of fall in the air. That fall day in particular was lovely with its colors of golden yellow and spice as tree leaves teetered on the verge of dropping. Café Les Deux Magots had a reputation as a rendezvous for the literary and intellectual élite in Paris so she studied not only her textbooks but the people as well.

She didn't quite expect that they would be studying her as well. Still relying on her wardrobe of theater rejects, she had a way of combining her clothes into an exotic bohemian style that was striking, along with her youthful beauty. The odd hats she wore added the final touch of eccentric flair, quite the opposite of how she perceived herself. In her mind, her style was one of desperation not choice. Money went for tuition and food, not for clothes, she once told her sister Louise.

One afternoon a middle-aged gentleman who'd been watching her, approached her table at the busy café. "Pardon, Mademoiselle. If I may, excuse me, please. I think you must be an American, am I right? I see you with your books in the afternoons and . . ."

"Yes. I come here to study." She looked up from her book a bit surprised.

"May I sit, Mademoiselle?" His thinning hair was windblown and over his ears, but his eyes steady; even kind. He sat without waiting for an answer. "I like blue. Most of my paintings are in blues and other happy colors. I noticed you because of your blue scarf but mostly because you have a Mona Lisa aura about you."

"A Mona Lisa aura? What does that mean exactly?" She pulled her book toward her in case she decided to leave. He watched her. Her hands were delicate and resting on the table.

"Ah, well it means that not everything is visible . . . there's much behind the smile." He leaned forward a little waiting for her reaction.

She hesitated. Talking with a stranger made her a bit uncomfortable but he had a vulnerability that made her feel safe. And, they were in a café so she thought there would be no harm.

Madeleine and Therese

"Can't that be said for everyone," she said. "Isn't there always much behind the smile?"

"Ah, perhaps, but some people are all out front with nothing left behind, or inside I should say."

"And what is it you want to see when you look at someone?" She put a marker in her book

"I think it's not what there is, but what there is not. That's the fascination. I'm Raoul by the way." He smiled.

"I'm Therese. Do you live and paint here in Paris?"

"Ah yes, although I am from Le Havre originally. I came here to study at the Ecole des Beaux-Arts. I paint but I also do designs for a textile company and do some ceramics and tapestries. But painting is what I like best. Are you a student here?"

"I study at the Sorbonne, French theater and languages, and I do some work here in Paris to pay for my tuition." She watched his face. It was expressive. He moved his eyebrows and nodded while he listened. "I've barely arrived so I'm getting to know my way around." She smiled and shrugged her shoulders, feeling a little embarrassed telling that to a stranger.

"Well, certainly you've been to Gertrude Stein's salons and met some of the artists and writers, no? Many of them are Americans."

"No, actually, I haven't."

"But Gertrude Stein is American and you must meet her. When you meet Gertrude Stein you meet Paris and every soul in it, at least the lost souls who come for the creative energy. Let me invite you to her salon tomorrow night. I can meet you there and introduce you to some of the people."

She reached for her hat. "I'm not quite sure what you want from me. I'm . . ."

"No, no, no" he said sitting back in his chair laughing. "My wife would have my head if she thought I was trying to meet young ladies in a café. What I want is to paint you, and mind you I generally don't do portraits, I'm more into landscapes and odd things like horse races, regattas, parades – anything with action and color. But you have an interesting quality, aside from being very attractive, of course, if I may say. I like the way you dress and your nervousness when being approached by a stranger. Even now, your eyes are darting back and forth and you keep reaching for your book or your hat. It makes you vulnerable. I would like to see if I can capture that quality on canvas."

He watched her expression but it didn't change; she just listened. "I can't pay you but I can give you one of my paintings if you'd like. And, I can introduce you to a Paris you might be missing," he said to tempt her. "It's the people that make the city not the other way around. Besides, I don't know very many intellectuals and you can introduce me to your way of life as well. We will be friends, no?"

"Tomorrow night?" She drummed a finger softly on the metal bistro table. "Ok, why not? Can you write the address on a piece of paper?" She pushed her notebook toward him.

He scribbled on the notepad and stood with a slight bow. "*Au revoir,* Therese. It was nice meeting you. Tomorrow then? And think about sitting for the painting," he said as he was leaving. "Maybe you'll be the most perfect da Vinci model. Maybe we will be famous together." His broad smile added to his charm, and she didn't fail to notice.

"Tomorrow," and she gave a slight wave. Gathering her books and the notebook, she saw that he wrote: 27 rue de Fleures, Gertrude Stein and Alice Toklas, and signed, Raoul Dufy.

The stone-blue lilacs along the brick foot path appeared frostbitten, victims of the frigid nights and she pushed her hands deep inside her coat pockets and stopped for a closer look. The dried petals swirled about, filling cracks and making colorful lines in a pleasant crisscross pattern along the walkway. She sighed and took her hands out of her pockets, looking at the address Raoul gave her. Stepping reluctantly onto the porch she knocked on the door, and then again. A short man with round eye glasses opened it briefly and then disappeared leaving the door ajar. So when no one else appeared she walked in and followed a hall into a small dining room with oak shelves lined with books, and drawings taped on a brick wall. One sketch was signed by Picasso, a name she recognized, and another by Matisse, a name she didn't. She took off her hat, a wide-brimmed felt salvaged from the pile of clothes at the New York repertory theater.

"Why do I think you are Raoul's new friend, the student from the Sorbonne?" A stout woman with very short hair and deep ebony-colored eyes stood in the doorway. She wore a long dark skirt almost to the floor and a brown tweed jacket that seemed too big for her frame.

"I'm Therese Bonney, so it might be me," she shrugged. "I'm supposed to meet him here. I hope it's alright to just walk in like this." She was no longer nervous, only curious.

"Of course, yes, everyone does even though we always say come by invitation. But this is Paris and no one follows the rules." Her voice was soft in contrast to her striking appearance.

"I'm Gertrude Stein by the way, and I'm so glad Raoul invited you. I've wanted to meet the young American woman accepted for doctoral studies at the Sorbonne. It's practically been a newsworthy event around here."

Therese fidgeted but smiled.

"Come into the studio; well, we call them salons or *ateliers* here in France. There may be some people you'd like to meet. Raoul is here, we talked earlier. Please, there are drinks and canapés on the table," she said, doing her best to put Therese at ease.

I must look nervous. Or maybe she's just being nice. Certainly not as intimidating as when she first walked into the room.

"Oh, and I do want to spend some time with you, Therese, so don't run off."

Several large pieces of furniture lined the walls of the atelier appearing almost too big for the room. In the middle, a long renaissance table with an interesting inkstand caught her eye. Beyond that she noticed several note books piled haphazardly on a nearby shelf, and at the end of the room was a cast iron stove that served to heat the atelier. A tea kettle rested on top. The focus of the room however was the art; paintings on every wall by different artists: Picasso, Matisse, Cezanne, Gauguin, Greco, Toulouse-Lautrec, and more. A few of the names she knew but most were unfamiliar to her.

"She's yet to hang my work; can you convince her?"

She turned to see Raoul. His hair was tidy and he handed her an aperitif with his smile. "I'm glad you decided to come this evening. Don't be nervous. These are all just starving artists like me. Let me introduce you," and he took her arm, gently. "There are some Americans here too, mostly writers. Maybe you know them."

"I doubt it, but I'd like to meet them."

Raoul introduced her as they walked through the room but the names all became a blur. Too many to remember, she thought. She did recall some names: Matisse, Man Ray, Picasso, Sherwood Anderson, a handsome young American named Ernest Hemmingway, James Joyce, T.S. Eliot, Ezra Pound, and Juan Gris. She met a poet, Mina Loy who arrived with another writer, Djuna Barnes, and she was introduced to Gertrude Stein's companion, Alice Toklas, and Stein's brother, Leo.

"So many of them are young," she whispered to Raoul.

"They're just getting started. That's why they're here, to join with other young writers and artists for support and I suppose inspiration. That's why some of us who are older are here as well. There is no age limit to creativity," he said with conviction.

She patted down her skirt. "I'm not sure I fit in. I'm not a writer or an artist."

"Oh, but you're young, Therese. You fit in since what you do is beyond the ordinary and takes courage. It's . . . it's all the same thing."

She grasped his arm. "Thank you, I needed to hear that."

"Do you intend to monopolize her for the evening?" Gertrude said with playful sarcasm as she appeared and stepped between them.

"Ah, I surrender her to you, Madame Stein," he said with an overly dramatic bow. He gave Therese a comforting nod and said, "Don't disappear without saying *bonne nuit*.

They sat by the iron stove talking long after many had left, discovering they had taken similar paths in their lives. Although Gertrude was twenty years older, both had been born on the East Coast, both moved to Oakland, California as youngsters, both attended Harvard, and both pursued graduate degrees, Gertrude in medical school and Therese now at the Sorbonne. Both were Francophiles and loved the language and culture, and both as bookish youngsters read everything they could. Gertrude lost her parents in her teens, and Therese had all but lost her father when she was young - so both had periods of depression and loneliness, and both found salvation in learning and school.

Therese found Gertrude warm and unassuming, but still somewhat mysterious. *How did she become the catalyst in bringing all these talented people together?* She didn't want to ask since s he'd just barely met her. At the end of the evening, Gertrude expressed a genuine interest in Therese's work at the Sorbonne, making her promise to be a regular guest at her salons. "You come even without an invitation each week. I will save a chair for you," she said as they parted. Therese made her way through the room looking for Raoul and saw him talking to the artist Matisse so she waited by the table. A voice behind her interrupted her thoughts.

"Excuse me, Mademoiselle. I couldn't help but overhear that you are a student at the Sorbonne? How impressive, if I may say so." He was a large man, or seemed so because of his black cape; that and his closely-trimmed beard added a strange aura.

"I'm Paul Poiret, a fashion designer here in Paris."

"Hello, it's nice to meet you Monsieur Poiret. What is it you design?"

"Women's fashions mostly," he said nodding. "I have an atelier in the Marias district and shops, well, all over. Judging by the creative way you dress and your stature, I'm guessing you are a model. We have a show coming up and we're looking for tall models who can wear dresses well."

"Me? Oh, I don't think I could do that, but thank you for asking. I'm really just a student and . . ."

"Well, don't students need money?" he said smiling. "We did when I was in school. You wouldn't need any experience; we'd show you what to do."

"Oh, well of course we always need money." She smiled. "When is your show?"

"It's next Wednesday at noon. We'd want you there by eleven. You have the perfect look, and we are short of models right now. You'd be doing us a great favor."

"Wednesday? Oh gads, I'm afraid that wouldn't work for me, Monsieur Poiret, I have an exam. Unfortunately, my studies and other obligations don't allow for much flexibility. The extra money would be wonderful, but, well perhaps some other time." She looked around to see if Raoul was free.

"Oh, too bad. You have the shoulders and slimness we always look for in this business. But I understand you can't jeopardize your studies."

"Well, thank you and I hope that you find someone. Excuse me, Monsieur, I see my friend."

"Just one more thing, Mademoiselle. If I may, I know another fashion designer looking for someone to help with fittings. It may not be regular work, but I think the times might be flexible."

"Well, thank you. I'm not sure if I'm interested . . . but I'll write down his name," she said to be polite.

"It's Madeleine Vionnet."

As she approached Raoul, he smiled and said, "Ah, I see you have a new friend," nodding toward Monsieur Poiret.

"No, not really."

"Well, there are several gentlemen here asking about you. Would you like to meet some of them?"

"No."

"No? My dear, you cannot be in Paris and not be in love."

Therese laughed. "I am in love . . . with Paris."

Raoul tilted his head and with a sly smile, "Ah, we'll see about that."

"Raoul, do you know of Madeleine Vionnet? Her name is familiar and Monsieur Poiret said she might be looking for part-time help. I didn't know there were women fashion designers here."

"Ah, I do know of her and yes, women are now rising to the ranks of couturiers but not many. My sister worked in her atelier for a time. She's becoming one of the important fashion designers in Paris and her dresses are in demand, selling for a fortune."

"Well, she sounds sort of interesting."

"Come, let's sit for a minute." They found a quiet corner. "Most of the fashion houses closed during World War I, including hers. There was no business since people fled because they were afraid of an invasion."

"Did you leave?"

"Yes, I did for a short time. Even leaving was hectic. The roads suffocated with thousands of people escaping to the south. Ah, what a mess. Fortunately, the fighting was limited to the trenches in the north where the German invasion was the strongest."

"Paris was saved, right?"

"Yes, but no one knew that at the time. Eight million men left for the front, the government evacuated Paris and set up in Bordeaux, and it seems the only ones left in Paris were the women and they took over, working in factories, running businesses, everything. I think that is what's happening now."

"What do you mean?"

"Women are definitely more visible, more involved. They're starting businesses and becoming . . . I don't know, maybe more flamboyant and carefree. It's something we didn't see before the war."

"Is that why Vionnet is successful, because she's a woman?"

"I think Vionnet is successful because she has a new way of thinking about fashion. Her dresses are different, actually shocking to some."

"In what way?"

"My sister tells me she wants to get rid of the Edwardian style of big dresses with lots of heavy fabric and those metal and stiff things that make the dresses stand out. She said Vionnet believes that dresses should be worn close to the body and that women will demand to be liberated now that the war is over and that means liberated in fashion too." He smiled and raised an eyebrow. "She was right, and now her dresses are all the rage. She might be interesting to work for. You should see if she's still looking for help."

"I appreciate all of this Raoul. I might go by. I can use the money."

Six

THERESE GLANCED at the address she'd written on a scrap of paper and stopped, seeing the number 222 etched on the glass door and *House of Vionnet* printed on a small sign in the window. The building, a typical granite two-story with a classical façade, looked like all the other establishments on rue Rivoli; that is, small and unremarkable. The door was ajar so she stepped in.

Once inside, the salon was a sea of activity with women moving in all directions in the noisy foyer. The summons bell on the front desk rang incessantly and the clatter of women's voices resonated off the walls and high ceiling with a clamorous echo in the small but crowded salon. "Over here," a woman at the desk yelled. Another pleaded loudly, "Will someone please close the door." Therese stepped aside and stood against the wall. Women wearing white smocks and aprons scurried about with measuring tapes hanging from their pockets and ushering patrons into rooms behind closed curtains. Two workers came from the back carrying several rolls of silky fabrics in a kaleidoscope of colors - soft blues, taupe, cranberry – and looked frantically for an empty table.

The receptionist looked up once but seemed distracted with a patron about a missed appointment, so Therese waited as women rushed past, elbowing their way across the room. The two women with the rolls of fabric finally found a metal table and dumped the rolls, propping the extras against the ochre-colored walls. The room smelled of cloth and spice and Therese stood wide-eyed taking in every scene.

A few minutes passed so she walked further into the salon. The high-coved ceilings and transom windows made the room look larger than it was and the lounge, beautifully decorated with art deco pictures, furniture with square pillows and angular steel tables, was the epitome of the new French modernity Therese had read about in all the French magazines. She thought of sitting but decided to stand just as a fashionably-dressed woman in a black crepe dress appeared.

"May I help you?" she said, looking quite surprised to see Therese standing there. She pulled a curtain to close off the workroom and foyer, and took the closed sign from the window. "We get so busy," she said apologetically.

"I have an appointment to see Madeleine Vionnet."

The woman looked at her from head to toe and hesitated before lifting an eyebrow. "With Madame Vionnet herself?" When Therese nodded she said, "Well, then come this way," and they walked between tables of fabrics in a blaze of colors and dodged women carrying large spools of thread and what appeared to be gauze patterns. The squeaking wooden floor seemed to twang beneath her feet with each step and she imagined the smell of oak as they walked quickly through the work room toward the back. On each side, were sewing areas with several treadle stitching machines and against one wall were shelves buckling with large wooden bobbins of thread. Several white smocks hung over empty chairs so Therese assumed the seamstresses hadn't yet started their day. A number of smaller rooms were partitioned off with curtains and only one room in the back had a door. The woman knocked lightly and then opened it slightly.

"Are you expecting someone this morning?" Therese heard a voice but couldn't make out what was said. The woman in the black dress opened the door wider and motioned Therese to go in. She walked slowly into the room, removing her wide-brimmed felt hat and took a deep breath.

The room was eerily quiet and dimly lit from an oil lamp on the desk. A row of tall French windows were all but hidden behind the closed heavy linen drapes - yet the room was light enough to see an unpainted brick wall with several photographs of models wearing formal evening gowns. The dresses were beautiful and shiny, and Therese thought the models extraordinarily slim like those she'd seen in silent films. A few more photographs sat on a table in the corner next to rolls of fabric leaning against the back wall, some partially covered but all in soft colors. A single ray of light escaped through the drapes and cast a grainy beam on piles of papers covering a desk and onto a small photograph, barely visible. Perhaps the most interesting item in the room was a wooden doll about two feet tall situated on a piano stool; quite unusual and with hinged arms and legs. She let her eyes rest there.

"Come in, please," a voice said, startling her since the room seemed empty. At that moment an attractive woman probably in her early forties stepped forward into the room and Therese squinted to see her more closely. *So, this is the famous Madame Vionnet!* Her dark hair with slight strands of gray was caught up in a French bun, with errant tresses falling slightly awry against her pale skin and the gentle angles of her face. Her eyes, dark as cinder, were surprisingly soft, betraying her impersonal expression. Therese thought there was something about her, alluring yet distant, almost impatient but not. The woman examined Therese for more than a minute as if measuring her for a gown. Therese blushed, not knowing what to say.

"I see you're admiring my mannequin," the woman said finally, looking over to the doll.

"Yes, I've never seen anything like it."

There was an awkward pause. "Really? If you're a skilled fitter, I'm surprised."

Therese took a forced breath and swallowed hard, shaking her head slightly, almost to herself. "Madame Vionnet, there must be some mistake and I'm afraid it's my fault." She blushed again. "I must admit, I'm not a skilled fitter. In fact, I don't even know what that is. I was just told you needed fitters and that the hours were flexible. I'm. . . well I'm a student and also a translator at the *Theatre Sarah Bernhardt,* and I also do various part-time jobs to pay for my rent and tuition." She wanted to leave but stood awkwardly talking faster than usual. She shifted her weight and fidgeted with the brim of her hat.

Vionnet watched her, slightly amused and Therese took note. *Is she smiling because of my embarrassment or something I said? Or just at everything!* Trying to hide her discomfort, Therese added, "I didn't know you were looking for skilled workers. I'm sorry, really, to have taken your time this morning." She turned to leave.

"Where do you attend school and what do you study?"

Therese relaxed her shoulders and turned. "I'm at the Sorbonne; my doctoral studies are in French theater and languages."

"I see . . . the Sorbonne. Well my dear, that type of education will not get you a job in the field of fashion."

Madeleine and Therese

Therese stifled a smile. "You're right. But that was not my intention. It was just to pay the rent."

Vionnet looked toward the window and then back. "I'm Madeleine Vionnet. I'm just now reopening my atelier," she said stepping closer. "I had my shop for two years and then the Great War broke out." Her tone was softer now, not as dismissive. "I need help since I'm trying to get started again but unfortunately I need skilled help."

"I understand." Therese stood impatiently by the door.

Vionnet studied her again intently and then disappeared into the darkened part of the room. The question came from there. "Don't you care about the way you dress?" The room became as still as a midnight hush and Therese stood silent, opening her mouth to say something but didn't. She looked down at her long black peasant skirt and boots, and the flowered scarf wrapped around her hips, her favorite hat in her hand. She had wanted to look nice that day.

Her face flushed and then she remembered where she was, the pictures on the wall, the clients in the foyer and how they were dressed. She let her hands drop to her sides and smiled. "I care about choosing the right shade of lipstick." She turned and left.

She heard the woman say, "Please close the door behind you."

Madeleine Vionnet sat at her desk tapping her finger. *Hmm, bright girl, clever, pretty.*

Two weeks after her embarrassing meeting with Madame Vionnet, Therese received a handwritten note delivered to the Sarah Bernhardt Theater and addressed to her:

Can you please come by the salon again at your convenience?
Madeleine Vionnet

Seven

THE ART DECO FOYER was abuzz again that afternoon and Therese waited by the door watching well-dressed women in gloves to the elbow prattling noisily and smoking from long ivory and gold inlaid cigarette holders. The smoke stung her eyes. *What are they all doing here, so many of them?* She overheard someone mention fittings, still not knowing what that was. She shook her head and smoothed the creases from her dress as she walk up to the desk.

"I'm Therese Bonney. Madame Vionnet said to come by at my convenience."

"Yes, she mentioned you. Come with me, please." A younger woman this time escorted her to the back.

The heavy linen drapes were open this time revealing the blunt end of an old brick building with a tarnished metal roof. The light flooded the room making it softer, more pleasant than before. Madeleine Vionnet stood by her desk clearly visible. Her white cotton floor-length dress with ruffles framed her face and her hair reflected the light from the window, making it lighter than Therese remembered. The contrast of her dress with the seductive evening gowns pictured on the walls was dramatic, but both equally appealing. Therese fidgeted with the scarf over her long straight dress and then sat down. She wore a black beret but took it off quickly, letting her dark hair fall to her shoulders. Madeleine looked at her and then away.

"So you're interested in unskilled work to help pay your tuition." Therese started to answer but Madeleine continued. "I can use someone for my draping."

"Draping?"

"Yes, you see, I don't sketch my designs like the others. I first drape small pieces of fabric on my wooden mannequin to see how the fabric falls." She walked over to the wooden doll and used her hands to illustrate. Therese noticed her hands were small and moved quickly.

"It's not altogether accurate but it gives me an idea, lets me imagine how I want a gown to look," she said, sitting down at the desk closer to Therese. "What matters though, is how fabric falls on the human body. Otherwise there's no perspective. Wooden mannequins don't move. Models do."

Therese wanted to know more but felt awkward asking questions. "I don't know much about the fashion business," she confessed.

Madeleine's smile was unintentional and she glanced at Therese's mismatched outfit. *Hmm, both bizarre and intriguing.*

Therese continued. "I've seen those busts in tailor shops. Don't they use those when making fashions for women?"

Madeleine shook her head. "No, never. At least not in my salon. I make very expensive gowns that my clients buy for the way they fit. My dresses are different, more fitted, closer to the body. It's my signature style; it's what makes the House of Vionnet unique. The busts you refer to are literally busts, from the shoulders to the waist. A beautiful gown must celebrate the hips, stomach, and all the way down in addition to the upper body, you see. Besides, those busts are made of cotton. Delicate fabrics, especially when cut on the bias, can't flow over cotton."

"And larger wooden mannequins?"

"Too difficult to handle, I'm afraid," Madeleine replied with a hint of a smile. "The most important point is that a dress should move with the body. When a woman smiles, so should her dress and it's impossible to know how the dress will move without draping the fabric first." She was quiet for a moment and looked out the window at a lone tree taking much of the light for itself. Therese looked about the room and studied her desk, a letter opener, a torn and faded photograph of a child.

"The others just don't get it," Madeleine said turning back from the window. "They sketch dresses and then wonder why they don't fit the way mine do." Her voice stiffened. "There are other couturiers more famous. Most buyers don't know me and actually I don't want them to.

I'm private. They just need to know that my gowns can make the ordinary woman look beautiful."

"You don't fit them? Is that the right word?"

"Rarely. I have fitters for that. Also, when my collections are shown I sit in the corner out of sight. If the client doesn't like it, she can go somewhere else."

Therese sat thinking, wondering how to respond as she looked at her. Vionnet was not what you'd call beautiful but her face had an unmistakable strength that made her appealing, attractive really, Therese thought as she eyed her cautiously. *She's somewhat rigid, though. I wonder if she laughs or cries easily.* "Are those your dresses, and may I look?" Therese walked over to the photographs on the wall not waiting for an answer.

"Yes, they are all my creations, and as you can see, gone are the bustles and metal undergarments."

"And this one, worn by the dancer?"

"That's a friend, Isadora Duncan. It was her Grecian approach to dancing that actually inspired my work. Isadora abandoned all the old ideas years ago, including what women should wear. She believed as I do, that sexy, soft flowing dresses unrestricted by undergarments are the most beautiful. "

"Oh!" *Without undergarments? Did I hear her right?* Color rose to her cheeks. "And, no shoes," Therese said looking closely at the picture. "She dances barefoot?"

"Yes, sometime less is more." Madeleine said coyly. "You can see from the photos, my dresses liberate women and eliminate the need for undergarments like those terrible metal corsets and brassieres; or worse yet, blanketing the figure in yards of heavy fabric. It just isn't beautiful or sensuous."

"Do most women still wear brassieres and corsets?"

Madeleine laughed. "Well, obviously you don't so I guess you've answered your own question. You can get away with it."

Therese blushed again. "Sometimes it's a matter of priorities. I'd rather buy a book than a brassiere."

Madeleine shook her head and chuckled. "You're a rarity, my dear. If any woman will keep her body trim and fit my dresses will do the rest.

The Great War is over and women want to be liberated, not only in life but in what they wear and how they look." She motioned in the air with her hands. "And where else can they be more liberated than in Paris wearing a Vionnet gown?" Therese noticed her eyes sparkled as she talked about her fashions. Like something on fire, she thought.

Therese sat again. The old photograph on the desk had disappeared and Madeleine was peering out the window. The light hit squarely on her face and Therese wondered what she was thinking. *There's something about her, an undefined quality or sadness, like something unfinished.* The light was too bright to see beneath the surface but it left Therese curious.

"So, are you interested in being one of my models for draping or not?" Madeleine said turning in her chair.

Therese took a quick breath. She was fascinated with Vionnet and her work, yet she wondered if she could really work with her . . . *the abruptness, coolness, being both aloof and stimulating at the same time.* She was trying to imagine what it might be like.

"I don't know, I . . . well, I wouldn't know what to do. I've had no experience and I know nothing about fashion . . . I mean, I wouldn't want to make a mistake."

Madeleine looked at her with interest. "Why do I think you're not the type to judge actions as mistakes? You're courageous to come to France on your own. You have your own style and you don't apologize for it. You seem to accept things as they are."

"Is there anything wrong with that?" Therese said.

"No, just unusual for someone like me. I'm envious."

Therese narrowed her eyes. "You don't apologize for your styles, and you have the courage to defy convention by designing dresses to be worn without undergarments, or at least the bulky kind. I just don't know how to be a model for your draping."

Madeleine's eyes fixed on her. *She's gritty, different, smart. Naïve like a child yet wise like a mature woman.* "You don't need to know anything. You're the perfect size for draping with wide shoulders, slim waist, tall, erect posture, and other than fidgeting a little, you appear capable of standing still and taking instructions. That's all there is to it. I do the rest." She waited, never averting her gaze. When Therese didn't respond, Madeleine added. "I can pay you 30 francs a sitting and will work around your other obligations. I prefer to drape in the evenings both with my wooden mannequin and a live model since that's when I get my inspiration and ideas." She stood and put both hands on the desk, leaning forward. "Besides, the interruptions during the daytime can be annoying and it's quiet here after everyone leaves. I would only ask that you not bring your dog if you have one, or food . . . you understand I'm sure."

"I don't have a dog." Therese wanted to laugh but the atmosphere was not jovial, but then not unpleasant either.

"Fine, then. You can see Madame Delacroix at the desk and she will take care of some paperwork."

Therese stood. "This will be a first for me," Therese said, putting on her beret.

"Well, this is after all, Paris, my dear."

When Therese left, Madeleine closed the drapes and sat at her desk. She thought about the time when she too walked into a couturier's atelier for the first time and she thought of Vincent and his kindness. *I must remember to pass that on and not frighten this refreshing young woman.*

Eight

A SOFT KNOCK at the door interrupted her thoughts and Madeleine turned in her chair. Lila Delacroix leaned part way into the room.

"Do you have a minute, Madeleine?"

"Yes, of course, Lila. Come in."

Madame Delacroix was not necessarily an attractive woman but always exquisitely groomed. Her narrow shoulders seemed out of proportion to her body just as her high forehead did to her small chin, but she wore her auburn hair loose around her face in a pleasant manner and chose her clothes with an artful eye. They met at the House of Doucet when Madeleine was a designer and Lila a *vendeuse* who presented the designers' fashions to clients. Lila and some of the other *vendeuses* refused to show Madeleine's styles, finding them immoral because they were designed to be worn without a corset. Madeleine eventually left, but not before telling a friend, "I lit a small torch, but it was rapidly extinguished in the heavy air of the *vendeuses* at the House of Doucet." Recently, when Madeleine reopened her own house after the war, Lila appeared and asked for a job. Madeleine hired her to manage the office but not to sell her fashions.

"I think there's been a misunderstanding with that young Bohemian woman who was just in here," she said, walking into the room. "She seems to think you've hired her as a model for your draping. She has no references or experience . . . she insists. I'm not sure what I should tell her."

"Lila, I did offer her a job. She'll be working as an occasional model. Just have her fill out the forms and . . ."

"But she has no experience! She wouldn't fit in here; did you see how she dresses? We have others here who can model. Why put someone else on the books when it's not necessary?"

Madeleine pushed some papers aside on her desk and tapped her pencil. She reminded herself why she hired Lila. The fashion business is small and competitive. Everyone crosses paths eventually and everyone needs jobs. Lila was out of work and came to her. It was that simple. And, sometimes keeping your adversaries closest is the safest.

"I've hired the young woman, Lila. That's all, thank you."

That afternoon Madeleine met her friend Marie Gerber for lunch at the Hotel Palais - a ritual they'd kept since Madeleine worked for her at Callot Soeurs and they became friends. Marie put her gloves on the table. "Ah, Madeleine, it's so good to see you - or I should call you Madame Vionnet now that you've reopened your own fashion house?"

An alluring woman with deep-set amber eyes, Marie Gerber wore her dark tresses swept up in a dramatic pompadour in contrast to Madeleine's simple style, but then Marie was decidedly more outgoing and promoted herself and her fashions in a more public way. That afternoon, her simple white lace blouse and black floor-length skirt defied her reputation as one of Paris' most notable designers. They chose a table where they could talk.

"You may call me whatever you like, Marie. You know I will always be your humble apprentice," Madeleine said smiling. "My experience with you was invaluable. You taught me that one must adorn women, not just construct costumes."

"Ah, I think you taught me that, Madeleine, and more. I'm wondering if that will still be the case now that we're starting up again after the Great War. What will post-war Paris be like for fashion? What do you make of it?" The waiter interrupted to pour champagne and take their order.

"It's new but I think it's also exciting. The garlands on the lamp posts and celebrations in the streets are refreshing after the grimness of war. I also see women . . . lots of women, everywhere even in America, who kept things together during the war and now feel empowered. I think they're ready to throw off the shackles and take the freedom they deserve - and that can only be good for us in the fashion business. I think women will still want to be beautiful, and sexy," she added.

Marie laughed. "You've been trying to get rid of the corset ever since I've known you, Madeleine, so now maybe your time has come."

"Oh my, I think the time came a long time ago but no one wanted to be the first to let women break free from their yokes." She thought for a minute. "They always said I loved women too much. Now I just want to free them. It's 1918 and it's about time." She leaned closer. "I have so many ideas, Marie, but I'm struggling. I need backers and more space and to get my name out there."

"You're known and respected in our business, Madeleine. Your salon is bustling."

"It just seems that way because I lack the space to spread out. I need to bring in more clients so I can grow. You and your sisters at Callot Soeurs have interesting clients, the wealthy Americans, French aristocrats, royalty from Spain, Austria, and Bavaria all come to Paris for your fashions. They order dresses by the dozens. I sell one at a time and work hard just to do that. If I expanded my business I could hire more staff and turn out more gowns."

"It'll happen, Madeleine. You're innovative and courageous while the rest of us are still languishing in the . . . the old Edwardian age. Your gowns have sex appeal and that's just now catching on." Marie looked at her coyly, and added, "It's not easy to find clients who are willing to wear your gowns without undergarments."

They both laughed at the thought.

"Well, certainly not the bulky type that imprisoned women in the past," Madeleine said.

"By the way, I've hired a young woman, an American, for some draping. She's not interested in pursuing it but she's different and certainly has the right figure for my gowns. And, she's eager to please. She actually has an unusual style; you know, original, not necessarily intentional. She dresses to please herself and I like that. It triggers my own creative impulses, keeps me on the edge.

"You're already on the edge, Madeleine. It's fun to watch your business grow. We must have lunch more often so I can find out what you're up to."

The foyer at dusk exuded a different mood with the lights dimmed and shadows from the remainder of the day slipping in through the front windows. Madeleine's note said to come at dusk and the woman at the desk said Madame Vionnet was busy and to wait, but an hour passed after the seamstresses and *vendeuses* left, and finally the woman at the desk locked the front door behind her. Therese sat alone until she heard the last door open and the wooden floor creak as the footsteps got closer.

"You're late. I believe I asked you to come at dusk."

"I've been here, Madame Vionnet. In fact I came early. The woman at the desk said you were busy and to wait, and then everyone left."

Madeleine drew a deep breath and shook her head. "Was that Lila?"

"I don't know her name. Her dark hair was pushed up high on her head and . . ."

"That's Lila," she said almost in a whisper." From now on just come to my office, don't stop at the desk. If there are problems with Lila, let me know." They walked to the back and into her office. "Do you prefer to be called Therese or Mademoiselle Bonney?"

"Oh, please, call me Therese. I'm . . . I'm a little nervous about this," she said quickly and almost relieved to have said it. "You'll have to tell me what to do. I want to get it right."

Madeleine seemed amused. "You will, Therese. It's not like getting your teeth pulled." Therese twisted a piece of fringe on her jacket and Madeleine glanced at the clock and sighed.

"You don't have to be nervous. Let's sit and talk for a minute so you can relax." She motioned Therese to sit near the desk. "So, how do you like Paris so far?"

"I like it, very much. There's so much to do and see. I'd probably find New York a bit stodgy after being here."

"And what about fashion? Does it seem different here?"

Therese hesitated. Madeleine was extremely well-dressed herself but not glamorous like the pictures on the wall. Therese wondered if the question had to do with her own mismatched style. "Fashion has never seemed important to me. I suppose that makes me somewhat of an outcast here, doesn't it?"

"No, that makes you independent. A lot of women would like to claim that."

"Well, New Yorkers like to brag that they get their dresses from Paris, so I'm sure style must be important here. It would be nice to have more exchanges between France and America so we could appreciate each other."

"Why not make that happen?"

"Yes, that's something to think about. People in America are curious about Paris and the lifestyle. I know I was. Right now my focus is school but it doesn't hurt to look ahead. I've been writing articles about Paris for American magazines, not under my full name of course."

"Why is that?"

"Publishers still think men are the experts in everything, I suppose. Women have a difficult time getting published unless they're writing about household chores or child rearing."

Madeleine nodded and sat quiet for a minute. "And you'd like to change that."

"Oh well of course, but in due time. Right now it's school and work," Therese said, letting go of the fringe on her jacket.

"Well, speaking of work let me show you a new fabric I think will be fantastic for a dress I have in mind. It's getting late but I'd like to see how it flows. We can do a short draping session and if the fabric works we'll continue with it next time."

They walked to the dressing area. "I'm sorry I didn't let you know I was here waiting in the foyer. I should have been more assertive. It's a little intimidating being here."

"You attend the Sorbonne and you find it intimidating being here?"

When they reached the dressing area, Therese sighed to herself, glad to be easing slowly into this draping experience. "Do I take off my . . . how should I prepare . . . ?"

Madeleine turned to face her, seeing how young she looked. "When I first started in this business some shops required models to wear black full-body undergarments when trying on clothes because they thought it was immoral to show bare skin." She shrugged slightly and smiled. "That was fine for clumpy dresses, but not for delicate gowns and not in my salon. There's already too much hidden in society anyway and the unadorned female body is so much closer to the truth, full of pleasure and power. Why hide it?"

Therese gasped and blushed at the same time.

"So, it's best to take everything off but realistically you can leave on your lower undergarment for this fitting. Once you undress, wrap yourself in a piece of muslin that you'll find hanging by the mirror, and then lower it as I drape the fabric. Are you comfortable with all of that?"

"Yes," Therese said, disguising any quiver that might reveal her nervousness. She unpinned her hat and undressed, putting everything on a nearby table. She put her boots by the door.

The fabric was called rayon. Madeleine explained that it was a man-made product still in the experimental stages. "It's of little interest to most fashion designers because they think it's too flimsy. They go for cottons and heavy brocades," she said as she put the roll of fabric on the table and unrolled it. It was a soft peach color and almost weightless. She held it up to the light as she walked toward Therese.

Therese dropped the muslin wrap and immediately realized her mistake. "Oh, goodness!" She put her hands over her eyes and squeezed tight as she stood nude except for her knickers. "I'm so . . . embarrassed."

Madeleine was surprised to see such a beautiful body for someone so childlike. She smiled, bending to retrieve the muslin. She wrapped it around Therese, pulling her hands away from her face and handing her the loose ends. "That's alright. You're new at this. You'll figure it out."

On the second try Therese felt a quiver as the fabric fell over her shoulder and bare breast under the careful hand of Madeleine. She let the muslin drape fall to the floor and at certain angles, she watched the draping process in a full-length mirror on the wall. Madeleine's hands were like magic, moving and shifting the rayon at all angles, stepping back to look.

"It helps if you stand still," Madeleine said in a whisper. At one point she asked Therese to move a certain way and twist the top part of her torso leaving her lower part in place. The fabric felt cool and fluid as it slid down an arm or over a hip floating with ease until it bunched up over her cotton knickers. "They make undergarments of rayon and silk also. I'll get some for these draping sessions."

"Are you pleased with the fabric and how it falls?" Therese asked, her voice still shaky.

"Very," Madeleine said, studying the feather-light fabric. She placed a few pins. "Now, you can walk across the room."

Therese took a few hesitant steps before following the instructions. "Oh, this is like walking through cool water except it's light as air." She closed her eyes half way as the rayon caressed her skin. It felt sensuous and dreamy, and she now understood. *This is what Madeleine had been talking about: the love affair between the fabric and the body.*

When she left that evening, Madeleine thanked her and reminded her to come directly to the office next time and to bypass the desk or anyone asking questions. She added, "You're a perfect model, Therese. That piece of fabric on you looked better than an exquisite gown on the best-dressed woman in Paris."

Nine

HE GRABBED HER shoulders from behind. "Where have you been, Therese?" Raoul Dufy peered around then sat at her table, taking her hand. "I haven't seen you. I feared you might have returned to America. Gertrude has asked about you several times; we've all missed you."

"Oh, Raoul, I've been busy at school and with my part-time work and other projects, but I'm so happy to see you. Today is my first day here in a long time. I'd hoped you might be here. "

"Well, tell me, how are your studies at the Sorbonne and tell me about work?" They talked for two hours, drinking coffee and leaning close to hear every word. Therese told him about the thesis she'd been writing on the moral ideas in the theater of Alexandre Dumas. She mentioned that she's still translating in both English and French for the Sarah Bernhardt theatre, and doing work for the American Red Cross, but gave no mention of her work for Madeleine Vionnet. Even though it's become one of her favorite ways to pass the time and earn money, she sensed Madeleine was very private about her life. Either that or she didn't have one. Madeleine never spoke of friends or anything personal; still, Therese didn't want to face questions that might compromise her privacy. Raoul talked about his painting and ceramics, and asked when he might paint her."

"Soon, Raoul. I'll have more time when I finish my thesis." She put her hand on his arm. "I know it takes a while to sit for a painting, but I promise you it will happen."

"Well then, at least come to Gertrude's Saturday night. There are a couple of American writers I'd like you to meet - Janet Flanner and Nancy Cunard. They're with a circle of writers and artists you might find

Madeleine and Therese

interesting. They struggle like the rest of us but have fun doing it," he said smiling. "Other expats will be there too like Man Ray, Peggy Guggenheim, Edith Wharton, and probably the usual French crowd. And, Gertrude will be delighted. She asks about you every time I see her."

Therese looked at him and took his hand. "How did I ever get so lucky to meet you, Raoul?"

"In the stars, Therese my dear. It was in the stars."

Although short at only five-foot two, Gertrude Stein seemed monumental in her stature just as Therese remembered her from their first meeting. Her dark corduroy skirt and grey woolen jacket didn't soften her presence in the room, nor did her colorful stories. People came to the salon as much for Gertrude's charisma as for her splendid collection of art and a chance to meet interesting people. Therese spotted her by the wood stove smoking a cigar and talking to a captive group of friends. Therese listened from across the room.

"France has so much to offer," Gertrude was saying. "There are so many talented artists and writers here but no one buys our work. If it weren't for the wealth and position of Mabel Dodge who published some my books, no one would be reading my work in America. I couldn't get anyone to take an interest." She paused and blew smoke into the room. "In Paris, we buy each other's work but it should be appreciated elsewhere. I'm not sure what it will take."

Therese walked closer. "Perhaps better communication between France and America - and the rest of the world, for that matter. How else will they know about French culture if someone doesn't promote it?"

Gertrude looked surprised and squinted through the room's smoky haze. Therese wore a pair of loosely-fit men's trousers and a black tunic, tied at the waist with a purple scarf. Her dark hair was windswept from the walk and added a spark of wildness to her statuesque figure.

"Ah, Therese, it's you! What we need is an analytical mind to solve the dilemma instead of our constant whining." Gertrude held out her arms. "Just where have you been hiding? We've looked for you."

"I'm sorry. I've been buried in my thesis and then there's work. I didn't forget your warm invitation to come every week. I just haven't been free to do it."

Gertrude snuffed out her cigar, while Therese watched laughing. "We all have our vices, my pet. What are yours, Therese?"

"I haven't had time to form any, yet."

They laughed as Gertrude took her arm. "You're delightful. And, I like your outfit. Raoul said you had an interesting look. Come sit. Talk to me. How can we promote our work abroad?" Gertrude pulled up two chairs as she does when she's serious.

"I'm not sure, really. I just know that I hear people talking about more exposure, more publicity. I also know that when I write home about what's happening here in Paris - the new styles of art and architecture, the new fashions, and everything modern - they just can't get enough. They ask questions, they're curious. I think now that the war is over people are thirsty for culture, for innovation. It's like a new beginning. I've been writing articles about French culture and they're still being published in American magazines, so perhaps I need to do more of that. I wish I could publish under my full name."

"That will change, Therese, I'm sure of it. Men are still getting used to the fact that we ran the country while they were away at war." Gertrude stopped to light another cigar.

She found Gertrude easy to talk to and open to new ideas. *I wish I had the same rapport with Madame Vionnet since I find her interesting too but enormously private.* She wondered what Vionnet had to hide, or was it just her manner from working her way to success. She tried to imagine what Vionnet might be like as a friend but nothing came to mind.

Gertrude blew a puff of smoke off to the side just as Raoul walked toward them.

"Ah, I see you two are at it again. Gertrude, we must find suitable friends for Therese so she won't leave us when she graduates. You can do your *tete-a-tete* another time. I promised to introduce Therese to Janet Flanner and Nancy Cunard and I just saw them walk in."

"Alright, Raoul, give us a minute and then she's yours. I promise." He smiled and disappeared in the room. She turned to Therese. "I like your idea, it has merit. Let's talk about this again. I know you're busy but this could be something only you can imagine since you've now lived in both France and the U.S., and you're smart," she added with a wink.

They stood and Therese scanned the room for Raoul.

"Therese, just one more thing," Gertrude said. "Janet Flanner and Nancy Cunard are both talented writers, but they party as well as they write. Just so you know."

Raoul appeared with two women, both immaculately dressed but distinctively different. Janet Flanner had a theatrical allure; her long face and exaggerated features could have served her well on the stage. She was tall and slim, and wore a shimmering grey pants suit of silk. Her classy look was marred only by her incessant smoking, toggling a cigarette between her lips as she talked while smoke curled up around her face. Yet her quick smile and sad eyes added an air of friendliness and Therese took an immediate liking to her. Janet confessed her love of writing and worked as a journalist, but she said she hoped to write a novel one day.

Nancy Cunard, on the other hand was petite, with thin lips and wide eyes made larger by heavy dark eye shadow and eyeliner. Her blonde hair was pulled tight in a bun and her pale skin was exaggerated by her bright red crepe dress. Her look and expensive jewelry made her conspicuous in a room full of starving artists and writers but she didn't seem to notice. Therese understood from their conversation that she was a poet and a British heiress, and came to Paris about the same time as Therese.

"We haven't seen you here, Therese. Raoul said that you attend the Sorbonne and have an interest in French theater," Nancy said.

"Yes, I also have couple of jobs and I'm writing my thesis right now, so I've only been here once. But I hope to change that once I finish at the Sorbonne and have more time."

"Really, at the Sorbonne? That's impressive," Janet said. "We were just talking about the accomplishments of women. Is it because we ran the country while the men were at war, or is it something else? Care to give us an academic perspective?"

"Oh gosh, probably not. As an American I'm just an observer, really. Paris does seem so much more advanced than the U.S. in terms of the experimentation here. I've been writing articles on modernism so I probably see the women's liberation in Paris as just another example of the modernist movement where individuals rebel against and reject the present culture, finding it stifling and repressive." Nancy and Janet listened and nodded so she went on to talk about women artists and writers and how they might be looking for alternatives to revitalize their own lives and culture through new ways of doing everything - like in art, architecture, philosophy, fashion, and even morality. "Ironically, women are getting the right to vote everywhere except here in France and that must incite the need to reject the status quo that prohibits them the vote. Maybe they're rebelling in terms of what they can control and that's their bodies."

Nancy watched her carefully, obviously enjoying the discussion. "It's archaic to deny us the right to vote," she said, "Especially after we ran the country, for gods' sake. I know women are forming close alliances right now. I guess there's strength in numbers."

Janet nodded without removing the cigarette from her lips and then took it out just as she began to speak. "I agree with Therese about the sexual revolution among women in Paris right now." She shook the ash from her cigarette, using a tray on the table. "With the vote thing and the desire to overturn the old ways, women are questioning all traditional values that have held them back. That's probably why we have the flappers who bob their hair as short as men's and shorten their skirts to reveal their bare legs. Anything to feel empowered," she added. "But the sexual liberation might simply reflect the creative spirit so rampant here, especially on the left bank. Creative people are usually bisexual, how can they not be?" she said, stubbing out her cigarette.

"Hmm, I'm not sure I agree with that," Nancy said, shooting her a glance. "But whatever the reason, it's about time women are rebelling. They're not going back into the kitchen after working during the war. I know I'm not."

Therese had a sudden thought about Madeleine. *She's a good example of someone who liberates women through fashion by coaxing them to shun everything under their Vionnet gowns. I wonder how she liberates herself. Or maybe she doesn't!*

"I suppose freedom and liberation have many faces," Therese said. "I'm afraid I've had my nose in the books too much to really know what's going on in France other than what I see. My biggest concern is finding a quiet place to study," she said shrugging. "But I do find this conversation stimulating."

"Well join us when you have time, Therese," Nancy said. "We get together with our literary friends and talk about all sorts of things: our writing, books, poetry, politics, the theater. We also go to parties, so maybe you'd like to join us for those too."

"Thanks, hope to do that sometime."

Therese thought about the conversation on her walk home. She kept hearing about the rebellious nature of women in Paris and their need for freedom. Even Janet and Nancy as women of privilege talk about the need for emancipation. She didn't quite understand how women become emancipated but she liked how close women were in Paris without the stigma associated with women bonding together or being who they want to be. *I wonder if that's what it takes to be a real Parisian woman. I wonder if I will ever be one.*

Ten

THERESE FOUND MADELEINE'S salon to be an education in *haute couture* and saw Madeleine as a genius with unbridled imagination and creative courage. Her gowns, the fabrics she chooses. her theme of liberation all seemed revolutionary and earned her the attention of the press and other couturiers. She was making fashion history by giving women a new look: more risqué, exotic, and beautiful - and women loved it!

Madeleine was also turning fashion into an art form, creating a new appreciation for original designs and the daring use of fabric. Those who could afford her gowns - and that meant the rich and famous - eagerly put their names on the waiting list.

But Therese struggled with Madeleine's mood swings, never knowing if she would be friendly or distant. Madeleine rarely shared anything about her life even though they spent hours in the salon together. Therese was curious about her. *Is she married? Where does she live? Who are her friends? I wonder what she wears around the house - certainly not baggy trousers and bulky sweaters!* Therese pictured the two of them having coffee someday and smiled at the absurdity. *I avoid the advances and interests of my classmates yet I want to have coffee with the famous fashion designer Madame Vionnet? Really?*

She put the thought out of her mind, although she did feel she could learn something from a successful person like Madeleine Vionnet. But she was grateful to be making rent money and did what Madeleine asked of her and avoided Lila who wasn't particularly friendly. Lila was usually gone by the time Therese arrived anyway, but one evening she was in the office when Therese came in. Lila seemed surprised to see her.

"Oh! I didn't know you and Madame Vionnet are draping tonight. I thought you had a class."

"No, not tonight. I didn't know you worked late, Lila."

"Well, I don't. I just forgot something so I came back." She closed her satchel quickly before rushing off.

Therese found Madeleine in the workroom putting chalk marks on a lovely crepe fabric.

"One more draping and I think we can pass this gown on to the premiere and the seamstresses," she said.

Therese often attempted some meager conversation but she never knew if Madeleine would respond, and she didn't want to be thought of as a nuisance. That night however, she did ask, "Where did you learn to speak English so well?"

For a moment there was no reply and then Madeleine said, "Where does anyone learn languages?"

Silence was Madeleine's way of setting boundaries. Therese thought it ironic that her dresses revealed almost everything about a woman's body, yet she reveals very little about herself. That night Therese observed her while she was working, her perfect posture, the impeccable way she dressed, her hands never faltering, her voice always clear befitting of a woman entirely in control. Therese wondered if she was ever spontaneous.

About an hour later when they were removing the chalk lines from the fabric, Madeleine explained, "As a young woman, I wanted to learn English so I could advance one day. During my first real job at the House of Vincent, a client said she knew of a position in London. Vincent said to go if I wanted so I was on an ocean liner heading for England with a recommendation in hand. I worked for Kate Riley in her atelier and learned English while I was there."

That evening they moved rolls of fabric blocking the aisles and made room for dresses waiting to be sewn. The work was piling up for lack of staff and space and Therese sensed Madeleine's frustration trying to get things ready for the seamstresses the next day.

"I can't slow down," Madeleine said with a surprising admission. "If

I want the business I need to put in the time."

Therese noticed that even under pressure, Madeleine still focused on every line and fold, every movement and bias of the fabric while being draped. Even the tiniest detail became important and significant and anything less than perfection was not a viable option for her. Therese understood that kind of dedication; it's what got her through years of schooling.

"I need more room, more staff, more seamstresses. I'm limited by what we can do in this small atelier."

"Can you move to a larger space, or do you even want to?"

Madeleine shrugged. "Well, yes and no. If I'm to expand I need a professional manager not just an office manager, and I'd need backers. But growth means giving up autonomy."

"Autonomy and growth don't mix?"

"Not when you have to borrow money to expand. I'm afraid to turn my business over to male backers. I entered a man's profession and I did it without their help. I don't want lose control of my company to them at this point."

"Control in terms of business decisions or creative decisions?"

"Hmm, well both. In theory, business decisions, but the two can be married." And then she added, "but not happily."

Madeleine talked about some of the hardships during her early apprenticeship as a child and later struggling to create her own designs while working for other *maisons de couture*. "I can't put myself in that position again. I just can't."

Therese was curious. "Can you make that part of the agreement, that you have artistic freedom? Why would any backer want to interfere with what you've created, especially when it means profit for them?"

"Ah, there's something morosely sinister about money. Backers are investors and yes, they should leave creativity to the artist, especially if the artist is successful. But money rarely comes without conditions and interference."

They sat in silence for a while. "I have some important decisions to make," Madeleine said.

"Yes, it seems you do." *Hmm, she actually shared some feelings, some fears, maybe she does have a human side.*

Eleven

ON A DRIZZLY MORNING in June Therese rummaged through her closet throwing one item of clothing after another on the bed. *A dress? Maybe a long skirt. Gads, what do they wear at these things? Defending a doctoral thesis shouldn't hinge on what I'm wearing!* She ignored the clothes and went over her notes again and then one more time. She glanced at the heap of clothes on the bed. *Something conservative, a dark long skirt to the ankles and a blouse. Oh, and a hat!*

She gulped as she entered the room. Her thesis committee sat at the long side of a dark mahogany table - five men, all her former professors, all looking down at their notes. She closed the door behind her, reminding herself to keep her head up. By the time she opened the door three hours later she had argued her point and answered their questions. She took a long measured breath and paced the hall, now quiet, and waited while they deliberated. She recounted the words she used and rehashed in her mind what she could have said but didn't. *Why did I blab on about my methods section? At least they didn't fall asleep. Could I have answered the last question differently? I wonder if I looked alright?* She looked down at her long skirt and tried to see her reflection in the window at the end of the hall while looking at her hair as well.

The door opened just minutes later. She thought the worst. It had been only thirty-five minutes. Her thesis chair appeared at the door looking somber and stepped quietly into the hall. She stood limp with her hands at her side.

"Mademoiselle Bonney, do you know that you are now the youngest person, only the fourth woman and tenth American to receive the honor of earning a *Docteur de lettres* degree at the Sorbonne? Come in so we can congratulate you."

It was 1921 and she was twenty-seven years old, having spent the better part of those years in school. Much to her surprise, she became a minor celebrity in the weeks to come as both the French and American press made a stir about her accomplishment at the Sorbonne. *I wonder if Father read about it. Probably not.*

Telegrams arrived from well-wishers and with offers for post-doctoral study and teaching positions, including one from her former advisor at Columbia University, Professor Agasty, who originally told her doctoral studies at the Sorbonne were for men only. His note asked if she would consider a teaching position at Columbia. She smiled and discarded the telegram in the trash. For the first time, she had no real plans, having gone as far as she can in school.

She kept to herself in the weeks to come, doing more introspection than celebration, and wrote to her mother: *I've been in school much too long and perhaps it's time to explore options other than university teaching.* She couldn't help but think her mother would agree. She also sent a note to Gertrude Stein asking if they could talk, and they agreed to meet at the Café Le Dôme in Montparnasse later that week.

"You must be basking in the limelight of your well-deserved fame, Therese. How exiting!" Gertrude kissed her on both cheeks before they settled into a quiet corner.

"No, I'm afraid I'm basking in confusion, Gertrude. It's been a long time without choices; I'm not sure what to do next. I was hoping to discuss some ideas with you, especially after our last talk." She slipped off her jacket and unwound her puce-colored scarf putting them on the chair beside her.

"You must be getting offers for teaching positions. Do any sound of interest?"

"Well, that's just the point. I'm rethinking a teaching career. I can't seem to get excited about it. Maybe I've been in school too long. It's strange but I've just graduated and I feel so . . . so incompetent."

Gertrude gazed at her through narrowed eyes and moved her chair closer. Her cropped hair revealed short strands of grey and the light from the café windows illuminated the fine lines near her eyes. She leaned in. "What excites you Therese? What do you think about every day?"

Therese sighed and stared out onto the street. "I keep thinking about our last conversation, Gertrude. I think I mentioned the idea of building an intellectual and cultural bridge between the U.S. and France, and that I've been publishing articles in some of the American magazines and newspapers on the French way of life. I'm so aware that modernism in art, design, fashion and everything else here is so different and new. What's happening here in Paris hasn't caught on in mainstream America but there's a curiosity. People ask scads of questions. They know France is different, way different and that's appealing to them."

"I couldn't agree with you more, Therese. As I told you, it's difficult to get published in America and our artist friends, Picasso, Matisse, Dufy are not known there so they sell their art for a few francs on the streets here and live in poverty. Can you imagine how it would be for them if Americans could see their work? You have a good start on this, my dear. You're already writing about French culture and creating interest."

"Yes, but slowly."

Gertrude laughed. "Therese, patience is not one of your virtues; that's one of the things I like about you. You're like a bolt of lightning underneath your quiet exterior. So tell me your thoughts." Gertrude settled back in her chair folding her arms in front of her tweed jacket.

"Well, this may seem unrealistic, but . . . but what if I were to start a real press service here; you know, like a clearing house gathering and disseminating the written word and illustrations depicting the Parisian lifestyle: the avant-garde, the artists, cooks, designers, the writers, people who inhabit the city, the modernism."

"Ah, now this sounds interesting." Gertrude unfolded her arms.

"The real Paris is almost unknown in other countries, not just in America. I don't really know anything about business, only that I want to explain the innovations in France to others. I want them to love France as much as I do. This so-called press service could distribute news of Paris by allowing newspapers and magazines in America and elsewhere to subscribe to the service. They'd get regular articles and illustrations and even request articles by subject." Therese sat up straight and spoke faster, her eyes bright as pearls. "It would be much like I'm doing now but on a grander scale. For one thing, I could finally write under my own name instead of a darn pseudo-name that hides my gender. The news and illustrations would show Paris after the Great War as it embraces modernism in the arts, the architecture, feminism, literature, philosophy, and, well just everything! I think people want to know what's going on here, don't you think?"

"Absolutely!"

"Making information available could even create an international society not just a totally French or American one; it would bring the two nations together. I'm not sure how this will work exactly, but . . ."

Gertrude reached over and grabbed her hand. "Do it, Therese, do it! It's a perfect idea, splendid in fact. How exciting and wonderful for you, for all of us. Only someone like you can make this happen, and what a wonderful way to utilize your expertise and cultural intellect. By damn, do it, my dear!"

Encouraged by Gertrude's enthusiasm, Therese rushed over to Madeleine's salon. They had been talking about their private lives more and Madeleine had let her guard down and shared her feelings on more than one occasion. They were beginning to take a genuine interest in each other's quest to succeed in a man's world so Therese was anxious to discuss her idea for a press service and to let her know that she wouldn't be leaving for a teaching position after all.

She knew something was wrong when she walked through the door. The staff huddled near the desk whispering, and two clients were being ushered out of the foyer and given appointments to return. Therese walked through the workroom toward Madeleine's office and heard loud voices. One was Monsieur Guillet's voice, Madeleine's business attorney. Therese had met him once before. But mostly she heard Madeleine, her voice almost unrecognizable. She turned to leave when the door opened and both Monsieur Guillet and Madeleine appeared.

Therese backed up. "I'll come back Madame Vionnet; it was nothing important."

"No come in, Therese." Monsieur Guillet left after they uttered something about meeting again tomorrow. When Madeleine closed the door Therese could see that her face was ashen with blotches of red on her neck not quite hidden by the high ruffles of her dress. Her eyes were red and moist as she handed Therese the fashion page from *Le Figaro*, one of the popular Parisian newspapers.

Double the Trouble, the headline read. Therese looked quizzically at Madeleine. "It seems someone copied the gown I made for one of my most important clients. Another woman appeared wearing a counterfeit version at a large reception they both attended earlier this week and a photographer snapped their picture both wearing the same dress."

"Oh, no." Therese realized the importance of originality in *haute couture*. She also knew that Madeleine was a perfectionist, a true artist who took pride in being original. She'd never seen this side of her though, how upset she was and angry. Therese felt a little embarrassed, like a voyeur looking upon someone else's tragedy. She stood by awkwardly, watching.

"This will ruin me, really ruin me," Madeleine said, tears streaming down her face. She covered her face with her hands, shaking her head. "Clients don't pay thousands of francs to find someone else wearing the same gown!" She slammed her hand on the table. "No one can replicate that dress without the pattern we made after the dress was cut. And look, they didn't even do a good job even though the fabric is identical." Madeleine threw the newspaper on her desk.

"No one can make the dress? Not even if they have a photograph of it? Perhaps your client might have worn it to another event and it was photographed."

"No, the pattern is missing. I just checked a few minutes ago with my attorney. The patterns are kept locked in the storeroom. Of course no one is taking responsibility. Besides, you know how I work Therese, how intricate my markings are to get the dress to fall just right. No one can duplicate that look on their own or from a photo. And I'm careful to lock up all the patterns, notes, measurements, everything."

Therese knew that to be true. She took a deep breath and felt a wave of agony. All she could think of was that night when Lila was in the atelier late and the satchel, and how surprised she was when Therese walked in. Maybe it meant nothing. And then again maybe it did.

"Do you have any idea who might have taken the pattern?"

"I spend my time behind closed doors. I detach myself from much of what goes on here so I can work. As long as everyone does their job, I leave it up to Lila to oversee the management of the salon."

There was a long silence.

"Lila?" Therese hated to hear that name coming out of her own mouth.

Madeleine sat down near the desk. She pushed her fingers through her hair then stood abruptly, slamming her fist down on the desk over and over. "Damn! Lila!" Her tears spilled onto the desk dampening the newspaper that spread the ill tidings.

"I hate to say this, Madeleine, but I saw her one night some weeks ago when I came in for a draping. I surprised her. She looked shocked to see me, and said she thought I had a class that night, but I didn't. There was a light tan leather satchel with a flap and some straps, I think. Lila played with the flap trying to get it to close. She said she'd forgotten something and came back for it. It was an odd encounter, but I didn't think any more about it."

"My god, of course Lila, that bitch!" Madeleine sat down at her desk and stared into space.

Twelve

WORKING FROM HER studio apartment on Saint Germaine des Prés on a meager budget, Therese started the Bonney Service to be promoted as the first American illustrated press service in Europe. She planned a New York office operated by her mother and sister, Louise, who were giddy with excitement to be part of a "family" business.

Therese couldn't wait to share the news with Madeleine but hadn't heard from her for over two weeks. She knew Madeleine was upset over the counterfeit dress so she stopped by to see if she could be of any help, and share the news about her new venture. Lila was at the front desk when she walked into the atelier and toward Madeleine's office but Lila stepped in front of her and crossed her arms.

"We were wondering when you might be in," Lila said with a strong stench of sarcasm.

"I'm not sure what you mean. I'm here to see Madame Vionnet. Is she not in, Lila?"

"You're no long employed here. You've been let go. Here's your letter of termination." She thrust something at Therese. "If you have any questions you can contact our attorney, Monsieur Guillet. I should tell you that if you make a scene, we're to call the gendarmes and charges will be made."

"What? What's going on, Lila? I need to speak to Madeleine."

"That's not possible, now please leave."

"What's this all about? What happening?"

Lila scribbled something on a slip of paper and thrust it at her. It was Monsieur Guillet's address. "If you don't leave immediately we will call the authorities. You're lucky to get off with just a termination. Now leave!"

Several clients milled about in the foyer and rather than make a scene, Therese rushed out the door and walked quickly to the address on the slip of paper, a short distance away, running the last half block. Guillet was just leaving his office when she ran up the stone steps.

"I need to talk to you right away," she said out of breath.

"Mademoiselle Bonney, I was just on my way out. Can it wait?"

"No, it cannot." She stood in front of him, feet apart, with a cold steely glare.

Therese sat stunned as Guillet spelled out what happened. "When Madame Vionnet and I decided to question Lila Delacroix about the disappearance of the pattern and her possible involvement in the counterfeit gown matter, she said she saw you take the pattern late one night."

"An absolute lie, Monsieur Guillet; I would never do anything to interfere with Madeleine or the House of Vionnet. Can't we go to the police?"

"Well, of course we can, but Madame Vionnet is trying to minimize the publicity of the unfortunate matter. That's why we confronted Madame Delacroix directly."

"Surely, Madame Vionnet knows the truth here; that it was most likely Lila Delacroix and certainly not me."

"Unfortunately, there's one more complication." He shuffled his notes. "Lila Delacroix brought forth another witness, one of the seamstresses, who said she also saw you take the pattern. If this was a matter for the police, two witnesses would be a very strong indication that their word would outweigh yours. Plus, you perhaps could be considered more motivated to sell the pattern for a sizeable profit since you're unemployed for the most part. I'm afraid the evidence would not be favorable for your acquittal . . . again, that is, if the matter was to go to the police."

"This is outrageous! Was the seamstress a friend of Lila's? Can't something be done?" She stood and paced in front of his desk. She stopped to pound the desk with her hand. "This is absurd, absolutely absurd! Can't we do something?"

"That's what Madame Vionnet asked. But given two witnesses and keeping the matter out of the press, I advised her to handle it this way. It seems the least damaging to everyone."

"To everyone?" She leaned over his desk. "Well, not to me!"

"That may not necessarily be true. It could be worse, Mademoiselle Bonney. You could go to jail and have your own fine reputation tarnished. Here's the official word from the House of Vionnet, and he reached for a slip of paper from a basket on his desk. It read:

An unnamed and unethical employee leaked the design and has been let go. Matters are underway to prevent the counterfeiting of any future designs.

"She has to protect her company, her name, at any cost. I'm sure you understand."

Therese bit her lip and wiped her face with her sleeve. "And how does Madame Vionnet see all of this?"

He paused and looked at her, his eyes softer. "She's devastated on all fronts. I can tell you that personally."

It was February, the frigid part of the year and Therese worked in her apartment wearing wool gloves and her herringbone scarf wrapped tight to stay warm. She walked through the small apartment, through the kitchen, and back and forth each day while work sat on her desk unfinished. At times she sat for long hours with her eyes closed. *It was just a job and now I'm accused of stealing - and from Madeleine, of all people; someone I wanted as a friend. I'll never understand this.* She tightened her scarf to keep her mind from unraveling.

"I'm so naïve," she whispered under her breath.

To keep herself busy and forget the disaster at Madeleine's salon, she began sending out press releases announcing the opening of The Bonney Service and wrote in earnest, anything about Paris and modernism of interest to American audiences. The notoriety from her previous success at the Sorbonne helped put her in the news again as the founder of the first illustrated press service in Europe. Yet, she still had to sell editors abroad on the idea.

Anxious to get away, she sailed to New York to finalize the details and meet with prospective publishers and editors to sell them on the press service. But when they saw she was a woman and doing the work herself they refused to subscribe. A few asked if she was working with a male partner or manager but she stood her ground, reminding them that they'd been publishing her free-lance articles all along under the name of T. Bonney.

"Journalism is a man's business, young lady," one admitted. "You know, gritty and demanding." He shrugged his shoulders. "Sorry."

Back in Paris she was at a loss. She took long walks looking in store windows and spent endless afternoons in the galleries of Montparnasse. She rode the new subway to any stop and then back again, pausing only to admire the art deco ironwork at the entrances. At dusk she'd sit by Pont Neuf, the oldest standing bridge to cross over the river Seine, watching book venders along the quay selling reprints of Voltaire and Rousseau while chasing birds off the displays and smiling at the tourists. Colorfully-lit boats floated lazily downstream leaving in their wake, small waves lapping against the canal and muffled only by the laughter of tourists. Frustrated and angry, she watched the world move around her. Fired by Madeleine and a failure at promoting her new business, she felt despairing. She wanted to blame someone but could only look to herself. A frigid gust blew off the Seine and she sunk deeper into her coat and pulled her hat down over her ears before walking home in the starless night.

One chilly afternoon she sat in a small park in her neighborhood, St-Germaine-des-Pres, bundled in her wool coat and black knit beret to stay warm. She smelled the savory aromas drifting from the nearby French patisserie and listened off and on to children playing games in the park, but mostly she dabbled in her notebook and tapped her pencil in agitation, thinking about what she would say to her mother and Louise. She wrote a few lines and crossed out words but nothing sounded right.

Her last draft said: *The abysmal rejection of the press service by the editors is cause for concern and I'm again considering teaching.* She crumpled that one up too.

If Madeleine were here she might have some suggestions for breaking this unpleasant news to my family. Well, she's not here so that's a moot point. She snapped her pencil in two and threw it in a waste can and thought about her mother. She had desperately wanted to provide some income for her, some comfort since she'd given up everything in life for her children. The press service would have been a family venture providing work and income for both her mother and Louise. *Now it seems I can't even provide for myself.*

She remembered their move to California many years ago when her mother woke them quietly before dawn one morning and whisked them off to the train station while their father slept. She counted out the fare for three using coins she'd saved. "All third-class tickets please," she remembered her mother saying proudly. Soon they were on the train sharing a wooden bench in the last car. They nibbled on small pieces of bread and apple and at night the girls curled up with their heads on their mother's lap, each cradling a small bag hastily packed with their clothes. They giggled and their mother smiled, but Therese never forgot the look of fear in her mother's eyes.

She got up slowly from the park bench and packed up her notebook, deciding to stop at the patisserie for an espresso before going back to her apartment.

The *boulanger* behind the counter was cutting pieces of a croissant as Therese entered. "*Voulez goûter notre croissant au chocolat aujourd'hui?*" she asked.

Therese eyed the appetizing plate of bite-sized pieces of a chocolate croissants. "No, no not today thank you."

"Go ahead my dear, these samples are free," the *boulanger* said in perfect English. "Once you try one you'll see how good they are," she said smiling.

Therese thought for a moment. "These are free samples?"

"*Oui, Mademoiselle.*"

After taking the last sip of her espresso she practically ran back to her apartment. Out of breath, she composed a short letter to those on her list of editors and publishers. By the end of the month almost all had signed up for the free trial offer for a subscription to the Bonney Press Service, offered with "no obligation." The following month over half had signed up for the actual paid service, with more signing each day.

Thirteen

THE DOORBELL RINGING at that hour surprised her and she knocked over a small aperitif sitting on her desk as she got up. She dabbed it with a cloth before going to the door. She was even more surprised to see Madeleine, looking elegant and undoing the top button on her beige wool coat. It had been months since they'd spoken, not since Therese was let go at the House of Vionnet. Therese replayed that anger as she stood there not knowing what to say.

She opened the door wider and Madeleine, hesitant at first, stepped inside and they stood awkwardly by the door until Madeleine broke the silence.

"Therese, may I sit down?"

Therese stepped closer, sorting through all her feelings of sadness, anger, and disappointment. She was abrupt. "I didn't take the pattern, Madeleine. I didn't take anything from you. I've never even told anyone I worked for you. I protected your privacy and in turn you betrayed me. You didn't even allow me to defend myself."

"I didn't betray you." Madeleine's voice quivered. "I understand how it might seem that way. Of course I knew you didn't take the pattern, Lila took it. But when she convinced or bribed one of the seamstresses, we knew it would be futile to prove otherwise. It would have been two witnesses against your word, Therese." Her eyes were searching. "And to be honest, I needed to protect my business and let everything settle down rather than have a lengthy legal battle that would have delighted the press and perhaps ruin my company."

Therese looked away trying not to get sidetracked by the words, or the feelings.

"I'm here to say I'm sorry, Therese. I never intended for you to get hurt over this, really I didn't. I thought I was protecting you from legal charges and protecting your reputation while protecting myself from more negative publicity. I should have contacted you sooner and I'm sorry."

"But you harbored the perpetrator and threw me out."

Madeleine sighed and shook her head. "Yes, although I wouldn't put it that way. This was a business decision. Firing Lila would have created more legal battles and publicity. Therese, you live by your principles and look for what's right and what's wrong. I live pragmatically, the opposite of your idealism. I look at what works best. Maybe it's the difference between our two countries. The French have very little room for sentimentality when it comes to business, or anything else for that matter. Americans are self-righteous, looking for blame or who is less than ideal. If you want to marry the two countries, then perhaps you need to understand who you are marrying. Again, there's no room for sentimentality if you want to sell us to the world. There was no room for sentimentality in the business decision I had to make. Again, I'm sorry."

Therese turned away and then looked at Madeleine again. "You claim you are not sentimental? How can you say that? What about that picture I've seen on your desk? You know the one that's torn and faded, that you put in the drawer when someone comes in. Is that your childhood picture? Isn't that sentimentality? Where's the pragmatism in that?"

Almost immediately she regretted her words. She realized that bringing something so personal into the conversation seemed stupid and unfair. She looked down while Madeleine buttoned the top buttons of her coat and let herself out closing the door behind her. Therese buried her face in her hands. She knew Madeleine was strong, complex, even flawed, but she wished she could take back her words. *What a mistake. Why did I have to muddy things?*

Madeleine walked back to the salon in the cold that night.

I shouldn't have been so blunt. I wanted to apologize, not give a lecture of the ways of the French. No one has been able to explain the French anyway so why even try.

Marie Gerber tapped softly on the door and Madeleine thanked her for coming. "Let's sit in the foyer. It's more comfortable there" They squeezed through bolts of fabric and around several sewing machines that left little room to maneuver in the already cramped quarters.

"I never thought I'd be running my own sweatshop," Madeleine said a bit amused and looking around at the cramped quarters, "but it's beginning to look that way." They sat in the well-appointed foyer and Madeleine got straight to the point. "I've been obsessed with my work, Marie, and my life and business are crumbling around me." She told her about the counterfeit dress and her fear of getting rid of Lila because of the trouble she might cause. "I don't have the time or the inclination to deal with it all."

"And you shouldn't have to, Madeleine. You're an artist. You're getting 10,000-15,000 francs for a gown. If American women are paying that for a dress, you've arrived! You should be designing not managing the drama that's inherent in this crazy business, but first tell me about that young woman. You said she got hurt in all of this Lila business."

"Yes, and it's my fault. You know I put business first. I tried to apologize but . . ."

"Why is this so important to you? She only worked for you on occasion, right?"

Madeleine rubbed her hands. "I liked her, Marie. I don't know why but I always looked forward to seeing her. She's different, authentic, and liberated in a natural way not the way some women try to be. Therese kept my mind in motion, spurring on my creativity. She's struggling to find her own way in life but I always felt a little more alive when she was around."

"So you hurt her and now you feel guilty."

"I hurt her and now I feel bad. There's a difference. "

"Give it some time, Madeleine, and then do something about it. I've never known you to be concerned over things like this. But right now I think your House of Vionnet is the priority. Investors are interested if you're open to that. You're the most talked about designer in Paris right now and everyone is waiting to get a Vionnet. An investor could help you expand."

"Oh, I know, Marie. I'm not sure why it's so hard for me to do that. But I either need to scale back or I need to move forward with a larger salon and more staff. I see the problem clearly, I'm just hesitant about the solution."

"What's holding you back?"

"I guess I don't want to give up my life's work and commitment to liberating women through fashion. I'm afraid I'll lose that if I take in business partners who may have their own agendas. Like you and your sisters, I've broken the barriers and entered a man's profession when they said it couldn't be done. To bring men into my business now seems like defeat. You can understand that. You've struggled with the same issues."

"Yes, but frankly, we paid our own way by having wealthy parents, whereas you've earned and created what you have on your own."

"Maybe I just don't want to admit there's a limit as to how far I can go without getting wealthy men to come to my rescue."

Marie sat quietly for a minute. "Perhaps you need to view the financial part of it as separate. You've become a renowned fashion designer and no one can take that away from you, and you don't have to share that with anyone. On the other hand, a financial arrangement is just that. Businesses borrow all the time to expand. Why shouldn't you? Use those financial backers. Use them to get what *you* want rather than the other way around."

M. Théophile Bader had a meager face; his small mouth shrinking into a pucker at the slightest provocation. His eyes, mere slits, sit beneath thin black eyebrows that underlined a continuous wrinkle along his brow. Besides that, he reeked of the smell of sour cigars. Madeleine feared his unpleasantness might foretell his disposition and business ethics even though he had already achieved success as a wealthy and shrewd retailer who owned the department store Galeries Lafayette and had investments in another, Monoprix.

Bader arrived late for the meeting and sat next to Henri Lillas, owner of the popular Parisian department store, the Bazar de l'Hotel de Ville. The third potential investor was an Argentinean, Martinez de Hoz, who was more famous for his beautiful wife than for any of his business accomplishments. Madame de Hoz was one of the most photographed clients of the House of Vionnet, especially when she wore one of Madeleine's most dazzling gowns. It was rumored that she married Martinez because he offered to buy her as many Vionnet gowns as she wanted. Madeleine asked Marie if she would sit in on the meeting and they sat together both unpinning their hats and placing them on the table.

Bader immediately sensed Madeleine's reserve. "I want to be clear," he said, "that our interest in the House of Vionnet is that of investors and for financial profit only."

Madeleine glanced at Marie and leaned close. "His wife probably wants to be assured of a constant flow of Vionnet gowns," she whispered.

Bader, along with the other investors, praised Madeleine for her accomplishments and added quickly that change is often necessary to stay in business. His face twitched before proposing a new venture he called Vionnet et Cie or Vionnet and Company where the three investors would act as silent partners and have limited powers.

"The operational decisions would be up to you of course, Madame Vionnet, and we would all share in the profits." He shifted in his seat before adding, "I will be the majority stockholder because of the size of my investment." Madeleine started to interrupt but he continued. "The money would go to fund a new establishment designed to outshine all other couturiers in Paris," he said grinning with pride. "You of course can hire as many seamstresses as you please and help design the layout of the space." He paused to shape his mustache with the tips of his fingers. "We will put up the money but you will run the company."

Lillas added, "You need a showcase, Madame Vionnet. Something . . . well, sensational! A venue that reflects your innovative styles; a salon with pizzazz! It's hard to believe someone of your fame works from a small one-floor atelier away from other houses of *haute couture*. You could be a global sensation if you accept our proposal," he said smiling and nodding to the others.

It was hard not to be dazzled by the offer. Madeleine and Marie Gerber sat long after the backers left. "This will put you at the top,

Madeleine. You can do whatever you want with the company given the amount of money they intend to invest."

Madeleine ran her hands through her hair and paced the room. "These men will own part of my company and my name. I abhor the idea! I've worked to get where I am on my own. Everyone said I'd never be a designer. I was told I'd be lucky to be a dressmaker."

"Madeleine, sit down. Listen, you are a designer and one of the best. The financial support will free you up to move forward." Marie leaned closer. "You could hire others to do the menial tasks. You'd be free to design *haute couture*. Isn't that what you want?"

Marie watched Madeleine twirling a pencil on the table.

"You don't need to decide this minute, Madeleine. Take some time to think about it. Let's talk again soon."

Fourteen

THE GLOW OF LIGHT from the back of the building shined bright against the darkening sky. Therese paused under a gas lamp wondering if Madeleine might be working late and imagined seeing her silhouette in the window and pictured herself standing next to her.

Just then a cold damp wind pushed tenaciously through the narrow cracks between the buildings and an unexpected gust took her thoughts and almost sent her felt hat whirling down the street. She shrugged and looked again but the fantasy had faded and the building seemed smaller and further away, the light in the window now obscure.

She stood there as a carriage passed, the clattering of hooves on the cobblestone street distracting her. When it passed she stepped into the street to cross, to go closer, maybe even to go in, but then she stepped back unsure.

Under the star-filled winter night a stranger on the corner wearing an overcoat and a brimmed fedora watched her as he fingered a cigarette before lighting it, tossing the match aside and blowing smoke that caught the last vestige of light from the slate-gray sky. She moved on, somehow thinking the walk would cure her melancholy.

Their last conversation hung like an imposter in her midst even though she tried to forget, and the familiar pang in her stomach was there again as she thought about their argument.

Words can never be taken back and maybe they shouldn't be. Some things need to be said. She stopped to watch a young couple buying roasted chestnuts from a street vendor, laughing as they juggled the hot treats in their gloved hands. Therese sighed and looked away. *I said what I needed to say to her. I could have added more though. I could have told her that I'd been living in a wilderness until I started working with her in the atelier.*

She joined her new friends Janet Flanner and Nancy Cunard as often as she could especially when she felt the need for company and even when they attended the wild and seductive parties at the women's salons. The soirées were curiosities to her but not of great interest, although she was learning about Paris after dark and about the women's liberation movement. She preferred instead going with Janet and Nancy to the tiny surrealist galleries near the *Jardin de Luxembourg* and talking about art and politics, topics more of interest.

On occasion she did go to Tamara de Lempica's soirees because she appreciated the Polish artist's paintings and taste in interior design. Lempica's parties were less artful than her well-designed apartment but never dull - the drinks were served by half-nude waitresses and cocaine and hashish were passed around freely. Therese observed that women often kept cocaine in their compacts instead of face powder, which she thought was clever but she nevertheless refused it when offered. She wondered if she was perceived as an outsider for not joining in, but then she already knew she was an outsider in many ways without judging it or feeling remorse. She saw herself as different and perhaps more studious, but not out of touch. Lempica's soirees grew more promiscuous as the evenings wore on and women paired and disappeared - which was just about the time she politely excused herself.

"You're new here," one elegantly-dressed woman said one evening, latching on to her arm as she turned to leave. Therese nodded and then slipped out the door. *Is that what it means to be a real Parisian woman? I guess I'm falling far short.*

As a writer of Parisian life she was learning that shock value was fashionable among women who considered themselves liberated. Tamara de Lempica was fond of saying, "I refuse myself nothing," which to Therese was the banner of the women's empowerment movement she observed in Paris and certainly at the women-only salons. Lempica's paintings reflected the freedom women took in their own bodies as if reclaiming them. Her painting *Group of Four Nudes* that hung in her living room was indicative of the acceptable chic attached to lesbianism in the 1920s in Paris, and Therese overheard the American writer, Mercedes de Acosta, say at one of the soirees that her lovers had included Isadora

Duncan, Greta Garbo, Marlene Dietrich, and Tallulah Bankhead. True or not, it sounded plausible given what Therese was learning about Paris after dark

Days passed into months and early one morning a note came in the mail as she brewed another kettle of tea.

I'm working on a special gown for an important client and I can't find the right model. Would you come for a draping Friday at dusk? I'll leave the door ajar.

Madeleine.

Therese read the note over and over, baffled at first but then with more interest. She paced the room feeling slightly nervous as she always did when seeing Madeleine at the salon, always a little uneasy and uncomfortable in her presence yet always lit with energy. *It's been so long. We haven't spoken since her brief visit to my apartment.* Just the thought of the stolen pattern stirred up memories of anger and betrayal that at the time had recast all her notions about life and fairness. Still, she felt the lonely void of not having a friend like Madeleine who gave her the courage to focus on what's possible in her own life. *Should I go? But what would I say?*

The late afternoon light was all but gone and the atelier was even more cluttered than she remembered as she entered quietly just at dusk. She paused for a long moment near the entrance, her thoughts and feelings churning inside as she wondered what it would be like to walk through that door, to see Madeleine again, and to work with her. Squeezing between the tables her heart beating fast, she found a small but cluttered aisle leading her to the back. The familiar scent of fabric and sensuous colors of silken material gave her an intoxicating quiver and she stopped long enough to run her hand along a piece of cream colored rayon spread on a table, imagining the aroma of vanilla.

A thin line of light coming from beneath the door led her to Madeleine's office and she hesitated then went in. Madeleine stood at her desk, her eyes darker than usual, her hair a bit longer, but the same contour to her face, strong and defined as always. She wore a long black skirt and a soft rayon blouse the color of dark wheat and smiled but only faintly.

Madeleine and Therese

Therese stood awkwardly by the door running her hands down her wrinkled skirt then slowly removing her beret, allowing her hair fall before she looked away. Her eyes fell toward the wooden floor, faded and worn from years of use. She didn't look up, embarrassed by her sudden emotion. She wanted to run from the room not knowing what to say or what to do. Madeleine tilted her head to one side, narrowing her eyes while watching her intently. She walked from behind the desk closer to Therese touching her face, lifting it to see her.

"Therese, we need to talk, I mean really talk." Therese took a deep and trembling breath and let her shoulders relax knowing that somehow everything would be all right.

They talked late that night, sharing their feelings, the heaviness of their business dilemmas, and sometimes just sitting together quietly. Because of the late hour, they agreed to postpone the draping session until the following evening and Therese took a carriage home. The cadence of the horse's hooves was soothing but not as much as seeing Madeleine. They unraveled layers of anger and disappointment to expose what really mattered but only subtly grasped before. They were both the better for it.

Fifteen

THE NIGHT SKY was lit with stars. Therese caught her breath as she rushed through the front door of the salon getting there right after dusk and anxious for their first draping session in months. Like a page from the past, Madeleine was spreading a roll of fabric on the cutting table.

"I have some good news," Therese said, her scarf hanging loosely while she unbuttoned her coat. "I just received word that all of the editors I queried have now signed up for the press service, every one of them!" Her eyes were alive and she waived her hands while talking, accidently knocking off her felt-brimmed hat.

Madeleine laughed and watched Therese whose excitement was like a burst of fireworks. She saw her as youthful and appealing, but no more so than her charm and paradoxically her tenderness at that moment. "It's wonderful news, Therese. The editors realized what they'll be getting. You do move like a locomotive when you set your mind to something."

"I can hardly imagine all of this," Therese said, still out of breath. "I can't wait to get started." Madeleine kept her gaze and smiled. *We've crossed a threshold, both of us easily and steadily moving in our destined directions.* She found the moment fresh and poignant and she sighed deeply. *How close we came to losing moments like this.*

The dim light flickered in the draping area as Madeleine unrolled a shimmering creamy-mint satin fabric and spread it carefully on the table, looking and tilting her head at different angles looking pleased. Her hand rested on the fabric. Therese watched the ritual, how Madeleine chooses her fabric carefully especially when creating a glamorous gown for an important client. Madeleine glanced her way. "Magnificent, isn't it?" Therese smiled and nodded as Madeleine held a portion of the fabric up to the light. "It's full of life, like champagne," she said smiling.

Therese untied the scarf around her hips and slipped out of her long skirt and bulky knit sweater, putting them aside with her heavy boots and hat. She shook her hair away from her face and wrapped the muslin around her, waiting until she felt Madeleine's hands laying the soft satin fabric over her shoulders. She let her head fall slightly.

Madeleine paused for a moment. "I was upset because of the distance between us."

Therese turned. "So was I. Do you want to talk about it?"

"No, do you?" Madeleine whispered. Therese shook her head and Madeleine waited a moment and then wrapped the satin fabric around Therese's midsection, making sure it was positioned on the bias. Therese felt a slight shiver when the satin touched her skin and let the muslin drape fall to the floor. Her sigh could barely be heard. "Are you comfortable with this?" Madeleine asked. Therese nodded so Madeleine draped the satin, gently fitting it over her breasts while making small tucks, securing them carefully in place with pins. She let the rest of the fabric flow to the floor before fitting it over the hips.

"Move a little and twist to one side," she whispered. Therese did what she asked. "Ah, lovely, now a couple of steps." Therese sensed her pleasure with the fabric and how it was responding. She listened for any instructions that involved moving or walking while Madeleine pulled the fabric carefully around her abdomen and over the hip bones allowing it to stretch, but only slightly. "Hmm, the beauty of the bias," Madeleine said softly.

Working more rapidly now, Madeleine moved the fabric in all directions, pinning it in place when she was satisfied and undoing it when she wasn't. She had Therese walk across the room, and at times would unpin and refit a section like a sculptor might adjust the clay to get the right effect. When finished, the fabric did the rest, wrapping itself around the legs and falling to the floor in soft folds like water poured from an urn in glimmering ripples.

Madeleine took a deep breath. "Here, look." She moved Therese toward the mirror. It was a stunning sight. The gown was so beautifully layered, so powerful, so dazzling that they both stood staring.

"How you can . . . well, how you can create this work of art from a piece of fabric is unbelievable. It's beautiful, Madeleine: it's . . . it is absolutely beautiful."

Madeleine stood behind her in the mirror. She made a small adjustment to the fabric and let her hands fall on Therese's shoulders. "Yes, yes beautiful," she whispered. For a moment a sensual warmth lingered between them as they stood there, neither moving, breathing in rhythm. Abruptly, Madeleine moved her hands away and busied herself with another small adjustment.

Therese turned her head to one side so Madeleine could hear. "You liberate other women," she said softly, "but not yourself."

After a long pause, "Yes."

Therese turned to face her. She chose her words. "I've . . . I've never been with anyone before." Her skin was pale in the dim light, her look vulnerable, ethereal, her lips a soft pink. A cascade of auburn hair fell onto her bare shoulders, and only her voice revealed her slight nervousness.

Madeleine stared, her dark eyes moving quickly, searching Therese's face for expression, something beyond the words. She watched Therese take a deep long breath, then an innocent quiver. She moved closer. "Nor have I, not really," she finally replied. The ambient light fell on rolls of fabric and on the ochre-colored walls, interrupted only by the two shadows eventually appearing as one.

Sixteen

HER THOUGHTS OF the previous evening were still vivid and scintillating when Therese returned to the salon for the few remaining measurements on the gown. She couldn't wait to see Madeleine again. For the first time, she felt like a real Parisian woman, truly grownup and a part of the liberation movement among women in Paris. Pushing aside a large role of fabric, she approached the back room and the light filtering from behind the open door. She felt a warm and pleasant quiver.

Madeleine turned from the window and motioned Therese to come in. "The fabric is cut so I just need a few measurements. It will only take a couple of minutes." Her voice was strained, detached, and the sparkle in her eyes the night before was gone. She talked about the fabric while measuring the waist and floor length, and about the client who plans to wear the dress at a special gala in New York soon. The surprising coolness in the room tangled the words - Therese heard only half of what she said. When Madeleine finished she looked away. The awkward silence grew into minutes.

Madeleine's face was strained, almost stern. Her hair was disheveled and her dress wrinkled as if she'd slept in it. "We should talk, Therese. Let's sit here in the office." Therese sat and leaned back, aware that her life was flickering like the end of a burnt candle.

Madeleine stared at her desk. "I'm not sure where to begin," she said finally looking up. "There are no *bon mots*, or adequate words for this. Therese, about last night after the draping session . . ." She took a deep breath. "It was lovely . . . so lovely in every way but I think we need to talk about it. I've been draping with models for years and this has never happened before. I'm older, I should have known better. It was my mistake."

The word traveled through her body before reaching her mind. "Mistake?" Therese blurted out. "It was a mistake to you?"

"Therese, I hope it won't stand in the way of our work. You are a perfect model, the best for my style of gowns. I'd hate to lose you over something like this."

Therese felt her breath deep inside and felt a wave of panic. "Something like this? It meant nothing to you?" She looked away, her eyes wide and moist. "Maybe we don't need to talk about it right now. There's a danger in analyzing too much. Let's just see in time . . ."

Madeleine shook her head. "Therese, sometimes these . . . these intimate encounters come with assumptions like, well like commitments, feelings, perhaps expectations," she said haltingly. "I can't speak for you but that was never my intention. We just got caught up in a lovely moment and let it go too far."

Therese sat rigid. "Don't you feel any . . . any closeness or caring?"

Madeleine stared at the light's reflection on the wall and heard the radiator hiss. "There's no room in my life for that. It's not safe to love anyone, you must know that."

Therese wiped her eyes on her sleeve. "I don't know anything about love, but I know I can. The challenge it seems is to be loved in return."

Madeleine sighed and rubbed her forehead. "Therese, an intimate encounter does not mean love. Look, we're both immersed in our businesses. Our personal and intellectual freedom is important if we're to succeed. You're young and . . . idealistic. Women, well some of us today want to vote, run businesses, have financial freedom and not be tempted into relationships or even situations that might, well, might threaten that liberation. You . . . you've talked about what goes on at those salons, casual encounters and then they go their own way. That's the way it is these days. We can't make this more than it is."

"It wasn't anything like those soirées."

"No, I can see it wasn't for you."

"And for you?"

"Therese, I don't attend those places. But the point is that we think differently about what happened. You obviously have some expectations, some assumptions, and you're clearly disappointed."

Therese ran her hand over her eyes again. "I don't pretend to know anything about this sort of, well situation, but can't something more meaningful come from this . . . this kind of closeness?"

Madeleine shook her head and shrugged. She sat for a while looking away. "In theory, perhaps. But not if there are other priorities like work and keeping one's freedom. Then something like this would stand in the way."

"Why? Does it have to?"

Madeleine searched for words. "Well, who can taunt themselves with one pleasure without wanting more? And before you know it . . . well, it just wouldn't work." She straightened her back and put her hands on the table. "This seems like a serious conversation over a one-time encounter. Again Therese, I hope this won't interfere with our work or our friendship."

Therese sat stunned, hearing words that cut like a broad sword. She looked around the room, aware that Madeleine had stopped talking. *She seems to be waiting for me to say something.* "Of course, yes of course," and she gathered her coat and hat and walked toward the door.

Madeleine groaned softly. "Therese if it's closeness you want, there are so many others out there and some day you will meet someone and marry. There's a whole world of happiness waiting for you."

Therese closed the door behind her, trying not to slam it. Madeleine listened to her footsteps fade and when she heard the front door of the salon slam she put her head down and wept. *What would she want with me anyway, a reclusive dressmaker?*

On the walk home, Therese thought how little she knew about life and the mysteries of human behavior. *Madeleine was right, that intimacy can come with expectations and assumptions.* She shook her head as she walked alone on the street. *How immature of me to assume that physical love was the same as emotional love. I feel so embarrassed, naïve. How could I have been so stupid? Madeleine must think me terribly immature.*

Hazel Warlaumont

87

Nevertheless, she couldn't help but think about that night, the breathtaking seduction, the tenderness, the delightful abandonment. At the time, she was sure she would never be the same. *How could something so exquisite be dismissed like a heap of leaves swept up after a storm — instead of the most beautiful experience of a lifetime? I'll never understand any of this. My first attempt at friendship and then something like this happens! It seems unfair to get only a glimpse of something so special.* The frigid cold air bit her face with a fury but she let her scarves hang loose. The music from an upstairs apartment and the beggar on the corner went unnoticed.

The House of Vionnet was busier than ever in the weeks to come and Madeleine put in long hours - many past midnight that included extra draping sessions. Therese was grateful for the extra work and nothing further was mentioned about their encounter or the discussion that followed. Therese decided not to dwell on the incident. It was something beyond her reach, beyond her knowledge and understanding. She'd spent her years in books not in life so she didn't feel like a martyr or a victim, but then not like a liberated Parisian woman either. She just simply didn't understand. Maybe that made it easier to accept.

Madeleine on the other hand worked quietly and was somber, almost morose. Her sullenness went on for weeks and she struggled with her guilt and regrets. She was reminded every day that she hurt Therese, someone she cared for. And she truly regretted her insensitivity during their discussion. She could have said that she had felt the same intoxication, the same elation, but instead she referred to it as a mistake. *How arrogant of me to dismiss it, to pretend it didn't matter. Why couldn't I admit that it did mean something to me?* She tried to put those thoughts out of her mind but couldn't. *Shutting down and detaching myself from unpleasant situations has always been my fall back. Damn, why isn't it working now?*

"I'd like to show you something before you go," Madeleine said one evening after one of their draping sessions. "I know it's late Therese, but can you come in the office when you're dressed?"

The desk drawer was half opened when Therese walked in and Madeleine had the old torn photograph in her hand. Therese put her coat and hat on the chair next to her and sat leaning forward. Madeleine didn't look at her but slid the photograph across the table.

"I don't share much, as you know," Madeleine said looking up. "It's not that I don't want people to know me." She paused and looked away. "Perhaps it's that I don't want to know myself for then I'd have to admit to my own mistakes and imperfections." Her slight smile betrayed her nervousness.

Therese thought about what she said. "I suppose that's true for all of us, isn't it?"

"Yes, but you mentioned the old photograph a while back; it was during our conversation in your apartment the night we had the disagreement. You were right in thinking there was some sentimentality attached to it. I'd like to explain."

"Madeleine, you don't have to . . ."

"I want you to know about this, Therese. I can't keep hurting you without letting you know something about myself." Therese picked up the faded photograph. The curly-haired child appeared to be barely a toddler of two or three.

Therese smiled. "How sweet, is this you?"

"No, it was . . . well, my daughter."

Therese looked again, closer. "Your daughter, really? You have a daughter?"

Madeleine rubbed her hands and entwined her fingers. "I did have a daughter. She died in a fall shortly after this picture was taken."

Therese blinked and looked at the photograph again before handing it back. "Madeleine, that's awful. It's terrible. You were married?"

Madeleine put the photograph back in the drawer. "Briefly, a long time ago. It was, well it was arranged. My father knew I was suffering at Madame Broussard's sweatshop and thought if I married I wouldn't have to work. But that wasn't the case. The man he chose for me couldn't support me, and Madame Broussard insisted that if I wanted to keep working, I had to stay with the others in the shop so I'd be available when she needed me. The man, well, my husband, picked me up for a few hours every day and took me to his boarding house. He . . . he was not kind."

She paused to look at the picture. "My father kept telling me to do what the man wanted and eventually he would take care of me. I . . . I just didn't know about such things. I was sixteen. I got pregnant and I felt desperate. That's what drove me to ask for the job at the House of Vincent the day I went to Paris with my father who didn't know I was pregnant at the time and I didn't want to tell him. What could he do anyway? He was already distraught. My hope was to have a decent job, a room of my own, and to care for my child. She was born while I worked at the House of Vincent."

Therese listened never averting her eyes. "How terrible! Didn't your mother stop this?"

"Oh, my mother. Hmm, she had left some years before when I was three. That's why my father couldn't care for me. He had to work so he took me out of school to apprentice with Madame Broussard."

"Goodness!" Therese sat shaking her head. "Having the child didn't interfere with your work at the House of Vincent and what about your husband?"

"No, not really. Vincent was a kind man. He helped me find child care and advanced me as much as he could, but knowing English in the fashion world was necessary because of our English-speaking clients. I had an opportunity for temporary work in England so I took the job for two months to learn the language. I had divorced my husband by then but kept in touch with his parents. They agreed to take my daughter while I was gone."

"Were you able to see her during that time?"

"No. No, I came home once and that was to bury her." She looked down at her hands, putting one over the other, squeezing gently. Therese wanted to reach for her hand but thought better of it. "I was told she died in a fall four weeks after I left and twenty-seven days before my planned return."

They sat in silence as the light flickered and the radiator grumbled. Madeleine stared out the window. "I don't talk about this with anyone, or nearly anyone. I have a friend, Isadora Duncan, who lost children. We've talked."

"Yes, the dancer."

"Her two young children were in a car with their nurse. The car stalled and the chauffeur got out to crank it but forgot to put the brake on. The car rolled down a hill into the river Seine. The children and nurse drowned before anyone could get to them."

"Oh, my god, how awful," Therese said.

"In her grief, she wanted to have another child right away so she got pregnant by someone she barely knew. Sadly, that child died a few minutes after birth. Isadora and I have spent long hours talking about losing our children but it's futile. It doesn't bring them back. You just build a harder shell around yourself. I keep the picture and look at it often. If I didn't it would be like letting her go. A mother never wants to let her child go."

Therese sat listening, shocked and numb. She couldn't find the right words. *A shell around herself! And why wouldn't she? Deserted by her mother, a father helpless under the circumstances, and her child's tragic death.* She wanted to soothe Madeleine's pain, to reach for her, but knew she couldn't. She now understood Madeleine's need to protect that fragile part of herself by getting lost in her work by redirecting her grief - and keeping everyone at a distance.

Madeleine leaned back in her chair. "I can't talk about this anymore Therese, but I thought you should know. I don't offer this as an excuse for hurting you or for pulling away. There is no excuse possible for that."

Seventeen

"I'M GIVING IN," Madeleine told Marie Gerber over the phone. "I can't hold off any longer. My clients are unhappy because I can't turn out the work fast enough to please them, and I need a lot more space, more seamstresses, more equipment, and more time if I'm to stay open. I'm at my wits end! My rivals are like wolves at the door waiting to drag my clients to their lair. Elsa Schiaparelli, Coco Chanel, and Paul Poiret are already imitating my work and trying the bias cut to lure clients away." She groaned. "I'm going with the backers and that's it."

"I was hoping you would, Madeleine. I'm sure you know by now that Elsa is expanding her line to include evening wear - which of course is your specialty. Coco is getting business through her self-promoting antics and her flamboyant lifestyle. It's hard to compete. I think you're making the right decision."

"Well, it doesn't feel totally right but I don't see that I have a choice. The backers are suggesting a dazzling salon, but they also want me to have a more public persona. They told me that everyone knows the Vionnet name but not the person. For god's sake, Marie, I can't be someone I'm not!"

Marie laughed. "You're a natural recluse Madeleine and you don't need to change. But you are the only person in fashion with international fame even though no one knows you. But so what? Your designs speak for themselves. They represent the new age, the 1920's, so you can understand why your clients want to see the woman who's designing the sexy gowns. Who knows, maybe your demand for privacy will add even more to your mystique!"

"Well, that's reassuring," Madeleine said. "You mean I don't need to perform for the public?"

"You wouldn't anyway," Marie said teasing. "Do what you want, Madeleine. It's still your company. Make it work for you."

It was agreed by all that the new company would be called Vionnet et Cie and headquartered in the large and luxurious building at 50 avenue Montaigne, one of Paris' most elite addresses. The building, chosen for its many rooms, enormous ceilings, and a dramatic staircase just off the foyer will have a second floor atelier where Madeleine will work. The newspaper, *Le Figaro,* reported that, "the décor will match her fashions and be tasteful, classically inspired, and innovative."

The press immediately dubbed it the "Palace of Fashion," designed by an impressive collaboration of Paris' finest architects, decorators, and artists, including the sculptor, Rene Lalique. The plans included an entry opening to a spectacular *Salon de Présentation* and a number of boutiques for furs, shoes, and accessories all under the Vionnet name. Madeleine's own upstairs quarters would be private but the downstairs would house several fitting rooms and a huge workroom designed for up to twelve-hundred seamstresses who would sew for the newly-created ready-to wear division. Several managers were chosen to oversee the daily operations, one of which would be in charge of hiring a multitude of employees. Under Madeleine's direction, his first task was to fire Lila Delacroix and her seamstress friend, and to "make their termination immediate."

At Madeleine's insistence, the salon would also have an adjoining and unprecedented medical clinic for employees, a child-care facility, an employee's lounge and cafeteria. The employees would receive regular pay raises, maternity leave, and no one would be hired under the age of sixteen.

The press was quick to report on the unorthodox and generous benefits, referring to Vionnet as "eccentric," and calling the benefits, "highly unusual for the French fashion industry often known for its sweatshops."

Théophile Bader was infuriated when he heard of the benefits and sent a note to Madeleine calling it a dire waste of money and ordered her to rescind the arrangement. Madeleine asked her attorney to send Bader a copy of the contract, underlining in red the part giving her the rights to run the business.

Several fashion houses also expressed concern saying the generous benefits might force them to offer the same. When asked to comment, Madeleine responded by saying, "Good, it's about time." When a reporter asked Coco Chanel about the Vionnet benefits, she said, "It can only lead to more employee demands."

When coaxed by the reporter to elaborate, she was quoted as saying, "The minute I turn my back there is unrest. Ungrateful bitches! Why should I give them more? Don't they realize that working for Chanel gives them a chance to meet rich lovers or even a husband? What more could they want?" When Madeleine read this in the newspaper she couldn't help but laugh at Coco's typical lack of decorum in exchange for press coverage.

While work was underway on the new salon, Madeleine and Therese continued their draping sessions in an effort to keep up with the demand. They often met for dinner or stayed late talking over a glass of wine on the nights they worked together. They kept their conversations cordial, mostly about their work but they made it a point to spend time together even when they weren't working.

"Do you feel better knowing you'll have the staff and extra room?" Therese asked one evening.

"Actually, my concern right now is about counterfeiters stealing my designs, the arrogant thieves! It's rampant and happening to everyone, and not the little deceits like Lila stealing the pattern but copying on a grand scale. They copy our dresses and sell them for a fraction of the original. It could ruin *haute couture*. We survive by producing original designs so I'm hoping to do something about it now that I'll have more time."

"What about legal protections for high fashion? We have copyright laws in the U.S. to keep someone from claiming another's work as their own."

"We don't have that here, unfortunately. Fashion has never been considered an art form so it's not covered by the laws protecting creative work. The exorbitant prices now for original gowns are tempting the copyists."

"Perhaps your managers will have some ideas. It would seem that would be their job. "

"Oh goodness, the managers? They have their sights on expansion with plans to open Vionnet salons internationally and we haven't even officially moved into the new salon. The managers want to introduce new products under the Vionnet name, like shoes and handbags, and perfumes. They talk about joint ventures with companies in the U.S. and the rest of Europe." She paused and rubbed her arms.

"It's going too fast, Therese. It's dizzying trying to keep up with their ideas. They're encouraged by the backers of course, who want to make money. It's certainly a sharp contrast from the simplicity at the salon on rue de Rivoli."

Therese could hear the concern in her voice like she was already on the train and wanted off but knowing it was too late. "Speaking of rue de Rivoli, I'd like to take some pictures of you working in the atelier there. It'll be part of history soon and will make a good article for the press service, if you're fine with that. And, I'd like them for myself as well, if I may say so – you know, a sentimental remembrance." Therese raised an eyebrow teasingly at her reference to a previous conversation about sentimentality.

Madeleine looked at her with concern, trying to read her mind and wondering if she should read something into Therese's comment. She wondered what Therese meant by a 'remembrance.' "Are you going somewhere?"

"No, no, of course not. But you'll be famous, Madeleine. More than you are now. Your life will be full of people, new models, clients . . . ." Therese shrugged her shoulders.

At a certain angle, the light from the street lamp stole through the window illuminating Madeleine's gaze. "You can take as many pictures as you like. But for yourself, trust me you will not need pictures. I'm not going anywhere and I hope you aren't either."

Hazel Warlaumont   95

Therese was quiet for a moment. "You use the word trust? Doesn't that suggest a degree of closeness? Didn't you once warn about making assumptions and also having expectations? Someone can get hurt from trusting too much. I'm sure you'd be the first to agree."

Madeleine hesitated long enough to look at her. "Ah. Yes, perhaps. But it's torment not to trust at all."

The evening ended with both of them wondering what the changes in their lives would mean to them. It was a haunting concern, one that would loom large in the weeks to come.

Eighteen

PARIS IN 1923 was marked by two major events: the opening of Madeleine Vionnet's plush "Palace of Fashion," and the death of Sarah Bernhardt, known as the *Grande Dame* of French theater. Bernhardt's funeral closed city streets as thousands of solemn mourners lined the roads to see her cortege pass down the Champs-Élysées. Therese and several of the actors from the Sarah Bernhardt Theater stood in the frigid rain with the others. For Therese, the passing of Bernhardt meant the theater would close. It wasn't just the loss of a part-time job, it was losing a friend.

As Therese stood in the street shoulder to shoulder with the others, she remembered her youthful enthusiasm when meeting Bernhardt in Paris for the first time four years earlier. In spite of her advanced age Bernhardt still performed and had a passion for the theater and French playwrights, and she and Therese often had long talks about their shared appreciation. As the cortege passed, Therese's somber homage spoke to how much she would miss her.

Without her part-time job at the theater, Therese spent more time working with Madeleine on the issue of counterfeiting in the fashion industry, now a nation-wide concern. With the opening of the new salon just weeks away, Madeleine had a growing concern the publicity and her notoriety as a popular designer would lead to more copying. With no laws to protect high fashion in France, Madeleine had cause to be worried.

"Then you'll have to be the first to establish those laws!" Therese replied when Madeleine expressed her concern.

A few weeks later after consulting with her attorney, Madeleine established the Anti-copyist Association to be housed in the new salon and under the supervision of Vionnet & Cie's managing director. All fashion designers were urged to register their garments with the association showing they are originals, and Madeleine herself introduced labels in her gowns with an original signature and an imprint of her right thumb to authenticate her gowns. Garments without these would be considered fakes.

"This business is becoming more difficult," she told Therese. "We never had to worry about protecting our designs or opening grand salons."

"Then why do it since it's not working for you right now?"

Madeleine thought for a minute. "It's our duty, all of us, to protect the fashion industry in Paris. It goes back to Napoleon's time. Half the people in Paris work in some form of the fashion industry. Besides, it's my life. It's what I know and love, but it used to be easier."

With more time on her hands now, Therese often stopped by to see Madeleine at the new salon even when they weren't draping. She'd bring a bottle of chilled champagne and a French baguette and brie knowing Madeleine would be working late and welcome a break. If all the workers were gone, they'd sit on the steps of the grand stairwell where the moonlight shimmered on the walls and silence was a welcome relief for them both.

Madeleine felt a little awkward at times being with Therese after that intimate evening. She was especially careful during the draping sessions, or when their hands brushed while working, or alone together over a glass of champagne at the end of the day. She liked Therese and they had long discussions. She found her easy to talk to especially after telling her about her daughter. Therese was a compassionate listener and Madeleine shared much about her life and struggle to the top - information she'd normally not share with anyone.

If Therese was uncomfortable around her she didn't show it, and it never came up in conversations. *Hmm, I wonder if she ever thinks about that night like I do?* Madeleine decided not to dwell on it; she was just grateful to have someone to talk to. "You bring sanity to my life, Therese," she told her on more than one occasion.

They agreed on a time for the photos at rue de Rivoli and met there one afternoon. The atelier was filled with bolts of fabric and equipment waiting to be moved to the new salon but still rich with nostalgia.

"Just imagine, this is where it all started for you, Madeleine."

"And, where we first met, don't forget. I'm not sure who would want to see photos of me draping my mannequin here but . . ."

"You're famous now; everyone will want to see where you started." Therese arranged the camera and altered the lights in the room before taking photographs by moving from one side to another and stashing the finished rolls of film in her pockets so as not to lose them.

"Be patient with me, I'm still trying to figure out how to use this camera."

"I thought you had photographers taking your pictures."

"I let them go a while back. They took pictures showing the outside of things without capturing the emotion inside."

She kneeled on the floor to get a shot of Madeleine at her desk and cleared the work table for a place to stand while positioning herself above Madeleine to snap a photo of her pinning fabric on her mannequin. At one point she tossed off her black beret, her dark hair falling wildly. When she finished, her sweater and tights were covered with bits of thread from the floor. Madeleine couldn't help but laugh. She watched Therese closely. *She has no inhibitions . . . so comfortable in her body, caring little about what people think of her.*

"The press will be snapping your photos at the opening, Madeleine, so you'll have to get used to this," Therese said, her eyes full of delight.

"I'm not sure I'll even be at the opening," Madeleine said. "You know how I don't like crowds of people around and that I'd rather be working."

"I doubt if Bader and your managers will let you get away with that," Therese said laughing. "You're their star and they'll insist you be the center of attention."

"Oh, my. I hope not. I want to work, not perform."

"Is there a date for the opening yet? I hope I don't miss it."

"Miss it?" Madeleine seemed surprised.

"Yes, I've been asked to show images of decorative arts and architecture at the Whitney Museum in New York. Some of the images will come from the press service but I'm adding to that collection." She moved in closer for one last shot of the mannequin before putting her camera in the bag. "The curators want to see the interiors of artists' and designers' apartments in Paris and they are particularly interested in photographs of anything showing modernism. It seems that Paris is considered the modernist capital of the world with all the new innovative styles in art and architecture."

"So you might be gone? What a wonderful opportunity to be invited to America to show your photographs. You are becoming an artist in your own right, Therese. I envy you. You're in control of your time and your life. I wish I could say the same. I think the opening will be the end of the month. I hope you'll be back."

"I hope so too. I realize it's hectic for you right now. Don't you think everything will settle down after the opening?"

"Oh, I don't know. The new salon seems overwhelming and I've really been longing for simpler times. We were cramped here on Rivoli, but at least it was manageable."

Therese closed her camera bag. "I know you miss the simplicity. It will come though. Just keep thinking that one day it will come."

Later that week Therese met Madeleine at the new salon at noon for more pictures. Their quiet midnight retreat where they draped after everyone left for the day was now filled with lights, workers, equipment, boxes, and noise. Therese arrived dressed in a slim flowered peasant dress with a long black neck scarf and a black broad-rimmed shaker hat. As usual, heads turned.

She spotted Madeleine immediately in the grand foyer talking to a very fashionably-dressed woman. While waiting to get her attention, she stared at the splendor of the huge building. A photographic tribute to Isadora Duncan filled one wall and photographs of some of Madeleine's gowns worn by Hollywood movie stars adorned another. A huge crystal chandelier hovered over it all.

"Ah, you two will finally get a chance to meet," Madeleine said as she and the woman walked toward her. Therese, this is Marie Gerber. Marie meet Therese Bonney," she said smiling. "Marie and I worked together during tough times and now we remain close colleagues and friends." Therese nodded and watched Madeleine who looked beautiful in a sage linen skirt and a white silk blouse accented against her string of iridescent pearls. Her grayish hair was pulled up and held with ivory combs. Therese thought how fashionable and groomed Madeleine always appeared, in a comfortable not formal way.

Marie Gerber held out her hand and smiled. "I've read and heard so much about you, Therese. I think you've been very good medicine for my friend, Madeleine."

"Thank you, I'd have to say the same for you."

"You two talk," Madeleine said. "I have to return these samples and I'll be right back."

"Well, is this spectacular?" Marie waved her hands in the air as she looked around.

"Absolutely, it's stunning really. I suspect this is somewhat stressful for her though." Therese looked in Madeleine's direction across the foyer.

Marie nodded. "I don't think any of us imagined it would be this large and elaborate with all the different vendors and departments, and the size of this place. It's overwhelming."

"And, Madeleine? Is she doing fine with all of this?" Therese knew but wanted to hear what Marie had to say.

"She's vulnerable right now, Therese. It's as if her worst fear has come true; that she's losing control and being pushed into the limelight at the same time. She just wants to design dresses not get caught up in the business of this elaborate showcase. And to make matters worse, her backers are making demands and trying to control things, especially Bader. He's constantly trying to run roughshod over her because she's a woman. The only good thing is that her business will thrive now that she has the room and help to keep up with demand so she can finally concentrate on designing *haute couture*."

Madeleine came up behind them. "And what are you two talking about? Isn't this unbelievable?" Madeleine stood looking at all the work going on and people rushing around. It's pretty amaz . . ."

"Good morning, Mademoiselles."

They turned to see a handsome young man coming across the foyer. His tie was loose and he carried a set of plans under his arm.

"Netch, what a surprise. I didn't know you'd be in this morning."

"They're doing the layout for my shoe salon, so thought I'd better be here. I see you are all admiring this exquisite palace. It's hard to know which is more beautiful, the new salon or its lovely couturier, Madame Vionnet." He leaned to kiss her on the cheek. Marie looked quizzically at Therese.

Embarrassed, Madeleine introduced them, explaining that Dimitri Netchvolodoff's shoe salon will be housed in the building.

"What style of shoes are you designing Monsieur Netchvolodoff?" Marie said examining him closely. He was in his late 20s or early 30s, his blonde hair fell slightly below his collar and his intense blue eyes were fixed on Madeleine.

"Well, the style that will go well with Madeleine's amazing gowns, of course." He winked at Marie.

"Where did you work before this?" Her tone was more serious.

He looked surprised. "Ah, well, I was in the military in Russia, and then I worked for my father who also designs shoes."

Madeleine interrupted. "We're taking pictures this morning, Netch, so you'll have to excuse us." Madeleine walked with Therese and Marie to the other end of the foyer.

"I know you're taking pictures and I'm just leaving," Marie said putting on her coat. "It was nice meeting you Therese. Madeleine we'll talk soon? Maybe lunch next week if you're free." They exchanged goodbyes before Madeleine and Therese walked up the stairs.

Once they were in Madeleine's office Therese said, "Is that young man a friend of yours?" Before Madeleine had a chance to answer,

Therese busied herself with her camera and after a short silence said, "No posing today. I'd like to take some spontaneous photos and then some of the salon, if that seems like a good idea to you."

Madeleine sensed something might be wrong - maybe Therese's uneasiness about Netch, the man she met in the salon. She wanted to ask her about it and had the words in her head but decided not to say anything. Instead, she changed the subject.

"Therese, can we talk about your trip to New York? Are you really leaving soon? When will you be back? I know I'm being silly but I've come to rely on you . . . in so many ways," she added.

Therese put her camera on the table. "I'll return as soon as I can, really. I'll spend some time with my mother and Louise going over ideas for the press service, and then do the exhibition. I won't be gone too long. We can send telegrams and letters; that would be fun. It will hardly seem like I'm gone."

Madeleine's eyes moved quickly not finding a place to land. She toyed with her fingers, feeling the tips of each one. Therese noticed and wondered what she was thinking. It was a look Therese hadn't seen before and one that would haunt her all the way across the Atlantic.

Nineteen

THE GRAND OCEAN liner, the RMS *Caronia*, sailed into Pier 54 in New York on a bright and crisp autumn afternoon. Louise and her mother waited anxiously for Therese to disembark for their first reunion since the Bonney Press Service. They planned to celebrate in style. Like three giddy girls getting together after a long absence, they dined at the Ritz and later stopped at Harry's bar at 47th street for a nightcap and jazz. The bar was noisy and crowded but they huddled at a small table in the back talking about ideas and celebrating their success.

Addie, who had been keeping track of money matters, took out a small notebook and reported the recent earnings as they swooned at the good news and raised their glasses. Giggling from too many Manhattans, they walked back to the apartment that night arm and arm. Walking along the streets in New York seemed familiar to Therese but for the first time, she realized that Paris felt more like home.

In the days to come, they outlined plans for the press service and Therese proposed a series of guide books on Paris she wanted to write with Louise.

"Oh, I don't even know Paris," Louise said, "and I'm not much of a writer. That's your area, Therese."

"We'll work together. These will be shopping guides for tourists, one on buying antiques and furniture and another on buying fashions. We can do a French cookbook too, one for American kitchens. Mother, you can help us with that one. You can both visit Paris later this year and we can get started."

"Oh, I'd better start making notes," Addie said. "We'll really be writing a cookbook?"

"It all sounds terribly exciting, Therese. I can't wait to see the Paris you've been writing about for so long," Louise said. "Imagine, Paris! Oh my, how exciting!"

Later that night before they settled in, Therese asked her mother once again about her father; if she sees him or hears from him. Her answer was the same as always, that she's had no contact whatsoever. "It is what it is, Therese." She gave her a warm hug. "Maybe it's for the better."

Therese and Madeleine wrote regularly sharing news of their work and lives. Madeleine lamented that Théophile Bader was becoming more difficult, and Therese wrote about the exhibition, and shared several good ideas the family had for the press service. Madeleine ended every message by asking: *When will you return?*

Therese reassured her it would be soon, and signed her letters: *With love (if I may say)*.

Three weeks into Therese's journey however the messages from Madeleine tapered off. Her notes were brief, with news of the grand opening and descriptions of new fabrics, but nothing about herself or how she was coping with the stress of business. When her letters weren't answered, Therese sent telegrams asking how she was and to send news of life outside the salon - but she seldom received a reply. Her last note was a plea:

Dear Madeleine, I would rather hear anything from you than bound volumes from anyone else. Please write. Therese

But to her dismay the messages stopped completely.

The Whitney Museum exhibit was a huge success; in fact, extended for another month. It seemed New Yorkers could not get enough of modernism in Paris. The exhibit opened opportunities for Therese –

invitations to present her modernist photographs in other venues, speaking engagements in New York, and lectures at major universities on the East Coast. She accepted an invitation to consult on a new proposed gallery for French art in New York City, and to act as the liaison for branches of the American Red Cross in France and perhaps other European locations. She was slowly being recognized as an emissary for internationalism, fueled by a desire from both the Americans and the French to cross cultural borders. She and the Bonney Press Service were both steps toward making that happen, but she was desperate to get back to Paris to find out why Madeleine's correspondence had stopped. She couldn't imagine why.

After a three-day voyage from New York aboard the *SS Olympic* she arrived back in Paris on a cold and rainy evening. It seemed an endless sail. Each evening on the ship's promenade she watched the dark sky in the west as it met the even darker Atlantic Ocean and wondered about Madeleine. It was after midnight when the taxi stopped in front of her Paris apartment. Finding it cold, she left her bags on the floor and took a walk after putting on an extra wool scarf and grabbing her umbrella. Knowing Madeleine would be asleep as that hour, she walked to St-Germain-des-Pres where she hoped the lights and night-dwellers might lift her mood.

The aroma of coffee lured her into La Tortue on Boulevard St. Germain and she sat drinking espresso and catching up on Paris events by looking through old newspapers stacked on a table. When the lights dimmed and she heard the clinking sound of dishes being washed, she put the newspapers back and gathered her coat and umbrella. While putting on her coat it immediately caught her eye. The name Vionnet in a small article on the bottom of page one in a previous edition of *Le Figaro* on the table. It was under the banner: *This Week in Paris*:

> *Famed Parisian fashion designer Madeleine Vionnet married Captain Dimitri Netchvolodoff, eighteen years her junior, in a civil ceremony earlier this week in Paris. Netchvolodoff, a shoe designer, has his salon in Vionnet's new and luxurious 'Palace of Fashion' and will be marketing his shoes under the Vionnet name. In another story. . .*

Gripping her umbrella and clutching her coat at the neck, she waited outside until she saw the lights go on at 50 Avenue Montaigne a few

Madeleine and Therese

hours after dawn. The window from the upstairs atelier where Madeleine usually worked was still dark so she waited another hour until a dim light appeared. To be unnoticed, she knew to sneak through the employee's entrance to the foyer and through some back rooms before using the stairs to the second floor. She waited at the foot of the stairs so as not to be seen, and then rushed up to the second floor and to Madeleine's atelier.

The door was ajar. She felt her throat tighten and her heart pound. Madeleine stood draping her mannequin by the window when Therese pushed the door wide open. Rainwater from her unopened umbrella dripped slowly on the floor as she stood in the doorway. Startled, Madeleine looked twice and then beyond the door, relieved to see no one else.

"Please close the door. Come sit down." Therese did neither but stood glaring. "Therese, please, close the door." Finally, Madeleine walked from behind the desk and shut the door. As she walked back to her desk, Therese took hold of her arm.

The rain dripped from her rain-soaked hair and down her face. "What happened? What possibly could have happened? I thought we were friends, confidants."

"Sit down please. I can't talk to you while you stand and glare at me. Please, Therese."

Therese sat as her umbrella slid to the floor and lay in a small pool of water. She leaned across the desk toward Madeleine, breathing heavily, staring, waiting, her jaw set, her gaze like forged steel.

Madeleine took a deep breath and then a long sigh, "I don't expect you to understand any of this." Her brow arched and she shifted in her seat. She put her hands on the table, then in her lap. "It was difficult when you left, Therese. You were my sanity, by muse, my friend, my . . . well, the one who brought me closer to the person I wanted to be." She lowered her head and ran her fingers through her hair leaving them there while looking up. Therese sat perfectly still, leaning forward, her gloved hands in front of her on the desk leaving small pools of water.

"It was chaotic here," Madeleine said continuing. "I needed help with Bader. He saw me as a mere seamstress with no business sense. He continued to make demands and challenged my decisions. Netch stepped in on my behalf on several occasions and Bader backed down each time."

Therese's chair flew back against the wall as she bolted from her seat trying to control the quiver in her voice. "You don't marry people just because they help you professionally, Madeleine. You don't. Why didn't you let me know?" She slammed the desk. "I would have come back sooner. I would have helped you get through that. Why did you have to marry him, for god's sake?" She waited but no response. She pulled the chair from the wall and sat back down shaking her head and pulling off her wet gloves. She strummed her fingers on the arms of the chair, letting the water drip down her face still flushed with anger. A naked light bulb on the ceiling flickered momentarily.

Madeleine started again. "I . . . I just didn't know how to tell you. I wanted to, I knew you'd be worried, but I couldn't write. I didn't know what to say to help you understand so I . . . well, I did nothing." She wiped her eyes and stared at the desk. "You and I had no arrangement other than friendship, and this wasn't about us anyway but I knew you'd see it that way. We're different people, Therese, and we make different decisions. We've both had to overcome issues, abandonment, difficult situations, working our way to the top in a man's world, but you were raised with the love and support of your mother and sister; I was raised to survive on my own. I lost my family, I lost my youth, I lost my child. How many loses can one endure without shutting down to emotion, to reason?" She rubbed her forearms and looked directly at Therese. "After a while you just come to expect that everything worth having will be lost; that nothing good can come from any type of meaningful relationship or friendship so why try?"

She reached across the desk to touch Therese's hand, but Therese pulled it back to her lap. Madeleine sat back. "Over the years I put my love, my emotional energy into my work, my business, and pushed everything else aside. Remember the conversation we had once? I said that you are the sentimental one and I'm all about business. That's ingrained, Therese. That's who I am. My decision to marry was a business decision. I can't put my trust in people, only in preserving my business so I don't end up in a sweatshop again."

Therese sunk into her thoughts and sat silently shaking her head. "No, you were starting to trust me, opening up, tender, and allowing

Madeleine and Therese

yourself to be vulnerable. We've been so much to each other, Madeleine. More than most women are. We've related intellectually and personally, and our draping sessions added a new dimension, an intimacy. We broadened the scope of how women can relate. Women's friendships don't have to be one-dimensional and they don't have to be temporary. They can be lasting, meaningful, but only if you stay with it, trust it."

Madeleine stared at her desk. Her voice was low, almost somber. "It's a mistake to trust that kind of closeness. I can only trust what I can control and that's my business, and even that's questionable at this point. Marrying Netch was not a romantic or an emotional decision. It was a business decision. That's all I can say."

Therese rose from the chair and turned to leave, but then turned and in one swift move swatted a stack of papers from Madeleine's desk across the room. "Nonsense! That's nonsense! Business takes place in the board room not in the bedroom, Madeleine. Don't tell me your marriage is about business or just having someone to stand up to Bader. Your attorney could have done that. I pity you, that you see it this way. And if it is true, how can you prostitute yourself with this . . . this Netch person just to have someone to fight your business battles for you?"

"I can't expect you to understand, Therese. Not you, especially not you and . . . about this." She spoke slowly. "I know I've violated our friendship by not telling you, and by taking away our precious times together by bringing someone in between us."

Madeleine watched Therese standing there alone soaking wet, heartbreaking in her rage, every part of her weeping the desolate cry of pain and abandonment, the angst of loss, rejection, and betrayal. Watching her, Madeleine thought her own heart would break.

After a long breath, she said, "I got scared Therese, afraid that I'd lose my business even more than I already had. I thought it would be taken out from under me. Bader was worming his way in, making decisions, inciting mutiny among the managers. There wasn't anything I could do or you could do. Bader backed down with Netch. Business is a man's game. That's the way it is. Netch wouldn't have continued to confront Bader and the others unless we were married. He would have lost interest doing it as a favor. I realize how strange this must sound to you, protected as you've been from this side of business and of life. You would have handled it differently I'm sure. You're much stronger than I am when it comes to courage and ethics. I have no courage, no feelings, no sensitivity."

Therese picked up her coat and umbrella and at the door, turned. "Yes, you do, Madeleine. You're just too afraid to show it, to trust it."

She stepped over her gloves on the floor and slammed the door behind her. The group at the bottom of the grand stairway dispersed quickly into adjacent rooms.

Twenty

IT WOULD BE A YEAR before Therese was to see Madeleine again. at least in person. The newspapers kept Madeleine in the headlines, delving into her personal life after she opened her extravagant new salon and married a younger man. *Le Figaro* splashed photos of Madeleine and her new husband sailing to America to promote her business and expand her list of clientele, and one photograph showed Madeleine with a number of Hollywood actresses including Jean Harlow, Greta Garbo, and Katherine Hepburn all wearing Vionnet gowns.

Therese wondered if the trips were all Madeleine's idea or her husband's - or Bader's, especially knowing that she rarely gave interviews or allowed herself to be photographed. She certainly never answered questions about her personal life. She was quoted as saying "no comment" more often than not, much to the frustration of prying reporters. More recent photographs showed Madeleine with her new husband at parties in New York, and one attending the funeral of her father. After a while Therese vowed to stop looking at photographs of Madeleine altogether.

Although curious, Therese avoided the Palace of Fashion on her evening walks, worrying she might see a light upstairs and be tempted to go in. Instead she chose to walk down by the river Seine or to the Bastille to watch the artists sketching under the street lamps, or to the flower markets in Montparnasse when she needed a break. It seems everywhere she went however she imagined seeing Madeleine. She welcomed work during the day, taking photographs of French art and architecture and selling the rights through her press service. The Bonney Agency now supplied as many as 350 photographs a month to publications in dozens of countries. In the evenings she'd see friends, especially at Gertrude's Saturday night salons where Raoul hounded her to pose and she did on several occasions. After seeing the first painting though, she protested. "I don't have a double chin, Raoul. Can't you paint over it?"

He laughed with eyes sparkling. "My dearest Therese, if we as artists wanted an exact copy then we would take a photograph. Paintings are interpretations," he said, waving his hands. "They are part fantasy, part surreal."

"Can't you interpret my chin without adding another beneath it?"

He laughed again and put his arm around her. "My lovely Therese, you are perfect. I've only added a little character. Next time I will paint you without a double chin, I promise."

"Next time? You think there will be a next time?"

Several artists painted her portrait once, but Raoul Dufy painted her three times, Georges Rouault, six times, and Matisse, twice. She never really understood why. Therese teased Raoul that he had to keep trying until he got it right. Gertrude Stein hung Rouault's portrait of Therese on the wall in her salon, and Raoul gave Therese a small painting of herself, finally more flattering to her than the first. She liked the informality of Gertrude's salons and the people she met there, especially the artists and writers who were unpretentious and laughed easily when they weren't huddled together discussing something serious other than their poverty or their work.

Going to Gertrude's was good medicine, she thought, but not a cure. She did her work and saw her friends, but the void in her life without Madeleine seemed like an excavation not just a thin crack. She had dared to leave her safe zone, her refuge in her work, and was now paying the price. *I've buried myself in my studies all my life but I can't hide from the world, from living, relating, and most important, from caring. Hmm, a scary thought. No more safety net!* The realization made her panicky, like getting lost with no sense of the way home.

One evening Gertrude took her aside and confided, "I'm glad you're spending more time with us. We miss you when you're not here." She put her hand on Therese's arm. "I see something new though," and she raised an eyebrow. "I know the press service is going well and your travels, your exhibits, and everything else I hear and read about you is good. You're a celebrity, but something's amiss." She kept her eyes steady.

Therese was fond of Gertrude and normally could talk to her. She wanted to say something, tasting the words in her mouth but couldn't get them out. "I'm not sure what to say, Gertrude," and she looked away.

"That means something is amiss. Do you want to talk about it? It must have to do with affairs of the heart or the soul, the only variables in life we can't control."

Therese smiled and shrugged. Gertrude let it rest.

"By the way, my new 1924 Ford will be delivered next week and Alice is planning a small gathering. We always have a celebration and name our motorcars, at least we did for the last one. You must come, Therese. This new one is easier to drive than the old one. I'll show you how."

"What? Drive a motorcar? I'm appalled at the suggestion! I've never done that before."

Gertrude looked at her askance. "Therese, we are women and this is Paris. It's 1924 for god's sake."

"Oh, alright, I'll do it," Therese mumbled. "What should I wear?"

Gertrude laughed. "Anything! It's just a motorcar Therese, not an airplane or a camel."

The glistening new motorcar dazzled everyone at the party but it turned out to be far less interesting than the stories behind it, ones only Gertrude could tell. After everyone arrived she told the history.

"We bought our first Ford, a used one, from a cousin in America in 1918 because we wanted to help with the Great War effort here in Paris. When it arrived we contacted the American Fund for French Wounded to say we have a car and want to deliver medical supplies and emergency provisions to wherever they're needed. The person I spoke to asked if I knew how to drive. It seemed a reasonable question since privately-owned cars during the war were rare and then typically owned by men."

"So what did you say?" Raoul asked.

"Well, I had to say no, I didn't know how to drive! He hung up on me."

Amid the laugher, Gertrude continued. "We knew a taxi driver who drove one of the two-hundred motorcars donated by Renault and used to deliver French soldiers to the front during the battle of Marne during the Great War. He said he'd teach me to drive. Not only did he do that, but he taught me to crank the car and repair it. He was very kind about it since I was a woman, I suppose."

Alice interrupted. "Are you going to tell them he taught you to drive but that you couldn't master the skill of backing up so we always had to go forward?" More laughter.

"Well, I guess there's no need to tell them since you just did, but I have to admit that's still the case. It's the damnedest thing, driving backward. But learning to drive provided a great adventure for us." She glanced at Alice. "Before the war, the furthest we'd been from Paris was Fontainebleau and suddenly there we were driving all over. Some of it was painfully sad though. I hope to never see another battlefield. As a result of our volunteer war effort we now drive everywhere. The motorcar has given us freedom."

"As women, the war gave us freedom as well." Alice said looking at Gertrude.

"Yes, that's true. After wars women always have more freedom, especially modern wars. Conflicts dislodge people from their old perspectives. Well, anyway, here we are with our second Ford. We've named her Godiva because she's a stripped down version of our first, but very adequate." Everyone applauded and cheered, and champagne was poured.

"And what are your plans for this motorcar?" Therese posed the question to Gertrude.

"Oh, nothing as altruistic as delivering war supplies. There's no need nor will there ever be if we can believe that the Great War was the war to end all wars." She drew a deep breath. "We will use this Ford for fun and travel, and to teach you, Therese, how to drive!"

"Oh, no," Therese said in her smallest voice.

Later that evening there were screams of laughter from a black model T Ford burping and chugging down the Champs-Élysées. A shrill voice could be heard yelling "the clutch, the clutch, not the gas . . . no, not the brake!" Passersby watched in amazement.

Twenty-One

WHEN IT SEEMED winter would never lose its icy grip, the purple tulip-shaped crocus pushed gallantly through the last vestiges of snow in time to bloom for spring. Louise and her mother, Addie, arrived in Paris in time to see and marvel at the showy display; and, even though their luggage was filled with work from the press service, Therese announced that this would be more than a working trip but a true vacation for them both.

Starting with the Eiffel Tower and the Arc de Triomphe they visited the sights of Paris, taking the new transportation system called the *Metro*, and walking endlessly through the captivating Parisian neighborhoods.

"It doesn't seem that long ago that you did bales of laundry just to feed us," Therese said to her mother, "and now you just crossed the Atlantic in a first-class cabin and had tea at the Ritz with your daughters in Paris!"

"I can hardly believe it myself," Addie said. "But you girls always pushed a little further than other children your age so I'm not too surprised, just pleased."

They worked in the east wing of Therese's new apartment at 82, rue des Petits Champs, comfortably but sparsely decorated with art deco furniture and paintings, and with lovely views of Parisian rooftops. When they weren't enjoying the sights of Paris, Addie helped catalogue hundreds of photographs while Therese and Louise worked on plans to write the series of books for tourists visiting Paris. They decided to start with *A Shopping Guide to Paris* intended to give shoppers an inside look at some of the city's luxury goods, especially the fashion boutiques and perfume shops - two areas of special interest to American shoppers.

"Americans are crazy about French fashions," Louise told Therese. "I've made a list of fashion houses and perfume shops mentioned in American magazines. I hope we can visit them and interview the fashion designers while I'm here. I've put stars after the most popular. Do you think it's possible, Therese? Can we start? I can't wait to meet them!"

Therese laughed at Louise's enthusiasm. "Yes, yes, of course, let's start with the ones you've marked as favorites."

"Well, that would be Vionnet, Schiaparelli, and the four sisters, I think their salon is called Callot Soeurs. Do you know any of them?"

Therese felt a chill. "Well, I've met them, yes, most of them."

"You have? What are they like? Imagine, they are all women! Who would have thought women would become famous couturiers."

"Yes, well these women are all quite exceptional."

"One thought, Louise. How would you feel about splitting the interviews? Perhaps you could interview the three major couturiers: Vionnet, Schiaparelli, and Callot Soeurs. That would be fun for you, and I can interview the others, those perhaps less interesting?"

"Oh my gosh, Therese, I'd be so nervous doing that without you. I don't know anything about fashion. You've met these women and I'd be at a loss for words. Can't we do it together?"

Therese hesitated. "Of course. Interviewing them separately makes no sense at all. We'll go together. It will be more fun that way."

Therese sat quietly at her desk that afternoon and studied the tree outside the window, barren but with tiny spectacles of green sprouting from the weathered bark.

What will it be like to see Madeleine after all this time? I wonder if she'll even agree to an interview? Louise would be disappointed . . . perhaps we both would. She leaned back in her chair. To her surprise, her anger and feelings of betrayal had faded. *Would seeing Madeleine rekindle all of that?* She sat tapping her pencil on the desk until the tip broke off.

Louise's eagerness to learn about the fashion industry pleased Therese so she took some time to answer her questions. She explained some of the etiquette of the major salons, like the practice of showing collections only twice a day always at eleven in the morning and three in the afternoon. The order of showing is normally sport dresses first and evening gowns last. Prospective buyers are assigned a *vendeuse* or sales person whose role is to stand by and take questions about fabric or price, and to make notes of the client's comments. Therese told Louise that dresses are usually identified by a name or number and generally, if someone is interested in a particular dress they make an appointment with their *vendeuse* to return the following day.

"Some houses allow changes in color and possibly slight alterations in style, but Vionnet for instance, never allows changes other that those needed to fit the dress to the size of the client."

Louise listened intently. "What about price? Does everyone pay the same?"

"In the finer houses, one is never to bargain about price unless they're an established client and even then, it happens rarely. Buying *haute couture* is not about negotiation. You don't attend a showing without the means to purchase."

"Well, everyone we contacted agreed to be interviewed," Louise told Therese. "I guess they realize it will be good publicity. The only disappointment is that Madame Vionnet does not do interviews but someone else from Vionnet & Cie will be available. I'm disappointed. I really wanted to meet her."

"I'm sorry, Louise, this happens," Therese said almost relieved. Still, she saw Louise's disappointment. "You might try sending the invitation again and address it to Madeleine Vionnet this time marked 'personal.' Be sure to sign both of our names."

A few days later, the invitation was returned with a note at the bottom saying, *Looking forward to seeing you. Madeleine.*

Twenty-Two

"WHO ARE ALL of these women?" Louise whispered as they entered the Palace of Fashion.

"Women with money," Therese said as she marveled at the sight in the grand salon along with Louise.

Therese read that Madeleine was still having serious problems with counterfeiters but judging by the number of clients in the foyer it didn't seem to affect her business.

"Take pictures, Therese. Lot's of them."

Therese whispered, "I should mention that much has been written about Vionnet fashions and her use of the classical for inspiration. You can see that in her gowns in the photographs here on the walls." Louise strained to look. "So whatever information we don't get in the interview we can get through our research."

"Are you sure you want me to ask the questions from our list?"

"Yes, you'll do a great job. I'll take photographs and also jot down her responses along with you."

"I'm excited, but also a little a nervous. Are you?"

Therese sighed. "Yes, both."

Madeleine greeted them at the door when they were escorted to her office. She introduced herself to Louise and asked a few questions about her stay in Paris and about the nature of the book, and invited her to sit down. Therese stood in the doorway, blinking hard and biting at her lip.

Madeleine walked toward her. Both seemed to be searching for words but there were none.

Therese smoothed her long slim dress and sat down next to Louise, watching Madeleine walk back to her desk and noticing that she was impeccably groomed as always and wore a soft beige dress as pale as her skin. The seams in her nylons were slightly askew, the only flaw. Therese looked down while Louise asked questions from the list, but glanced at Madeleine on occasion without being obvious, seeing her face drawn, the darkness around her eyes, her uncertain lips that moved at times but said little.

Madeleine graciously answered every question and gave Louise a catalog from her last showing. She was animated when telling Louise about her "hygienic atelier" as she called it; a place where her seamstresses have access to a gymnasium, a dental and medical clinic, and child care facilities.

"I want to make sure my workers have every opportunity for a normal and healthy life," she told Louise. "I worked in a sweatshop as a girl and my greatest satisfaction now is not this edifice to fashion," she said looking around the room, "but that my employees are treated with care and respect."

"Was that a terrible experience working in a sweatshop?" Louise asked a question not on the list.

"I actually started as an *arpette* or pin-picker." Seeing that Louise looked puzzled, she explained. "It's the first job given an apprentice in the dressmaking business. You crawl around on the floor picking up pins dropped by the seamstresses. The job went downhill from there." She shook her head. "It was hard and demeaning work but it doesn't have to be, at least not in my salon."

Louise nodded and made a note. She looked up. "I've read that you don't meet with clients or do fittings, is that true?"

Madeleine thought for a moment and nodded. "Yes, it's true for the most part. My job is usually finished once I create a dress. There are others to attend to the fittings and discussions with clients unless they are friends and then I occasionally meet with them."

"I've also read that you don't give interviews. Why did you decide to give this one?" The question was a surprise.

Madeleine smiled with pleasure. "I can see you are indeed a Bonney. You are tenacious like your sister, going after what you want. I like that quality."

Louise laughed, a bit embarrassed. "But, well you didn't answer the question."

Therese stood and put her hand on Louise's shoulder. "Louise, I think Madame Vionnet has been most generous with her answers, so we probably have what we need."

Louise stood also. "Yes, it's just that she has been so candid, and I was curious."

"Your question deserves a response, Louise." Madeleine rose from her desk. "I consented to be interviewed because I care for and respect your sister, and now you. I'm happy you came today. I wish you well with your book project." She came from behind her desk to see them out, brushing her hand against Therese's arm but nothing was said.

At the bottom of the stairs, Louise stopped. "You didn't take photographs or say anything! She seemed to know you. Do you know her? She was so nice and I wanted to ask questions about her life and how she got to where she is. Can you believe she used to pick up pins from the floor?"

"Louise, Louise, so many questions, so much curiosity. I was here before the salon opened so I have many pictures, even some of her working with her mannequin that we can use in the book."

"But she was so nice. Is she always like that? I thought she was a recluse."

Therese took her arm and walked her briskly from the lobby onto the street. The cold took her breath away and numbed her face but evidently not her feelings. She wanted to apologize to Louise for her curtness.

"Madeleine and I were friends at one time but something came between that friendship. I'm sorry, Louise."

"I sensed some tension in the room but I wasn't sure what it meant," Louise said looking at her with earnest, still a bit puzzled. "Don't wait too long, Therese. We've had too much sadness in our family, too many wounds to be letting go of good people."

Therese stood in the cold inhaling deeply, shaking her head slowly before turning to Louise and putting her arms around her.

Therese and Louise worked late that night long after their mother went to bed. Louise was still ecstatic after their day of interviews and sat working on her notes.

"Louise, you live closer to mother than I do. Does she ever talk about father? I've asked her on several occasions if she hears from him but she always says no. Has she talked to you about him?"

"Not much. I don't know if she's ever heard from him but if so, I doubt if she responds. I suspect leaving him was a hard decision. I think she cared for him but she was afraid for us, and maybe for herself too."

"Why doesn't she talk to us about it?"

"I'm not sure. She probably doesn't want us to feel guilty because we're probably the reason she left him. She put us first but I do think she loved him, at least at one time."

"I've always felt guilty because I'm the one he hated. I've had to struggle with that."

"You know Therese, I think you took the brunt because you could bear it. He was an angry person and had to take his frustration out on someone. You were able to bounce back, we probably weren't. I think mother is happy knowing we are fine, happier than if she'd kept the family together. She'd never have forgiven herself for staying because the abuse would have continued."

"I'm glad you think mother is happy."

"What about you Therese, are you happy?"

"I'm working on it."

Twenty-Three

THE CARD OF appreciation was signed by both of them, but the note scribbled at the bottom was written by Therese.

Thank you for your kindness at the interview. Warm regards, Therese.

A few days later, Madeleine responded.

I know you are busy with your family but I'd be most pleased if you would stop by when they've left. Regards, Madeleine.

At their farewell dinner in Montparnasse, Therese, Louise, and Addie popped the cork on a bottle of champagne and toasted their accomplishments during their month-long visit. The interviews went well and Louise was present for them all, asking questions like a professional - and Addie organized all of Therese's negatives and had all the finances in order by the end of the visit. At the dock after lingering hugs, they agreed that more time together was the number one goal in the future. Therese hated to see them go.

To avoid igniting the sparks of their explosive meeting in Madeleine's office a year ago, Madeleine and Therese agreed to meet downstairs after everyone had left for the day. Therese walked to the salon, wanting time to ease her tension and think about what she wanted to say - or not say. The last thing she wanted was to upset Madeleine or suggest she change. *Why try to smooth something that is so beautifully textured? I only wish I could understand her.* Madeleine met her at the door and they sat in the foyer. The light was dim but Madeleine noticed how lovely

Therese looked in a simple print dress and no makeup but looking thinner than usual.

"You look . . . "

"Is your work . . . "

They laughed and both relaxed into a smile. A long strange moment passed. "This is hard, it's been so long," Therese said trying not to stare. "I've seen your light so many evenings and . . . well, I'm just happy to see you."

Madeleine sat next to her on the velvet divan, reaching for her hand, searching her eyes, seeing them bright and steady like the magnetic pull of something yielding and profound. She shook her head slowly. "I had no idea how important you were to me until I lost you. My world just now, this minute, stopped spinning out of control."

They talked for hours about their work and Therese's family visit, the new salon . . . well into the night. Therese was careful to not ask about her personal life. It was none of her business and even if it was she didn't want to hear about it.

"Business is up and profits are good," Madeleine said, "and I finally have more staff to help with orders so clients are happy. But it's different now, Therese. The exuberance, the excitement is gone. I feel far removed from my work - and that's not a good thing."

"I read that you've built some vacation homes and have new stores opening, one in New York, I think. Isn't that exciting?"

"Those things don't feel important to me, I suppose."

"Then why do them?"

Madeleine studied her hands. "I do them to appease those around me because I'm . . . I'm entangled with them and that's the price you pay. It's what I feared. In trying to save my business I sold myself to the devil - or devils, I should say. I sold out, compromised. I think only you can understand that. I have more, but I also have to deal with more people, more problems, and more anxiety. Most of it seems so unnecessary and almost all of it without meaning, to me at least."

"I thought you were given control of the business; that you would be directing the orchestra so to speak."

"Therese, it's too big now for me to handle on my own. Bader continues to squeeze in and . . ."

"Isn't that what your husband is for, to be an intermediary between you and Bader and the issues." Therese regretted saying that but it seemed like a valid response.

Madeleine put her fingers to her temples and moaned. "It was that way at first but Bader has the money so the managers cater to him, and Netch wants the vacation houses and lifestyle so he too caters to Bader. What suffers is the artistry, the organic, the simplicity, the intimacy of owning a business and making it work yourself."

"Then where's the value for you, Madeleine? Is there any pleasure in any of this or in your life?"

Madeleine was still. "In my business? I'd have to think about that. In my life?" She paused. "I think you know the answer to that. It's been a difficult year and I don't know if I've ruined it for us. I told you once that you are my sanity, by muse, my friend, the one who brought me closer to the person I wanted to be. When I foolishly pushed you out of my life by not confiding in you about Netch, I lost all of that."

Therese sat quietly for a minute rubbing her fingers. "Well, I guess we both have a history of closing ourselves off for emotional protection. We turn to work instead, especially when it's work we believe in. It sounds like you don't believe in your work, your company. Is there any aspect of it that still moves you? Perhaps finding that and making it your focus will make it seem worthwhile again."

"You know, Therese, my door at the salon on rue de Rivoli was always closed. Nobody had the right to come in. I was free, tranquil. I did my best work there. I wish I could recreate that here, to get back to designing beautiful gowns. I also want to continue my work on defeating the copyists. They're going to ruin this industry. I hired managers to take care of business, including the copyists, but they're not doing it, they're loyal to Bader who wants to run the company."

She thought for a minute. "I'd like to close my door to all these weasels and get back to what's important to me."

"Then do it, Madeleine."

"Hmm, yes, I just might."

Later, they walked to the door together. Madeleine turned to her. "You didn't respond. Have I ruined it for us?"

Therese took a long breath. "You're married, Madeleine, and your time now belongs to someone else, as well as running a very large company. I . . . I don't know."

Madeleine's gaze was penetrating. "Therese, have I ruined it for us?"

The room was still, just the sound of their breathing. "No," Therese said in a whisper.

Madeleine moved a step closer. "I've thought of a thousand ways to say I'm sorry but none seemed good enough."

Therese's eyes were soft, brooding. "That way sounded good enough." They hugged and held each other for a long time.

Therese took a carriage to her apartment that evening. As usual, she liked hearing the horse's hooves clacking on the cobblestone late at night. Looking back at the Palace of Fashion she saw a dim light upstairs and pulled her scarf up to her chin. She thought she could still smell the scent of Madeleine's perfume.

Twenty-Four

HER OFFICE DOOR was closed for the first time since moving to the new salon and she tacked up the small printed sign: *S'il vous plait frapper,* or "please knock." In the weeks to come Madeleine took charge of the company she owned. She held meetings for managers and employees making clear they understood the salon's priorities, including the issue of counterfeiters. Prominently displayed plaques in the grand salon and in the work rooms alerted both employees and clients to the dangers of copyists. They read:

New ideas are like sparrows being pursued by buzzards.
Let's work together to defeat counterfeiters.

She called on her managers to shift their emphasis from profit to protection, and at one meeting insisted that a manager be present at each showing to prohibit copyists from entering.

"This should preferably be Monsieur Durand, the manager in charge of protection, but if not, one of the others," she said.

"Is this necessary, Madame Vionnet?" Durand protested. "Haven't we better things to do than watch women model clothes."

"Monsieur Durand, you of all people should know that copyists attend showings and either sketch or memorize the dresses. Sometimes even several attend, each one memorizing a different part of the dress and then sketching that part when they leave. They pool all the sketches and have the complete dress. This is just one way our dresses are being copied and if you attended the showings you'd know this. These replicas are sold to New York department stores by the dozens and the copyists are making a fat profit while ruining our businesses."

"Preposterous," he huffed.

"Really? Tell me, Monsieur Durand, since it is your job to prevent counterfeiters and copyists, just what have you done to thwart them? What have you been doing all this time?"

"Well, Bader wants me to spend my time . . ."

"Bader? Bader is telling you what to do? May I remind you that you work for me not for Monsieur Bader."

"Yes, but he thinks it's a waste of time to prevent copying. In fact, he says copying is more profitable; that it makes better sense to sell 100 dresses for less, than one at a higher price." He sat back in his chair smiling and looking back and forth at the others.

Madeleine's face turned red as she walked toward him putting both hands on the table and leaning close. "Monsieur Durand, let's be clear. This is *haute couture* and I'm the designer. We have a separate division for ready-to-wear. And, I am in charge of running this company."

She looked around at the others. "Does everyone understand that?" She turned back to Durand. "And lastly, Monsieur Durand, please gather your things and leave the premises. You no longer work here."

"You can't do that. You can't fire me."

"I just did."

Marie Gerber poured more tea as they sat in the garden at her home. "That jackass! What nerve to tell you he's working for Bader."

"Well I thought you should know in case he comes to your doorstep asking for a job. You know, Marie, I think we need to form an alliance. If they're stealing my designs they're stealing others."

"Of course they are. Copies of my dresses are showing up all over and Chanel is irate about what's happening to hers. What about a replacement for Durand, will you hire someone else?"

"Yes, in fact I wanted to talk to you about that. Do you remember Simone Claire who worked for me before the war? She was principled and easy to work with, and concerned about copyists even back then. I think she would make a good manager. I wonder where she is right now, do you know?"

"No, I don't, but a woman manager? I like the idea! I'll ask around and let you know. You have my full support, Madeleine. You're going up against some powerful and greedy businessmen."

Two weeks later Madeleine hired Simone Claire as the new Manager of Intellectual Property Protection at Vionnet et Cie. The news of a female manager in a high position in business caused an uproar. The Paris newspapers called it revolutionary and Bader immediately sent a threating note to Madeleine demanding that Madame Claire be fired immediately. Madeleine's receptionist was instructed to hang up if he called the office.

Together, Madeleine and Simone created a long list of deterrents to copying. Admission to showings would now be monitored, and non-buyers and unscrupulous agents would be denied entrance. Madeleine started an organization called *Protection Artistique des Industries Saisoniers*, or P.A.I.S. that soon had seventy-five members from couture, millinery, and textiles.

As a favor to Madeleine, Therese used the library at the Sorbonne to research legal issues pertaining to copyists. She found two outdated laws, one in 1873 and another in 1884 suggesting that couturiers could take action when they suspected copying. While *action* was not defined, Therese thought it could be interpreted to mean raids and law suits. If so interpreted by the courts, copyists could be sued for damages and those damages could be for amounts far exceeding mere penalties.

"We're getting close to what we need," Madeleine told Therese. "The difference between mere penalties and damages could break the backs of copyists and be the best deterrent yet."

When the door flew open late one afternoon she turned quickly from her mannequin to see Thèophile Bader in the doorway. "Did you not see the sign on the door, Thèophile?" His face was red and his voice growled with fury.

"Oh I saw it alright and I've heard what you've been doing behind my back." His voice trembled enough to make his mustache quiver. "Just what right have you to fire Durand? He's been a good friend of mine for years. And, hiring another manager without consulting me and a woman at that? It's absurd!"

Madeleine turned back to her draping. "If you're finished bleating, please close the door behind you."

"What right, woman? Have you gone mad?" His foot tapped uncontrollably.

Madeleine swung around. "What right?" She opened the top drawer of her desk and took out a copy of their contract. Holding it up close, she said, "I'm the one responsible for company decisions. I believe this is your signature, Monsieur Bader." She took his elbow and prodded him out the door and then slammed it so hard several bobbins of thread fell from a nearby shelf and rolled to the other side of the room.

Twenty-Five

WHIRLS OF TURKISH cigar smoke hovered over the table leaving the putrid aroma of bitter leaves. Thèophile Bader coughed and searched the room for a spittoon and Henri Lillas drummed his thick fingers on the mahogany conference table and tapped his foot. Within minutes, the Argentinean, Martinez de Hoz, rushed into the room bowing and scattering apologies to the others for being late.

"So, what's going on Thèophile, why the meeting? Are we in some sort of crisis? I have a business to run." Lillas' impatience was obvious.

Thèophile Bader sat hunched down in his chair, his narrow shoulders barely wider than his thick neck. "We're having trouble with Vionnet."

Lillas look at him quizzically. "What kind of trouble, for Christ's sake? We're making an enormous profit from this venture. By all appearances the salon is being run successfully, and her dresses are more popular than ever."

"She just fired Durand and hired a woman in his place. It's absurd! I can't believe it." His hand shook as he blew cigar smoke into the room. "Not only that, she's stepping up her vigilance against copyists and counterfeiters and she's trying to get the other designers to join her. She even has Chanel and Schiaparelli in on this. The woman is overstepping her bounds; she's inept."

"Wait . . . just wait a minute here." Martinez de Hoz stood slightly from his seat and then sat back down. "Isn't this just effective management? Isn't this the agreement we had with her; that she runs the company and we put up the money and stay out of the way? Thèophile, this woman is the most respected couturier in Paris. She's not only protecting the company and our investment, but she's also protecting *haute couture*. Isn't that why we invested in this company? Copying is turning into a major problem. I don't see any issue with her."

Bader chewed viscously on his short cigar. "She's stifling growth and making decisions without consulting me, ah . . . well, us. We're retailers, we could profit from carrying copies of her fashions in our stores."

"My god man, are you suggesting that we should condone counterfeiters?" Lillas glared at him. "Wouldn't that be like shooting ourselves in the foot? We'd be sabotaging our own investment. Vionnet & Cie is about high fashion and that means one of a kind, not ready-to-wear."

"I agree with Henri," Martinez de Hoy added quickly. "I think she's on the right track with this."

Bader stood. "Can't you see what she's doing? She's trying to take over. She knows nothing about business, absolutely nothing. She sews clothes, she's just a seamstress. Do you want her controlling our investment?"

Lillas leaned toward Bader trying to avoid the billows of smoke. "Quite frankly, I do. You seem to have some personal vendetta against her. As an investor, I vote to leave her alone and let her do her job. She knows this business better than any of us."

"I vote with Henri, absolutely," Martinez said. "As long as profits in this company are soaring, and they are, we need to stay out of the way. She started this company and got this far without us. That's why we bought in, for her creative and business savvy. I'm not interested in interfering with her in any way, and I mean any way."

Bader took the cigar out of his mouth. "Let me remind you both." He stood and waved his cigar at them scattering ash on the table. "I own one more share of this company than anyone. It's my company and that's it." He grabbed his satchel and huffed out of the room.

Henri Lillas put his hand on his forehead. "Oh, god."

"Yeah, what have we gotten ourselves in to?" Martinez de Hoy stood slowly and brushed the ash from his suit.

Twenty-Six

WHILE NOT EXACTLY friends - Madeleine once referred to Coco Chanel as just a "hat maker"- they were steadfast colleagues when it came to protecting fashion and the industry from copyists. When they heard that replicas of their dresses were selling for as little as twenty dollars in New York department stores they decided to take action. The following year they won a landmark suit after a raid on a copyist's shop revealed scores of Vionnet and Chanel counterfeit dresses.

It was a small but significant victory; small for the epidemic copying rampant in the lucrative fashion industry in Paris in the mid-1920s, but significant for future couturiers who would now be allowed to sue for damages. But perhaps the real victory was the high court ruling that the combination of fabrics, colors, and designs in *haute couture* constituted real works of art and entitled to the same protection as other creative endeavors. In other words, high fashion was now considered at art form. Madeleine and Coco celebrated together over a glass of wine, one of the few times they were seen together in public.

Madeleine later told Therese, "I'll fight the fights I can but this piracy thing will continue no matter what. It's a losing battle."

Therese knew of Madeleine's deep devotion to her craft and its historical and economic significance in France. Madeleine placed far more importance on that than personal monetary gain. She is a true Parisian woman, Therese thought; staunchly loyal to her country and her profession.

"I can understand your frustration Madeleine, but look what you've done. You've started this whole movement to combat fashion piracy and even more important, because of you *haute couture* is now recognized as an art form, as it should be. So perhaps a losing battle ultimately, but for now *haute couture* is still alive and thriving in Paris, thanks to you."

"You know, my dear Therese, you help me get in touch with what's important. You are my muse, and so much more."

The summer light bore through the east window of Madeleine's office like rays of wheat, turning rolls of fabric against the wall into shades of soft sand dunes and warm hues of Indian tea. She let the newspaper drop from under her arm to the desk, and sat her croissant and coffee alongside before flinging her jacket on the spare chair. The sun felt warm and she stood interlocking her fingers in front of her, letting it warm her body still cool from the early morning walk. Then she sat sipping her coffee, leafing through the newspaper. She stopped on page three. Staring in disbelief, she read the brief announcement in the middle of the page.

> The *Galeries Lafayette owner Théophile Bader announces the grand opening of an ultra-new in-store boutique offering copies of original French designs. Among the list of designers whose work will be replicated are Madeleine Vionnet, Coco Chanel, and Lisa Schiaparelli. All are prominent designers in Paris.*

Shocked, she ran her hand over the fold to make it flat and read it again and again, her coffee sitting cold. By ten o'clock a frantic assemblage of people including her attorney Anton Guillet and her five managers paced the floor while other designers listed in the article rushed in one by one. The announcement, read aloud several times, boasted: *Galeries Lafayette will be the first department store to offer line-for-line copies of French couture.* Sighs and outbursts echoed in the room and the questions came like shots from a cannon.

"A legal precedent has already been set by the high court in the last counterfeit case won by Madeleine and Coco," Guillet said. "Plus, you may not know this, but Madeleine has just been nominated for a *Legion d'Honneur* award for her work to protect *haute couture* in France so that will humiliate Bader. He can't possibly get away with this," he reassured everyone in the room.

"He already has," Madeleine said. "We'll sue him and he'll lose, but the damage is already done. He'll sell copies of our fashions in the meantime. This is not about selling copies, it's about revenge."

"We'll try to get an injunction, Madeleine. This is new territory so I can't promise anything," Guillet said.

That afternoon Therese appeared at Madeleine's office out of breath. The door was closed and one of the receptionists sat nearby to deter visitors. Therese knocked lightly on the door and opened it a crack. "Madeleine?"

"Oh Therese, come in, everyone just left." Makeshift ash trays and empty coffee cups littered the room and extra chairs lined the walls in disarray, some with crumpled copies of the newspaper still on the seats, some on the floor.

"Are you . . . well, this is terrible, Madeleine." They pulled chairs together and sat by the window.

"I'm better now. At some point you just let go." Madeleine ran her hands over her face and through her hair leaving fluffs of it astray. She sat looking at Therese, studying the perfect shape of her face and her slim legs shown through her tights. She smiled. "Everyone is working on this. Others will step in but much of the damage is done." She shrugged slightly. "You talked to me recently about focusing on what's important and I intend to keep doing that but I don't see how we will ever avoid piracy. I'll do what's within my reach and in my own salon."

Her voice revealed defeat but Therese saw the strength in her jaw and the square of her shoulders. "Are you concerned that Bader will come here? He's obviously unstable."

"Not really. He's a coward. The people downstairs know what to do if he shows up. I want to know about you, Therese."

"Do you really want to change the subject?"

"I do. What's done is done. And if I'm to focus on what's important then I want to know about you."

They talked until the sun shifted the shadows on the wall. "Since the press service is going smoothly and I can now wire my articles and photographs from anywhere, I'm working on a correspondence exchange between the war-wounded children of Europe and the children in the United States. It will be like having pen pals. I'll be traveling some to help set up Junior Red Cross groups. It's volunteer work, but it's something I want to do. The real victims of the Great War were the children left homeless or maimed. It's been almost ten years since the war and some are still homeless, if you can believe that."

"Hmm, let's hope that was the war to end all wars. It's frightening to read about troops here, troops there. It would be terrible to recreate the travesty of the Great War. As for the children, if I can donate . . . money or anything, I'd like to do that."

Therese watched Madeleine's sadness as she spoke, clearly defeated but wanting to move on, to change the subject, to escape. It had been a difficult day and now they were talking about children. *What more could possibly upset her?* It was hard to anticipate Madeleine's moods or know what she needed, but at that moment Therese could see the exhaustion in Madeleine's empty stare.

"I have an idea. Would you like to ride in a motorcar?"

"A motorcar, are you serious?"

"Yes, my friend Gertrude has one and taught me to drive - well sort of. She said I could borrow it anytime. Let's do it, Madeleine. Let's go for a drive tonight and see the lights. What do you say?"

"Oh, my. Are you sure you know how to operate it?"

They agreed to meet in front of the salon at dusk, "Dress warmly," Therese said as she rushed off. Madeleine sat looking confused. *Did she really say a motorcar and that she knew how to use it?*

The sun was just setting when Therese drove up and waved from Gertrude's black Model T. Madeleine didn't recognize her so Therese tooted the horn and pushed the passenger door open to get her attention. "Get in. Hold your hat," she yelled. Madeleine climbed in and slammed the door. Therese wore a leather helmet with ear flaps and a purple scarf that billowed behind her, part of her stash from the wardrobe pile at the theater.

Madeleine laughed and lifted one flap, "Are you in there?" Before settling in her seat, she examined every aspect of the vehicle, touching the knobs, feeling the padded wooden seats, and even reaching over to toot the horn.

After a few jump starts Madeleine held on to the passenger handle and the car took off down the middle of rue Montagne spewing a billow of smoke and making a symphony of grinding and popping noises. Madeleine screamed, "Oh, my goodness, we're in a motorcar!"

They laughed and Therese tooted the horn again while holding the steering wheel tightly as they passed the horse-driven carriages trying not to spook them. She glanced at Madeleine who had a frozen look of amazement.

As the sun dipped behind the Eiffel Tower the lights burst on the moment they approached the intersection of Quai Branly and Pont d'Iéna in time to see the spectacle spread across the sky. "Oh, my, look at that! I've never seen it so beautiful," Madeleine yelled.

"Let's drive around and see it from the other side," Therese shouted, trying to find the right gear and watching for carriages and pedestrians.

After the Eiffel Tower, they drove down by the river Seine and Pont Neuf to watch the lantern-lit boats along the canal. The clacking noise from the engine drowned out the music near the canal but the ambiance was still magical. Therese slowed so they could take it all in and at one point, Madeleine lifted the ear flap on Therese's leather helmet. "It's wonderful," she yelled, trying to be heard.

From there they drove around the traffic circle near l'Opera laughing and honking the horn the entire time as Madeleine held on to her hat with both hands. They stopped long enough to let a parade of carriages pass, the horses' hooves almost in unison, then on to Place de la Concorde and Place de l'Etoile and they gasped at the Arc de Triomphe ablaze in lights. They drove in circles for the next several minutes just to see it again and again and then they took a quiet street back to the salon

When the Model T stopped in front of the Palace of Fashion, Madeleine removed her hat and took Therese's hand in a gesture of impetuousness, holding it to her cheek before letting go quickly and saying goodnight. As she watched Therese drive off she stood for a moment, intoxicated from the evening and by the carefree way Therese lives her life, her sensitivity, the risks she takes, her clothes, her choices, but mostly the size of her heart. She knew the evening had been Therese's way of showing concern, of removing her from the pain of the day's events. She thought how much she loved being with her and that it was not fame, but connection she desired and intimacy she craved.

On the way back, Therese thought about the evening and wondered if Madeleine's husband was in Paris with her or at one of their vacation homes. *Madeleine never mentions him and he wasn't there when Madeleine received the news about Bader's new boutique. Did she need to explain to him where she was tonight? It was late and wouldn't he wonder?*

Since it was past midnight when Therese returned Gertrude's motorcar, she left the keys on the dashboard and a bottle of wine and some cigars on the front seat.

Twenty-Seven

WHILE OTHER designers previously tried and failed, Madeleine's company was the first to successfully open a French house of fashion in New York City - and on swanky Fifth Avenue. Her first clients included the glamorous Hollywood stars and wives of senators, and almost overnight Madeleine became an instant success in America. The new vernacular in American fashion included terms like *Vionnet types, Vionnet inspired,* or being from the *Vionnet School of Design.*

Her reluctance to put herself on display however didn't change her adamant demand for privacy and ironically, her reclusiveness added to her fame. The American press became infatuated and referred to her as *the mystery woman, notoriously private,* or described her as the *reclusive* Vionnet. During one incident when she was cornered by the press and forced to comment on her work, she replied much to the reporter's chagrin, "How I work and what I work on is nobody's business but my own." Her comment was reported all over the newspapers and Therese laughed when she read it, knowing that Madeleine was still was setting boundaries in her own ill-tempered way.

Madeleine did make herself available to new designers wanting to learn from her. She opened a school within her salon to teach young apprentices how to create clothing using the bias cut and taught most of the sessions herself. She also allowed students to use her wooden mannequin for practice and allowed them access to the state-of-the-art equipment in the salon. When he heard of this, Bader sent a terse note: *How dare you open the salon and give away company secrets to new designers,* he admonished. She crumpled his note and threw it in the trash.

Just when Madeleine's life and her work were going smoothly she received word that her long-time friend and muse, Isadora Duncan, died in a tragic accident in the south of France. According to the newspapers, Duncan was trying out a new motorcar on the Promenade Des Anglais in Nice when a gust of wind blew her long neck scarf over the side of the car entangling it in one of the wheels and dragging her out onto the roadway. Her neck was broken. Madeleine ordered the salon closed for a day of mourning and it was another week before she would return to work. It was Duncan's classical style that influenced her designs but it was her friendship and the similar tragedies they shared that meant more. When Therese called Madeleine to see if she wanted to talk, she replied, "No," and hung up.

Madeleine and Therese's business trips to New York occasionally coincided giving them a chance to travel on the same ocean liner - Madeleine in a luxurious stateroom and Therese in any room big enough for her and her camera equipment. That was to her liking. Therese hesitated, but once asked Madeleine why she didn't travel with her husband.

"It's not that kind of marriage," she replied. Therese didn't pry but she did know that her husband, Netch, was seldom around and spent most of his time at one of their vacation houses in the south of France. *He was probably less in love with her than in her status; but still, how could she be intimate with someone who was not around that much?* It struck her as odd. *Well, what do I know of marriage? Actually, what do I know of intimacy?*

Sailing together on the *SS Olympic* to New York that spring gave them time to relax. They played shuffleboard on deck even in a storm, and drank champagne in one of the lifeboats just for a new experience - and to get away from people. They were both celebrities, Madeleine more so and decidedly more insistent on protecting her privacy. Traveling together also gave them time to talk about their work. Sitting on the deck one evening Madeleine expressed some concern.

"What do you think will be the repercussions of this new Wall Street crash everyone's talking about? We haven't felt it in France; in fact, our economy has never been better. But I have some concern, do you?"

"It's hard to imagine that wealthy Americans would suffer much from a bad economy. Aren't they the ones coming to France, or now to New York, to buy Vionnet gowns? They'll probably keep buying."

Madeleine turned her face toward the sea and a salt-infused gust of wind pushed against her. "Yes, well, I'd rather see the market right itself and rebound soon."

Therese shrugged sensing her concern. She thought for a moment while the ends of her scarf tattered in the sea breeze. She wasn't sure how to put Madeleine's mind at ease. The news was bad on all fronts.

"I think the more impending threat is what's going on in Europe right now," Therese said. "The political issues seem to be heating up again. France's insistence that Germany pay for the Great War still creates anger in Germany so maybe it's coming back to bite us. Supposedly, it's one of the reasons the Germans want to rearm right now."

"Oh goodness, maybe that's why this Hitler and his party are becoming so popular. He's counting on public anger."

"Hmm, yes, no doubt," Therese said, grabbing at the ends of her scarf.

Madeleine's wish for a quick rebound in the stock market didn't materialize and a global depression in the 1930s dampened any hopes of recovery, quick or otherwise. Businesses failed, banks closed, and coupled with the political unrest over Hitler's rise to power, the decade stumbled into uncertainty. Madeleine ordered her staff to be alert for economic and political news and bought one of those new radios everyone's talking about for her office, a small Philco.

Both Madeleine and Therese were grateful the global depression didn't hit France as hard as it did other countries. Germany, already struggling with reparation payments from the Great War, was now dealing with massive unemployment and the rise of Adolph Hitler and his Nazi Party. Editorials around the world expressed concern.

It was 1931 before the global depression finally hit France and by that time even wealthy Americans were reining in their spending on luxuries like *haute couture*. Before long fashion houses in Paris began to suffer as clients everywhere either lost their fortunes or had their funds devalued. By Madeleine's calculations, French fashion exports fell by an unprecedented seventy percent.

"What will you do, Madeleine?" Therese expressed concern. She knew from what Madeleine had told her, that Chanel, Schiaparelli, Poiret and others were already using cheaper fabrics, more basic designs, and ultimately lowering their prices.

"I refuse to compromise," was her usual reply to Therese or anyone for that matter.

She told one reporter when asked about downgrading her fashions, "I didn't go into this business to make smocks for bar maids." Instead, she sought hard to reassure her clients through her usual elegance and sophistication.

She confided to Therese, "My sexy and exquisite dresses give women something to hope for, a means to escape the dismal economic and political reality. In essence, I'm selling a dream, a dream of prosperity, of romance, of better times ahead." So she continued with her flowing and sophisticated designs of chiffon, silk, and Moroccan crepe, and while sales were down she held her position as the top fashion designer at the time, while others closed their salons.

"I may not sell as many," she told Therese, "but I know there are women who will continue to want my gowns rather than settle for some drab outfit that costs less and everyone else is wearing."

A contemporary of Madeleine's, Elsa Schiaparelli, called on Madeleine one afternoon in her office. "I want to compliment you on your fantastic salon, Madame Vionnet, but I also wanted to get to know you." She held out her hand. "Thank you for seeing me on short notice."

While waiting for her to sit, Madeleine noticed that her long dark hair, pulled starkly in a bun, was the exact same color of her large brooding eyes. She was petite and wore a conservative dark knit suit, one of her own creations. Madeleine also knew that Schiaparelli was fast becoming one of the most important fashion designers in Paris.

"How can I help you, Mademoiselle Schiaparelli?

"Elsa, please. Well, as you know I've opened a small salon here in Paris and probably at the wrong time if one can believe the news." She crossed her legs and sat back in the chair. Madeleine noticed that she wore the finest in silk hosiery. "With the depression and some political fears . . . well, I'm not sure if any of us will have any future in *haute couture*. I was just wondering what you think?"

"Mademo . . . Elsa, none of us can predict the future, and certainly not me."

Elsa blinked and took a quick breath. "I thought perhaps you could advise me. We're not really competitors; you design evening wear and I design more casual fashions and formal knits, but I'm not sure what direction to take right now. Who will be buying dresses anyway? I'm wondering what will sell in troubled times?"

Madeleine narrowed her eyes and folded her hands in front of her. "Well first, this is what everyone must decide for themselves." She leaned forward in her chair. "You can't really ask other designers for ideas, least of all me." Madeleine relaxed and sat back. "I don't follow trends and fads; in fact I abhor that part of the fashion world. Someone decided that styles should constantly be changing and clients, poor souls, fear they'll be out of fashion if they're not always buying something new."

Schiaparelli shifted in her seat. "I suppose the rationale is that fashions will keep selling if they keep changing."

"That's not part of my philosophy, Elsa. I care about making women look beautiful and the rest falls into place. I design for what's lasting, and that's beauty. Women want to be beautiful in good times and bad." Madeleine was quiet for a moment. "So, if you don't know what to design, then don't."

Elsa looked around the room to avoid Madeleine's gaze. "So . . . that's why you continue to design expensive evening wear rather than what the rest of us are doing; that is designing for austerity?"

"Let me ask you a question, Elsa. What do you care about the most as a designer?"

"Well making money, of course."

Madeleine gave in to a slight smile and stood. "It was nice meeting you, Mademoiselle Schiaparelli, and good luck."

Madeleine heard later that Schiaparelli was adding evening wear to her collection. *At least now we'll be competitors. That would end any further annoying visits fishing for ideas.*

In the months to come Madeleine's worst fear, although not entirely unexpected, would came true. Fabrics were quickly becoming scarce. The textile industry could no longer withstand the economic upheaval raining down on every sector and Madeleine, like the rest, was finally forced to cut back on production. Along with that, sales at her New York salon hit bottom. She thought hard, unsure about where to turn next.

Madeleine invited Therese to have dinner with her at a small restaurant nearby, suggesting they walk from the salon on the lovely spring-like evening. She valued Therese's input and her surprising good sense and logic now that she was becoming renowned in her own right, and making decisions about her life and work that were propelling her into the spotlight. While they were both careful to avoid anything other than friendship, clearly they enjoyed each other's company. The intimate evening in the salon was never mentioned although they both thought about it, even when they tried not to.

"This is a nice surprise," Therese said as they walked to the restaurant along rue Montagne, she in a pastel dress the color of soft orchid and bracelets dangling from her arm. Her beret was positioned to the side and her hair loose and blowing slightly in the evening breeze.

"I thought it would be nice for us to get out of the salon for a change. Sometimes I feel I live there."

"You do," Therese said teasing.

The neighborhood flower shop on the corner of rue du Boccador was just closing as they passed by. The aroma from large fragrant bouquets in tall tin vessels drew them closer and the florist, a young woman, brushed her hands against her leather apron and smiled, raising a bouquet along with her eyebrows.

Madeleine shook her head. "We're just enchanted with the colors and fragrance, but thank you."

The restaurant was small and it was early so they asked for a table in the back. Madeleine seldom went out and when she did, she liked her privacy. Knowing that, Therese smiled as they walked toward the hidden table. They ordered a bottle of red wine and crepes, and took off their hats after Madeleine put her cloth coat on the spare chair. Therese was surprised to see her low-cut silk blouse as she turned back toward the table, instead of the high ruffled dresses she often wore.

"These times seem like *déjà vu*, Therese. You weren't here during the Great War but everyone was wondering what to do next. We could count on nothing, just like now. I feel like this is the time to decide if I want to go through another war or save myself the grief."

"You left and waited out the Great War in Rome."

"Yes, but there's more at stake now. I'm established, I have clients, and a responsibility to somehow keep the fashion industry alive - which is getting difficult because of fabric shortages. And then there's the copyist issue. The counterfeiters must be stopped or it could ruin the whole idea of fashion as an art form." She took a deep breath.

"Well, you have money now, Madeleine, and the satisfaction that you accomplished what you intended. Would it be so hard to retire? If there is a war, it could be more complicated. Paris could be destroyed this time. It could be dangerous."

Madeleine blinked and turned her head, distracted by the *garçon* pouring more wine. She leaned back in her chair, lowering her chin. She said almost as a private thought, "There's still so much to do. I couldn't stand the thought of leaving."

"Haven't you just answered your own question?"

Madeleine smiled. "I suppose I have. What about you, Therese? Your life seems centered more in New York right now with your exhibits and lectures. Surely, you will go back to America if war does break out."

Therese watched her face, the raised brow, her dark eyes moving nervously as if she wanted an answer but not; a look of concern, even if slight. *Draping models are easy to find so why does she have this look?*

"It's too soon to tell. My work can be done here or in New York. As of now, I'm not going anywhere." She noticed a slight smile, more than Madeleine usually reveals. *I wonder what she's thinking.* Therese dared not ask.

Twenty-Eight

DESPITE THE GLOOMY economic forecast, ironically the 1930s saw the christening of several new luxurious ocean liners representing the ultimate in modernism. Therese was hired to photograph the lavish and avant-guard interior of the *Ile-de-France* so she and Madeleine took the opportunity to coordinate planned visits to New York and booked their passage.

Therese found the opulence aboard the ship a stark contrast to the downsizing and shortages rampant throughout France. "Obviously all of this was planned before the Great Depression became a reality," she said to Madeleine.

Their first night on board they walked around the decks bundled to stay warm in the icy Atlantic air. Therese shared her long wool scarf with Madeleine, draping it around them both as they walked.

"I sense a quiet desperation in Paris, an undercurrent," Madeleine said as she slipped her arm through Therese's. "It's strange because on the surface everything seems normal. Do you feel that too?"

"Yes, definitely. I even see it. People look distracted, serious. At Gertrude's salons the conversations are more about Hitler than about art. Everyone seems to be bracing for something, hopefully not war."

"Hmm, so much uncertainty right now, but also so much excitement for you with all your exhibits in New York, and now as director of the Gallery for French Art at the Rockefeller Center. I suppose that means you'll be spending more time in New York.

Therese squeezed her arm. "Not necessarily. I can come and go. And you?"

"The New York store is losing business. I need to see what's going on and if something can be done. I'm told by my managers that if I did personal fittings or at least met with important clients, business might increase. They never seem to let up on that, do they? They want to drag me into the public eye." She sighed and shook her head. "I didn't get into high fashion to be popular. Otherwise I would have gone into prostitution."

"Well I hope not, although with the prices you charge for your dresses you'd be the highest paid trollop in the world." They laughed while running for shelter from the sudden downpour. "I have a bottle of brandy in my state room, let's go where we can get warm," Madeleine said, pulling Therese out of the rain.

Therese slipped off her boots and held her wet panama hat in her hand, not wanting to put in on the luxurious furniture in Madeleine's suite. Her dark hair fell around her face in a charming disarray and she shook the rain from her hat in the sink and left it there. Madeleine watched, smiling. She was always amused at the way Therese dressed, her hats and turbans and baggy trousers. That night Therese wore a bulky cerulean-colored sweater draped with brown beads. They settled on the divan and sipped the smooth brandy.

Madeleine leaned against her shoulder after slipping off her shoes. "It's funny, we've talked about the economic situation and at first I was worried, but now I almost relish the thought of a slowdown. I feel a weight lifting. The problems with Bader and copyists, and now the shortage of fabrics, the desperate competition . . . I almost wish I could go back to a small salon like the one on rue Rivoli. It was simple and meaningful."

"Hmm, you can, you know."

Madeleine poured more brandy and leaned back deep in thought. Therese liked watching her at times like this when she leaves the conversation. It used to bother her but now she understands it's only her musing and nothing else. *It gives me a chance to really look at her without being noticed. She's eighteen years older than I. Her hair is rimmed slightly with gray and her face wears the stress of the last few years. But she is still beautiful, the way any fine treasure ages with time. Her skin is pale and flawless, her mouth relaxed and her hands soft.*

"You're not wearing your wedding ring!"

Madeleine looked at her ring finger and then at Therese, searching her eyes. "Do you really want to talk about that?"

"I don't know, do I? Will I be upset?"

"What would upset you?"

"Well, if you said that it's at the jewelers being enlarged with an emerald inset and implanted with a special adhesive that will weld it on your finger forever?"

Madeleine threw her head back laughing and then she searched Therese's face with a prolonged intensity. Madeleine had seen that look before, the innocent child wanting reassurance. She remembered when Therese told her of her father's abuse and her confusion about that as a child. Madeleine was seeing the same bewildered look, the yearning to be loved and not left or hurt.

Madeleine reached for her hand. "No, the ring is not at the jewelers; it's in a drawer somewhere. I won't be wearing it again. I asked Netch to move out. He's at the house in the South of France and has taken his things." She thought for a moment. "It's one more immense boulder I've lifted from my shoulders." Therese nodded but was quiet. She rubbed her face on the sleeve of her bulky knit sweater.

The House of Vionnet on Fifth Avenue was empty except for the manager and a vendeuse. Some of Madeleine's dresses were displayed beautifully near the entry, and photographs of her gowns lined the soft green walls of the boutique. She spent the morning going over orders and cancelled orders with the manager and concluded that the New York salon was doing better than most, but the economic depression had put even the wealthy in a conservative spending mood. Not only was the salon not meeting expenses, it was a drain on the company.

She met Therese for lunch that day near Rockefeller Center where Therese was meeting with the Center for French Art, and earlier with publishers about some book ideas. Madeleine watched her approach the

Madeleine and Therese

café and looked twice to make sure it was her. Therese wore a dark slim dress with open-toed pumps and a red silk scarf that quivered in the breeze behind her with each step. Her dark hair danced on her shoulders and her tall slim figure moved rhythmically with her long and easy strides, shoulders straight, chin up, and mesmerizing to watch. Madeleine was reminded why she chose Therese for a draping model and why every artist in Paris wanted to paint her. She was like a chameleon, changing her look to fit her mood. Madeleine watched as did everyone else nearby.

"I was looking for trousers and an oversized sweater, and here you are in a beautiful dress." They kissed on both cheeks before sitting.

Therese smiled. "A gift from Elsa Schiaparelli after I included her in *A Shopping Guide to Paris*."

Madeleine tilted her head to one side and looked askance. "Well, it's beautiful on you even if it is a Schiaparelli." She thought Therese extraordinary, looking every bit like an elegant model.

Therese put her satchel down and took off her gloves. Her hands were delicate with slim fingers, and Madeleine didn't fail to notice. *Hands that could touch someone tenderly,* she thought.

"How were your meetings, Therese?"

"Good, actually I signed a contract with *Life* magazine to do a story and take photographs inside the Vatican. It will be a first." She shrugged. "I guess people have an interest in the secrecy and intrigue. It's been an enigma even to Catholics, so I'll have an opportunity to demystify the unknown with my photographs, I hope." She smiled. "It should be an interesting project and might even turn into a book later on."

"This seems a departure from building a cultural bridge between France and America," Madeleine said.

"Well, yes, but when you look around," she scanned the room, "here we are sitting in a café in New York with French metal bistro tables and crepes on the menu. The cultural exchange is happening, but news is fickle and French modernism almost seems passé right now. People are interested in what's happening today. The world is changing; there's conflict brewing now, shortages, strikes, borders being challenged. I'm not sure what it means but maybe documenting it might be more important than cultural bridges right now. What do you think?"

Madeleine lifted her chin. "I'm wondering if it's safe being in the middle of all of that. You've been focused on the beauty of modernism and now global conflict?"

Therese sensed her concern. "Yes, it is a switch. I'll just see what comes up. There's no global conflict at the Vatican. It should be peaceful and insular. What about you, did you visit the store on Fifth Avenue?"

Madeleine nodded, still a bit distracted in thought. "Yes, it's financially insolvent. I need to close it. These days if women can afford a Vionnet, they can afford to come to Paris and buy one. Bader will balk. He's more interested in image than profit at this point. I think he'd rather bankrupt the company than give me the satisfaction of making a profit anyway."

Therese leaned closer making eye contact, and said with a slight smile, "Is this the first step in downsizing to the point of returning to the old days on rue Rivoli?"

"Let's just say it's part of unloading more annoying boulders right now."

Twenty-Nine

BY LATE AFTERNOON the news was all over the streets of Paris as newsboys on every corner yelled, "Nazi's Attack! Nazi's Attack!" Madeline watched from her office window as scores of people from homes and stores lined the streets to buy a newspaper.

"Seen this?" one of her mangers said, poking his head in her office and sliding a newspaper across her desk. "Nazi Germany just invaded Czechoslovakia and Austria."

It would be the first in a chain of events to rattle the world. Months later Italy invaded Ethiopia and Japan occupied China. Fear hung over Europe and the world, and the whole of Paris was stunned wondering if France would be next.

Madeleine remembered the tumultuous exodus during the Great War of 1917 along with shortages, carnage, and disruptions. Once again, she shuddered at the thought of being in the middle of another world war. Therese also followed the news closely; it was hard not to. On every street corner, freckled-faced news boys waved the latest editions shouting "global war on the horizon" and "Hitler on the move." The headlines in *Le Figaro* warned of the impending danger and urged Parisians to brace for war.

Before leaving for Italy on the Vatican assignment, Therese gathered boxes of her photographs depicting the modernist movement in France during the 1920s and 1930s and donated them to museums in New York. She urged Madeleine to preserve what she could as well. "If the news is correct, Paris may not be as lucky as it was in the Great War. The city was spared then, but the new weapons, the size of this new German army, who knows what will happen?"

"Ugh, I have other things on my mind right now. I'm trying to find fabrics. There must be some, I just don't know where. Anyway, the Germans seem to be focusing on rebuilding their country and boosting their armies. What would they want with Paris?"

"Well, isn't that the nature of war; the lack of reason?" Therese tried to speak without sounding overly concerned but she was. "I do wish you would take this more seriously. You have your dresses, your patterns . . . your history. It all needs to be kept safe."

Madeleine sighed with frustration. "Therese, you're responding like an academic. What needs to be preserved is keeping Paris as the fashion capital of the world, not bundling up our dresses and closing our doors while the Germans dance in our streets."

Therese rolled her eyes and looked away. Madeleine went on. "If we lose our reputation as the fashion capital we may never get it back. Both Britain and the United States want the honor; we have to stand firm." She let her hands run astray while she walked back and forth. "The world has always looked to France for fashion. It's been that way for centuries. Those of us in the business have an obligation to preserve that. Not just to save our own companies but to preserve the reputation of the industry itself. We need to keep producing in order to keep our skills and pass them on to future generations. But without fabric we can do nothing. Absolutely nothing!"

Therese knew that look, the clenched jaw, the fiery eyes, the pacing back and forth digging deep into her own thoughts, and being right. Madeleine had an uncanny way of being right when it came to fashion. And while the odds may be against her, especially if there is a war, Therese knew she would persevere right up to the end. It was one of the qualities she most admired about her.

"Yes, I understand, Madeleine. There's also the matter of personal safety that perhaps we could discuss when we meet again after I return from the Vatican. There may come a time when staying here in France may be unsafe." Therese waited for her to respond but instead Madeleine shot a cynical glance, dismissing Therese with the wave of her hand.

Therese knew when to let most things be, but she did wanted to have that conversation with her at some point. *Just not now while she's agitated. Whew!*

In the coming weeks, Madeleine searched desperately to find fabrics, even surplus stock. She'd always demanded the best in textiles; it was her hallmark. The silks, rayon crepes, crepes de chine, were all light enough to cling when cut on the bias, whereas many couturiers traditionally sought the heavier fabrics used during the Edwardian period. Some did use more delicate fabrics though, and for that reason she hoped there might be stockpiles of silks or crepes somewhere unused, and if so she might be in luck.

She purchased her own fabrics through the firm, Bianchini and Férier founded in 1888 in Lyon. She dealt mostly with Charles Bianchini who headed the design section in the Paris office at 24 bis, avenue de l'Opéra. Monsieur Bianchini admired Madeleine and her work, even purchasing some of her dresses for his wife and daughters. He always gave Madeleine his undivided attention and even wove fabric in wider dimensions to accommodate her bias cuts. Normally, he came to her salon to take fabric orders, but today she made an appointment to see him at his office.

"Bonjour Monsieur Bianchini." She slipped off her glove and held out her hand when he greeted her at the door. He was a large man with thinning straw-colored hair and bright ocean-blue eyes – and was quick to smile.

"Madame Vionnet, what a pleasant surprise to have you call on me at my office. And, after all these years, when will you start calling me Charles?"

"Well, when you start calling me Madeleine." It was a pleasant ritualistic conversation they'd had many times before and they laughed as he invited her to sit on the divan. His office was small but tastefully decorated in what might be called a "manly" style . . . dark woods and chestnut colored leather chairs with dark green brocade pillows. He waited for her to sit then seated himself near her. She was dressed in an elegant taupe dress with an ivory-shade silk scarf and she put her gloves on the seat beside her. He watched with obvious admiration.

"You know why I'm here, Charles." She said unpinning her hat.

"Yes, of course I know. I have your orders on my desk, on top of the stack in fact." He sighed, and then looked at her. "It's the fear factor, Madeleine; first it was the economy and the real consequences of that. Spenders tightened a grip on their wallets and businesses suffered and closed. But now it's the talk of war. Again, people are holding off on spending and businesses are closing or cutting back on production." He shook his head, rubbing his hands together.

Madeleine saw the worry in his eyes. "And we're not even at war," she said.

"No, but what we are seeing is this: the insatiable juggling of material goods by Nazi Germany, Fascist Italy, and Imperial Japan are indications that war might be imminent. Millions of tons of raw materials were recently imported by each country, possibly to prepare for warfare. In response, material goods were also being shipped to adjacent countries to prepare for defense against attacks. In short, all of the fabrics and raw material were bought up by countries rather than the fashion designers. In a way, we in the textile business are in a more privileged position to observe this shift in raw materials. In my mind, this usurping of raw material can only be interpreted as preparation for something . . . probably for invasions and defenses."

He gathered his thoughts and went on. "My contacts tell me the fabrics are being used for uniforms, tents, and whatever. The silks you want are most likely being used for parachutes."

Madeleine took a deep breath and let it go hastily. "What about synthetics like rayon? I suppose they're being used as well."

"Exactly. And for specialty fabrics like you want, it's too costly to gear up our machines and we can't get the raw materials to do it even if we could. You know I'm sure, that many designers are either closing their doors or fleeing to the south of France. The fabrics worn by ordinary people are easier to come by. They're cheap and plentiful. Your crepes and silks, Madeleine, are not, unfortunately. If there's a war, even the cheaper fabrics will be rationed and importing and exporting of all fabric will be forbidden."

"Yes, I remember during the Great War it was the same. Styles were altered to save on fabric. There could be no fabric-wasting pockets or cuffs, and clothes were slimmer and shorter. People didn't mind."

"You're right, Madeleine. They were grateful to get utility clothing, as it was called. Staying fashionable just didn't seem that important when bombs were dropping."

"Ah, but without *haute couture* during bad times you run the risk of losing the skills - something even Napoleon realized," Madeleine said. "To revive the silk-weaving industry in Lyons after the French Revolution, Napoleon placed orders for fabrics and ordered his subjects to wear silk and lace to preserve the skills needed for working with these fabrics."

"Yes, well he was no fool," Bianchini said.

She pushed her hair from her face and paused. "That is my main concern, Charles. Ready-to-wear clothing will be the thing of the future. Styles will be more practical. But French *haute couture* is one of the artistic achievements that defines France and keeps it at the forefront of fashion. It's good for the French economy and for the many talented designers who think of fashion as an art. We wouldn't tell painters to stop painting because of a shortage of oils and canvasses. Glamour, even during war, empowers women and offers hope of a better life."

"I couldn't agree with you more, Madeleine. My wife would no sooner give up her Vionnet than she would groceries in the cupboard. But the reality is that the raw materials are not available for us to weave, and that may very well be the last word."

They sat quietly for a while, and then spoke at the same time.

"Do you think . . ."

"I'm wondering . . ."

Charles gallantly motioned for her to speak.

"To leave no question unanswered, are any fabrics stored at the Lyon mill that would be suitable for me? You know my work, Charles. Do you have anything I can use even in the narrower widths that I can piece together; silks, rayons, chiffons, anything?" Her eyes were wide and inquiring.

"Well, I was just about to say that I will personally look myself to see what's there in the crepes and silks, even the synthetic rayons that might work for you. I'll gather everything I can find, even remnants."

"I would be most grateful. I'll downsize but I've been in the fashion industry all my life and it's times like these that we need to keep working. If for no other reason, in defiance of warmongering."

"I understand. And know that I feel the same. As you know, my family has been in business for a long time. I've watched *haute couture* grow into the second most lucrative industry in France, next only to film making, partly because of designers like you. It's a shame what's happening right now."

"Well, hopefully this will pass." Although she secretly suspected it would not.

The next step was to summon the financial backers with the goal of restructuring and downsizing the business. The thought of seeing Bader made her nauseous. *I wonder if Therese will be back from the Vatican.*

Thirty

THE SECRETIVE AND walled Vatican propelled Therese on a new and exciting path as she demystified the headquarters of the Catholic Church in Rome through hundreds of photographs. The exhilaration of being there prompted her note to Madeleine:

This might be my entre into global reporting, I like being here; it's all fascinating. Wish you were here to see it.
Affectionately, Therese.

Knowing the public's interest was moving toward global issues reaffirmed her shift in focus. With talk of war and the economic blight, the vibrancy of Paris was grinding to a depressing halt and it was obvious to her the interest in its modernism was fading fast.

Letters from Madeleine kept her informed while she was in Rome but Therese sensed a new urgency in her notes, especially the most recent:

When will you return? I have to convince Bader we need to downsize. It's easier to slay Goliath with more than one rock nearby.

Warmly, Madeleine.

Therese smiled at the thought. She knew which one would be Goliath and it wasn't going to be Bader.

Therese returned that week to be the other rock and they agreed to meet at a restaurant at dusk her first night back. Therese glowed with excitement over her Vatican project and the prospects of more global reporting. Madeleine watched her with interest. The late setting sun ignited Therese's eyes into a luminous green and Madeleine relaxed just seeing her across the table and knowing she was back. *How quickly our lives are changing. So much going on and how we're both struggling to adjust just to keep our edge. I want to tell her how much I care for her and how afraid I am that something might change.*

Instead she asked, "Did you get to see much of Rome when you were there?"

"Some, but the Vatican project was pretty intense," Therese said. "I know you're worried about Bader and downsizing, and whatever might be next. How can I help?"

Madeleine looked away deep in thought. "You know, Therese, I have houses in the country. We could go to one, be safe. Let this entire war business pass over us." Having said that, Madeleine took a long, deep breath and pushed back her shoulders. After a short silence they both laughed.

"Lovely idea, I'd like to see that," Therese said with a note of sarcasm in between the laughter.

Madeleine shook her head. "I'm not sure where those thoughts came from. Fear I suppose. You and I are not ones to cower in the corner and I know that. We need to be involved. If we escaped to a house by the sea you'd be out on the beach looking for a story to write about clams and I'd be making dresses out of tablecloths."

Therese knew Madeleine was upset about the rapid changes. She leaned closer to her. "It will be alright. There are changes, but only on the outside. We will stay the same." She touched Madeleine's hand for a brief moment.

After dinner they walked along the Seine, stopping to hear jazz at *La Chambre Bleu* where people stood at the bar faking less stressful times. Sitting on the bridge they talked about the upcoming meeting with Bader. Madeleine said she hoped he might agree to downsize and liquidate the furnishing in the Palace of Fashion.

"I just want a small shop again, Therese. My textile supplier may be able to come up with some fabric, enough for my special clients. I also want to continue with my workshops if anyone is interested. It's important to pass these techniques on to the younger couturiers. What about you? If you let the press service go, what's next?"

"Well, a lot hinges on what happens with the economy and if the war comes to France. I'll make sure my mother has enough income and that Louise can keep some aspects of the press service to provide an income for her. Finland is preparing for the next Olympics and I'd like to cover the preparation. I can sell that story to a number of newspapers. It's all so uncertain right now. It's hard to predict the future." She glanced at Madeleine. Her face still reflected concern. She slipped her arm through Madeleine's and held it tight.

Later that week, Therese sent word to Gertrude that she'd like to talk to her and Raoul. The note that came back said:

We've been thinking of you. Come this Friday. Raoul will be here.

Yours, Gertrude and Alice

When Therese arrived the table was set with Gertrude's hearty soup made with bounty from her vegetable garden, and a block of warm peasant bread sitting next to a bowl of melted butter. Alice poured glasses of red table wine and left the jug on the table where the four of them sat near the old wood-burning stove. They asked about Therese's trip to the Vatican and when the prospective book will be out, but the conversation turned to their concern about the rapid deterioration of the economic and political situation.

"I'm convinced there will be war in Europe," Gertrude said. "Why else would Hitler annex Austria and rearm in spite of the Treaty of Versailles that forbids that? His anti-Semitism is no secret. He wants to wipe out the entire Jewish population in order to establish a pure race, as he calls it."

"Well, we don't really know if that's his agenda," Alice said. "I think he wants resources to build a stronger Germany. The papers say he's already pilfering Austria for food and weapons for the German troops, even sending Austrians to work in German factories to replace Germans recruited for the military."

Therese looked at both Gertrude and Alice. "If Germany goes to war with France, what will you do? You've been through a war before so you probably know what to expect. You're both Jewish. Will you go back to America?"

"Ah, we've talked about it," Gertrude said nodding. "But we rent a vacation house in the south of France in Bilignin so we'll probably go there. Of most importance though is finding a caretaker for our art since we can't take it with us. There's too much. As for us, I'm counting on our celebrity status to protect us. I know it can be very unpopular and demoralizing to citizens in general when invaders tangle with well-known people. Besides, we're American citizens not French, so we might have some added protection even if we are Jewish."

"Gertrude is checking on all that now," Alice added. "It helps that her family is somewhat prominent on the East Coast in America and have political connections. It may not do any good, but it may help if we do need to get out of the country. The question we've been wondering is what you intend to do, Therese. We think it best for you to return to America for now."

"Yes, we all feel strongly about that," Gertrude added. "I know you are very capable but you are still here alone."

"I agree, Therese," Raoul said. "It may be too early to make that decision but if Germany does march on France, no one knows how much protection Americans will really have."

Therese smiled. "One minute you're glad I'm here and the next you're telling me to go! Seriously, I appreciate your advice and concern. You are more experienced in this. What I know is that I want to stay connected with you no matter where we are. My press service, is winding down out of necessity and I'm going to Finland soon to cover the preparations for the upcoming Olympics. I'll keep my press credentials so I should be able to make that happen."

"Well, we'll vow to stay connected and help each other," Gertrude said, looking at each of them. They lifted their glasses.

"I have a question," Therese said. "If Germany somehow invades France, what will happen to French citizens?"

"That's hard to say," Raoul chimed in. "Marching on France would be quite different than bombing France, of course."

Gertrude nodded. "During the Great War, the Germans didn't invade Paris like they did in other parts of France. We all had shortages and rationing but generally they didn't waste their bullets killing civilians;

they just tried to use them or take what they had to send back to Germany. Are you worried about friends here?"

"Oh, just curious I suppose."

Thirty-One

ON A QUIET SEPTEMBER morning the song *Parlez-Moi d'Amour* played softly from the small radio in Madeleine's office as she cut a piece of fine chiffon on the bias. When the music stopped abruptly she turned and stared. *We interrupt this program* . . . It wasn't the words that that first caught her attention but the hint of urgency in the announcer's voice. *Nazi Germany has just invaded Poland!*

Madeleine felt a chill; she knew the significance of the invasion. Both Britain and France had treaties with Poland, meaning they would declare war on any invader. To honor that agreement they would be forced to declare war on Germany. In turn, Nazi Germany would almost certainly invade France and if possible, Britain.

She pushed her fabric aside and walked out onto the walkway. Shopkeepers, barmaids, families and farmers had taken to the streets bewildered, unsure of what the news would mean for them, for their families, for their businesses. They gathered in groups talking in low murmurs like mourners at a wake. Strangers were hugging, mothers pulled their children close, and others just stared blankly. *They've not been through this before. Too young, or too old to remember the Great War and what it was like to have their lives upended, their businesses lost, the camps, and for others even death . . . so much to think about, so much to mourn.*

She watched a woman striding through the crowd, crossing the street and then walking faster toward her direction. Wearing a pair of black tights and a black beret, her colorful scarves flowed behind her as she tried to catch the tail ends and pull them closer to speed her journey. Madeleine sighed deeply and whispered, "Oh, Therese. Thank god, it's Therese."

The news of war with Germany came at a time when Therese had finally taken the world stage as a truly prominent photo journalist. *The Vatican,* her recent book exploring behind the scenes of the mysterious institution was just published to great acclaim. Her success however felt bittersweet that morning after hearing the news about Poland and she rushed to find Madeleine. The realization that France would soon be at war came as a surprise even though it was almost inevitable. She had received a call early that morning from Louise.

"We've just heard the news, Therese, and we expect that you will return to America right away."

Therese hesitated before she spoke. "I need to settle things here and, well Louise, any military action if any will be a long way off so there's no real need for concern right now."

"What needs to be settled there?" Louise's voice trembled with impatience. "Mother and I are worried. You've already sent boxes of business from the press service to us here in New York."

"I must confess that I don't know what needs to be settled. This is new to me, war that is." Therese offered a forced laugh.

"I see. Well, hopefully you can take care of what needs to be done very soon, don't you think?"

"As an American I'm sure I'm safe here, Louise. Germany's not at war with America, and actually not really at war with France, yet."

"But they soon will be and I don't think bombs distinguish between nationalities."

Therese smiled. "I understand your concern, Louise. I'm going to Finland soon to do a story on the preparation for the upcoming Olympics there. I'll see how things are here when I return."

Louise questioned persistently. "Is it safe traveling to Finland?"

"Yes, yes I'm sure it is. I've read that the Germans will be focusing on the Balkans and the south, not countries further north. I'll keep you and mother informed of my plans." She paused. "And Louise, it will all be fine. I'm sure you'll see me in New York soon."

"Do be careful, Therese."

"Yes, yes of course."

Madeleine's door was ajar when she heard Therese bounding up the stairs two at a time before standing in the doorway out of breath, her beret in her hand. Madeleine pulled her into the room and closed the door. They hugged like two frightened children in the dark.

"I must say that I'm worried and a little afraid." Madeleine buried her face into Therese's shoulder and felt her heart beating from the sprint.

"Yes, me too. This is unnerving. It's not knowing what to expect. Will bombs drop tonight or will they come marching into the city any minute?"

Madeleine walked to the window and put her hands on the glass. "I feel like all those people down there wondering what's next. Will we lose everything we have, all that we've worked for and accomplished? Will it all be gone, destroyed, with nothing left? I didn't have that much to lose in the last war, but now . . ."

Therese walked over and stood right beside to her, their shoulders touching. "You know things will change, Madeleine, but we won't. We've survived everything else - our family situations and struggles with our businesses - we'll survive this."

"I hope so. We out ran them in the Great War but now with different weapons, planes and bigger tanks . . . well, this will be different. Of course you'll be leaving for America. Have you decided when?"

"What? No, it's too soon. Germany will need time to mobilize and I haven't decided what I'll do. And you, will you be leaving for your home in the south of France? That's where everyone seems to be going."

Madeleine hesitated.

"Won't you?" Therese asked again. "Surely the Germans can't destroy all of France. They'll go right for Paris at least in the beginning."

"Therese, Netch is there at the home in the south of France. He's been living there as part of the agreement of our separation. He can't go back to Russia at this point."

Therese sat down near the desk. After some time Madeleine sat as well, watching Therese play out some scenario in her mind, toying with her fingertips, looking very young, and as if the boat was sailing without her.

It was the first time Madeleine had mentioned Netch after she said they'd separated. Therese heard rumors that he was quite the playboy in the south and popular with the ladies, and that he evidently gave up his shoe salon in the Palace of Fashion. Madeleine once referred to herself as his "banker" and so Therese assumed they never divorced or Madeleine probably would have mentioned it.

Therese sat nodding. "When the time comes, you need go to the south of France, Madeleine. No matter what."

Thirty-Two

THÈOPHILE BADER insisted they meet at the Palace of Fashion but Madeleine sent word they would meet in the office of her attorney, Anton Guillet. She invited Marie Gerber to join them.

As usual, Bader arrived late. He entered with a heavy-set man towering above his diminutive stature by several inches. At first, Madeleine thought it might be a body guard and tried not to smile, but Bader introduced the man as Monsieur Doucet, his personal attorney.

Bader spread out some papers in front of him and flicked the ashes from his cigar on the floor. Anton Guillet leaned across the table and whispered, "Monsieur Bader, please, there is no smoking in our conference room. Thank you." Bader stared at him and then snuffed his cigar out on the conference table leaving it sitting there next to his briefcase.

"Thank you all for coming," Madeleine began. "As you know, there are a number of dire circumstances that are and will adversely affect our company. The global economic depression has eroded our list of clientele and talk of war and rearmament has caused devastating shortages in materials, specifically fabric.

Bader interrupted. "Nonsense, I'd like some proof of that. It's your. . . . your doing."

Lillis rose part way. "Let's hold our comments, Thèophile. Let her finish." He sat back down and Bader wiped his mouth with his sleeve.

Madeleine continued. "Not only do we have fewer clients and almost no fabric, we're seeing the entire fashion industry shutting down.

Many couturiers are leaving for the south and the reality is that, well, fashion and war do not mix."

"If I'd been allowed to copy your fancy dresses we could be selling copies for a fraction of the cost and selling lots of them. We can still do that . . ."

"That isn't relevant, Thèophile," Martinez de Hoz said loudly. "If there's no fabric there are no dresses. So perhaps we can stay on the topic." Marie Gerber sat shaking her head and glanced at Madeleine.

"I agree," Lillas sided with de Hoz. "I'd like to see us focus less on the past and more on what's happening right now. Madeleine is alerting us to some urgent issues. I don't know about the rest of you, but I want to limit my investment losses here and I want to know what's happening with Vionnet et Cie."

Madeleine whispered to Marie, "I'll let de Hoz and Lillas take on Bader." She continued to the group. "I should mention that even if we did have fabric it would be confiscated or rationed. Based on what we're seeing in Austria and Czechoslovakia, and soon Poland no doubt, is that all fabric is being sent to Germany. The bottom line is that we need to close our salon and liquidate our assets. We need to let our staff go and I think we need to start that process now. I'd like reasonable separation pay for our loyal employees; the ones who have really been doing the work, and . . ."

Bader jumped to his feet. "Preposterous! They'll get no pay. We're already in the hole because of the way they're pampered. Cushioned seats, medical care . . ." Bader's attorney reached for his arm, pulling him down in his seat. Bader sat but reluctantly

"I'm asking for your approval to close and liquidate," Madeleine concluded.

"Agreed," both Lillas and de Hoz said at the same time.

The room grew tense as Bader groomed his mustache with his thumb and forefinger. "Ha, what fools," he said. "Have you forgotten that I own one more share than anyone in this room. This is my company and . . ." His attorney turned sharply, whispering something to him in private. Madeleine's attorney had been sitting quietly but pushed his chair back and stood.

"Monsieur Bader, I'm sure your attorney has informed you by now that the company is essentially bankrupt, or will be soon, and the shareholders, at least three of them or seventy-five percent, have just agreed to liquidate. As a shareholder, I'm not sure why you would want to prevent the liquidation since you will all share the profits from selling off the assets. But with a majority in agreement already, your vote is not needed for anything right now."

Madeleine rose on that note. "Our meeting is adjourned. We'll keep you informed of the liquidation progress. We still have clients we're serving and the process will take some time, but it will happen. This is the beginning." Bader sat stunned and was finally led out of the room by his attorney, who also picked up his snuffed cigar and dropped it in Bader's briefcase.

Madeleine sighed after everyone left the room and turned toward Gerber. "I never thought I'd see the day."

"We're closing too, Madeleine. It's bittersweet. As you know, I've been ill and I'm ready for a rest but what a fantastic time it was for fashion."

"Yes, I know Marie. And, a rest for you is in order. Anyway, ready-to-wear is taking over as fashion moves more toward the masses, the middle class and not just the elite. And while we are at war, New York might take over what's left of *haute couture* where we left off."

"What'll you do, Madeleine, what are your plans?"

"If I can get fabric remnants I'd like to have a small boutique salon just to keep working. I hope to stay in Paris as far as I know. This is my home. If the city is bombed I might change my mind and go to the south of France, but who would want to bomb Paris anyway? I can see taking it, but to destroy it? I can't imagine. If there's interest, I'll teach young designers. That's about all I know at this point. I'll do anything to keep Paris as the fashion capital even if it means stitching by candlelight. And you, Marie?"

"My sisters and I plan to stay together as a family and close the salon. If France is occupied, we'll probably stay. If war is fought in the streets then we'll have to leave. You too, Madeleine."

"Yes, we'll see. We'll see what happens."

Thirty-Three

THE FRIGID AIR bit her cheeks and stung her nostrils as she stepped off the train in sub-zero temperatures that icy afternoon. Shivering uncontrollably she pulled her woolen coat close and stood freezing by the tracks looking at Helsinki for the first time whitewashed in snow like a bleached canvass. The linen sky completed the stark-white picture of a city literally on ice. Therese slipped off her gloves to reach for her camera but flinched and quickly pulled them back on with a hard yank. A young porter stood by smiling. "You can't get by without gloves in this weather; it's the coldest winter in a hundred years, and that's the truth." His breath curled around his face making him almost obscure.

"I'm beginning to think I can't get by with this coat either." She grabbed the collar and pulled it tighter to her chin while stomping her feet to stay warm.

He was lanky and young, and wore a tightly-knit wool hat with ear flaps that hung loose, swinging back and forth against his face as he led her toward the station. Her icy breath drifted upward like smoke in a film-noir movie and she followed in his large footprints before they quickly filled with snow. "Snow suits," he yelled over his shoulder.

When they reached station, she said, "Snow suits?"

"Yes, it's the only way to stay warm here." He motioned her inside and before entering she noticed the temperature gauge on the wall was stuck at 20 below zero. She took a deep breath and relaxed her shoulders when she felt the warmth in the crowded waiting lounge.

"Snow suits and waterproof boots," he said again. "It's the only way. Go to Stockmann's department store." He looked her over. "I see you have a camera bag so you'll probably be out taking pictures. You won't last long in what you're wearing." His cheeks were crimson and bits of snow hung precariously on his eyebrows.

"You're very kind, thank you. I'll get a snow suit right away . . . at Stockmann's," she added. She handed him some Finnish markkas before heading to the Hotel Kämp, a distinguished hotel in the center of town famous for its long history of prestigious visitors. She chose it because it was recommended to foreign correspondents in town to cover the preparation for the upcoming summer Olympics. A press room with wire services and equipment were set up in the hotel just for that purpose.

After a short taxi ride, she found the hotel and checked in, relieved to get out of the cold.

"Oh, and this was left for you, Miss Bonney," the receptionist said, handing her a note along with her room key. Therese read it while she waited for a bellman to help with her bag.

Dear Miss Therese Bonney. We are pleased to welcome someone with your distinguished credentials to Helsinki. Please let us assure you that we will do everything we can to facilitate your work, especially reporting on the upcoming 1940 summer Olympics. You'll find our press room will have whatever you need and a car and escort will be available to show you all the Olympic facilities. Please come to the reception in your honor this evening at 7 p.m. in the lounge so you can meet with the Olympic Committee and other officials.

Regards,
Henrik Klaas, Chair
Finland Olympic Committee

She thought for a moment. *Oh my goodness, someone knows I'm here!* After unpacking and heeding the young porter's suggestion, she dashed out to find warmer clothes.

"Good god!" she muttered under her breath as she stepped from the hotel onto the street piled with snow.

The department store was within a block, but already she felt the snow creeping into her shoes and socks so she walked quickly hearing the icy snow crunching under her feet and sending chills to every nerve ending. She found Stockmann's in an attractive art deco building with a huge modernistic clock on the façade. She thought of running back to get her camera but realized the late hour and her painfully frozen feet so she rushed inside. Within minutes she found everything she needed and more. She couldn't wait to tell Madeleine that snow suits and boots are the *haute couture* in Finland!

Searching through her canvas bag back at the hotel, she looked for something to wear to the reception. Spotting her new snow suit on the bed she paused and then shook her head. *Hmm, wishful thinking.* Instead, she wore a long slim black skirt and sweater, hoping the reception wouldn't be too formal. Her bag was filled with film not clothes.

The large rock fireplace warmed the dark-paneled lounge and a man at the bar stood when she entered. "Ah, Miss Bonney, I recognized you from your photograph. I'm Henrik, Henrik Klaas, from the Olympic Committee." He offered his hand and a rather kind smile. His ruddy complexion and blue eyes seemed a good fit and he wore a suit but no tie. She smiled, a bit relieved it wasn't a formal affair. "I hope you've had time to get settled in your room. You arrived by train this afternoon, correct?"

"Yes, and I've already had a lesson in how to dress for the weather so I went shopping this afternoon. And please, call me Therese."

"Indeed, Therese, this is an unusually cold winter right now, even for us. Let's get a drink if you like, and some food," he said leading her toward the buffet table. "We're pretty informal. I want to introduce you to some people who might be helpful during your stay but first I'd like to give you a little background." He poured a hardy red wine, just what she would have chosen.

"Let me say first, we're overjoyed to have you here. We know of your work and reputation. I'm sure you're aware we were second in the bidding for the summer Olympics, losing to Japan after all our effort." He shook his head and rolled his eyes. "Now with the war in the Pacific, well, we were awarded the honor of hosting by default and the world is watching to see if we can pull it off; that is, be ready in time. That's probably why you're here. We're also hoping of course to publicize the Olympics and our homeland, Finland. The publicity will help."

"I'm sure everyone knows Finland will be a superb host. I think the interest now is just in the logistics given that you've had so little time to regroup and prepare."

"I can assure you we will be prepared, and we want visitors to come for the Olympics although we're not getting much publicity or press right now."

"Quite honestly, Henrik, after Nazi Germany invaded Poland, news about the Olympics may be the last thing on people's minds."

"Yes, well that may be true; the war has taken center stage. We still want to think positively and we hope for a full house for the Olympic events. It's very good for business. You'll see that this is a beautiful country with hospitable people. We hope you can convey that in your stories and images."

"Of course." Therese hesitated. "But since Europe is at war or will be soon, isn't there also another story here, Henrik? What position will Finland take?"

He blinked several times and chose his words. "We'll leave that up to the commanders. Our job is to prepare for the Olympics not war."

Some thoughts are worth postponing, but she couldn't help but think he was mulling over his answer. Then he added almost in a whisper, "The reality is that given Finland's geographical location it's dancing with two suiters: the Soviets and the Germans - both with non-aggression pacts. But as they say, agreements are written in sand if the stakes are high enough." She watched his expression. He changed the subject but still looked pensive. "Well, let me introduce you to some people, Therese."

Over the course of the evening she met Finnish journalists, employees of the Ministry of Foreign Affairs, local politicians and industrialists, along with Christopher Mehlem, the Chairman of the International Journalists' Association. *Why are all these people invited to the reception? Surely, not to meet an American photojournalist interested in the preparation for the summer Olympics. Perhaps there's something else.* When introduced to the last guest to arrive it became clear.

"Therese, I'd like you meet the Commander-in-Chief of the Finnish Army, Commander Mannerheim."

"Oh . . . well, I'm pleased to meet you," she said while staring at the brass stars on his epaulet and the medals on his chest. He had entered the room with three armed soldiers who stood by the door. "And a little surprised," she added.

"And why surprised, Miss Bonney? Don't you have the military in America" He smiled coyly and seemed to enjoy her embarrassment.

"Yes, although they normally don't show up at my events. I mean they could but I don't know why they would. This leads me to ask that question of you."

He laughed. "Why am I here? You're brave to ask. We all have an interest in the Olympics because they provide a significant stage for a country's spirit and they help to build national pride. The Olympics are also good for business and tourism, and that's good for the economy."

"Hmm, did you answer the question or side-step it? What is your primary interest in being here, Commander?" She decided to be point blank.

"Ah, indeed, you are American aren't you?" He smiled, and looked friendlier than his uniform and armed guards suggested. "My interest is keeping Finland safe and independent. We're in a precarious situation, politically and logistically. My hope is that if we need help, America and Britain will come to our aid. It's really that simple. As an American photojournalist, you're in a position to help convey that message."

Therese nodded, but thought it best not to respond. She didn't know much about global politics and already felt in over her head, but she liked his playful combativeness, his willingness to engage.

After everyone left, she looked for Henrik to thank him. He reappeared and let out a long sigh. Evidently, there was still tension lingering in the room.

"I just want to share some things you should know, Therese, not to alarm you."

"Could I possibly be more alarmed Henrik, what's happening here? I came here expecting to hear about the Olympics and the talk is about everything but that – and especially about the war."

Henrik's laugh seemed forced. "Mannerheim and his guards are a little intimidating. His role is to keep us safe and we're thankful for that. Everyone wants publicity for one thing or another. But now getting back to what you should know, Helsinki has quite an extensive civil defense system so in case of problems, at least within city limits, you'll hear a loud siren. There are shelters in all high-rise building basements. These are just basement rooms with reinforced walls in order to withstand bombing, so basements in tall buildings are the places to be if you're unsure about anything. Also, this room has been reinforced."

"Really?" She looked around. There were steel beams at key points and wire mesh against the windows. *What have I gotten myself into? Why is he telling me all of this?*

"You should also know that you are under no obligation to stay."

"I see, well you must be reading my mind. But why would I leave now that it's just getting interesting?"

Thirty-Four

DAYLIGHT HOURS IN Finland in the winter were precious few – each day darker than the last. Therese photographed the Olympic facilities mid-day so she could shoot without a flash and even then, the light was often lost to blustery weather. On her third day after returning from a visit to the new Olympic stadium just outside the city limits, she asked her escort to drop her near the edge of town so she could take photographs of hardy farmers trying to work in fields covered in snow.

"Thanks, I'll walk back," she shouted and waved the driver on. Strolling along the icy road she stopped for a while to watch a group children playing ice hockey on a frozen pond. It was too cold to stop for long so she kept walking while zipping her snow suit to the top, wrapping her scarf around her face, and pulling her hat down over her ear muffs. *Hmm, that's better!* Further along she photographed a family scattering hay for their cows over the snow while the children threw snowballs at long icicles hanging from a dilapidated barn and cheered wildly when they knocked one off. She waved and clapped her hands but with gloves on they could only see her enthusiasm and waved back. As she got closer to town she took pictures of a group of children throwing small rubber balls into huge snow drifts and then diving in after them screaming with delight. It made her cold just to watch but she laughed with them as they emerged looking like miniature snowmen posing for her and her camera.

For the first time since arriving in Finland she felt relaxed. She was happy to see the families and children of Helsinki, and the snow added an illuminating beauty to everything, especially when resting precariously on wire fences and old tractor parts. It was beautiful she thought, to see the ice coating the tips of branches turning them to glittering sparklers, and she breathed deeply with the smell of smoke filling the air, imagining warm houses with kettles of soup on wood-burning stoves and gloves drying on a mantle nearby. She stopped to photograph the ivory white sky being infiltrated by a huge black cloud. There was thunder in the distance and as it got louder and closer, she packed up her camera and stuffed the half-used film down the inside of her snow suit to keep it from freezing. She quickened her pace toward town and as the thunder got louder, she ducked under a small bridge. *How strange. What's happening?*

The noise was deafening even with her ear muffs, and the ground shook surprising her. She suddenly felt clammy and then felt herself moving, tossed about and then landing on the ground near the bridge with bricks everywhere, some on her legs, some in a nearby heap. She choked and coughed, the stale smoky air burning her eyes, her nose. Her ears felt plugged and then open to the rhythm of the pounding noise. Dust floated in the air and stole the light like thick fog in a valley, only it was dry, burning dry and thicker by the minute. *My camera bag? Where's my bag?* She pulled her gloved hand free, running it over her body and felt the bulky bag with the strap still around her neck and at her side. The dust coated her mouth and she tried not to swallow but then felt sick to her stomach, retching, bringing up nothing. The smoke reeked of rancid air, hot and piercing and she tried to cover her face with her gloved hand but her whole body hurt to move. Rolling on her side, she heard more bricks tumble to the ground with mounds of dust.

Where are my legs? She tried pulling them from the rubble but had no sense of where she was or which way was up or which way was down. Propping her back up against something she struggled to find her breath. The air was gone and what was left was tight and dirty. The cold was her first sensation and then the pain. She worried her eyes would freeze in the sockets or that she would suffocate. Gasping for air she closed her eyes, scared and unable to cry. After a while she felt something moving and opened her eyes to see a small gray rabbit. She closed her eyes and then opened them again. It huddled in some bricks, its fur fluffed and wavering. She reached and brought it close, cuddling it in her arms. "There, there." She rocked gently. "There, there," she whispered.

In the pitch of night the light was bright, so blinding that she turned her head blinking uncomfortably several times. There were voices, men's voices. She was still rocking when a hand reached toward her. Through the haze she recognized her escort but not the others. "Miss Bonney . . . Miss Bonney." After a while, she heard his voice again, more distant. "We've found her. Yes, near the bridge, she was rocking back and forth. I think so . . . maybe hypothermia . . . we're getting her out now."

He appeared again. "Miss Bonney, do you think you can walk?" He put a helmet on her head while others moved bricks and timber.

"I think so," her breathing was faint. She looked down and then on each side of her. "Let's take the little rabbit. We need to take the rabbit."

"What rabbit, Miss Bonney? There are no rabbits here," her escort said. "They could never survive the sub-zero temperatures unless they burrowed deep underground. Some do in the forest, but not here. There have never been rabbits here."

She looked around the rubble at her side. "Are you sure? Oh, of course you're sure. You would know. Was it a big storm? I remember hearing thunder."

"No, Miss Bonney. We've been attacked, the entire country, by land, sea, and air. They bombed Helsinki late this afternoon. You were just on the edge where one of the bombs landed. It took out part of the bridge.

"Are German troops here now?"

"We weren't attacked by the Germans, Miss Bonney, we've been attacked by the Soviets, and no, there are no troops. Not yet. Let's get you out of here."

Wrapped in a blanket and protected in the slow-moving armored vehicle as it made its way along the road, she watched the steady stream of people, some holding the hands of children, some barely dressed, and others collapsing in the snow. She sat up straight and wiped the haze from the window. "Stop! We need to stop for them. This is inhumane," she yelled as she slammed her hand repeatedly against the window of the armored truck before one of the corporals draped a cloth over the window. She let her head fall back, and the tears finally came.

Hysterical guests in the hotel elbowed their way to the desk, some looking for rooms, others rushing to leave with bags half closed and asking questions. She pushed through the crowd, a few moving away when they saw the blood and her snow suit torn to shreds, the helmet still on her head. Slipping into the lobby restroom a soon as she could, she stood looking in the mirror. Her hands shook as she fumbled with the strap on her helmet, finally getting it off. Staring blankly, she saw her face frozen in fear and blackened with soot, and eyes she didn't even recognize. *My god!* She grabbed the rim of the sink as the dry heaves wracked her body until her stomach muscles ached and she gagged on nothing. She looked again. The person in the mirror was a replica of someone she might have once known.

She wiped some of the blood and grit from her face and rubbed her temples to soothe the pounding in her head, and then took the stairs to the second floor expecting to see mobs of reporters in the press room. Surprisingly, it was empty except for the information receptionist she'd met her first day.

"Where is everyone, the other reporters?"

The receptionist stared. "You're the only one, Miss Bonney. Other than a few local reporters, you're the only international journalist here. We don't expect that to change any time soon." She stood wide-eyed. "We've heard it's practically impossible to get into the country right now." She kept staring. "Are you alright? Do you need some help?"

"I'm alright, but my god, I need to find out what's going on so I can send out wires. How can I reach an information specialist with the military?"

"Commander Mannerheim asked about you a couple of times already. He's been in and out with his staff all afternoon using the equipment here. Since the bar lounge is reinforced as a shelter, he and some of the military higher-ups are also using that room. I'll see if I can find him, if you like."

"Don't they have an official base of operations here?"

The receptionist smiled nervously. "This is tiny Finland. We barely have an army let alone a base. I'll try to find him."

"Thank you. Also, I'm wondering if there's some way I can get some winter clothes? These are . . ." She looked down at her ripped and stained snow suit.

"If you write down your size or maybe even cut the label from that one, I can send someone over to Stockmann's first thing in the morning. Just make a list of anything else you need."

"Will they be open?"

"They will be for us. We're the government."

While waiting for Mannerheim, Therese sent a wire to the editor she knew at the New York *Times,* her hands still trembling.

Finland reportedly attacked by air, sea, and ground this afternoon by Soviet forces. Helsinki bombed but damage unknown. Details to follow. I believe I'm the only international journalist here in Helsinki. I'll be sending reports and images soon. Let me know what you want.

Therese Bonney

Hotel Kämp, Helsinki, Finland.

At midnight, Commander Mannerheim and several of his staff arrived at the press room looking weary, his pristine uniform wrinkled and his tunic unbuttoned. "We were worried about you, Miss Bonney, especially when you ditched your escort. I pulled a detail off duty to find you." He looked at her carefully. "I'm glad they did, do you need a doctor?"

"No. Thank you. I had no idea, was this expected?" She tried to sound upbeat although her pounding heart and shaky legs would tell a different story if noticed.

"You're asking me to give away military secrets," he chided. His eyes were heavier than three nights ago, even melancholy. She knew he needed her support and her contacts, although he also seemed genuinely caring. Whatever it was, she was grateful.

"One question," she asked, her voice still shaky. "Why would they bomb Helsinki and not just the military positions?"

He exhaled and shook his head. "Breaking the heart is sometimes more potent than breaking the back." He raised his chin and looked serious. "We're being attacked right now. The Soviets are a formidable military force and we're a very small army with barely any equipment."

He shrugged his shoulders and leaned toward her. "We're looking for a military transport to take you to the train station so you can get out of here."

She thought for a moment and looked around the room. Her body ached and she desperately wanted a hot bath, even a glass of wine maybe. She pushed away those thoughts of people displaced in the snow along the road with no shoes and clutching the hands of children, but the images kept coming back.

Her entire body was still shaking. "The real question is can you provide a military transport so I can stay? I'll need a way to get around."

He probably hadn't shaved in two days. She saw that his mustache needed trimming because it seemed to fall slightly over his upper lip. But underneath she detected a slight smile. He nodded and his eyes looked younger but only briefly.

"Get some rest, Miss Bonney. Let's meet in the morning and work on a strategy for daily briefings, even hourly briefings if needed. You can then tell the story to the world."

She nodded and gathered her things.

"Oh, by the way," he said. "I sometimes need to imagine a small helpless creature too, like a little rabbit, to find some humanity in the horrors of war."

Thirty-Five

THE PHONE RANG twice waking her with a start. She fumbled with the receiver while trying to look at the clock on her desk. *A little past midnight.*

"Hello . . . hello." She tapped the phone to see if the static was on her end.

"Madeleine?"

"Oh, my god, Therese! I was hoping you'd call. I waited here in the office, thinking you might call here."

"I know it's late, I didn't expect you to answer."

"Therese are you alright, are you still in Finland or on your way home? Were you in Helsinki when the bombs fell? The invasion is all over the newspapers."

"I'm still in Helsinki and wanted to leave a message that I'm . . . I'm good. I don't know much more than that. How are you?"

"When will you be here? I can meet you at the station or wherever . . . I've been worried, terrified really."

There was a pause. "I can't come home right now. There's so much to do. I'm the only international journalist here; the others can't get into the country, and . . . well, I'll be home at some point. I just had to call you. I knew you'd be worried."

"I have been, horribly so. Your post in the *Times* has been reprinted in all the newspapers so at least I knew you were alive."

"People are roaming aimlessly, Madeleine, with inadequate clothing, children have lost their gloves, and some have fallen and are down in the snow . . ." Her voice cracked. There was a long silence.

"Oh, Therese, are you sure you need to be there? I suppose I don't need to ask." She waited. "What's the name of the hotel again, I know you wrote it down for me before you left."

"Hotel Kämp in Helsinki. It's the press center for both the military and foreign correspondents. Are you alright; is everything the same in Paris?"

"Yes, Paris is the same. I wish . . . well, can you call me again or can I call you?"

"I think I can, I'll try. It's hard to know what each day or each hour will be like. Expect to hear from me soon though. Can you call Louise and my mother for me and tell them I'm alright? I left that number for you."

"Yes, I'll call them when it's light there. I'll tell them you're fine. You are fine, aren't you?"

"I'd rather be there. I have to go."

"Therese . . ."

"I know."

The call ended and Madeleine dropped her face in her hands. She looked at the newspaper on her desk, tapping her finger nervously.

Finland reportedly attacked by air, sea, and ground this afternoon by Soviet forces. Helsinki bombed but damage unknown. Details to follow. I believe I'm the only international journalist here in Helsinki . . .

During the next several weeks Madeleine plotted Therese's locations in Finland based on her articles and photographs in the newspapers, everywhere from the front lines to the small towns and villages left in the trail of destruction. Therese brought to life the heroic effort by the small but ill-equipped Finnish army fighting on snow skis and on foot against the mighty Soviet invaders, and occasionally by tossing Molotov cocktails into the turrets of the invading Soviet tanks. Her most poignant observations, as Madeleine soon realized, were through the lens of her camera. She showed the world the devastating effects of war on civilians, especially children and the most vulnerable.

Madeleine circled the city of Vasa on the map where the pictures captured the essence more clearly than words: children and the wounded walking through snow into the countryside to avoid the bombing and flying glass, some wearing only pajamas or skimpy clothing in sub-zero temperatures. The less able were photographed sitting on cold stones or school stairs waiting for help. From Helsinki the images showed a family huddled in a barn watching their house burn, and a broken hockey stick next to the body of a child face down in the snow.

The vivid photographs stirred anger and Madeleine read that even Roosevelt and Churchill implored the Soviet Union to stop bombing civilians. Obviously, their pleas were in vain. The world watched in horror and Madeleine shook her head at each tragic picture knowing the pain Therese felt with each click of the camera's shutter. Yet, she knew it would be unfair to coax her to come home. We each have our lives, she thought, and we need to live it in our own way.

She busied herself with work. Dismantling Vionnet & Cie proved a daunting task. Bader demanded his share of the profits immediately, even before the assets were sold, and he threatened to sue Madeleine if she didn't sell everything that week and fire the workers. He also demanded an itemized list of every bobbin and measuring tape that was to be sold and wanted his people to do an inventory, including the contents of her desk.

"Thèophile, we can't sell the assets until we finish processing all the orders," Madeleine said when he called. "We have an obligation to fulfill the requests. These are our most important clients."

"Damn the clients. Just sell everything this week unless you want to be pulled into court."

"Pompous ass," she muttered before hanging up on him. She refused to take his harassing phone calls after that.

These business matters seem so senseless and mundane given what's going on in the world! She wondered what Therese was doing at that very minute. She thought of that first day when she walked in to her office looking for a job. Madeleine suspected that innocence has now been lost on some snowy battlefield.

In spite of what she told Therese, Paris was not the same. The evacuation left closed shops, locked bakeries, and abandoned *maisons de couture*. Empty cafes and bicycles left by the side of the road were all signs of the impending war and mirrored her own desolate emptiness. The city was being deserted but she was committed to staying.

She focused on work as usual. Orders were still being placed by the optimistic and in spite of Bader, she accepted them if she could find the fabric. Her supplier, Charles Bianchini, followed through on his promise to look for remnants and odd rolls, so every week he came by with whatever he could find.

"Hold on," he would say. "Don't give up, Madeleine. We are still the fashion capital of the world and we need to stay that way." She liked hearing him say that because they both shared that belief and it felt good to hear someone else say it for a change.

Late one afternoon when she returned from lunch the receptionist buzzed her in her office. "There's a man on his way up and he wouldn't leave his name." Madeleine prepared herself for Bader or one of his henchmen but when she opened the door, Netch was standing on the top step.

"Hello cutie."

Three years had passed since their separation and even though he lived in her house in the south, she'd had no contact with him.

"Netch, this is a surprise. What brings you to Paris?"

"To see you of course, my dear." He moved closer to kiss her on the cheek. He looked older, she thought, with his neatly trimmed beard and shorter hair, but she also noticed he hadn't lost his good looks. Evidently, other women thought the same. He'd become quite the lady's man at all of the summer resorts, according to friends. She motioned him to sit.

"You look good, Madeleine. Is the business going well?"

"What can I do for you, Netch? It's not like you to come all this way just to say hello. If you need money . . ."

"No, no, baby, that's not why I'm here. I wanted to say hello and, well things are changing quickly in Paris and I'm sure you're preparing to leave like everyone else."

"I have no plans to leave. If you're concerned about the house, I told you before you can stay there. Besides, where else would you go?"

He shrugged. "You'll need to leave Paris at some point, Madeleine. I mean, let's be practical. Paris could be bombed or occupied at any time. It wouldn't be pleasant or safe." He inched his chair closer to her desk and lowered his voice. "It would be wonderful if you could come to the summer house. You know, like old times." He reached for her hand but she pulled it back.

"I don't remember those old times being so wonderful, Netch. I appreciate your concern but there are other options."

"Well, you can't go to the north, babe. During an invasion, the Germans would probably attack through Brussels. At least in the south there are escape routes, to Spain perhaps or Portugal. Practically everyone fleeing Paris right now is coming south. I doubt if Hitler wants the French resorts. He wants Paris."

"It's hard to know what he wants," she said sighing. "My plan right now is to stay in Paris."

"Sweetie, we could start all over." He reached for her hand again but she pulled it away. "I made mistakes. I'd like a chance to make things right. After the war, we could come back to Paris, get back in the business. . ."

"I'm neither a 'sweetie' nor a 'babe,' Netch. You'll have to excuse me but I have some matters to take care of this afternoon." She stood and walked to the door to show him out.

"Just give it some thought. No need to make a decision right now." He put his hand on her shoulder before leaving and winked. She heard him whistling down the stairs as she closed her door.

Thirty-Six

THE FINISH SOLDIERS looked imposing in their all-white snow suits with white capes and rifles flung over their shoulders - the standard winter uniform. Therese once lamented that the Arctic aspect of the war created a lack of contrast between the Finnish soldiers and the snowy landscape, making the almost invisible Finnish soldiers difficult to see or photograph. Commander Mannerheim teased her saying, "That's the idea, Miss Bonney."

She traveled throughout Finland as one of the few foreigners authorized to do so and when she had a chance, she tagged along with military transports to the front - at least that's what they called the border between Finland and Russia. In reality, the front was everywhere given the massive attack on the small country. Her goal was to document the displaced and wounded, and to show the dire aftermath of the invasion. But she also took on humanitarian work along with everyone else, distributing supplies and offering aid to those in need.

The packages from Madeleine were a surprise. Several large boxes of winter clothing miraculously found their way addressed to her at the Hotel Kämp by way of Sweden. Madeleine had sent hundreds of small mittens, about the size her daughter probably wore as a toddler. Therese personally handed them out. "*Varten nuorille,* for the young ones," she would say. She kept one pair in the pocket of her snow suit as a keepsake. More boxes soon arrived from Madeleine, some with blankets and woolen hats, and some with packaged snacks along with a generous donation.

The International Red Cross and hundreds of volunteers from Sweden sent medical supplies and clothing. Knitting became a national pastime in Sweden as women made woolen gloves and socks to be sent with supplies. Soon boxes came from all over the world. Therese and others braved the snow and bombs to distribute everything to shelters, empty barns, church basements, and to those fleeing along the roads.

To give people something to do in the shelters, Therese brought rags and bottles and taught the people to make Molotov cocktails.

"Just tear the rags in strips and stuff them into the bottles," she'd tell the people in Finnish. With the eager help of Commander Mannerheim, the bottles were picked up regularly and delivered to the field where they were filled with gasoline and oil and thrown into the mighty turrets and trucks of the advancing Soviet army. The results were miniscule but the people felt better doing what they could to defend their country.

To the horror of everyone, hundreds of bombs continued to fall on Helsinki in a barrage of shattering destruction. During the long hours of darkness, Therese watched the bombs appear like comets flying from the air. At times they lit the sky in an array of dramatic fireworks as if competing to see which explosion could be the biggest, brightest, and deadliest. The illumination replicated daylight and the chilling wail of sirens became as commonplace as traffic on a busy street.

Therese still ducked for cover when she saw the enormous Soviet aircraft drop from the clouds as the sirens deafened the hum of life in Helsinki. They flew so low that she felt she could touch them if she just reached high enough. Without anti-aircraft guns to deter them, everyone and everything was a target. She learned to stuff her camera in her bag and run to the shelters shouting at everyone she saw, "Ajaa, Ajaa, run, run," while at the same time her heart raced in tempo with the sound of their feet pounding in unison through the snow. The experience never became comfortable, but it did become familiar. Her anger stayed close to the surface. *How much is enough? How inhumane to continue to break the legs of the fallen!*

With only a few daylight hours in winter, Therese usually returned to the press room by late afternoon writing and often sorting negatives. The entire first floor of the hotel resembled a war room with maps and charts and officers huddled together, some unshaven, some in dirty uniforms. Empty coffee cups sat on tables, boots were often seen scattered about the floor, and dishes rattled as the hotel staff brought food or cleaned up empty plates. Under different circumstances she'd be sitting there writing stories about the Olympics instead of the displaced and forlorn. She shook off the thought. *People don't survive by thinking about the tragedy they're seeing — but about the work they are doing.*

"Ah, Miss Bonney. I was hoping you might be here." Commander Mannerheim usually found her at the end of the day so they could talk. It was the best part of the day for her. He was a cultured and educated man who spoke both English and French and their conversations frequently drifted into topics beyond war, a welcome change for both of them.

His eyes brightened when he smiled. "Did you by any chance know your photographs are being torn from newspapers and nailed to posts around Finland to spur on the Finnish resistance?"

"Really? I wasn't aware of that but I'm glad to hear it. I hope it's working," she said while moving a stack of papers from the empty chair so he could sit. "I'm amazed at what I see every day here, the sacrifice and comradery, and now this outpouring of support from all over the world. We have more supplies than we can distribute," she said.

He sat down and turned his chair to look at her. "Why do you stay?"

She shrugged and looked off into the room. "I don't know. I really don't know. Is it necessary to understand everything in life?"

"No, of course not. I think feeling everything is good enough."

She nodded.

"Miss Bonney, would you join me for dinner tonight? I have a meeting right now but I'd like to meet you in the lounge around eight. Everything should settle down by then; that is, if you'd like to join me."

She looked surprised. "Yes, yes, I'd like that. I'll see you at eight."

She dressed that evening in a pair of black knit tights and a lavender tunic - something she crammed in her bag with the film before she left - and let her hair fall naturally after scrubbing it with some hotel shampoo she found in the room. She threw a scarf over her shoulders even though it was comfortably warm inside the hotel.

He stood at the bar talking to one of his corporals when she walked in. The waiter cleared off a table as they walked in that direction and Mannerheim held the chair for her. He was tall and not a handsome man but with good features and expressive eyes. He looked younger than his sixty-some years and slim and fit. He'd changed his tunic and looked clean shaven, although his boots were still dull and damp from the snow, something she guessed people got used to seeing there.

He spoke first. "You look stunning. I wouldn't have recognized you in the field. You'd appear as an apparition."

She laughed. "I hardly recognize myself. My snow suits have been my constant companions."

He narrowed his eyes. "Have you recovered from your fateful experience under the bridge? I have soldiers who experience shell shock in battle and it sometimes takes a while to get over. It seems to reoccur unexpectedly. You know, we seldom have correspondents, especially a female journalist, in the field with us so this is new. I hope you've been given the proper care."

"Yes, yes. It was frightening since it came out of nowhere, but just a few bruises and scratches, and the jitters once in a while. Every day now is better than the last, probably because I keep so busy and there's so much to do. I can only empathize with those who are permanently scarred; I was lucky." She shook her head. "Will it ever end?"

He poured from a bottle of French wine. "Cheers hardly seems the right toast," he said lifting his glass.

"Well then, peace," and they smiled, touching their glasses together.

"To answer your question, yes it will end. The Soviets thought the invasion would be a cake walk and last a day or two. They have 450,000 troops at our border and we have 40,000 to stop them and almost no weapons. The terrain is fortunately split by lakes, rivers, swamps and the rest is almost entirely covered by forests. We hope the terrain and the weather will stop them, since we certainly don't have the means."

"This can't go on forever, can it?" she said.

He sat back in his chair and let his head fall back. "No, and it won't." He leaned closer. "Our decision to fight is making headlines around the world, and thank you by the way for your reporting and for telling of and showing our resistance. The need for photographs and news is always helpful because they create international interest, and in our case poignancy. We're the underdogs still being attacked and you've shown that to the world. That along with the weather and the terrain can put pressure on Russia and shame them into retreating. At least that's our hope."

"And if they don't retreat?"

"Then we'll deal with that when the time comes." He shifted in his seat. "I've talked too much about war and I want to enjoy your company as if we are somewhere else instead of in the middle of a battlefield. I rarely have an opportunity to dine with anyone other than my staff."

"Do you live here in Helsinki?" She obliged and changed the subject even though she found his observations about the war fascinating.

"I had a home here although a soldier's home is where he is at the time I suppose. My wife passed away a few years ago. It wasn't much of a marriage. I was gone most of the time and she said I always seemed like a stranger to her when I came home. Does your husband feel that way when you return?"

She hesitated. "I'm not married."

He lowered his head and looked at her. "What do you do for sex, Miss Bonney?"

She held back a gasp. She wanted to tell him the question was inappropriate, but she found herself enjoying the conversation. She felt an interesting intimacy when they first met that seemed to pave the way for honesty and candidness - and not the usual protocol and formality between strangers. She wondered if the urgency of war demands that kind of straight talk.

"I focus on love instead, I guess."

"Who do you love?"

Her eyes widened but she didn't want to retreat now. "I love . . . life."

Containing a smile he looked at her askance, and let the comment slip by.

That night he escorted her to her room. At the door he leaned down and kissed her for a brief moment on her lips. "Even though you probably wouldn't be tempted, I doubt if either of us can do love and war at the same time," he whispered before leaving her.

In March of 1940 the exhausted Finns reluctantly ceded territory representing eleven percent of their land and thirty percent of their economy to the invading Russian forces. Finland retained its sovereignty and enhanced its international reputation but it was still a bitter loss. The historic 100-day Winter War finally came to an end.

Shortly after, an article appeared in the international press:

The Finnish government bestowed upon Therese Bonney Finland's highest honor, the White Rose of Finland, for service to their country and bravery in the field. Her photographs were the only record of what is now known as the Winter War.

At the ceremony, Field Marshall Mannerheim was chosen to place the medal around her neck. His eyes never left hers.

Thirty-Seven

OLD AND RICKETY, the #748 train in Helsinki was miraculously spared from the Winter War, probably just by coincidence. It stuttered slowly from the station on time that morning and her compartment was empty so she pulled off her boots and let her head fall back against the seat, her camera in her lap as she watched the bleakness of a country in ruin. She put her feet up and stretched, surprised to see that her socks were torn. *How did they get so tattered and why am I just now noticing?* She took a deep breath and pulled off her gloves and loosened the top buttons of her snow suit while watching the condensation form and trickle down the window, meandering around a hairline crack in the pane. She wiped at the moisture with her sleeve and felt an unexpected emptiness as she watched the landscape begin to change.

The train creaked and rattled past the buildings in Helsinki, past mounds of rubble near the tracks, and past bricks and metal twisted into odd shapes as far as she could see. Beyond the tracks, Stockmann's department store stood out amid the rubble. Her breath misted the window and she wiped it again to look more closely to see where the large clock used to be; the pieces now in a heap on the sidewalk amid broken glass. She thought about the irony of sunlight reflecting off shards of broken glass in the street like sparking candles on a birthday cake, but without a celebration.

The train picked up speed so she settled back in her seat watching pockets of people huddled together along the tracks in makeshift shelters on the edge of town; some dusted in snow, some clutching children, and some just staring blankly. Instinctively, she raised her camera but then put it down, leaving her nothing to do but watch helplessly. Soon they became a blur like a piece of film being rewound as the train sped south. The thought of people alone in the rubble made her sick to her stomach but then she remembered - that feeling went with the job.

The Paris Nord train station was a turbulent sea of activity with travelers scurrying about in all directions, some to catch trains and others rushing out of the terminal dragging luggage in search of taxis. Trains arrived one after the other mostly from the north in anticipation of the impending Nazi assault on Belgium, and mothers frantically herded their children and men with briefcases buttoned their overcoats as they ran through the noisy terminal. Therese stood blinking and looking in all directions, everything whirling around her with noise going in and out of her head and at one point wondering where she was. People pushed to get to their destinations and she could only stand and stare in some strange stupor. Gripping her bag, and still holding her helmet too bulky to pack, she wasn't sure if it was her head spinning or her surroundings.

"I have a car and driver." Someone grabbed her arm.

Therese swung around.

"Come quickly," Madeleine said and took her by the arm while her driver grabbed her bag. "I know you said you'd get a taxi but . . ." They climbed in the back seat and the car sped from the station, leaving behind chaos and masses of people.

Therese sat staring wide-eyed. The crowds, the confusion, the flashbacks of bodies and bombs, seeing Madeleine after months, being back in France, she felt like she'd fallen down a deep well and finally reached the bottom to discover she was still alive. It all seemed surreal now that she'd left it behind. When she felt the comforting hand of Madeleine and heard her reassurances, she put her head in Madeleine's lap and sobbed until she heard the car door open.

Madeleine pried the helmet from her grasp. "You're home now, and safe." Therese looked up to see Madeleine's town house. "You'll stay here with me for a while. Everything will be fine now. Just fine."

That night as Therese surrendered deep into the soft bed linens, Madeleine stood by the bed and watched her bouts of fitfulness, the indecipherable muttering in her sleep and finally her breathing, slow and quiet. *This probably won't be easy for her,* Madeleine thought. She reached down and kissed her softly before leaving the room.

Therese recuperated at Madeleine's town house for the next several days, sleeping late and sorting her negatives. She called her mother and Louise to tell them she's back and all is well. She was sullen and quiet at times and Madeleine knew it was just the experience slowly unfolding as Therese realized what she had been through. Their long walks along the Seine gave them a chance to talk.

"What stays with you, what's making you pull inward?"

Therese sighed and shrugged.

"It's good to talk about this, Therese."

"I know," she said sighing and straightening her shoulders. I'm not really sure but part of it is just the jarring difference of being there and now here, and some of it is just delayed reaction, I'm sure. When I take photographs I'm working and somehow protected somewhat from the weight of anger and compassion, and sorrow, and the enormous calamity of helplessness. The camera seems to protect me or insulate me from that." She wiped her eyes. "When the reality sets in, after the camera is back in the bag, it all starts to sink in. I feel so helpless."

"But you did help . . . your humanitarian work, receiving the medal, Finland's highest honor . . . ."

Therese stopped and looked at her wide-eyed. "It's never enough, ever, ever." Tears ran down her face. "It can never be enough. If it was enough no one would suffer. That picture of the child face down in the snow next to the broken hockey stick?" Her chin quivered. "I watched those children playing hockey on the pond just a few hours before the attack. I can still hear them." She put her face down and cried into her hands before looking up. "The picture of the family huddled in the barn watching their house burn? I saw them earlier on my walk that afternoon. They were working in the field and the children waved. Then their lives changed, for all of them, in a matter of minutes. Some died, some were maimed, some were walking in the snow without shoes and some left behind, separated from family . . ."

Madeleine watched the tears run down her face while Therese interlocked her fingers and swayed back and forth with the searing stare into her own inner thoughts. Madeleine put her arms around her and

Madeleine and Therese

rocked her back and forth. "I understand this, Therese. I understand perfectly." She looked into her eyes. "I understand how you must feel. It's not unusual for people who witnessed tragedy to bring the horror home with them."

Therese wiped her face and shook her head. "It's just that it's still new, still raw. Being caught in the bombing myself only brings it closer. I know the terror and confusion those people must have felt."

"Were you afraid?"

Therese took a long searching breath. "I was told I was in shock so," she paused, wiping her eyes, "I don't think I knew much, at least I don't remember much. But in looking back it wasn't that I was afraid to die. It was the thought of dying alone. I still think about that. It haunts me." She cried softly. "If my escort hadn't looked for me, I would have frozen there in the rubble, alone." Her voice trailed off. "It's a sobering thought. I'm more afraid now that I think about it than I was then."

Madeleine squeezed her hand. "But you weren't alone. You had the little rabbit." She smiled. "You're a survivor, Therese. Instinctively, you knew what to do."

They walked in silence for a while. Therese slipped her arm through Madeleine's and said, "We're both survivors. We've had to be."

They settled into a comfortable routine. Therese slept long hours and began to relax. They took leisurely walks every day in different neighborhoods exploring alleys and small boutiques and quaint cafes for afternoon tea. They cooked together and searched for the freshest fish, the most exotic cheeses, and the finest wines; a pastime of most Parisians but soon to give way to shortages and rationing as the fear of war came closer. Their thoughts were on each day and they vowed to live in the present as much as possible which helped Therese come to terms with her unexpected thrust into the horrors of war, and for Madeleine to deal with her own anxiety about her business and the impending invasion. During those days they felt content to just be together, even when doing nothing.

"I could get used to this," Therese said over coffee one morning.

"I already have," Madeleine said, a little embarrassed at her own candor.

Within weeks of her return, offers came from the Library of Congress and the Museum of Modern Art in New York, both wanting to exhibit her historic photographs of Finland's Winter War. She was surprised by the outpouring of public interest. One newspaper called the photographs "the most moving and shocking portrayals showing the effects of war." Therese tentatively agreed to go to New York as curator and lecturer. There was also talk of a traveling exhibit and a book as well.

"It doesn't seem right to use the photographs in this way," she confided to Madeleine. "The receptions, the publicity . . . all seem a little sacrilegious or exploitive for a topic so somber."

"Perhaps. But the exhibits are in America and could stir American sentiment. It seems every European country is hoping for American aid, especially those countries being overrun by the German army right now."

"I suppose. If I go to New York to promote the photos, it would be wonderful if you could come too just to get away for a while, or even to stay. The tension here in Paris is growing. We're seeing it in everyone's eyes." She looked for some reaction in Madeleine's face. "Don't you think you should think about leaving Paris?" she added. "Hitler just bombed a naval base near Scotland and Nazi troops are gathering right now near the borders of Denmark and Norway. The waiting is just torment."

"I know, Therese, and New York would be a lovely break from the gloom here, I agree. But really, I must stay."

Therese didn't need to ask why, but she did anyway.

Madeleine hesitated for a moment. "Because I'm a French woman and this is my home."

Therese nodded knowing that was that.

A week later Therese sailed for New York and the exhibits drew enormous crowds. One major newspaper wrote "It was about time someone was showing the human side of war and that should be a lesson for us all." Therese went to the receptions and did the interviews but secretly she yearned to put it all behind her. It was like reliving the events every time she was asked to talk about the photographs. *I didn't expect any of this. I went to Finland to cover the preparation for the Olympics. I wish they would stop asking question, stop wanting details.* In spite of her feelings, an interesting offer arrived that would set a different course.

The telegram was from the Carnegie Foundation offering her a grant to continue her photographic work in Europe; this time, documenting the war and the devastation left behind as a result of Hitler's rampage. The only stipulation was that she deposit a copy of each photograph in the Library of Congress to be used for historical research and educational purposes.

Ugh, do I really want another experience like Finland? Probably not. She knew there were a dozen reasons why she should say no, but in the end she surprised herself by accepting, not really knowing why.

Across the Atlantic and working under a dim light that night, Madeleine made some adjustments to a dress so the client could pick it up the following day. She'd just heard from Therese and about the Carnegie offer. She put the dress down for a moment and thought about Therese's decision. She sat staring without noticing the dress had fallen from her lap.

Thirty-Eight

THERESE KNEW the Carnegie grant was an opportunity to make a worthwhile contribution but she woke more than once with thoughts of going to the Franco-Belgium front. She replayed her Finland experience over and over in her mind, falling back to sleep only to wake again. *Just typical travel jitters . . . or maybe I've made the wrong decision! Waiting out the war in New York might be a better option, and safer too.*

When the alarm rang in the morning she bolted out of bed, feeling resigned to go. After checking her camera and lenses she made notes on a detailed map of Europe, underlining twice in red the strategically important Franco-Belgium border. That evening, her last before leaving, she and Madeleine dined at a small restaurant in St-Germain.

"Your decision to accept the Carnegie grant surprised me," Madeleine said as they ordered wine.

"Hmm, it surprised me as well." They looked at each other for a long time. "You know, Madeleine, we're in this whether we like it or not. We've been thrust into this place and time and war and we do what we do because we can. We're able and capable. If not, it would seem like we're shirking our duty."

That was all she said and they agreed to avoid the talk of war. Instead, they watched people laughing and enjoying themselves in the popular Bohemian neighborhood and they walked every street arm in arm late into the night watching people in dance halls and cabarets and like them, pretending it was just a typical evening in Paris. That night they didn't say goodbye. Everything they could have said was in their eyes and in their long embrace. Therese packed her knapsack later that night with her accreditation papers from the War Department and her passport, and endless rolls of film. She left early in the morning before she had a chance to change her mind.

The *Maginot Line*, according to the briefing, was France's defensive line that runs along the border between Belgium and France and the main obstacle to a German invasion into France. The heavily-armed French 2nd Army stood ready to stop any attack. Therese used her wartime pass and correspondent's credentials to catch a ride on a military transport to join the 2nd Army at the front, her camera ready and her pack full of film. It almost felt routine, but the flutter in her stomach told her this was serious business. It was around midnight when the transport from Paris dropped her off near the Belgium border and pointed her to a path leading to the commander's headquarters.

A sliver of moonlight guided her in that direction until she heard a noise in the bushes. Standing motionless she listened until she felt something cold on the back of her neck. Glancing quickly over her shoulder she saw a rifle pointing toward her face. Turning the other way, she saw three soldiers, feet apart and weapons drawn. *Oh, my god!* Perspiration trickled down the inside her blouse as one of the soldiers stepped forward blinking rapidly and trying to hold his weapon steady. His chin had the straggly beginnings of a beard and they shared the same frightened stare. He tightened his hand around the grip.

"*Hande hoch,*" He waved the tip of his rifle up." *Hande hoch!*" he said again with more force and with a youthful French accent.

Therese put her bag down slowly and raised her hands. When she looked again she saw that his uniform was French not German. *They must think I'm a German!*

"*Je ne suis pas allemand. Je suis Americain,*" she said.

"*American?*" one of the soldiers said looking relieved.

"Yes, I'm an American correspondent here in France. I'm expected by Commander Huntziger of the 2nd Army. Would you like to see my papers?"

"The 2nd Army? No, no. We're the 9th Army not the 2nd. This is Ardennes on the east side of the French-Belgium border. The 2nd Army is at least 200 kilometers from here."

She stood blinking and speechless.

Field Commander Andre Corap of the 9th Army was a frail man. She guessed him to be seventy at least and his white mustache and beard matched his thinning hair. He put his hat on when she entered his tent and she thought that odd, although his hat was adorned with decorations so she thought it must be official protocol. She was surprised he spoke English so well.

"Young lady, what in devil's name are you doing here? Are you lost or something?" He squinted. His eyes were tired and his face seemed too placid to be commanding anything.

Therese explained the circumstances and showed her credentials. "I was told the transport was taking me to the 2nd Army. I'm here as a photojournalist."

"Well, this is no place for a woman. What were they thinking? They send a woman to cover the invasion?" He waived his arm in some imaginary direction and stood panting before his eyes softened. "Given that you're wearing a dark jump suit and a helmet, the guards thought you were a German parachutist. We apologize, Miss Bonney."

"No need to apologize. The 2nd Army was expecting me but you weren't. Is it possible to get to that part of the Maginot Line? Is there a transport going that way?"

"Possibly, but not for a few days at least. As a photojournalist you obviously want to be where the action is." He finally took off his hat and she contained a smile. "You won't see any action here, young lady. It's very unlikely the Germans will try to get their tanks and troops through the forest at this part of the line. I'll certainly be sending back-up troops wherever there's action and you can ride along if that's what you want to do. I can also get you out of this whole mess. We have trucks going back and forth between here and Reims, and from there you can get to Paris."

"If you don't expect the German invasion here in Ardennes, why are you here?"

He chuckled. "Well, sometimes we ask the same question. Actually, we're a decoy unit. Half my men are over forty and the other half under eighteen. The military has to cover every scenario, even the implausible ones. I have two trucks leaving for Reims in the morning for supplies. Do you want a ride back? You'd best get yourself out of this part of the world."

Therese sighed and fumbled with the strap on her camera bag. "Hmm, no, I'll stay thank you. I'll wait for a transport to the 2nd Army." She picked up her bag, muttering something under her breath as she left the tent.

The next two days dragged by with nothing to do. She explored the surrounding villages and ventured into the forest to photograph wild mushrooms and lichen on the trees just for something to do and imagined how beautiful the area would look in the summer with fields of flowers and people boating on the lakes. In between her walks she sat outside the post waiting for a transport and took pictures of the soldiers relaxing in the sun.

As she was cleaning her camera one afternoon, the young private she met the night of her arrival stopped by on a military motorcycle with heavily-treaded tires and the number 54889 stenciled on the gas tank.

"Hey, *Americain!*" It is me, Étienne. How are you? I am fine. I am seventeen years." He inched his motorcycle closer and she could see he still had fuzz on his face and cheeks blushing with youth.

"I'm happy to meet you, Etienne. My name is Therese."

"Good, you will teach me English, yes?" Just then a corporal walked by and tapped the fender of his motorcycle. Etienne grinned and rode off to do his duty whatever that was.

Again, the following morning she sat outside at the camp waiting for transportation. To pass the time she emptied her camera bag and sorted rolls of film while watching for a truck going to the 2nd army post. *Oh, maybe waiting around here is not such a good idea, I could be home doing something else.*

She looked around the post. Several soldiers slept while others played cards in their tent. A group just beyond the commander's tent played basketball with a makeshift hoop made of wire, laughing every time they missed a shot. She counted her rolls of film, stacking them on a wooden table before rearranging them in her bag. One rolled off and she stooped to pick it up and then another fell. She felt a slight vibration and then the ground rumbled beneath her feet. The faint rustle of movement and a dull grinding noise echoed in the forest just beyond and she sat up straight, her back rigid. The base became eerily silent and then over the loud speaker, "*Attaque! Attaque!*" Soldiers ran from tents, truck engines started, and officers with their shirts still unbuttoned shouted orders and waved their arms. Dust billowed beneath huge tanks as they were moved away from the post and shouting from every direction drowned out the ominous commotion coming from the forest.

Tossing the film in her bag, Therese sprinted toward Commander Corap's headquarters while shoving her helmet on her head, the straps slapping across her face as she weaved in and out of men grabbing rifles and flinging ammunition belts over their shoulders. The command tent was loud and chaotic with officers everywhere and she grabbed the sleeve of one and looked quizzically. His eyes were wide and sweat dripped from beneath his hat. "German panzers are approaching, not just in Ardennes but all across the Maginot Line," he gasped. We're the first; the bastards are coming through the forest!"

"What? How can that be?" she said still clinging to his shirt until he broke loose. She stood there numb and confused, her heart pounding. Several officers in the tent shouted into phones while others just shouted to anyone within hearing distance. On the other side of the tent, she heard Commander Corap screaming at a group of officers and waiving his hat. "They've concealed a huge arsenal of armored divisions right under our noses! The forest is teeming with Rommel's panzers and Nazi German troops!" He slammed his hand on the desk. "Right under our noses! How could we have missed this, who was on watch?" The sweat poured from his face and his eyes were wide with fury.

Therese didn't wait to hear the answer. She ran outside gasping for air as thick dust swirled and stung her nostrils. All she could hear was "*Retraite! Retraite!*" echoing all throughout the base and over the loud speaker. *Oh, my god, they're not going to fight. They're retreating!* Instinctively she reached for her camera and filled her pockets with extra rolls of film and began to capture the chaos. She stopped to steady her hand and then turned her camera in all directions shooting as fast as she could, stuffing finished rolls of film down her blouse. Swirling orbs of dirt obscured her view and in between she saw soldiers jumping into transports carrying whatever they could. A corporal whose eyes were afire as sweat beaded on his face caught her by the arm. "I'm to see that you get on one of these transports," he yelled in English. "Come with me."

"I'll wait." She slipped under his arm and ran into the crowd of soldiers, remembering a hilltop vantage point from her walk a few days ago. *If I can get higher I can see all of this.* She didn't wait for permission but ran through the camp keeping low and following the trail up the hill, slipping back again and again and grabbing bush limbs to pull herself up. She stopped once to catch her breath. Her heart was pounding and her blouse was soaked with sweat. The top was in sight, only minutes away. She stumbled again as she reached the top but pulled herself up and then stood in awe. Her arms fell limp.

As far as she could see the entire rim of the forest was a dense concentration of grey-green armored German panzers; hundreds, thousands of them. Some had broken through the forest while others could be seen moving among the trees and getting close. The sight stretched for miles, all across the Maginot line. *My god! My god!* she repeated over and over. She lowered her camera and stared in disbelief. The might of the German army caught her breath. She started taking pictures at every angle with several lenses, walking back and forth along the ridge documenting the massive movement of German tanks and troops. She stopped to put more film in her camera as her hands shook. She dropped a roll, picking it up with a handful of dirt. She kept stuffing the spent rolls down in her blouse for safekeeping.

At one point she pointed her camera down toward the base to capture the retreat and scanned it back and forth. Puzzled, she looked without the lens. *What the . . . !* The camp was in disarray but empty! *Where is everyone?* All she could see was dust filtering down over abandoned tents and equipment. The transports and troops were nowhere to be seen! She looked again seeing puffs of dust in the distance. Grabbing her long distance lens she saw what she feared: the small army had evacuated on the road leading from the post leaving only a trail of dust. She stiffened and her hands felt clammy. *How long have I been up her?* The rolls of film stuffed in her blouse were her answer.

Patting her pockets to be sure her unused film was safe she grabbed her bag and looked for the trail down. It was all a blur; the brush was all the same, plants, trees, tightly woven. *Oh, gads! Where's the trail?* She walked back and forth brushing the perspiration from her face with her sleeve and looking back over her shoulder. The forest was alive, the noise louder. Finally, she spotted a clearing with trampled plants. *Ah!* She ran down the hill without stopping, sliding the last part of the way.

Her eyes spanned every direction hoping to find someone, anyone. Her throat felt dry as she looked down the empty road and then she started running. She stopped once out of breath and bent over with her hands on her knees, her chest heaving. She looked up and saw clouds of dust in the distance so she kept running until her legs quivered. After about a mile she caught up with a group of villagers evacuating with what they could carry, some without any shoes and others dragging precious possessions that would soon no doubt be abandoned by the side of the road. She alternated walking and running, keeping the dust ahead in sight. Perspiration soaked her clothes and her legs were now bastions of spasms.

She stopped to adjust her pack and thought she heard a motor. She stood still until she heard him.

"*Americain, Americain.*" She turned to see the boy on the motorcycle, Etienne, from the base. "You must get on. I find a truck for you," he yelled. "Come, quick. *Rapidement!*" He held out his arm and she climbed on the back as they sped off down the road.

"Thank you!" she shouted, her voice cracking as her head fell on his shoulder. She patted him on the back. "Thank you." Her heart never stopped pounding.

A few miles down the road he stopped. "Look!" They got off and stood by the motorcycle on the side of the road to see hundreds, maybe thousands of airplanes overhead; so many they darkened the sky. "Stukas," he said as he pointed. She could see his concern. In the distance she heard the bombing and recognized the familiar smell of burning rubble.

"What are Stukas?" she yelled.

"Luftwaffe. Germans. Airplanes. We go, *rapide*! Now!*"

The piercing squeal from the motorcycle was lost in the clamor but the smell of scorched tires suggested his urgency. She grabbed his waist

Madeleine and Therese

and clutched her camera bag until her fingers ached. Burying her face in the back of his leather infantry jacket, she pinched her eyes tight as they sped past an endless trail of evacuees, a sight she'd seen so many times before and didn't want to see again. When the landscape changed and the strafing and blasts became faint, the boy slowed to a normal speed and she loosened her grip. She felt his shoulders relax and thought she heard him mumble something. They were approaching the town of Meuse and before crossing the river, a 9th Army military transport passed them on the left. The boy turned his head toward her and pointed.

"*Arrêter, arrêter*! Stop!" he yelled, while pounding on his horn and waving until the truck finally slowed and pulled over.

"You come too." Therese straightened her helmet and checked to see if she had her bag. "Leave the motorcycle."

He smiled. "I still have duty to do."

"No, please."

He didn't move and the transport driver honked impatiently. She paused and then ran. After turning to wave she jumped in the back as the transport jerked forward. She squeezed in between two soldiers, pulling her bag close and letting her shoulders fall slightly as her whole body shook as if it would fall apart. As she watched from the truck, the boy turned the motorcycle around to go back but a blinding flash and cumulus clouds of heavy steel-colored smoke destroyed her view. When it cleared faintly, a wheel-less motorcycle was turning cartwheels in slow motion high in the air.

Thirty-Nine

THE RETREAT OF the French 9th Army down the Meuse River valley was never supposed to happen. By all accounts, the Maginot line was impenetrable. But everything about that day seemed like a frightful dream to her, something that wasn't supposed to happen. When her transport stopped in the town of Meuse she and the others worked through dense smoke and ear-shattering bombs to evacuate refugees from nearby villages until the situation became too intense. By that time hundreds of aircraft flew above, some British, some French, but mostly German Stukas. Neither the French nor the British were a match for the colossal onslaught by the German Luftwaffe. The battle at Meuse was lost in just five days and Therese realized the unspeakable truth: there was nothing left to stop the Nazi German forces as they marched toward Paris. When she was forced to flee, she jumped on a military transport heading to Paris and at three o'clock in the morning banged on Madeleine's door. When it opened, she said, "They're coming."

The ambient light that morning streamed through the window and settled on two empty coffee cups sitting on a small table near the divan. Madeleine sat in her negligee against a stack of cushions and Therese in a borrowed robe, her dirty jump suit and helmet in a clump by the door, her knapsack full of film nearby.

She confided to Madeleine, "I never imagined being on the front line during the actual invasion. My job was supposed to be taking pictures of the preparation and the aftermath, the refugees and children, the destruction. This is beginning to seem eerie. Like Finland, I was the only foreign journalist at that part of the line – and by mistake! Who would have expected the Germans to break through the forest and surprise the 9th division? I used all the film in my bag," she said shaking her head.

Madeleine poured more coffee. Therese watched her hand shake slightly as she dripped a few drops on the table. "Damn," is all she said before blotting it with a cloth. Therese could see she was upset. The anticipation had become a reality. The Germans were marching on Paris.

"You okay?" Therese asked.

"Yes, are you alright? It must have been a terrifying experience."

"Yes, I'm alright," Therese said pushing her hair away from her face.

"Were you afraid?" Madeleine studied this lovely woman sitting across from her, wondering how she could be so calm and not hysterical.

"Yes, I was afraid, panicky even when I was up on the hill – it was my own fault. I got caught up in taking pictures and lingered too long. It was stupid really, and scary. I could hear the German Panzers coming through the forest and actually see them. At least I found the trail back to the base." Therese ran her fingers through her hair and down the sides of her face, rubbing an ear still plugged from the explosions. She waited for a few minutes and then, "What are your plans, Madeleine? I mean . . ." she hesitated, "I think it's important that you leave Paris. If there's no battle and France surrenders, well then come back and deal with the occupation. If nothing else, maybe you could stay with Marie Gerber and her family."

Madeleine shook her head. "I haven't had a chance to tell you, but Marie passed away ten days ago, a long illness but a quick ending."

"Oh, no, I'm sorry." She reached for her hand. "I know how close you were. That's terrible news." Therese knew this was hard for Madeleine since she and Marie were confidants and had been for years. They sat without speaking until Therese said, "I don't want to change the subject but as for staying in Paris, there are other options. You have other houses."

"Yes, other than the one in the south, the other two are north of Paris - probably right in the path of the onslaught." She shook her head and stared off into the room.

"Then the house in the south is probably the safest," Therese said quietly.

Madeleine sat pensively for a while. Her eyes followed the ray of light from the window and she took a long breath. "Are you suggesting I go to the south of France knowing Netch is staying in the house there?"

The words lingered in the room. Therese looked down and ran her finger along the rim of her coffee cup. She felt stripped of her armor, transparent, embarrassed even that her feelings about Netch and their marriage was so obvious, that her weakness was laid bare.

"Yes."

"I don't think you really mean that."

Therese thought for a moment. "I've just seen the force that will befall Paris."

"And you? Can I suggest that you take safety in America?"

Therese sighed with the slight hint of a smile. "We've had this conversation so many times before. Why do we keep coming back to it? We know that friends don't have the right to make decisions for each other."

"It's just that I know you will be there when the Nazis march on Paris, taking pictures and filing news reports. And you know I will stay because I am French and Paris is my home. We both know that about each other."

There was a long silence. "Then it seems we will both be here," Therese said.

"Yes. If there are bombs and tanks and fighting in the street, we have enough sense to flee to a safer place," Madeleine said almost questioning.

"Yes, agreed."

Therese never quite understood her own feelings about Madeleine's marriage. They lived apart, he in the south of France in Madeleine's house. Madeleine rarely mentioned him or went to him, as far as she knew. *But anything is possible. After all, they did get married. Was it romantic?*

Did they fall into each other's arms? It could happen again. They could reunite. After all, they never divorced. If they did reunite, what's the worst that could happen? I'd lose the only friend I ever cared for. Would that be the end of the world? Yes.

Forty

BEFORE DAYLIGHT WOKE the city, quickly-tied bundles of *Le Figaro* appeared in front of every store and shop across Paris displaying an unprecedented quarter-page headline: *FRANCE INVADED*. Within hours newsboys in wool caps and short pants screamed on every corner, "Nazi Germany Invades France. War! War!" Radios on kitchen counters and in small shops crackled static amid the news: *German troops pour into France in great numbers with tanks, planes, and heavy artillery. The 2nd and 9th Armies retreat, unable to stem the onslaught. The German blitzkrieg marches toward Paris. War is upon us!*

For the disbelieving, it was the sharp echo of gunfire and the billowing smoke to the north that spoke the loudest and truest. The pungent smell of rubber and burning rubble sent thousands fleeing, jamming all roads to the south and abandoning along the road what they couldn't carry. The French had fought valiantly from Meuse to Paris but the meager French forces were no match for 130,000 German troops and 1,222 tanks supported by a thousand aircraft. To protect the landmarks and save Parisians from unnecessary battle, the French government surrendered immediately and declared Paris an *open city;* that is, open to occupation with the agreement that the city will not be defended nor will it be attacked.

Therese made copies of every photograph she'd taken of the invasion and turned them over to the government, and Madeleine acted swiftly that afternoon, calling a meeting of fashion designers and fabric suppliers in Paris including her own supplier, Charles Bianchini. They gathered in the conference room in her salon.

"Aside from all the losses, and there have been many starting with the global depression and now this tragic event, the obvious becomes clear - we're at war which means we are faced with losing our edge as the fashion capital in the world. Without a doubt, these war-mongering lunatics will usurp our fabrics for their war games and chase away our clients, leaving New York and possibly other major cities to pick up where we are forced to leave off. As a result, we'll have to close our businesses or already have. The question remains, how can we protect our reputation in the fashion world while at war?"

Paul Poiret spoke up. "I don't think we can, Madeleine. Clients certainly won't be coming to Paris and the economic blight has already chased most of our clients away. Fabric has been scarce and will no doubt be rationed . . ."

"The Germans will take what they want anyway to send back home just as they're doing in Poland right now," Elsa Schiaparelli said, interrupting.

Coco Chanel stood. "I'm worried too, but there's our personal safety and that's my concern, not saving our reputation or the future. Yes, Paris is now an open city so hopefully there'll be no fighting but that could change any day. This is not a safe place to be, reputation or not."

"Still, we need to keep out name out there," Madeleine said. "Our clients come to Paris for French fashions. That's been going on for centuries. Half the work force in Paris is employed in some aspect of the fashion industry. I think we have an obligation to protect and ensure the tradition. I'm hoping you have some ideas."

"It's a dead horse, Madeleine," Germaine Krebs, a designer in Paris said. "Our hands are tied. There's a war and we can't change that."

"Yes," a young designer responded, "but if we give in, we're sure to lose our reputation and that could come back to haunt us after the war, especially for those of us who want to open our own salons after the war." There was some mumbling in the room.

"I don't see that we have a choice. We have no workers and no fabric, let alone clients," Poiret argued. "People are thinking of war not fashion."

"I'm not convinced that's the case," Madeleine said. "Women will always want to be beautiful, especially in the drabness of war. Many of my clients are from America where they're somewhat removed from the daily thoughts of war. Look, I understand what you're all saying. Let me suggest this. I'd like to buy any fabric you have that's appropriate for my gowns . . . silks, rayons, chiffons, whatever. It's my intention to stay here in Paris as long as it's safe, and to continue making dresses if there's a demand."

Coco stood. "You're selling more dresses than any of us right now, Madeleine, but aren't you liquidating the Palace of Fashion?"

"Yes, but I don't need a large salon to make a dress. Even if I make only a few, it will keep Paris fashions alive."

"Hmm, I doubt if you'd be allowed to keep a stockpile of fabrics," Poiret said. "We'll all have to surrender what we have."

Madeleine looked at him. "Trust me, Paul, I have no plans to surrender fabric to anyone."

"Fabulous, I'd rather sell to Madeleine than surrender what I have to the Nazis," he said, looking at the others. "She's just received France's highest honor, the *Légion d'Honneur*, and a gold medal from the city of Paris for her work protecting the fashion industry here. We should be indebted to her. Madeleine, you are welcome to whatever fabrics I have."

Most agreed and in the end, Madeleine bought eighty-six rolls of fine silks and rayons, enough for over a hundred and fifty gowns.

Forty-One

AFTER DECLARING Paris an open city, the French government fled to Vichy in the south of France and within hours - much to the horror of Parisians - the *Blutfahne* or blood banner with the black swastika blazing on a red background was flying from the Hotel de Ville and the Eiffel Tower. The mood of defeatism hung in the air like a stagnant odor and the humiliation only deepened when in the weeks to come the *Blutfahne* appeared on the walls of neighborhood cafés, private residences, and local businesses. The only consolation for the people of Paris under the terms of surrender was that all fighting would stop. Within days, the city was swarming with Nazi German forces drinking French wine and eating crepes at sidewalk cafés.

On one dark and misty morning during the week of surrender, a small private plane landed at an obscure airfield just outside of Paris. Three black Mercedes sedans stood waiting. Adolph Hitler rushed from the plane and stepped into the first sedan. With him was Albert Speer, his architect, and a bevy of body guards. The cars drove slowly in the pre-dawn dark with only a hint of moonlight to light their way, passing through the suburbs and toward the opera house. Hitler and Speer sat talking in the back seat.

"Take a good look, Albert. This is what I envision for Berlin - the wide streets, the beautiful monuments, the architecture, only better, much better."

Speer nodded and mumbled. When the first car pulled up to the opera house, the driver hurried briskly inside and a few minutes later the opera house came alive with bright lights as if on opening night. Hitler could be seen in the back seat clapping like a child at a circus. From there the caravan drove down the Champs Elysees and turned on Avenue Montaigne, stopping at number 50, the Palace of Fashion. They sat in front for a while before driving on to the Eiffel Tower where Hitler got out and posed with a victory salute for one of the cameramen in the last car.

The mysterious caravan continued slowly through Paris for the better part of an hour, stopping momentarily at various monuments and sights so Hitler could pose for pictures. When the first lights came on in cafes and people appeared from nowhere walking toward street cars, the caravan sped off quickly back to the airfield. As they walked toward the plane, Hitler turned to Speer and put his hand on his arm. "See, Albert, isn't Paris beautiful? Berlin must be made like this, but far more beautiful. Berlin will be the new Paris. I'm counting on you to do that."

In the months to come, Nazi soldiers in their green- grey uniforms appeared on every corner, in every café. They commandeered the grand hotels, enjoyed the best wine, the finest food, and demanded the best seats at the opera. They also destroyed art and books, banned plays and films, and shut down establishments run by Jews. Able-bodied French workers were transported to Germany to fill factory or farming jobs, or disappeared altogether. Radios were banned, although both Madeleine and Therese like many others kept radios hidden in closets or under floor boards. Food was rationed along with everything else and the French stood in long lines with ration coupons in hand, only to watch food and other supplies being loaded onto rail cars destined for the German homeland.

For some, black-market goods could be found but only for those able to afford the exorbitant prices. Madeleine gave her ration coupons to her staff, and sent her assistant to buy what little food she used from black-market peddlers. Whenever Therese ventured into the war-torn countryside to take pictures, she often returned with fresh vegetables from the fields stuffed tightly into her pockets and camera bag, enough for her and Madeleine to make a special meal from what she found and what Madeleine could get from the black market. Once, Therese returned with a live chicken but neither could kill it so they gave it away.

In a desperate attempt to keep her important clients, Madeleine wrote weekly notes of reassurance, promising to do everything she could to fill orders in spite of restrictions. Smuggling dresses out of the country would be another matter but since she owned a home in the unoccupied zone in the south of France, she had a permit to go back and forth from Paris to that *zona libre*. From there she could ship her dresses via Spain and Portugal.

When her staff fled Paris, she decided to sew the dresses herself. "I was once a seamstress," she told Therese, "even an *arpette* or pin-picker. I can certainly do it again." For the next several months she worked quietly at her salon designing and sewing dresses mostly for her American clientele and unnoticed by the occupying German forces.

One afternoon, however, while working on orders in her office she heard yelling coming from the foyer below. Rushing to the door she saw at the bottom of the staircase a high-ranking German officer surrounded by six gun-toting soldiers in battle helmets arguing with her frightened receptionist. The officer banged on the oak desk with his baton as the receptionist sat horrified and speechless.

"Is there a problem?" Madeleine asked, walking down the staircase.

The officer swung around, his face contorted. "And you are?" he blurted out, narrowing his eyes.

"I'm Madeleine Vionnet and this is my establishment. What is it you want?"

"Well, well, isn't that nice. Madame Vionnet herself," he said with a forced smile. "I'm General Dietrich Schneider, one of the Commanders in charge here." He clicked his heels. His knee-high boots fit snuggly below his billowing trousers and were polished to a glistening shine. Beneath the rim of his hat strands of blond hair clung matted against his pale face which seemed in a permanent scowl of contempt. Service medals hung evenly from his tunic and the iron cross swung rhythmically from a pin at his neck. The soldiers wore fewer medals but were equally intimidating in their helmets, and rifles hanging from their shoulders. They all smelled of damp leather and stale tobacco.

"How can we help you?" She didn't smile.

He straightened his back and lifted his chin. "I want to examine your work force."

"And what work force is that? We are essentially closed."

He walked toward her shaking his thin baton in front of her face. "Madame, you have 1200 seamstresses. Where are they? They must surrender to work for the Führer. A slight facial tic caused his eye to twitch. When she didn't respond, he stomped his foot. The receptionist inched her chair closer to the wall. "Well?" he demanded.

"That was many months ago before the economic collapse and before the threat of invasion. You know, the German invasion." Her tone was unmistakably sarcastic but he didn't flinch.

He nodded at his subordinates and they moved quickly to his side. "We'll look for ourselves." His lips were pursed.

"Well then please, let me show you our work rooms." She walked slowly across the foyer and down a hallway, stopping at each door while they peered inside to see that all were empty with white work smocks hanging in long rows against the walls and the work tables and sewing machines unused.

"There, you see?" she said, leading them back across the foyer. He stopped several times to look at the high ceilings and stunning staircase. "Hmm, very nice." He looked at her again.

"Where are the workers, I demand to know?"

"They probably fled to the countryside."

"All of them? You are still here though, aren't you? What's upstairs?" He motioned with his chin.

She stopped cold. *Oh damn, the rolls of fabric I bought from the others are stored in my office!* She cleared her throat. "Nothing, just my office . . .and, and janitor supplies." She felt the heat rising from her neck to her face and hoped he didn't notice. All she could think about was eighty-six rolls of fabric leaning up against the walls of her office. She coughed and put her hand on a nearby table as if to steady herself.

"You'll have to excuse me. I've been ill, possibly influenza."

Commander Schneider stepped back several steps and then motioned his men toward the door. He narrowed his eyes and spoke slowly. "We'll return again when you are feeling better. Next week, perhaps." When he reached the door he turned. "Next week, Madame Vionnet," he said defiantly.

"Yes. Yes, of course. That will be fine."

When the door closed she ran upstairs, glancing in a mirror. Her face was flushed as she suspected. She dialed Therese and then heard a tap on the half-closed door. She put the receiver down and stared. Commander Schneider stood in the doorway. "Let's make it official. Monday morning at ten. Just so there is no misunderstanding. Is that clear, Madame Vionnet?"

"Yes Monday at ten," she said, her heart pounding. When he left she replayed the scene again and again. The rolls of fabric were against the wall to his right. *Did he look that way?*

"Therese, I need your help," she said into the phone minutes later, panic pinching her throat.

That evening they went through the entire building looking for a place to hide the fabric, deciding on a locked storage closet off one of the workrooms.

"He probably won't look in this area again," Madeleine said. "He spent time here but went on to admire the building."

"He admired the building?"

Madeleine let out a long deep breath and ran her hands down the sides of her face. "Good grief. They could take this building, couldn't they?

Therese nodded. "They've taken just about everything else in Paris worth having, and if they do you'll lose your fabric for sure. What about your town house?"

"They could go there as well, especially if they suspect anything. That fabric is worth its weight in gold right now, to me and to them. They're using the silk for parachutes. We're supposed to surrender everything."

"I've heard that some people are hiding their valuables beneath the floorboards in their apartments. I know of some artists who are doing that with their art."

"Well I do have loose floorboards in my study. They squeak and toddle every time I walk on them. Actually, it makes sense. I'd have access and can work from home, especially if they appropriate this building." She stood nodding. "I don't know how we'd get those rolls to my apartment though. The Germans are everywhere, they see everything. They're forming Gestapo units who barge in whenever they want."

"What about your fabric supplier? Didn't he pick up all those rolls and deliver them here?"

"Yes, but that was just before the Germans arrived. I wouldn't want to put him in jeopardy now. He has a family and . . ." her voice trailed off. "The trucks and vans are gone. The Germans took most of them and the others were used by the French to escape from the city. Damn!"

Therese tapped her fingers on the desk and they both sat in silence. "I have an idea but it's chancy. "Do you have some sheets or cloth we can use to wrap the rolls in bundles? They'd be easier to transport that way since we'll have to be quick."

"I have the muslin we use for making patterns. In fact, some are already wrapped in that."

"What's it like here in the early morning, have you noticed? Do the Germans patrol this area?"

"Well, not really. I haven't seen patrols, just soldiers on the street and in the cafes."

"What about near your town house?"

"It's quiet on the street but I sometimes see them in the square about a block away. Therese, this is all a bit crazy. I can't get you involved in this. I don't know why I'm so obsessed with this fabric."

"For the same reason I'm obsessed with my camera. It's what we do, Madeleine."

Forty-Two

THERESE WAITED in the dark by the loading dock at 14 Boulevard Haussmann, the building housing the French newspaper, *Le Figaro*. She glanced at her watch. *Precisely 4 a.m.* She knew the schedule from her years as a free-lance contributor to the newspaper and hoped it hadn't changed. To be less conspicuous, she wore a pair of dark trousers and a black jacket and she hid her hair under a tweed cap. When she saw a vehicle turn the corner, she moved closer to the dock just as the panel truck with *Le Figaro* stenciled on the side pulled into the parking area. Therese was swift. As a young man stepped from the van she greeted him with a wave and smile, and flashed her press card.

"Bonjour, mon amie! Les cles du camion," she said putting her hand out for the keys and stepping forward.

He stood motionless, his brow furrowed as he stared. She looked at her watch and shrugged. *"Les cles, s'il ous plait,"* she said reaching for the keys and nodding reassurance. She put her other hand on his shoulder and looking puzzled he let the keys drop in her hand. She nodded and smiled.

Sliding onto the grey cloth seat littered with snack wrappers, she started the van. *Please let me know how to drive this. The clutch, yes, and the brake, just like Gertrude's auto.* It started with the first try and she watched him from the mirror, standing there looking puzzled. The van jerked and bolted out onto the street and she drove west toward the roundabout. *Good god! Thank goodness there are no cars this morning.* Her heart pounded erratically as she turned on Place Saint Augustin. The steering was stiff and the van felt bigger than she imagined. Her knuckles glowed white on the steering wheel. *God help me!* She held her breath until reaching rue

Montaigne and drove until the saw the side exit to the Palace of Fashion. Madeleine was waiting in the dark.

The bundles of fabric were still by the side door where they put them the night before and not wasting any time, they carried them to the van after scooting over three tied bundles of newspapers to make room. "Probably extras," Therese whispered. "I'll drive, you can get in the back. Newspaper deliveries are made by only one person so best to keep your head low."

Therese took side streets to avoid being seen and watched for Gestapo patrols but didn't really expect to see them at such an early hour. She turned down *rue La Boetre*, normally a quiet street, and struggled with the gear stick before looking up. *What? Oh, god, a barricade!* She wiggled the gear shift again to find reverse and then gasped as a German soldier stepped from the shadows and walked toward the van. *Oh no, for god's sake!*

"We have a little problem. Stay down Madeleine and cover if you can," she said quickly over her shoulder. Therese took a deep breath and got out of the van, waving at the soldier before opening the back. Madeleine was nowhere to be seen! She whispered quickly, "Wherever you are, please stay down." As the young soldier walked closer she grabbed a bundle of newspapers, closed the back, and walked toward a corner store.

"Hey, *hallo*," he said, walking toward her with his rifle.

"*Bonjour.*" She smiled and waved.

He motioned with his hand. "*Zeitung.*" Her language skills did not fail her.

She yanked a newspaper from the bundle and handed it to him before dropping the stack at the store. She walked back to the van, motioning toward the barricade. He nodded and walked that way, opening a space just wide enough for her to drive through. *Holy mother of . . .* Perspiration dripped from her face. She wiped at her brow and swiped her damp hand over her trousers before gripping the wheel and inching through the small opening.

She tried to catch her breath. "Are you back there?" she said over her shoulder.

"Barely," was the only reply. Madeleine's voice was like a child's at her first recital.

The street was dark as she approached Madeleine's townhouse, and quiet with no one around so they unloaded the bundles of fabric without talking, leaving them just inside the entry hall.

"You stay," Therese whispered. "I need to return the van. I'll come back this evening."

Madeleine grabbed her arm. "Just park it on the street somewhere. It's too dangerous. You can return the keys with a note saying where it's parked. "

"I don't want the delivery boy to get in trouble," she said in a hushed voice. "There's nothing in the back now except newspapers so even if I do get stopped . . ." Therese didn't wait for a discussion. She ran out and climbed in the van. Madeleine watched the exhaust billowing from behind as she drove off.

Therese took the main boulevards back to the *Le Figaro* loading dock where she parked the van in the same spot with the keys in the ignition. She got out and felt her legs wobble. The edges of the sky were just turning into daylight and she pulled off her cap and let her hair fall, shaking it vigorously. *Have I got a motorcar story for Gertrude.* Her heart continued to pound as she walked back home.

The note said come in the afternoon. Gertrude and Alice were leaving Paris that week and invited a few close friends for a farewell drink and to help with some last minute packing. A friend of theirs agreed to hide their art in his apartment so each piece had to be wrapped carefully. Therese arrived early and met Raoul as she was walking in.

"Therese, Therese, my little soldier." He hugged her for a long time.

"I was hoping to have a few minutes alone with you," she said. "Everything is happening so fast, people are saying goodbye, and . . . well, I'm glad you are here today."

"Ah, and I'm happy to see you too, my dear Therese. I wasn't sure if you were still in Paris. You are now famous and your photographs are everywhere. I want to hear all about it, everything."

Therese shook her head. "Stories for another time, Raoul. Today I just want to be with all of you. Who knows when we'll see each other again.

They walked arm in arm and sat nearby the stove with Gertrude and Alice who were opening a bottle of French champagne. They laughed at Therese's story about the borrowed van. Gertrude took her hand. "We first saw you as a shy American student and now here you are a famous photojournalist and a motorcar thief!"

"I'm not sure which was more stressful," Therese said laughing.

"You don't talk about Madame Vionnet, so thank you for sharing the story," Alice said, while glancing at Gertrude.

Therese thought for a moment. "She's a very private person and a friend so it's not for me to share anything about her life, but I did want to tell you of the story of the 'heist.' It's all because Gertrude taught me how to drive. Well, sort of anyway. I'm still getting the hang of it."

"So is Gertrude," Alice said and they broke into laughter.

"That caper happened because you had the courage not because you knew how to drive," Gertrude said. "You know my dear, we've followed every step of your reporting and the photographs, and thank you for your notes from Finland, by the way. We were indeed comforted by them especially knowing how dangerous it was there."

"Well, we're all experiencing danger," Therese said. They sat quiet for a few minutes while other artists and writers drifted in, Picasso, Matisse. Janet Flanner came in, followed by a number of others.

"We'll all exchange our new addresses today before everyone leaves," Gertrude said, once everyone arrived. This is a small group today, a special group, our family." Gertrude's voice faltered. Therese sensed her vulnerability for the first time, the antithesis of her strong character and stout persona. As the afternoon wore on, everyone talked about the war and drank glasses of champagne or hot cider while packing up the art.

"As Jews will you be safe in the south of France?" Raoul asked. "I've heard the Vichy government is following the same nasty regulations as the Nazis."

Gertrude nodded. "Our cottage is in a quiet village, I think we'll be fine. We're known and liked by our neighbors and that offers some protection, at least we hope it does, and we're not really going into hiding since the south is still the free zone. I think as Americans we don't fall under the rules of the Nazis anyway since America hasn't entered the war, at least not yet. If that changes, we'll have to reconsider." She paused to look at Alice. "I may be wrong about this, but I think high profile people have some added safety even if they are Jewish. Their mistreatment becomes known around the world."

"The American Embassy said that all Americans should report there for safe passage home. Why not go back to America?" Therese asked.

Alice looked at Gertrude and thought for a moment. "This is home to us. Our things are here, our art is here. You can understand; you're staying - and even putting on a helmet and following the troops to the front. We didn't know bravery was one of your virtues."

"It isn't," Therese said. "I don't have any courage. I just happened to fall into these experiences. Being in Finland was traumatic but came as a surprise. It's strange though, while you're in the midst of danger you get sort of calm. Maybe it's because you need to think clearly. It's after the fact that the panic is felt deeply. I suppose by then the adrenalin has worn off. But also, you're there doing a job and that becomes the focus. Every photo, every child, every person displaced . . . it's all tragic. Documenting it seems important. So I focus on that and not on the fear. People need to see the results of war, the results we tend to ignore." She smiled and shrugged. "Don't get me talking about war. What are the rest of you doing, or going to do I should say? I know some of you are leaving Paris."

"I'm staying even though I could go back to Spain," Picasso said. "The thought of leaving behind my art . . . well, it's just not going to happen. I suppose what's even worse is having it confiscated right from under my nose so I'm doing what I can to hide most of it."

"Well, I'd like to see you all leave Paris," Raoul said. "I'm taking the family and leaving for the south of France soon - near the Spanish border. But I'd like to think that one day we'll all gather here again and pick up where we left off. I still can't believe what's happening."

The room fell silent. Everyone raised their glasses and the evening ended with hugs and tears. Therese was touched by the comradery and sad to be leaving friends. *This too is the tragedy of war.*

It was damp that night and almost dark. The moon beamed just enough light to see her way to Madeleine's townhouse and she shivered under her light cloth coat, gripping at the neck. The smell of burning coal filled the air as she walked alone on the quiet street wondering how long it would be until the coal was gone too, rationed or loaded onto trains to Germany. She also thought about the young soldier earlier that morning on the barricaded rue La Boetre. *His uniform and rifle frightened me, but in truth he was just a young man doing his job, probably bored, wanting to pass the time reading a newspaper. He too probably had to say goodbye to friends.* She thought how fortunate that it didn't turn into anything more than it did: a simple encounter between two people wanting to be somewhere else.

As she reached the square near rue de Brentagne, an elderly woman with a cane and a flowered head scarf tied tightly under her chin, stood on the corner peddling hot apple cider from a coal-lit bucket. The fragrance, pungent and spicy, caused Therese to pause for a moment and push her hands deep inside her pockets to stay warm. The woman lifted the ladle and a cup. Therese smiled and dropped a few coins in the box but walked on.

Madeleine's townhouse was glowing with lights at the end of the street. Therese quickened her pace anxious to be in the warmth of her home. She felt a quiver and took her hands out of her coat pockets and rubbed them together. At the top of the steps, Madeleine greeted her at the door wearing a pale blue linen dress and lavender apron - and with a wooden spoon in her hand! Her forehead was damp from standing over the coal-fed stove.

"I'm so happy we're doing this tonight," Madeleine said as they kissed on both cheeks. The scent of provincial spices drifted from the kitchen and the house was warm and lit with scented candles.

"This couldn't be more perfect," Therese said.

The rolls of fabric were still bundled on the floor and Madeleine stood admiring them, obviously pleased. She leaned against Therese's shoulder. "This fabric would not be here if it weren't for you."

"If it weren't for us," Therese corrected her.

"No, really, it's because of you." She squeezed Therese's arm, still leaning against her shoulder. "We've known each other for almost twenty years. You have a way of always breathing new life into mine."

A moment passed. "And you into mine, Madeleine." They stood there until smoke billowed from the kitchen.

"Oh no, my soufflé!" Madeleine grabbed her spoon. "Tonight we celebrate," she yelled as she ran to the kitchen. Madeleine's house was elegant, luxurious even, and yet she would give leave to her staff and cook in the kitchen when Therese was around. Usually they cooked together but Madeleine insisted she prepare the meal that night.

"The food and champagne are from the black market, but the candles are from my collection I keep hidden in a drawer for special occasions," Madeleine said as she lit each one on the table and took off her apron. "In war and with shortages even the simplest comforts can heal the soul," she said smiling. Therese thought how lovely she looked that night lighting the candles, seeing the reflection sparkle in her dark eyes. Madeleine poured the champagne as they sat at the table, both wondering if this would be their last celebration.

"Let's toast to life tonight and act as though there is no war," Therese said holding her glass in the air. They touched glasses. There was a soft dignity in their look, their way with each other, and all that is lovely between two women, two friends, even though strikingly dissimilar. Madeleine watched Therese at the table and how the light from the candle softened her face, her hair, and how beautiful she was when she leaned forward a little over the French porcelain bowl to reach for her glass. Madeleine was fascinated with her aura, her look; her purple and blue print dress with a green turban wrapped loosely around her dark hair. Underneath that façade though, always fragile, always a little afraid. They lingered at the table as the ivory candles burnt half way and waxy remnants hung like tiny bulbs along the candle shafts.

Giddy from the champagne as the night wore on, they laughed as they relived the bizarre caper that morning and toasted to their success and to Madeleine's fabric, now safe. They also proposed a toast to the unsuspecting young man in the delivery van probably still wondering about the mystery woman who took the keys and van.

"I just have one question," Therese said trying to contain her giggles. "Where did you disappear to in the back of the van? I was filled with dread when I opened the back, expecting to see you in plain sight."

Madeleine could hardly get the words out for laughing. "I rolled myself into a cigar and slid beneath the long bundles of fabric." That image put them both into fits of laughter. Therese's request for a demonstration was met with resistance, although Madeleine did say she might show her one day.

Amid the tears and laughter that night, the emotional release, the joy and fear and caring, there was also contentment - a rare emotion in the throes of war yet one destined not to last. They cleaned up the kitchen and spent the rest of the evening pulling up floor boards, laughing, and drinking champagne. The many rolls of fabric fit neatly under the floor in Madeleine's study and when covered with a small rug, were entirely unnoticeable.

Forty-Three

NAZI GENERAL Schneider arrived promptly a ten o'clock Monday morning with an entourage from the Gestapo and three Nazi officers. Without introductions they scattered in all directions while Madeleine stood alone in the entrance near the front desk, her small staff purposely given the day off. The Gestapo stormed the work rooms and every room upstairs. Whatever was locked was pried open, whatever was Madeleine's was now theirs. They stripped the walls of valuable art and loaded the sculpture into large military trucks lined up near the entrance. She turned away.

"And the dresses, where are the dresses, Madame?" Schneider demanded.

She shrugged. "There are no dresses. As I told you last week, we were forced to close our business."

"No dresses?" He tapped the baton in the palm of his hand. "I find that hard to believe, Madame Vionnet." He walked over to the officers speaking in a hushed voice before turning to face her. "Then we will start up production again," he said with a saccharin grin and raising his voice. "Our officers would like to send Vionnet gowns to their wives and women in the homeland." He looked over at the officers, "Ja?" One of the officers whispered something to him. "Oh, and of course the Führer will want gowns for Eva."

Madeleine counted her heartbeats. "I'm no longer designing dresses. I am now retired." She clenched her jaw.

Commander Schneider walked closer to her until their faces almost touched. His breath of pork fat and tobacco caused her to turn her head to one side in disgust.

"Look at me! You don't make those decisions. Do you understand?" He waited for a response and then raising his voice, "Do you understand?" he yelled. The purple veins in his neck bulged beyond his stiff collar and beads of perspiration appeared above his lip. He stood and then glanced briefly at his men.

"I am now retired," she repeated. She glanced at the others and then back at him, unsure of his reaction.

He swung around and gave an order to a member of the Gestapo standing by the door who then disappeared and returned quickly carrying three rolls of yellow fabric. Schneider motioned and the corporal dropped the rolls on the floor.

"We will bring you out of retirement, Madame Vionnet," he said, his eyes pinched almost tight. "You will start by making yellow badges - the Star of David that all Jews must wear to identify themselves. You will cut the fabric and bind the edges," he said enunciating each word and raising his chin with smug satisfaction. "Welcome back to the work world, Madame Vionnet," he smirked. "Is that clear?"

She said nothing but stood firm against the desk. *Why give him the satisfaction of an argument?*

He beat the baton into his hand as his face turned red. "Do you have a hearing problem, Madame Vionnet, because you don't seem to understand anything I say?" He paced in front of her.

Her shoulders rose as she took a deep breath. "I am retired and no longer work," she said firmly. "I am also French and I don't betray my people, Jews or otherwise." She looked directly at him. "Nor will I participate in humiliating them. Now if there's nothing else I have things I must do."

His eyes widened and his nostrils flared as he raised the baton over his head.

"Dietrich!" one of the officers said sharply and rushed over to whisper something.

Madeleine turned and walked slowly up the stairs which by now were littered with items from her office. She turned at the top of the stairs. "And don't forget your fabric," she said, her legs trembling but hoping it didn't show.

The following morning when she arrived at her salon, two huge Nazi *Blutfahnes* hung from the columns in front. The black swastikas, boldly visible and accented against the red, waived back and forth as the flags fluttered in the breeze. "Swines," she murmured as she went inside.

Hours later Thèophile Bader screamed into the phone. "Now you're commiserating with the Nazis? Have you gone mad, woman? How dare you hang Nazi banners on my building?"

"Well first Thèophile, this is not your building or mine. We lease it, remember? And, second, if you don't like the banners outside you can contact the German high command and ask that they be removed, since they're the ones who put them there. And lastly, please don't bother me with your misguided ignorance." She slammed the phone down hard, surprised it didn't break to pieces.

Therese, my god, where are you? I could use some strength right now. Then she remembered, Therese was in the field taking photographs.

Two weeks later a note came by courier.

I would like to request the pleasure of your company to meet for lunch on Thursday at one o'clock in the dining room at the Hotel Ritz. Please let me know if you would like me to send a car. Otherwise, I look forward to meeting you then.

General Otto von Baumann
Commander in Charge, Paris.

She immediately called her attorney, Anton Guillet. "Anton, what is going on? Why are they harassing me?" She told him about the visits by the Gestapo and her refusal to start up the business again. "Oh, and they wanted me to make those dreadful Star of David badges. Can you imagine?"

"Actually I can, Madeleine. The *hoden* of the leader dictates the behavior of the followers."

"Hoden?"

"That's German for balls, Madeleine. Sorry to be so crude but look what Hitler is doing. He's trying to take over the world. None of it makes much sense."

"Well, who is this von Baumann and why does he want to meet for lunch?"

"I have no idea. He's the highest German in command here, in charge of occupied France actually. What he wants from you, well, I suppose you'll soon find out."

"If they want the Palace of Fashion can't they just take it? They've taken the art and already have their flags flying in front so essentially it's theirs now. I have everything out of there I want, although I didn't expect them to take the art."

"If you're asking me if they have any legal right to take what's yours or make you design dresses, it's not really a legal issue. They invaded and we surrendered. We're their captives, more or less. It's that simple. You can of course refuse, but there could be consequences. Madeleine, I can offer to go with you but that might suggest you have something to hide. Are you afraid to go alone?"

"No, not yet. Schneider was scary and probably showing off for his officers but I can't imagine that's what this is all about. I'll let you know."

"Yes, please do. If I don't hear from you by Friday . . . well, I'm sure I will."

She paused on the cobblestone walk after stepping from the taxi. The massive array of armored cars and tanks lining 15 Place Vendôme seemed daunting, especially in front of the once lavish Hotel Ritz, now the unofficial headquarters of the German high military command in Paris. She shook her head in distaste at the Swastika flags draped over the entrance and soldiers instead of doormen. Dozens of armed military troops patrolled the street while neatly-uniformed German officers came and went from the hotel like high society. *After all, it is theirs now, I suppose.*

She walked toward the steps through a maze of men and metal before a tall uniformed soldier carrying a rifle stepped quickly in front of her and muttered something in German. She took Commander von

Baumann's invitation from her coat pocket and thrust it at him. He nodded and she was escorted briskly to the lobby where two members of the Gestapo searched her purse and patted her down while holding her arms behind her back.

"Is this really necessary?" She pulled her arms free and straightened her coat before being led to the dining room. A lone German officer sat at a table in the corner and stood when she approached.

"Madame Vionnet, we've heard the name for so long and now finally a chance to meet the person. I'm Commander von Baumann." He bowed politely and motioned her to sit. "I've ordered some champagne, one of the best reasons to be in Paris."

"Actually, the only one, if I may say so. I'm not sure you should be here at all."

He smiled and tilted the bottle toward her glass but she put her hand over the rim. He paused and then put it back on ice without pouring for himself. He studied his hands. She guessed him to be around sixty or so. His grey hair was cut short and his thin but angular face defied the hardiness typical of the younger Germans seen in the occupied zone. His light blue eyes and uniform though were familiar sights, and his voice was soft but she remained cautious, wringing her hands as they lay in her lap.

He seemed unsure of what to say. "Let's clear the air right away, shall we, Madame Vionnet?"

"Yes, let's. Why am I here?"

He took his time. "Well, for a couple of reasons. First, I want to apologize for the rudeness of one of my officers, General Schneider. There is no excuse for his behavior during his visit to your salon. While I can't undo what he did or said, I am trying to gather the items taken from you, especially the art, and will see to it that it's returned. Several of my officers also reported that you were threatened, and I apologize for that as well. Commanding by fear has its place, but your salon isn't one of them."

He paused as a number of dishes were brought to the table and the waiter stood by to serve them. Commander von Baumann motioned to her and she shook her head. He pointed to a few and they were carefully placed on his plate. He lifted his fork, but put it down and looked at her.

"You were under no obligation to meet for lunch, Madame Vionnet. Perhaps another locale might have been more appropriate. I can understand why you might not want to eat. I'm sorry for misjudging the situation. I don't usually get myself into these . . . these matters."

"Which matters?"

He took a long deep breath. "Dealing with sensitive topics. I'm a military commander so I'm far removed from other duties. The main reason for our meeting is actually to pass on a request from the Führer. You may already know this, but he greatly admires your creations and your stature in the fashion world." He tapped his finger on the white table linen and thought for a moment. "In spite of what people know or think of him, he's enormously appreciative of the arts. He's also quite taken with Paris and all it has to offer; in fact, it's always been his favorite, and, well, now his prize I suppose. He likes the architecture, the art, and the fact that Paris is the art and fashion capital of the world. In his mind, you and your fashions, your beautiful gowns, personify real class, more so than the others. Every woman in Germany wants a Vionnet gown -but few can afford one," he added smiling. "*Haute couture* I think it's called. Everyone wants it, the glamour, the richness, the pinnacle of beauty. Those are pretty much his words since I know very little about fashion," he said a little embarrassed.

"And the request from Hitler. What is it? I've been forced to close my business. I have no dresses."

"Yes, well the throes of war, unfortunately. He has a vision. He sees Berlin as the new Paris and he has a sense of how that might look. Among other things, he wants Berlin to be the fashion capital of the world, with the finest designers, the most beautiful salons, a place where women flock to see the latest styles and buy the most beautiful fashions in the world. He wants you to be the first one, to come to Berlin, now. He promises you all the fabric and workers and equipment . . . everything you need. If you come, the others will follow. He is prepared to offer you anything you want. A glorious lifestyle, riches, fame, safety for you and your family . . . anything. And, I'm to convey this message."

She felt the color drain from her face like liquid from an urn. Her brow tightened and her eyes widened as she looked at him in disbelief. *To occupy Paris, kill and maim and torture and ruin lives, and shut down businesses, and execute Jews . . . all of this so Hitler can turn Berlin into another Paris? And to think I would even consider this because some madman wants his fantasy? What does he think I could I possibly get in Berlin that I haven't already achieved here in my own country? What lunacy! What absolute lunacy!*

She caught a glimpse of something in his expression. *Surely he must know this is ridiculous. His look of compassion and embarrassment, how could he not know?* She pushed her chair back and stood to leave. He stood as well, letting his napkin slide to the floor.

"Absolutely not," she said looking at him, her gaze full of fire.

He stepped in front of her and spoke quietly. "Madame Vionnet. I was asked to pass on this message since I'm the highest in command here. That tells you how much the Führer wants this. Be aware that if I cannot make this happen he will call on someone else to do his bidding for him; someone perhaps . . . how can I say, less cordial. I only say this because," he stopped, fumbling for words, "well, because I'm sorry we couldn't have had a nice lunch and talked about something more pleasant." He bowed slightly as she turned to leave.

Forty-Four

THE TELEGRAM arrived just as Therese was packing for another excursion into the war-ravaged countryside as part of her Carnegie grant.

Dear Miss Bonney,

We would like to appoint you as the official photographer for the French army with full privileges to travel in the unoccupied zone. We hope you will accept and continue to document the situation in France. If you accept, please keep this with you to obtain access to transportation, supplies including film, and key personnel.

Cordially,

Marshall Pétain,
Vichy Government, Vichy, France

Oh gads, this just as the Carnegie grant is winding down. I'm so tired of war; I've seen too much of it already. She knew that documenting the plight and devastation in France might draw America into the war; France's only chance of survival given its small army and lack of resources – and she knew the situation was dire. She had watched as more than half the food was being shipped to Germany and what was left was scarce even with ration coupons.

She admired the French, especially the women trying to hold things together while the men were shipped off to work in German factories or went underground to join the resistance. She saw how Parisian women fashioned shoes out of old cardboard and used every piece of cloth or exchanged it like currency. They created a new look called *la robe a mille morceaux* - a dress of a thousand pieces - sewn together using remnants and rags. These women in France are like Madeleine, she thought, proud, courageous, and resourceful. *Maybe this is what it takes to be a real Parisian woman.* After some deliberation, she decided she would take the French government up on its offer

In the months to come she used Marshal Petain's letter to gain access to an old Red Cross truck left behind in battle, and foraged through Army depots to find a huge metal drum for storing petro. She had it put in the back of the truck and filled to the brim at an army base since finding petro in the countryside was near impossible. She carted around a tattered map and drove to where the stories were, even covering the French who fled to Spain and Portugal or lived in the hills away from the watchful eye of the Gestapo. Wherever she went she helped with evacuations, delivered medical supplies, and listened to stories of survival - not just of bombs and weapons, but of hunger and abandonment.

Her long sojourns in the field were tiring, and she welcomed retreats back to Paris and time spent with Madeleine. They leaned heavily on each other for support and comfort, as always.

"You have a phone call, it sounds important," Madeleine's receptionist said after knocking lightly on her door. Madeleine lifted the receiver to hear a familiar voice.

"Madame Vionnet, this is Otto von Baumann. I was going to stop by but feared you'd probably had enough of us in your salon. I want to say first that I'm sorry our luncheon meeting was upsetting to you. I didn't plan it well and do I want to apologize."

"Did you actually think I would accept Hitler's offer?"

"I wasn't sure. I know you were forced to close your business and deal with shortages and the occupation. Berlin would have given you what unfortunately had been taken away. Many might have jumped at the chance. I think we have a lot to learn about the French and about you."

"Yes, I think you do."

"Well, I do have some good news. We've gathered what I hope are all of the items taken from your salon including the art. I'm wondering if you would like them delivered to your salon or somewhere else. Before you answer, confidentially may I suggest that you have them all delivered somewhere else. I'm sure you know what is happening. The beautiful buildings like yours are most often appropriated for the administration. I understand your salon is a very special place, if you know what I mean. You should prepare yourself for this."

"I see. How long do I have?"

"Think of days rather than weeks."

"Oh, my." She caught her breath. "Then please return the items to my townhome. If I'm not there, someone will be."

"Very well. I'll have the items delivered sometime this week. And, Madame Vionnet?"

"Yes?"

"If you would like to try for lunch again, I would be most honored."

She paused and thought for a moment. "That won't be possible. Goodbye and . . . well thank you," she said softly.

His words reached deep; she was stunned although not surprised. *They will take the Palace of Fashion!* The flood of memories . . . her seamstresses, the clients, her draping sessions with Therese, their time together there, and the beautiful gowns created in that building brought sadness.

Every day that week Madeleine packed satchels and bags with bobbins of thread, pins, needles, measuring tapes, patterns from her files, and lists of clients. At one point, she remembered her draping doll! It was still in her office so she bundled it in cloth and carried it like a child as she walked back to her townhouse hoping not to be seen by the Gestapo. Surely they would find some way to accuse her of hoarding.

Once she had what she needed, she alerted her three backers that the building will most likely be seized by the German high command and if they wanted any fixtures or furniture they should come immediately. Martinez de Hoy had already fled to Argentina and Henri Lillas sent word that he had been ill and wished her luck. That left only Thèophile Bader, who went into such a tirade over the possible appropriation of the building that his doctor had to be called.

Madeleine also called every artist, architect, interior designer, craftsman and vendor who had originally worked on the Palace of

Fashion. Before the week was over the entire building had been stripped of its magnificence. Gone were the huge chandeliers, the designer wall coverings, the art deco furniture, the glass lamps, the equipment, and the fine carpets. When it was back to the original style, she took one last look and closed the door.

The following month she was once again summoned by the Nazi high command but this time to 11 rue des Saussaires without any explanation other than to come at the designated time. *Oh, what do they want with me now? Therese is still away, I wish she was here; my nerves are like bolts of lightning.* Her attorney offered again to accompany her. "Not this time, Anton, but I'll take your number with me." He cautioned her to say as little as possible.

A summer rain drenched the streets leaving messy puddles so the taxi stopped close to the curb. The humidity was unbearable so she wore a simple cotton dress and a wide-brimmed hat but no gloves. She folded her umbrella as she walked up the steps to face the swastika and eagle emblem hanging over the door and four German soldiers standing near the entry sweltering in their woolen uniforms.

"I'm here to see Major Karl Reimer," Madeleine said, snapping her black umbrella closed and showing the summons. The building, an appropriated older mansion situated on the right bank in the 8th arrondissement near the Champs-Élysées still had lace curtains in the windows and a child's swing in the yard. The rooms on the main floor were fitted with desks and Major Reimer's office was the last room on the right. The sign on the door had his name and *Chef der Gestapo*.

He sat rigidly at his desk without looking up and she sat uninvited. "My first question for you," he began still looking down at his papers, "is what happened to all the furnishings in your salon at 50 rue Montaigne? I understand that was to be the exquisite property of the high command."

"I vacated that property since my business was forced to close. I don't know what happened to it after that."

He looked up and raised his eyebrows, staring. "You don't have the items? General Schneider said there was a large chandelier and some fine furnishings throughout when he was there."

"There was. I remember them well, but I don't know what happened after I left." She felt no compulsion to be truthful or helpful. On the contrary, she could hardly contain her anger but heeded her attorney's advice to say as little as possible. Major Reimer continued to stare without expression, his face stone-like, his eyes hollow. His mouth barely moved when he spoke. "Do you know why everything disappeared, where it all went?"

She could read nothing by looking at him which made her uneasy. "No, I don't." She shifted her feet and fingered the clasp on her purse.

"Strange, don't you think?"

She shrugged but didn't respond.

He ran his hand over his mouth and shifted some papers on the desk, his first sign of movement. "You are aware of the Fürher's wish to move the fashion center to Berlin, is that correct? I believe Commander von Baumann spoke to you about that and the Fürher's choice for you to lead in that effort."

"Yes, I'm aware of that but I'm retired and no longer work."

"But surely it takes little effort to design a dress. It's not like building a bomb or painting a building."

She felt cautious, not sure how he might respond nor did she want to find out. "The effort is mostly mental not really physical. It takes concentration."

"Well, how can we convince you to work on your concentration?" He leaned forward and looked at her with an insidious stare.

She shifted in her seat seething with anger but trying to stay calm. "Well I think age is often the determinant of concentration and not will power, don't you agree?" She offered a slight smile.

His eyes narrowed and his body twitched. "I'm the one asking the questions!" he yelled, slapping his hand on the table. She could see it didn't take much for him to uncoil. His shoulder jerked as he tried to regain his composure.

"Madame Vionnet, are you aware of the *Service du Travail Obligatoire*?"

Giving her no chance to respond, he continued. "It's the transfer of French workers to Germany for the German war effort. Sometimes the workers are put in work camps or factories, or even agriculture, wherever they're needed. It's hard and grueling even for the most hardy." He squinted and smirked at the same time.

"You see, Madame, we don't have to ask you politely to work for the Fürher. You have an obligation, and we see to it that you serve in the ways that *we* determine, not you. Am I making myself clear? Is this too difficult for you to understand?"

She sat for a moment taking in a long breath, her face burning with anger, her finger taping on the arm of the chair. *A work camp? How dare he threaten me! They want to control by intimidation*

She stood slowly. "It's not difficult to understand at all. What's puzzling though is your inability to see the consequences of taking one of the most respected women in Paris, sending her to a forced labor camp in Germany, and expecting her to create the fashions that made her famous worldwide. First of all, do you think the entire French nation, or the world in fact, would stand for that? And do you really think any creative person would use their passion to support this . . . this Nazi madness?"

He bolted from his chair, his eyes darting in all directions. "Sit down! Sit down and be quiet!" Saliva formed in the corners of his mouth and his face turned crimson red.

"Do you know who I am? I'm the head of the Gestapo. No one talks to me like that! No one!" he yelled.

She felt her body tighten but kept her gaze "I'm a French citizen, a world-renowned fashion designer. You can confiscate our food, our belongings, and invade our country, but you cannot take our spirit or talent, and you certainly can't turn us into little Nazis catering to your Führer."

She noticed the rhythmic throbbing in his neck and his mouth yelling words but she heard nothing as she turned and walked from the room, slamming the door so hard several SS soldiers came running down the hall as she left the building.

A sudden gust of wind caught her hat, twirling it down the sidewalk and she paused for a brief second, and then got into a waiting taxi and slammed that door as well.

Later that afternoon her attorney, Anton Guillet, confessed into the phone, "I can say this, Madeleine, you certainly are one of my more interesting clients."

Forty-Five

"I'M HORRIFIED," Therese said when she arrived back in Paris. "We need a way to stay in touch while I'm gone. I wish I'd been here."

"You were, in a way," Madeleine said smiling. "I'm obviously a target since I won't give in to Hitler's wishes and they probably won't give up until I agree, which of course I won't. I'm grateful I have some notoriety since I'd be in one of those work camps by now, or worse. I'm not sure how much longer I can put them off, Therese. My nerves are shot. Little by little, I'm trying to meld into the woodwork. The salon is out of my hands now so neither the Nazis nor Bader will be harassing me about that. And I've made it clear I won't work in Berlin. The thought of it! How naïve they are."

"They seem to prey on fear, Madeleine, so perhaps they think intimidation will work. Little did they know who they were dealing with!" Therese smiled coyly. "All the same, any one of them could snap so best to be careful. I just heard that Germany invaded Russia of all things so maybe that will keep their minds busy."

"How much longer can this go on? How can Hitler think he can take over the entire world?"

"Well, I'm sure everyone is waiting for the Americans to enter the war instead of just sending occasional aid. I sure wish they'd hurry. Have you thought any more about leaving for the south? Who knows what the Gestapo will do to you next. You're obviously not making any friends among them."

"Shhh," Madeleine said playfully. "I plan to stay here for now. I'll know if it's time to leave."

Madeleine dimmed the lights that night and for the first time, pried up the sturdy oak floorboards in her study, carefully removing the planks piece by piece. When she pulled the protective muslin sheet aside, the fabrics in luscious colors and hues caught the glint of light and shimmered majestically. She smiled as she chose the fabric for her first dress, a backless gown for Greta Garbo to wear in a dance scene for the MGM Hollywood movie, *Two-Faced Woman*. Garbo wanted silk so Madeleine chose an orchid-colored silk chiffon and Therese came for a draping session later that evening. Using the floor of her study, Madeleine cut the fabric on the bias and draped it over Therese's graceful figure, sculpting it into one of her most gorgeous gowns.

"It's stunning, Madeleine, absolutely stunning," Therese said as she glanced in a nearby mirror. "I can't believe you can do this even from home and under duress," she added while staring at the gown.

A few weeks later the gown was finished and sealed in a mailing pouch. She kept an account in a New York bank and it was agreed that payment for the dress would be deposited there. A former seamstress living in the south of France agreed to act as courier to get Madeleine's package to Portugal and mailed from there.

The orchid color was a knockout on Garbo and the dress was a sensation - so much so that she also wore it to the Hollywood premier of the movie and the press caught it all on film. A photo of Garbo appeared on the cover of *Life* magazine and the caption read: *Garbo sizzles in new Vionnet gown.*

A few weeks later her attorney, Anton Guillet, called her at home. "Thèophile Bader has filed a law suit demanding his share of the profit from the Garbo dress and also filed an injunction forbidding you to use the Vionnet name."

"What? That's my name!"

"Well, he contends that he owns the Vionnet name for commercial purposes since he's the major stockholder in the business, with one share more than anyone else."

"Oh, for god's sake, Anton. Can he really do this? Vionnet et Cie is over, bankrupt. If I start a new business without his investment, isn't that business mine?"

"It gets tricky but here's the bottom line. His legal suit isn't going anywhere given the German occupation. If and when the war ends and we become France again, it will take the courts years to get caught up. I wouldn't worry about Bader to be honest. I would however worry about the Gestapo. You've claimed all along to be retired and here you are putting France on the map again as the place for high fashion."

"I know, I've thought about that but who's to say these are new dresses? Garbo's dress could have been made years ago. I refuse to be under their thumb, Anton, and I refuse to stop working. It's my right."

"Unfortunately, that's what war does, Madeleine. It takes away people's rights."

"Well, they're not going to take mine away. I've worked to get here and I'll continue as long as I have the fabric."

"What if they search your house? Won't they find some evidence that you're making gowns? I'd be careful here, Madeleine. They want you to design fashions but in Berlin not Paris. They could make things difficult for you."

"Yes, I know, but it's hard to stand by without living life, without having passion, and without showing some resistance." She thought to herself how absurd that must sound to an attorney who deals with reality.

"Yes, well, be careful. Mailing pouches could get you in trouble and taking orders . . . well, communication can be monitored and will probably cease soon anyway. Don't you have contacts in New York who can act as agents?"

"Yes, and these are all good points, Anton. I can make some of them work. I've been stubborn, wanting to do this my way to keep from feeling powerless. The store manager of our now defunct shop in New York would be more than happy to take charge of orders and I'll deal with the communication problem in some way. I'll continue to design and make gowns right up to the end though. We can't give in to them, Anton."

"I admire you for that, but . . ."

"But what?"

"Just keep my number close, Madeleine."

Therese shook her head when she heard about Bader. "Doesn't he ever give up? I mean, he has his own companies, his own money, so why does he pick bones with you, especially over your name?"

"It's his nature. He'd fall apart if he couldn't be obstinate, or admit that women can run a business too."

"I suppose. I do agree with your attorney about the Gestapo and turning some of the logistics over to others. You never know what they will do so I hope you will be careful. Oh, by the way, I'm doing a story on Gertrude Stein in exile for *Vogue* magazine so I'll be in unoccupied territory in a town called Bilignin for a few days. If the phones work, I'll call you."

"Maybe we should get carrier pigeons."

"Maybe we should just spend more time together," Therese said smiling.

"Hmm, you're the one running off in that abysmal Red Cross truck all the time, and even sleeping in it. Really, Therese, can't you find something more . . . more ordinary to do?"

"Ha! Listen to you!"

Madeleine rose and took her morning water. As she was getting dressed she heard a loud noise and then pounding on the door and then at every entrance. Throwing on a housecoat she ran to her study and there on the floor lay a piece of fabric she'd cut the night before, along with the roll it came from and some supplies. While on her hands and knees she shoved them into the cavern beneath the floorboards and hastily nailed the boards back before rolling the rug in place and pulling a chair and ottoman into the center. Running her fingers through her hair and buttoning her robe, she hurried to the front door feeling her heart skipping beats with every step. She opened it to see the man she dreaded the most, the Gestapo Chief, Major Karl Reimer.

Pushing her aside, he shouted something to his men and they stormed through the house weapons drawn, ransacking every drawer, every closet until the floors were piled high with her belongings. Cushions were thrown from the divan, bedding was stripped from the beds, and clothes from her armoires tossed aside. The rugs in every room were rolled up and the Gestapo agents bounced on every floor in their knee-high boots - even in her study until she feared she might faint. She avoided the temptation to speak, instead held her breath to contain her anger and she finally sat down. Major Reimer stood in front of her with his arms folded.

"Where are you making your dresses?" he said circling around her. "Where are your fabrics and supplies?" He snapped his boots and the thud reverberated throughout the room.

She blinked rapidly. "This is my home where I live, not a salon."

"The Führer is losing patience," he shouted as he paced in front of her. "He wants all of this fashion business moved to Berlin and he wants it done now. Why do you hesitate?" He stood in front of her again, feet apart and firm. "The Führer knows about your gowns, that they're still being made, still smeared on the covers of magazines making a fool of him, making liars of us!" He turned and banged his fist against the wall and a small picture fell to the floor shattering the glass. "What have you to say?"

She shook her head. "My dresses are everywhere. I was in business for well over twenty-five years. I can't stop women from wearing my gowns or selling them to others." *He can prove nothing, the pig!*

His face tightened and he raised his voice. "Women are claiming to have new Vionnet gowns from France. How can this be? We control France!" He kicked over a table, its contents tumbling onto the floor.

She shrugged, determined not to be coerced while he paced waiting for an answer, his shiny boots leaving scuff marks on the floor.

"Well?" he yelled.

Stay calm, she reminded herself.

"I'm waiting!" he said, but she sat without speaking. Infuriated, he yanked his gloves from his belt and whipped them hard across her face. The metal buckle stung and drops of blood dripped onto her lap. Shocked, she rose and walked toward him holding her face.

"Swine," she said glaring.

He yelled to his men and within seconds they grabbed her by the arms and quickly walked her to their waiting car. It sped off accompanied by several motorcycles and in minutes pulled up in front of a large stone building with a Nazi flag hanging limp from the heat. She recognized the building, the Ministry of Aviation, now used by the Gestapo. The infamous cellar houses the Gestapo execution and torture chamber, or at least that's what she's heard. Two agents pulled her from the car and strands of her hair covered an eye and her cheek throbbed from the gash. She struggled to free one hand and tried to pull her blood-stained housecoat down to cover her thighs. As they walked her up the steps, a group of German officers were leaving the building.

"What . . . what's going on here?" She looked up to see Otto von Baumann, the Commander from their ill-fated lunch. He bent down to look at her face. "What happened here?" He motioned to Major Reimer and they stepped aside. She heard raised voices and saw them facing each other, the brim of their hats almost touching. A few minutes later, von Baumann draped his jacket over her shoulders and helped her up the stairs. They went into an empty office where he offered his handkerchief and asked an aid to bring some water.

Her face was pale and her lips dry. "Don't be afraid," he said and waited until he saw her shoulders drop a little. "I'm sorry this has happened to you. As you can see, we lack so much in terms of people skills for a country with such a strong army," he said as he sat at the desk across from her. "Major Reimer does his job well, that's why he's the head of the Gestapo. He just doesn't always know who the enemy is."

He watched her closely and pushed the glass toward her. She shook her head. "While it may seem trite to give so much attention to the matter of fashion, we are all under pressure to obey the Führer's orders. His mind works far beyond the present. He's focusing on a particular outcome - that of winning everything and Berlin becoming the pinnacle of art and beauty - while the rest of us are still struggling with the 'winning' part." He bent his head to look at her eyes and sighed. "I did warn you this might happen, didn't I?"

She nodded slightly but remained silent. He continued. "I can only protect you so much, Madame Vionnet. I understand you have houses outside of Paris. I know you have a strong commitment to stay here and to resist. I admire your courage. But . . . think about it. You at least have

Madeleine and Therese

somewhere else to go." He straightened his back. "If America enters the war, everything will look different. The American army will try to liberate Paris and we will fight them. Who knows what could happen here." He sat thinking, and then took a pen from the desk and wrote something on a scrap of paper. "Here's a number where you might reach me. If not, leave a message. I can't tell you what to do, Madame Vionnet. But please be careful. I'm still hoping for that lunch someday," he said smiling. "I'll get a car to drive you home. I don't think you will need stitches but you might want a doctor to look at that cut." He walked over and helped her up and then walked her to the car.

Forty-Six

GERTRUDE ONCE TOLD Therese that in the heat of summer, she and Alice would load up the car and head for the tiny village of Bilignin near the Swiss border to enjoy the cool air from the Alps. So it seemed a logical choice now that Paris was swarming with Germans and Gertrude and Alice were Jewish.

Stepping off the train with a canvas bag over her shoulder, Therese spotted Gertrude and Alice waiting in their familiar and faithful Model T Ford. They honked and waved madly before jumping out and gathering her in their arms. The drive to their cottage was magnificent. The sun ignited the landscape of rolling hills and orchards along the winding country road, and endless fields of pastel-colored spring flowers and rich farmland were visible as far as the eye could see. Therese breathed deeply, feeling the tension drain from every limb. Gertrude and Alice waved at neighbors near their 'home in exile,' and hushed their barking dogs as they went through the iron gate to their picture-perfect country cottage.

That afternoon, they lunched in the garden on vegetarian Panini and iced tea, and took in the stillness of the countryside with birds chirping in the distance and crickets keeping rhythm. The air was warm and sweet, and Therese watched the heat rippling in waves from endless fields of hay. She thought of taking a photograph but felt too lazy to even open her camera bag. She thought of Madeleine and wished she could be there to enjoy the peace. She would find out later that Madeleine was being dragged into Gestapo headquarters at that very moment.

Gertrude sat in the shade after settling herself into a large chair wearing her usual dark corduroy and tweed even in the simmering summer weather. In contrast, Therese sat nearby in the sun in a brightly-colored peasant dress and a wide-brimmed navy blue straw hat, every limb soothed by the heat and luscious landscape, and the chorus of sounds that always seems to accompany the suddenness of a hot summer afternoon in the country.

"We're comfortable here but it's isolating," Gertrude said. "We have our dogs, our radio, electricity and plenty to eat but we miss our friends in Paris - or wherever they are. The mail is censored or infrequent, the phone lines have been cut like everywhere else, and we miss our salons, the exhibitions, and the excitement." She looked wistful, even melancholy. "Raoul is nearby and he'll come for dinner tonight since he wants to see you. His wife and family left for Sweden to be safe. He's been having trouble with his hands, so hopefully we'll find out more. We hear from Picasso and the others when the mail comes through, which isn't often. What's it like in Paris now?"

"Tense. It's always the unknown," Therese said. "The people suffer and the Germans are skittish with talk of American's joining the war. I'm gone much of the time, either to New York and my exhibits, or in the field doing relief work and taking photographs. So, nothing as peaceful as this," she said smiling.

"How's your friend, Madeleine?" Alice asked. "We've read the Germans want to move art and fashion to Berlin but no one's going. They've put pressure on Picasso and now he's wondering if he should have gone to Spain instead of staying in Paris."

"Yes, it's stressful for everyone. Madeleine closed the salon but wants to stay in Paris." Therese was careful not to say much about Madeleine, respecting her privacy as usual. "The Germans are taking or destroying so much of what's beautiful. They closed most of the bookstores, looted the Louvre, and are burning books and art that's supposedly subversive. It's madness, ruthless."

Alice put her hand on Gertrude's sleeve. "Speaking of books, tell Therese about your novel. Maybe she has some ideas about how to get it out of France."

"Yes, I've written a book, *Mrs. Reynolds,* that I know would be burned if the Germans knew it was really about Hitler and Stalin disguised as two fictitious characters I'm calling Angel Harper and Joseph Lane. My publisher wants to read it but I can't send it through the French mail system because it's a package and will be checked."

"And sending it via Portugal?"

"A long drive to get there from here and petro is scarce, if even available."

"Is it your only copy? I could possibly try to smuggle it to New York the next time I go. But if it's confiscated . . . well, that would be that."

"Hmm, it's a thought. It is my only copy, but . . ."

That evening Raoul arrived having hitched a ride from Ceret, an artist's colony near the border of Spain, and they all drank heavily from pitchers of the local wine of Provence and laughed about old times. Gertrude cooked her famous hearty stew from her garden pickings and Alice baked an enormous loaf of peasant bread which they ate with fresh butter from a local dairy.

After dinner Therese and Raoul walked arm in arm along the flower-lined road. "What's happening with your hands, Raoul?"

"It's a type of arthritis, the debilitating kind. The doctor called them rheumatic attacks or some such thing. I'm strapping a brush to my wrist since I can't hold anything for long. But I keep painting because that's what I do," he said with a grin. "It's ironic that I left Paris so the Nazis can't control what I paint, and I end up barely able to paint anyway."

She squeezed his arm. "Is there a treatment, have you seen a specialist?"

"No to the treatment, yes to the specialist. There's not much that can be done. It's a degenerative disease. I'd better start painting fast, don't you think?" he said laughing, but Therese knew it was not a laughing matter. Art was his life, his passion.

Every day the four of them took walks, sometimes all together, sometimes with each other, and then they huddled together in some philosophical conversation before preparing a real country meal from

Gertrude's garden. After several long walks and a number of memorable meals, Therese finished the notes for her story and took several photos showing Gertrude and Alice in their charming home and garden, and several of Raoul for a story on him as well. She left two days later after more hugs and tears, and with the only copy of *Mrs. Reynolds* tucked under her arm and a small painting, a gift from Raoul.

Therese called Madeleine the minute she returned. "I'm back and I have a canvass bag full of fresh vegetables. Want to roast them tonight? I also have a bottle of red wine from Provence."

"I am so glad to hear your voice. I'm just so glad you're home." Her voice cracked.

"What is it Madeleine? You sound different. What's wrong?"

"Nothing, I just missed you. Can you come now?"

Therese stared in disbelief when Madeleine opened the door. By then, her eye and one side of her face had turned black and blue and the cut on her cheek was a thin red line with three black stiches. "The doctor said the stiches would keep it from scaring, even though probably not needed," she said as Therese hugged her.

"Who did this? Who could possibly do this?" She turned away and blinked several times and paced the floor.

"Come sit. It's nothing that won't heal. Therese, we can't give them the satisfaction of letting them upset us." Therese sat down next to her and Madeleine turned to look at her. She knew Therese at that moment. She could see her fears and child-like look, her bewilderment, her hurt, her tears. "Listen to me. I'm taking chances with my business and it's not without risk. I know that and I want you to know that too. These are my choices and my consequences. I know this is upsetting, but believe me, it's a small price to pay. I'm doing what I want to be doing, what I ought to be doing."

Therese nodded. "Yes, it's just that . . ."

"I know, I know." She looked at Therese for a long time and they sat in silence both grasping the seriousness of war when it comes this close. "My dearest Therese, I know," she whispered.

"I would like you to tell me the name of the person who did this. That's all, just the name. I should know who is out to get you just in case," Therese said softly.

"It was the head of the Gestapo, Major Reimer, when they were here ransacking the house. You know, Therese, I don't need to tell you this - you of all people - but courage stretches life beyond imagination. You and I both live our lives without shying away from controversy. You know that. We can't undo the wrongs, though. I want you to forget about Reimer. What I need from you is comfort and understanding right now, not anger."

Therese took a deep breath. "Yes, yes, of course." She touched Madeleine's bruised face carefully. "They say scars build character. In fact, someone once said the strongest are those bathed in scars."

There was a sad kind of laughter. *What does war do to people?* Therese thought. *I take pictures of the outside, but what's really happening inside? Is this how it feels?*

They dined on roasted vegetables along with a baguette and fresh butter Therese brought from her trip to the countryside. Madeleine lit tiny candle stubs at the last moment, trying to add some ambiance to their simple meal. "I'll be so glad when this damn war is over. I'm going to buy candles by the dozens."

It was midnight and they were still talking over wine. Madeleine took Therese's hand. "Tell me again about the countryside, what color were the flowers?" Therese saw her exhaustion, the wasting away of spirit with little to hold on to at the moment, so she repeated everything she could remember about the trip, including the peaceful fields and flowers in every color of the rainbow. She vowed to herself that she would no longer suggest that Madeleine leave Paris. She finally understood the importance to her of staying and what she was willing to risk.

Madeleine was one of the few couturiers to stay in Paris and she felt the void. She sometimes felt she alone carried the industry on her shoulders so she was surprised and a little pleased when Coco Chanel called inviting her to lunch. Never close friends, in fact sometimes antagonists, but they did work to keep the fashion industry alive in Paris. They agreed to meet at the *Café La Chain's*.

"I think we're about the only ones left in Paris, Madeleine. I admire your courage," Chanel said as they waited to order. She was dressed in one of her smart knits and looked refreshed. Madeleine was curious about the meeting but waited for Chanel to speak first and she did. "I heard you've had some problems with the Gestapo."

Madeleine shrugged, putting her hand to her face. "It's healing."

"And your work? I understand you're still making your beautiful gowns." It was well known that Chanel was living at the Hotel Ritz with a German officer and drawing much criticism because of it. *Is she trying to get information for the Gestapo? Is this what this meeting is all about?*

"Like everyone else, Coco, I was forced to close my business. What about you, are you still trying to work?"

"No, no, everything is on hold right now. Why did I think you were still making dresses? I saw the photograph of Garbo on the cover of *Life* Magazine. It's a beautiful dress by the way, and luscious color. I thought it said a *new* Vionnet."

"It may have said that, but nothing is new these days. Like your fashions, mine stay in vogue and are even resold. We should feel lucky."

"You were trying to buy fabrics the last time we all got together. Did that ever happen? I don't make elegant gowns like you, only knits so I had none to sell."

Madeleine thought fast to dodge the question. "No, no one had any to sell that I could use and without my salon and staff, it would have been too difficult to continue. By the way, I understand you're having a romantic liaison with a Gestapo officer. Will that put you in jeopardy once the war is over?"

Chanel's face flushed. "It's probably just a . . . well, a temporary thing."

"You know, Coco, this war won't last forever and that's when we'll all come together again. It helps to keep on good terms in our profession - you know, to watch out for each other."

Chanel's face was strained. "Yes, of course," she said with a weak smile.

Forty-Seven

"*PROCHAIN, MADEMOISELLE*," so Therese moved forward in line at the airport wondering if she'll be searched. *Please don't look at Gertrude's book*. As an afterthought, she put her press pass on the counter and the soldier stared for a moment and then waived her on. She exhaled easily knowing Gertrude's book made it through the Nazi censors and she couldn't wait to tell her. She rushed to get her plane to New York and the reception for her new book, *Europe's Children*.

The contrast between New York and Paris was more pronounced than ever. She moved about Manhattan without looking over her shoulder or hearing the boots of the ever-present Nazis. People talked and laughed freely, the restaurants were full, and street stands overflowed with fresh vegetables and other delicacies. Therese couldn't help but think about Madeleine though, alone in Paris, vulnerable, and under the vengeful eye of the Gestapo. If they discovered she was making gowns right under their noses, she would surely pay the price.

"Miss Bonney, I presume?" Bill Donovan held out his hand while spilling wine on his tie with the other. "Oops," he said as he brushed his coat sleeve over his tie and set his wine glass down nearby. "I recognized you from a newspaper photo. Congratulations on yet another important book, *Europe's Children*. I was hoping to meet you here at the reception; in fact, that's why I'm here."

"Thank you, and you are . . . ?" She guessed him to be around forty or so. He looked like someone's dad or perhaps a parish priest. His sandy-colored hair was thinning but he was muscular and had a pleasant smile.

"Bill Donovan. I'm the Director of the OSS."

"The OSS?"

"The Office of Strategic Services. We do all the cloak-and-dagger work for the government. Actually, somewhat similar to what you do."

She laughed. "Oh, really? And what exactly do I do? "

"Well, you go into war zones and gather information. Yours is in the form of photographs and reportage whereas ours is often in codes and other forms of mysterious espionage."

She liked his easy manner and quick smile. "I suppose you're right, except I don't work for the American government."

"Well, how would you like to? That is, work for the government?"

She straightened her shoulders and blinked. "Work for the United States government? Doing what?"

"You're friends with Field Marshal Carl von Mannerheim and you can . . ."

"Wait, how do you know that? What makes you think we're friends?"

"Miss Bonney, we know everything. It's what we do. We're the intelligence arm of the U.S. government and you can imagine we are quite busy these days putting our nose in other people's business. Besides, your picture was all over the newspapers when he decorated you with the White Cross medal. Congratulations, by the way. They don't give those out on a whim."

She looked at him suspiciously. "What could I possibly do for the OSS?"

"Finland is what we call a cobelligerent, or something slightly less that a full-fledged ally of Nazi Germany."

"Yes, but only because Finland wants protection from the Soviet Union."

"And so does Nazi Germany; it wants Finland as a base of operation against the Russian Army."

"Wouldn't it be nice if everyone left Finland alone?"

"Ah, you're an idealist. Finland is small and everyone loves Finland. But it's strategically located, bordered by both Germany and the Soviets. We would like you to convince Mannerheim to break away from Hitler and become neutral."

"And why would he even consider that?"

"To stop Hitler. It's really that simple. Germany would be more vulnerable without using Finland's strategic location. The U.S. and the rest of Europe are trying to stop Hitler and would be very grateful for any effort in that direction."

"You surely don't expect someone like Mannerheim to listen to me or anyone else. He'll make decisions based on what's good for Finland not as a favor for a photojournalist."

"Not a favor for a photojournalist, but from someone carrying a personal and confidential message from America. We don't have anyone else who has a personal relationship with Mannerheim that can get access to him. You'd be the messenger." He paused to study her face. "It's not without risks, I should mention. But then I'm sure you know about risks."

"Hmm." She leaned closer. "I don't know if even I have access to him."

"We think you might. At least it's worth a try." He leaned closer. "For your country, Miss Bonney, and for France too since I know that's your adopted home."

That night she called Madeleine from her hotel room, surprised she could even get through.

"Is it safe returning to Finland?" was Madeleine's first response.

"As safe as it is in France, I suppose. The Germans have been in Finland ever since they invaded the Soviet Union. They formed an alliance with Finland. The Soviets left Finland for the most part and are elsewhere fighting the Nazis. It sounds like a board game doesn't it? I'm not sure anyone is able to understand war. It seems so silly if it weren't so tragic for the innocents who suffer."

"These are your decisions, Therese. I just want you to be safe."

"I think it will be fine. The OSS will get me to Finland and then back to Washington, D.C. I'll be home after that. Be careful there in Paris, Madeleine. I worry about the Gestapo."

"Therese . . ."

"I know."

Forty-Eight

DONOVAN'S LAST words would come back to haunt her. "Therese, remember that flying during wartime is a bit different; let's say . . . more challenging."

In spite of the warning, she was unprepared for the labyrinth and intrigue of flying in enemy skies. She slept soundly on the transatlantic flight to England where she was driven to an airfield outside of London to wait for a Royal Air Force plane heading for the North Sea. Since German forces held all of Norway, the only transportation to Stockholm was on an occasional military flight at night in the dark, so she stood waiting alone on a dark airstrip in the starless night, shivering in the cold until she saw a small plane land without lights and taxi close. Two men appeared out of nowhere and lifted her into the plane as it continued to inch along the tarmac before abruptly taking off.

"Where shall I sit?" she said, seeing no seats. No one answered so she sat on the floor along with a shipment of airplane parts and slid back and forth once in flight until the co-pilot attached her to a cargo hook with a makeshift strap.

"Really?" is all she could say.

For the next leg of the trip she waited in a damp hotel with instructions to be ready before dawn, when a bearded man in dark clothes picked her up on a motorcycle and took her to another darkened airfield. He spoke no English and she tried a number of languages but no response. *This is beginning to feel strange. Who is this person and where am I?* She stood bundled in a blanket from her first flight until he motioned toward a small airplane sitting at the far corner of a vacant field. As they walked toward the aircraft, he handed her a canvas parcel with straps.

"What's this?" she whispered before climbing into the small plane in the dark of night. He pointed to the sky and slipped it over her arms.

"A parachute? Are you serious?" He just shrugged.

The small plane sputtered and taxied across the field and took off as she gripped the straps on the parachute in the pitch-black plane. *Gads, we must be flying over a battle field!* She put her head back and closed her eyes. Her stomach growled with hunger and she tried to loosen the parachute straps to reach some crackers in her pocket, but couldn't get them loose. She slept instead and six hours later she woke in time to see Stockholm bathed in the early morning light. It was her first glimpse of daylight in three days.

As she stumbled out of the plane, a man in a dark suit carrying a leather valise approached her on the tarmac. "Your flight to Finland won't leave for a while, Miss Bonney, so come have some breakfast and we can talk."

"I'm sorry, I didn't get your name." She fluffed her hair and ran a hand over her face, wishing for a hot bath.

"Karl Westman, I'm the Finnish ambassador to Sweden. It's my job to screen everyone entering Finland; I hope you understand. Even though your trip has been arranged, I'll need to see your papers and visa." They walked to a small hotel just yards away. "Please, I'll get us a table in the dining room if you'd like to get refreshed."

How refreshed can one get in five minutes? I'd give anything for a hot bath and a comfortable bed. She stretched and ran cold water over her face in the restroom and rejoined him just as the waiter poured their coffee.

"Since England and Finland are at war, you are fortunate to have an American passport and therefore can get into Finland. I'm told you are on assignment for an American magazine?"

"Yes, for *Collier's.*" The magazine was her cover arranged by the OSS. She carried a letter identifying herself as a journalist writing an article on Finland's arts.

"I should caution you, Miss Bonney, there is grave danger in Finland. It's my official duty to discourage your visit since we are of course occupied by German forces."

"Yes, thank you."

"I should also say unofficially though, we welcome your visit. You have our distinguished White Cross and are always an important guest in our country. It is dangerous, however. That's the bitter twist."

"Yes, well I'd like to see Commander Mannerheim while I'm here. I know there's been some attempt to make arrangements for us to meet but nothing has been confirmed. Can you help?"

"Hmm, he's been in the field but I'll notify his staff immediately. Where will you be staying?"

"At the Hotel Kämp in Helsinki." Just saying those words brought back a torrent of memories. The excitement of her past experience mixed with the pain of what she saw and experienced there left her feeling a bit unraveled. *It seems like ages ago. I was young, so inexperienced. Well, maybe I still am.* "What's the situation like in Helsinki? Is it safe to move about?"

"It's hard to tell. There are few visitors, almost none in fact. The Gestapo might be curious about you, a woman traveling alone. I'd be especially careful about taking pictures. They are strictly forbidden."

"I left my camera at home, but thanks for the warning."

Helsinki looked much like it did when she left almost three years ago. New rubble has replaced old rubble, but instead of cars the streets were now filled with German military vehicles and artillery. Sadly, the Hotel Kämp was adorned with Nazi banners and the lobby was teeming with German officers in field dress and Wehrmacht helmets. They glared menacingly at her when she entered. It was no surprise they had taken over the nicest hotel in Helsinki, she thought, just like in Paris.

Her room was simple and drab with more dust and fewer towels, unlike on her previous visit but the water was hot and that's all that mattered. She bathed and dressed, and took to the streets, curious to see Helsinki now after three years. The department store, Stockmann's, where she bought her snow suits was still closed, and the bomb shelters where she once herded victims were now boarded shut with weathered timber. The most noticeable difference was the weather. It was the fall of 1941 and still warm unlike the sub-zero temperatures she had known in the winter of 1938.

The other difference was that she now had constant companions. The Gestapo trailed her every move. They ransacked her room each time she left the hotel, tore through her suitcase, checked her trash for notes, and searched the pockets of her clothing, leaving everything strewn on the floor. *Ugh, I must remember to pick my battles. I don't want any trouble while I'm here.*

On her second day, she received a hand-written note delivered to her room by a young woman.

Therese. Please wait under the clock at 4pm tomorrow. Try to come alone.

Carl

She remembered the big clock, that traditional landmark that hung in front of Stockmann's and was destroyed when the Soviets invaded Helsinki. Evidently its reputation as a meeting place remained - but only to those who knew about it and hopefully not to the Gestapo!

Forty-Nine

THE SOUND OF heavy boots on the cobblestone walkway was disappointing. Suspecting the worse, she glanced over her shoulder to see two uniformed Gestapo agents trailing close behind less than twenty yards. *Oh gads, not again!* She quickened her pace and tried to remember the shortcut to the big clock but nothing looked familiar. *Cripes! Where is that street near Stockmann's?* Just then one of the agents stopped to light a cigarette, igniting the match on the sole of his boot and she darted quickly down an alley and into a tight-knit web of streets crisscrossing back and forth until she spotted a familiar landmark. From there she remembered the shortcut around a giant pile of rubble that brought her out on a street near Stockmann's where she stood in a shadow catching her breath.

At precisely four o'clock she stepped from the shadow in time to see an unmarked black Mercedes pull to the curb. A hand waved her closer and she walked quickly to the car just as the back door opened from inside and she stepped in. The man in the back nodded and the car drove off slowly.

The three men dressed in black were strangers. "I was expecting Commander Mannerheim."

The driver nodded, looking at her through the rear view mirror. She leaned forward. "And you are . . . ?"

"The Commander said you'd know the code word." He met her eyes in the mirror.

"Well, I don't have a code word; no one gave it to me."

"No, we have it. He said you'd know it."

"Okay."

"Snow suit."

She smiled and settled back in the seat as they drove in silence. The rubble diminished once outside of Helsinki and the countryside was serene and peaceful except for some occasional German convoys and the usual checkpoints where they were ordered to show their passports. She didn't recognize the area but then everything looked different without snow and she wondered which landscape was more appealing. About an hour later the sun eased toward the hills changing the light and the car turned into a long gravel driveway where Carl Mannerheim waited in front of a lovely villa framed by velvety hills and a stunning muted purple sunset.

She straightened her dress and tried to see her hair in the rear view mirror but couldn't so she fluffed it anyway and straightened the seams in her stockings. As she reached for the handle he opened the door and smiled at her through the window glass. He looked different without his uniform and more relaxed in his casual slacks and sweater. She was aware of his intense gaze as she stepped from the car.

"I couldn't be more pleased to see you, Therese," he said taking her hand and kissing it lightly. "The war has not taken its toll; you look lovely as ever."

She smiled. "It's good to see you too, Commander, and you seem to have survived as well, I see."

"Carl, please. Let's dispense with the titles, and welcome to my home. I'm so happy you're here." He took her arm as they walked slowly toward the house, past a Roman fountain near the veranda where birds splashed and chirped, and a lovely stone walkway aged with patina that led to the house. Beyond, the sky held the sunset draped perfectly across the hills and fading only slightly by the minute.

"It's beautiful, Carl, and what a lovely setting here in the foothills."

"This house has been in my family for years and I'm just now getting a chance to enjoy it. I'm here because there's little fighting in this area, at least not right now. That makes my job as Commander-in-Chief a little easier." He opened the front door and they walked into a beautiful room with massively high ceilings and a view of the hills from several large windows along the back wall. "So I use this house as my command headquarters and as a place to just relax before things change again."

"Change again? And when do you expect that might be?"

"Ah, do any of us know? You were here when the Soviets invaded and now the Germans. It gets weary as you can imagine. Can I pour you a drink? I hope you didn't mind the long drive," he said as he walked toward the bar. "You probably know by now, the Hotel Kämp has been taken over by the Nazis."

"A little white wine please, and yes, I'm well aware of the situation at the hotel. Members from the Gestapo rummage through my room and follow me everywhere I go. I don't know what they're looking for."

"I doubt if they know either. They're tense like everyone else. Shall we take our drinks out on the veranda? The housekeeper is preparing dinner."

"I didn't expect such a nice welcome, so thank you. I thought we might meet as our jeeps crossed in the snow like we used to. Those days were so bitter sweet."

"Now Therese, are you going to steal my heart again?" He walked over and took her left hand. "Still not married? What's the matter with those Frenchmen?"

She sighed and smiled a little. "I think you said it nicely before: it's difficult for love and war at the same time."

His eyes were dancing and intense, and she looked away. "It might be nice if you could prove me wrong," he said with his unwavering gaze.

The housekeeper announced dinner and they sat inside while he told her about the political situation in Finland. "I'll be drafted as the next President and that will mean new responsibilities but there's no one else to do it. But tell me about you. How is your life in Paris and your plans if America enters the war?"

"Well, I'll stay as long as I have the freedom to move about, I suppose. My press badge allows that now, but if America does enter the war, I'll be considered an enemy and I don't know how that will change my situation."

"Do you need to stay in Paris? Wouldn't you be safer in the U.S?"

"I think of Paris as my home, Carl. I have friends there. But also my work is in Europe documenting the effects of the war and Paris is a good home base for that."

"And when the war is over?"

"Will it ever be?"

They took their coffee on the veranda. "I want to tell you why I'm here," she said, sitting down next to him. "The OSS has sent me to convince you to break ties with Hitler and Nazi Germany."

He reached to touch her hand. "Oh, you'd make a terrible spy, Therese," he said laughing. "You're not supposed to reveal the purpose of your mission."

"I'll take that as a compliment because I don't want to be a spy, and especially not here in Finland. I would never do that, ever."

"I know and I already knew the purpose of your visit. We have an intelligence arm as well," he said smiling. He turned to look at her. "You know Therese, things have changed since you were here. When the tension between Germany and Russia became evident, we saw in Hitler a possible ally in gaining back the territory we lost to the Soviets."

"I remember you had to cede key areas as part of the cease fire agreement."

"Yes, and that's why we allowed German troops here in Finland while they prepared for their invasion of the Soviet Union. We were actually a part of that invasion because it was in our best interest. As a result, we were able to take back large portions of land we'd previously lost and that obviously was important to us."

"I can see the precarious position you're in. On one hand I'm sure you'd like support from the U.S. if it enters the war, but on the other, Germany is actually protecting you from another Soviet attack and the loss again of your territory."

"Exactly, and that's why we cannot and will not sever ties with Nazi Germany right now. I know your OSS will be disappointed, but l will see that you get some intelligence information that may help the U.S. without jeopardizing our position. Ultimately, we'd like the U.S. to enter the war because that would probably bring an end to this entire mess.

"Hitler's unrealistic dream of world domination may end it even sooner," she said. They both nodded at the irony.

"I like our talks, Therese, and just being with you. It amazes me that I can feel so far from the battlefield and the political turmoil when I'm with you. I remember that from our time together in Helsinki during the Soviet invasion."

She looked down, a little embarrassed. She felt the attraction, the chemistry, but something held her back and she couldn't quite figure out why. She chose her words. "I'm always so happy to see you, Carl. You've, well, you've meant so much to me and you're always so helpful in every way."

"When the war is over, the president, Risto Ryti, will resign, as I mentioned earlier. I'm slated to fill his shoes. Finland can be a wonderful place to live . . ."

She felt the conversation becoming too personal and suddenly she wanted to leave. It was all becoming too complicated, too far ahead into the future when her focus was on the present.

"We can't have this discussion right now, Carl." She looked away. "It's also getting late and I should be getting back."

Some of the fire left his eyes although they were still kind, still penetrating. "I'd like you to stay, there's a guest room . . . but my drivers will also be glad to take you back to Helsinki tonight if you prefer."

She reached for his hand a bit relieved. "I think that's best. But thank you for a lovely evening. They always are with you."

They walked to the car and said their goodbyes. He kissed her while holding the car door open and she surprised herself by kissing him back.

Fifty

THE DARK MERCEDES sedan pulled to the curb about fifty yards from the Hotel Kämp shortly before midnight and the door opened just long enough for her to step out before it sped off into the night. She walked briskly along the darkened street to the hotel and into the lobby, and that's when she felt an arm around her neck and being pulled off her feet.

As the arm hold tightened she heard someone say, "Here, in here," and she gasped for a breath while being dragged struggling and kicking. She felt a sharp pain down her back and felt her shoe tumble to the floor. She tried to scream out but a hand that smelled of stale tobacco smothered her mouth with such force she thought she'd faint.

She gripped the doorway with one hand and held tight until her hand slipped and she was dragged into a darkened room and heard the door slam shut with such a force the noise lingered in the room. Several voices whispered in German. *The Gestapo, of course!* The smell of boot polish was disgustingly familiar. Someone pushed her into a chair and one agent yanked her bag from her shoulder and emptied it on the floor while two others searched her coat pockets.

"What are you doing in Helsinki, Therese Bonney?" She recognized the Gestapo uniform but not the short stocky officer looking through her documents. His smile was more of a smirk.

She coughed and held her throat. "I'm here with permission of the Finnish government to write a story for *Collier's* magazine on Finnish arts." She coughed again and tried to hide her fright. She looked at the door but decided it best to just answer their questions.

He walked back and forth. "And, so that takes you out at night, in some mysterious car to some unknown destination?"

"You should know what I do since you follow me everywhere."

He bent over her and glared, narrowing his eyes and putting his face within inches of hers.

"Ah, but you were too clever for us tonight. Don't try my patience!" he said raising his voice. "I'll ask you again. Where were you tonight?"

She put her hand on the back of her neck where it ached. "At a violin recital."

"There are no recitals!" he yelled, his brow bunching up.

It . . . it was held at a private residence, for my magazine article."

"Give me the information, the address, who was playing? We have no record of such an event."

She tried to think fast but her body ached and her neck hurt. "It was prearranged with the magazine before I arrived. I was just told where and when to meet my transportation."

He glared and then stepped away. He and the others whispered something in private and then he turned. "Aren't you in fact a Soviet spy here for information? Who's giving it to you and where is it?" He stood with his feet apart and his hand on his pistol holster.

She wanted to laugh at the error. *What paranoid insecurity.* "Of course I'm not a Soviet spy! I'm an American citizen and a journalist for *Collier's* magazine in New York. You have my papers and an approval from the Finish ambassador in Sweden to enter the country. I'd like my shoe back. It's late and . . ."

"Search her!"

"What? Well, isn't that what you just did?" she said looking at the contents of her bag scattered about the floor.

He nodded and two Gestapo agents grabbed her by the arms and dragged her to a table in the room.

"No!" She struggled to pull loose from their grip, kicking and twisting but they held firmly and slammed her face-down over the table while another agent lifted her dress and ripped off her panties.

"Stop it! Stop it you cowards!" she screamed.

She felt a gloveless hand exploring her and heard the others in the room laughing. Fearing the worst she closed her eyes tight and tried not to vomit.

"*Nichts, da ist nichts.* There's nothing," one said in English. They let go and moved away from the table as she slid to the floor inches from the officer's boots as he stood in front of her, feet apart.

He looked down at her. "Don't think you've won," and he stepped on her hand, grinding his boot into the flesh until she flinched and doubled over. "You'll be under our watch and next time it might not be so pleasant."

She reached for the table and stood up, pulling her dress back in place. Seeing his sardonic smile she took a step forward. "You filthy coward," she said as he lunged at her.

In the scramble three Gestapo agents held him back while his face contorted, almost turning blue.

"*Nein*, stop, leave it be, let it go," one of the agents said to him. "We can't cause trouble, we have no proof."

She watched as they left the room, two of them still holding the Gestapo officer by the arms as he squirmed. She gathered her things and after a hot bath in her room, placed a call to her contacts. "I'm done here. Get me out."

The rain delayed her flight but when the storm lifted, she walked out onto the tarmac at the Finnish airfield to board a small plane waiting at the end of the runway. A man in a beige rain coat waited nearby and then walked toward the plane, handing her a thick manila envelope.

"It's from the Commander, Mannerheim. Have a safe trip, Miss Bonney."

Tightening the buckles and straps on her pull-down seat in the small aircraft, she leaned back and took a long breath, the envelope in her lap unopened. After a bumpy takeoff, she watched Helsinki grow smaller and then out of sight. She remembered her other harrowing experience there three years ago during the Soviet invasion. *My first loss of innocence.*

What would that experience have been like without Carl Mannerheim? Our frequent meetings and dinners, our time in the field made it palatable, even enjoyable.

She picked up the envelope and peered inside sifting through charts, maps and reports with notes and arrows in the margins. *Intelligence! I guess they call it that for a reason. It makes no sense to me but I suppose Donovan will be pleased.* A note slipped from the bundle of papers and she saw her name.

My dear Therese: My day is as empty today as it was full last night. Nothing seems quite the same. Please keep an open mind and think of returning when this damn war is over. With love, CM.

"Hmm," she whispered under her breath. She let her head fall back on the seat, keeping it there until the plane landed in Stockholm.

The next portion of her flight from Stockholm to Scotland had her sitting straight up, hands gripping the seat. "Cinch up your parachute, cinch up your parachute," the pilot kept yelling.

What good will a parachute do in this weather? Seat belts might be a better choice. At one point, the turbulence blew the plane back and forth sending her flying into the aisle. She held the vomit bag close until the plane finally set down in an obscure field in the middle of nowhere. A black sedan waited nearby and she was driven to a remote air force base where she was to pick up the flight to London - but no plane was in sight!

"They're all being used," she heard someone tell the driver. "Don't you people know there's a war going on?"

Six hours later, an unidentified private plane taxied down the runway stopping just long enough for her to climb on board before it left for the short flight to London.

"Get ready for a quick stop, sister," the captain yelled.

When she saw the shelling and explosions over London she realized why. The plane barely stopped and she was whisked off and onto a British Air Force plane that took off from London in a sky reminiscent of the fourth of July. Twenty minutes into the flight she heard "rat- tat-tat" and heard the pilot say "Oh, Christ."

She gulped. "What was that?" she yelled to the co-pilot.

"Flak, some German U-boats are right under us in the Atlantic." She felt the plane take a sudden turn and her hand went from her seatbelt to her parachute as she took an inventory just in case.

"What actually is flak?" She raised her voice to be heard.

"Anti-aircraft fire."

She felt the color drain from her face. "I see," she yelled, gripping the straps on her parachute once again.

After changing course a number of times, the pilot finally found a safe route and the plane arrived in Washington, D.C. several hours later. She was still gripping her straps when they helped her from the plane.

Not wanting to spend any more time in Washington than necessary, she called right away to schedule an appointment with Bill Donovan. They spoke briefly and arranged a time to meet in the morning.

"By the way, Therese, I may have forgotten to tell you but those flights can be a little sketchy."

She blinked several times, "I hadn't noticed." She could still hear him laughing when she hung up the phone.

The roar of aircraft buzzed annoyingly in her ears as she stepped into a long steamy bath. She shook her head from side to side. An hour later just as she was beginning to relax and her hearing was returning to normal, room service appeared at the door with food and a bottle of red wine, compliments of Bill Donavon.

She smiled. "Hmm, he's going to owe me a lot more than this," she mumbled under her breath.

She set the alarm for her early morning meeting with him and settled in, glad to have the trip behind her. Stretching out on the bed she read Mannerheim's note again. *I like him, and then there's the attraction.* She knew him to be kind and decent, and she certainly liked Finland. *It would be a fairy-tale life, easy and interesting. Hmm, what's holding me back? Wouldn't every woman jump at the chance to at least try it?* She'd never thought much about marriage. She couldn't remember a single day when her parents seemed happy.

She glanced at the clock sitting on the night stand. *Madeleine will still be up but the phone lines may be cut. I'll try anyway.*

She heard "hello" and after some static, she said, "Madeleine?"

"Therese? Thank goodness it's you! I'm so glad to hear your voice, where are you?"

They talked until late, sharing news and making plans for a trip to the countryside to buy vegetables and good bread, and about the gowns Madeleine made while Therese was gone, and Finland, and the flights. She didn't tell Madeleine about the incident with the Gestapo, figuring she had her own worries to deal with. *It'll be a story for another time, perhaps.* It was hard to hang up the phone that night. She realized that Madeleine challenged her, awakened and stirred her senses. They understood each other's needs and wants, and both needed challenges and moving beyond the ordinary. Therese knew they had a strong energetic connection, but beyond that, it was the beauty of uncertainty, the endless possibilities unscripted, the boundless and vastness of experiences and closeness they both desired and could find with each other.

When she hung up she dialed the front desk. "Do you know where I can buy some candles here in Washington?"

Fifty-One

IN SPITE OF THE danger, Madeleine continued to create spectacular new gowns, sending them out of the country by private courier to clients and vendeuses in major cities everywhere. Unfortunately, every time a gown was worn in public by someone important, the Gestapo was at her door.

The sadistic Major Reimer no longer accompanied them and she thought he might have been reprimanded by Commander von Baumann because of his abusive treatment. With him gone, she reluctantly came to accept the raids as routine and refused to be intimidated. When she heard boots stomping on the stairs she immediately stashed her fabric and gowns under the floorboards and put everything back in place. Usually four or five Gestapo agents made a quick sweep of her home and left. So she was surprised that afternoon to see a black Mercedes pull up in front with one German officer walking up to her door

What now, pray tell? She reached for the door knob feeling the familiar fear fluttering in her chest. "Commander von Baumann," she said, quite surprised. "Don't tell me they've sent you to sift through my things today?" She found him approachable, even kind at times. *If there's a sheep among the wolves he is probably it.*

He smiled. "I haven't been demoted to searches yet, Madame Vionnet. May I come in for a minute? I'm sorry to come to your home but I do need to talk to you."

They sat in the parlor and he took off his hat and held it in his lap. "My fellow officers don't always share my view about how to treat people, as you know. You are not easily intimidated and that angers them." He thought for a moment. "I happen to think it's a mistake to harass people here in France. It will only drive them underground and we're already seeing signs of an active Resistance movement in Paris and elsewhere, for that matter."

"I have no plans to join the Resistance, Commander, if that's why you're here," she said concealing a half smile.

"No, I didn't think so. You are an icon though, and famous and wealthy."

"What is it you'd like to say?"

"You may know that art and valuables are being confiscated from wealthy Jewish families here in France. Some of it goes to the Führer and some to Goering, but much of it becomes part of the private collections of the German officers."

"I'm not Jewish, so why are you telling me all of this?"

"Yes, well because of their eagerness to add to their private collections, I hear that many German officers are claiming that collectors or the wealthy are Jewish and that gives them the right to confiscate their valuables. The victims become intimidated and don't resist. Since you've angered the Gestapo and since they've been in your home and seen your art, I wanted to warn you so that you can be prepared."

"Prepared?"

"Yes, many people don't know this but all you need to do is show some documentation that you are not Jewish, a birth certificate or anything with your family name, to discourage them. They want art not trouble or reprimands."

"Well, they've already taken art from my salon and with your help it was returned."

"Yes, in that instance, they didn't take it because they thought you were Jewish. They took it because they were greedy and felt they had the right. That kind of behavior is now strictly forbidden, but confiscating from Jews is not."

"Well, I'm not Jewish but my family papers are in storage at my summer home."

"If I may say so, Madame Vionnet, it might prevent some trouble if you had something here. We both know they have a way of making your life difficult. You are not alone, by the way. They do this to others as well."

She nodded slowly. "I'll get some documents this week. May I ask why you came here? I mean, why you are trying to help me?"

He studied her face and sat silent for a moment. "We're not all insensitive and sadistic, although I can imagine you might think so." The mood in his eyes changed and he leaned forward. "Most Germans here are just people. We have families and farms, and want to go home. My wife is a school teacher and I am - or was in the Berlin Philharmonic. My daughter is getting married soon, but I won't be there. Some of us have feelings. That's why I'm here."

Madeleine hoped for a brief trip - just time to get the papers at the summer home and leave to avoid Netch. She looked at her watch and drummed her fingers on the wooden bench. The train to the Riviera was several hours late. She watched travelers rushing through the terminal at Gare de Lyon and to pass the time, she tried to remember where she put the box that held her father's papers. *In the attic, a drawer maybe?* She did a mental inventory of drawers, cupboards, different boxes in the closets. *Maybe Netch will remember.*

She looked at her watch again. Her mind shifted to Therese, on her way back from Finland only to leave again this time for northern France to take more photos. *We'll find some time in between all this moving about.* She glanced at the arrivals board but still no train. *Oh darn, I'll arrive late.* A few minutes later, some static from the overhead speaker muffled the announcement, but it was something about the southbound train now boarding.

It was dusk when the train arrived at Gare de Nice five hours late. She hailed a taxi to her summer home feeling full of dread, knowing she'd already missed the returning train to Paris and the next one wouldn't leave until the following day at noon.

Netch expected her and greeted her at the door with a hug. "Train late? It usually is, I should have warned you." He was bronzed from the sun and well-toned as usual. His blond hair was greying at the temples but only slightly, and he seemed more subdued.

"You look well, Netch."

"Yeah, well you know, lots of tennis, water skiing. It's what people do here."

"Yes, I suppose. Since the train was so late, it's not going back tonight. I'll have to stay over. I hope you don't mind."

"Mind? I was actually hoping that would be the case." He took her bag. "Where, my room?"

"In the guest room." She wanted to add *if it's free* but didn't. It was no secret that he entertained and had an active social life there on the Riviera.

"Too bad," he said smiling as they walked toward the guest room. "I'll fix us a drink. Take your time, I'll be in the kitchen." He paused and turned. "Actually, I was hoping you might like to have dinner out tonight. You must be going through hell in Paris. Are you up for a little fun tonight?"

The unoccupied zone in the south was lively and liberating. People actually moved about without being watched - or searched. Food was plentiful and the mood was optimistic. Netch knew all the clubs and they ran into old friends, Henri and Lily, and ended up listening to jazz with them until late into the night. Madeleine was reminded that the Riviera lifestyle was never of great interest to her but it was to him.

When they married, he was fun and the Riviera was a long way from her business and her responsibilities as Paris' premier couturier. She occasionally escaped those responsibilities with him. So when he suggested building a summer house on the Riviera she agreed and when they separated, she allowed him to stay there and sent him a monthly check - out of guilt.

She confided to Marie Gerber that she never loved him nor did she pretend to. He'd helped her with Théophile Bader and was her escort throughout the entire parade of parties and social events during the opening of the new salon. In other words, it was a marriage of convenience, mostly hers.

Madeleine and Therese

The following morning after finding the papers at the house, Netch drove her to the train station and urged her to leave Paris, at least until the war was over. She told him about the fabric under the floor boards and how that allowed her to continue her business in hiding even though she was harassed and searched, and always under suspicion.

"Perhaps I can help you find a way to get your fabric out of Paris and brought here to the summer house where you can work. It would be easier to get your gowns out of the country from here since we're closer to Spain and Portugal. You know, Madeleine, it's no fun staying in Paris and it just might actually get worse. Everything could shut down and transportation could stop abruptly. Your fabrics could rot under the floorboards for years. You've said over and over again that work is more important to you than anything so why not do it here at the summer house on the Riviera? What do you say?"

He often had a way of making sense and her voice was strained. "I don't know, Netch. I don't know anything right now. I'm just taking a day at a time." There was some truth to what he said and he had been decent to her during her visit and even fun. But then there was Therese.

Fifty-Two

THE TRAIN BACK to Paris arrived on time and she moved briskly through the station to find a taxi, but not before noticing groups gathering in the main terminal. Strangers were talking to each other in close whispers unlike the typical moans upon hearing of late trains. Curiously, she edged closer to a group of men near the ticket counter. One turned to ask if she'd heard the news.

"Japan has just attacked Pearl Harbor! This'll bring America into the war," he said. She nodded and continued out the door. *What about Therese and the other Americans in Paris?*

The following day the United States officially declared war on Japan, and she read again three days later that Germany declared war on the United States. It was early in December, 1941 and it rained every day that week.

Several days passed before Therese was able to return to Paris. Flights in Washington, D.C. were cancelled repeatedly and in some cases postponed indefinitely because of America's entry into the war. Phone lines were tied up and wire services were reserved for government officials only. With the help of Bill Donovan she finally got a late night flight to Paris and she went immediately to see Madeleine.

After a long embrace they sat on the divan and talked. Madeleine was able to get a bottle of red wine and they sat quietly without words, Madeleine swirling the wine in her glass and Therese pensive.

"Are you worried as an American? There's so much confusion and speculation right now," Madeleine said. "I just heard the Germans are arresting American men under the age of sixty and sending them to internment camps and putting others under house arrest. But oddly, many other Americans have been left alone. There seems to be no pattern. The American Embassy is telling all Americans to leave for the U.S. and they'll help with transportation."

"But nothing about American women?"

"No, I haven't heard anything."

"I have press credentials so maybe they'll leave me alone. What's been happening with you while I was gone? More visits by the Gestapo?"

"I'm trying not to answer the door when they arrive. They pound for a few minutes and then move on. I think they're getting as weary of the visits as I am and besides, they have other things on their mind now that America has entered the war."

"That must be a relief. What else are you doing?"

Madeleine looked away. She didn't want to break the trust they'd taken so long to build, even if it meant saying something hurtful. She started with the visit by Commander von Baumann and then her haste to get her family papers from the summer house, the late train, and staying over.

"Was Netch there?"

Madeleine knew that would be her first question. "Yes, and he drove me to the station the next day."

Therese fell silent without looking at her. "Did you spend time with him?"

Madeleine sighed. "Not that kind of time, Therese. We went out and met friends and had dinner and went to a jazz club. That's all. It was fun and good to be in the unoccupied zone. Netch and I have a marriage of convenience. I've told you that many times. He may be able to help me get all my new gowns out of the country. There's talk of closing off the unoccupied zone to everyone soon, which means it will be extremely difficult to get my gowns to Portugal to mail. If he can help, then I'll accept his offer. My relationship with him has always been about business, Therese, just business." She took a long breath.

"Yes, business in bed just like before when you ran off and got married. You have an interesting way of looking at business."

"Therese, let's not do this, not now. We're both stressed and we don't need to add more angst to our lives." She took Therese's hand.

"You are the most important person in my life. That doesn't mean we don't need others as well for whatever reasons."

Therese was abrupt. "Yes, as usual you're right." She stood and looked toward the door. "I'm going home to get some sleep."

Madeleine was aware of Therese's abandonment issues and her own as well. "You don't need to be afraid that you'll lose me or lose our friendship. That will never happen. I want to assure you of that. Why don't you stay here tonight? I can see that you're tired."

"No, I'll go home."

"Therese, what's happening?"

Therese didn't answer but walked to the door, leaving the box of candles on a desk near the coat rack. Their scent lingered behind her.

When the door closed Madeleine put her face in her hands and then folded her arms over her head, feeling the tears stream down her face. *Damn, why did I have to talk on and on about Netch? Won't I ever learn?*

When Therese reached her apartment the notice was nailed to the door:

All American citizens in the Occupied Zone are required to register with the nearest German Kommandatur by 6 p.m. on December 17, 1941. All American journalists in Paris will be interned with other American correspondents to await deportation to the U.S. Be prepared to leave.

She stood breathless. *My god, they must know who I am and where I live!*

The next morning she walked briskly to Shakespeare and Co., the American bookstore in the 6th Arrondissement where she'd met the owner, an American named Sylvia Beach, at Gertrude Stein's and often bought books at the shop. Sylvia was well-connected with the American community in Paris. If anyone knew the plight of Americans, she'd be the one. Heavy planks of wood sealed the front entrance to the shop and the sign in the front window said *closed* so Therese took the side stairs to

Sylvia's apartment above the store. When the door opened a crack Sylvia recognized Therese and pulled her in quickly. Her sweater smelled like burnt coal and they talked over tea in stained cups.

"I'm registering with the Gestapo since it's hard to hide the fact that I'm American," Sylvia said while pouring more tea. "I closed the shop a few weeks ago and hid all the books and names of customers, and now I'm waiting to see what's next."

Therese showed her the note from the door. "What do you make of this? Do they really have time to fight this war and monitor Americans' whereabouts in Paris?"

"I can't imagine it although they're interning American men, maybe because they seem more of a threat and the same might be true for journalists. That could explain the note on the door. Your work and your name are well-known here, Therese. Some Americans are staying in Paris, either collaborating with the Germans or resisting, but most have gone into hiding." She breathed a deep sigh and sat blinking. "I'd leave if I didn't have this shop. What are your plans Therese? I thought you'd be gone by now. Is there a reason you want to stay?"

Therese was silent for a moment. "I don't know, it's complicated."

They wished each other luck and Therese left more uncertain than ever. She wondered if she should leave for the countryside to continue with her work, but then as an American she'd never get back into Paris. *We're now the enemy whereas before we were just a nuisance.*

She walked for a while and found a bench in the park, and thought about her oft-troublesome friendship with Madeleine. A small part of her was happy there was someone, even if it was Netch, who would probably take care of her if she could no longer stay in Paris. Even if she did stay, he might help her mail her gowns so that Madeleine could continue with the work she loved. But the ache, the dreaded anticipation of a possible reconciliation between them filled her with grief and fear. *Why is this so hard for me? I can't stake claim to her, her time, her person - that would be morally wrong if not frustratingly impossible. There is a stark honesty about her at times even if I don't want to hear it, especially if it has to do with her husband. Nevertheless, it seems to trigger something in me. It makes me feel so alone, so deserted.*

She walked again, and wanted to run to Madeleine's, to soothe things, to set it straight but she still felt hurt, and scared. She stopped to look at people in a long line near rue de l'Odéon just beyond the metro station. As she got closer she could see they carried honey tins hoping the honey wagon might show up, Wishful thinking, she thought. It had been weeks and no wagon or honey. Sights like that were familiar all over Paris and the food shortage was worsening.

In the next block she crossed the street to get away from the stench of rotting garbage piled at the curb. Ahead, she saw the unmistakable *round-up* truck with swastikas on both sides and German soldiers following on foot close behind. She stood behind a tree as two Germans escorted a woman from an apartment building clutching her shawl while the rest of it dragged along the ground. When they lowered the truck gate she saw a group women huddled close together. She walked closer and recognized Katherine Emory, an American painter she'd met at Gertrude's salon, and two other American women she knew from the Red Cross.

When the truck moved on, she hurried back to the bookstore banging loudly on Sylvia Beach's door. When Sylvia appeared, Therese said out of breath, "The Germans are picking up American women in a large truck. I just saw them just a few blocks away."

"Come in, quickly. I just heard. They're interning them in the old zoo north of here, even American nuns, anyone American. That's all I know." She peeked through the curtains. "I'm sure they'll come for me too."

"Do you want to hide somewhere, I might know of some empty buildings. My place is no longer safe."

Sylvia shook her head. "Given the shortage of food we may be better off with the Germans right now. I'm sure this is temporary," she said squeezing her hands together. "They seem to be going after the Americans and not the Jews right now." The two stood looking out the upstairs window. "Have you decided what you'll do, Therese?"

"No, not really. I plan to keep my lights off and the door locked for now. I know that for certain."

It was dusk when she climbed the stairs to her apartment and ran her hand along the smooth wall feeling for the light switch, and then she remembered: *No lights! Keep them off!* She walked into her dim apartment and closed the door behind her and that's when she saw the intruding black boot preventing it from closing.

Fifty-Three

SHE WAS TAKEN away with only a hastily-packed bag. The Gestapo allowed her to keep her camera but confiscated her film and maps with directional notes. Fortunately, she had sent everything else of importance to her publishers and family in New York months ago. She glanced back as she was led away and saw a pair of baggy pants and a scarf on the bed and dishes in the sink.

Two Gestapo agents prodded her into a truck that smelled of urine and in minutes she was herded into a remote building where she recognized two other American journalists; one from the *New York Herald Tribune* and another from the Associated Press. Both sweated profusely in spite of the cold. She approached several German guards asking to use a telephone but they just looked away.

"I need to get a message to someone," she pleaded. "Please, I need to make a phone call. *Ich brauche einen telefonanruf zu tätigen.* You can listen in but I desperately need to tell someone I'm leaving. I'm Therese Bonney and . . ."

She continued, but if they did answer it was always the same: "*Nein, Nein, Nein.*"

She moved away from the others and when no one was looking, inched closer to the door. *My god, can I really do this?*

She took a step outside long enough to see armed soldiers swarming in all directions. She rushed back inside and leaned against the wall, then slid to the floor putting her head in her hands. She hated how she'd left it with Madeleine, what was said, her own sudden departure after hearing about Netch. *How stupid of me! I had no right to expect anything, anything at all. They're married and I'm the one who kept telling her to get out of Paris, to leave for her summer house, to be safe . . . and now this. No chance to say goodbye, no reassurance, no way to reach her.*

She looked up and eyed a young soldier standing nearby who smiled when their eyes met briefly. She got up and walked over. Reaching for whatever francs she had stuffed in her coat pocket, she said in a whisper. "Can you deliver a message for me." She held out the handful of francs. "It's a short message. Please." He looked around and then nodded, but just then a group of helmeted Nazi soldiers stormed into the room with rifles pointing. *"Bewegen schnell! Bewegen schnell!"* They were being told to move quickly. She glanced at the young officer who just shrugged as she and the others were whisked away.

After several hours of waiting at a remote railway station on the outskirts of Paris, the journalists were led to a long line of rail cars. With a sliver of light from the moon, Therese stumbled over each section of the track trying to keep close to the others until one by one they were being pushed up into a darkened rail car. When it was her turn she felt a rifle in the small of her back so she moved quickly. The musty smell of stale urine stung her nose and she wiped the perspiration from the back of her neck as she looked for a way out, only to be pushed further into the dark interior. After the last journalist was in, the door rolled shut with a jolt. Hearing the click of the padlock took her breath away and the journalists looked around and then briefly at each other. They huddled together on the floor, eight of them, and felt the train shudder before the wheels started to rumble over the rails in a monotonous rhythm. *Where are they taking us?*

Once her eyes adjusted to the dark she noticed a child's stuffed doll amongst the debris on the floor and she reached for it. The journalist from the Cleveland *Star* half smiled then looked away. Another found a dark sweater and draped it over his shoulders as a buffer from the cold. Everyone stared. Stitched on the front was a gold Star of David.

"This is one of the trains to Auschwitz! This is the Jewish train to Auschwitz!" one of them blurted out. "We've got to get out of here!" He crawled to the door, inching his fingers into the crack where the door was latched and tried to pull it open, then he clawed at the clapboard wood siding trying to squeeze his fingers between the boards where fine lines of moonlight seeped through.

"Coleman, Coleman, it's alright." A reporter who knew him reached over and grabbed him by the shoulders, pulling him back to the group. "We're going to America, that's what they said. Stay calm, now. Just stay calm." The man put his face in his hands and sobbed. A few glanced at Therese. As the only woman in the group perhaps they expected her to comfort him. It was all she could do but sit quietly and deal with her own fear.

They rode through the night and into the next day. When the train slowed late that afternoon they held hands, some trembling. When the door rolled open, light beams with specks of dust burst into the rail car as they squinted to see. A German soldier yelled. *"Aus, Aus."*

"They want us out," one said, and they helped each other once their eyes acclimated to the light. Most stood and stared, for in the distance was an airstrip and they knew at that moment they would be going to America.

Madeleine called every hour. *It was a terrible way to end the evening.* She wanted to say she was sorry and assure her that she was not getting back with Netch and that she would never abandon her. She thought about the irony of Therese's courage in her work, yet the depths of insecurity when it came to her private life. *I know I lost her trust when I married but how can I change that?* She called all the next day and by the following morning she was desperate. *Why isn't she answering? Agh. I should have consoled her instead of filling her with doubt. Why can't I get this right?*

Mounds of feather-light snow filled the crevices of the iron gate, and settled onto the cobblestone walkway. She pulled her coat and scarf close to her chin when she stepped from her townhouse, squinting to keep the cold from stinging her eyes. The street was quiet except for a man selling small tins of coal on the corner, his wool hat pulled down to his bushy eyebrows. A few military trucks sat vacant at the curb and the broken sign in a café window blinked "-*afé*" off and on.

She walked through the snow and quickened her pace the closer she got to Therese's apartment. Out of breath, she grabbed the hand rail and walked up the stairs to the second floor. Therese used her apartment for business and her unit took up the entire floor. On the last step Madeleine stopped abruptly. Therese's door was wide open, papers were scattered on the floor, and drawers were pulled from their cases. Therese and her camera were gone.

Racing back down the stairs and onto the street, she pushed through the snow like a weighted ox and took a shortcut through the park, losing a glove along the way. Snow flurries scattered in curling eddies landing in small mountains of snow on the barely visible cobblestone walkway, and the distant smell of burning coal came and went with each breath. The snow blew softly against her face, and the bitter cold sliced painfully through her coat. She put her hands deep in her pockets and pushed until her shoulders ached. The park was empty; *everything is empty, barren, gone. Everything that matters is gone.*

She ran the rest of the way, breathless and sweaty as she bolted through her front door, her hands numb, and her coat on the floor as she searched for the number and then dialed.

He answered. "*Hallo, ja.*"

"Commander von Baumann, I need your help, please. This is Madeleine Vionnet."

Therese Bonney's name was on a list of journalists returned to the United States with no known address, he told her when he called back that afternoon. "It's all I could find. Mail, phone, and wire services have been suspended so you probably won't be hearing from your friend any time soon. I'm sorry Madame Vionnet. I sensed this was an urgent matter for you."

"Yes, thank you so much for checking on this for me." Her voice was lifeless. Then she asked, "Not Auschwitz, can you assure me?"

"I can assure you, Madame Vionnet, not Auschwitz."

She hung up and put her head down on the desk, pulling the box of Therese's candles close to her

In the weeks to come it poured every day and there was nothing left but glistening streets and rain drops on the windows. Madeleine made a list of every contact Therese had ever mentioned in New York, including her publishers, the museums, the universities where she lectured, and her newspaper contacts. She didn't have the address of the family home in New York but she wrote down Louise's name even though she'd moved to upstate New York when their mother died. She added Gertrude Stein and Raoul Dufy to the list but they were in France, at least she thought that's what Therese had told her.

Every day she wrote a letter to someone on the list, even if the address was incomplete, asking that they pass a message on to Therese Bonney if they knew her whereabouts. The message was short: *Please tell her someone in Paris is waiting for her return.* All of her letters came back stamped *Pas de service de messagerie - no service* - but that didn't stop her; she still wrote every day. On some level she knew it was useless, but for her it was better than doing nothing. The memories of her life with Therese were vivid. She tried to forget but found that impossible.

She worked less and had trouble finding her creative spirit so she talked to colleagues and friends but found those conversations less than heartfelt. The connection she missed was the one she once had with Therese, who reminded her that she was not just one in the universe but part of it; that the true gift was to find one to share the minutia of everyday life as well as the deepest and most profound inner self.

The American journalists arrived in Norfolk, Virginia from Sweden by private plane as part of a reciprocal agreement to exchange eight American journalists in France for twelve German nationals in the U.S. Therese and the others were given money for emergency food and clothing and for travel to their destinations. Therese asked to call Paris, but was told the Germans had commandeered the lines in France and no calls could go through. Exhausted, she took a train into New York to the family apartment, now empty. The following morning she called the OSS director, Bill Donovan.

"Therese, where in the heck are you? Hopefully in the U.S."

"Bill, can you get me back to Paris? I was rounded up with the other journalists and returned to the U.S. I need to get back to France."

"Whoa, why on earth . . ."

"It's personal, Bill, please don't ask. You owe me a favor and I need your help."

"Therese, there's no safe way to get you back into France, at least not now. You know we plan to . . . well, expand our reach there but it won't be any time soon. Once we are there and the Germans retreat I might be able to do something."

"What about going now to do espionage?"

"Too risky. We're using local people, mostly in the Resistance. Our American agents are at risk of being sent to camps, in fact some already have."

"And getting a message to someone in Paris? I can't get through," she said anguished.

"No, no to that as well. Every message is considered a threat and jumped on by German code breakers. We do have contacts there and ways to reach them but we can't jeopardize their anonymity. I'm sorry Therese, war is war unfortunately, and we're in the thick of it right now."

She was silent for a moment. "Well, what about this? I'd like to go along as a military photojournalist if and when America sends troops to France. I know of course that's the plan so don't deny it. I have the credentials, Bill. Can that be arranged?"

"You don't give up, do you?" he said chuckling. "That might work. Let's talk again when the time comes. In the meantime, welcome back. At least you won't be dodging bullets here in the States, although I rather think you enjoy that."

It was 1942 and while the world was at war, Madeleine and Therese were on opposite sides of the Atlantic Ocean after twenty-three years together. Therese once told Madeleine they met in order to challenge and awaken each other's spirit and they did, struggling and succeeding like few women ever had. Before Madeleine, Therese never knew what it was like to have a close friend. Now she was finding out what it means to lose one. *What happens to people when close friendships end? Do they forget each other in time? Will I forget Madeleine? Will I forget her laugh or the fragrant scent of candle wax on her table? Will this cavern of emptiness ever go away?*

Fifty-Four

DAYS AND NIGHTS dragged slowly into months for both Madeleine and Therese. Following the Allied landings in French North Africa in November 1942, Hitler ordered the occupation of the Vichy free zone - meaning all of France was now occupied by German forces as the Allies inched closer by the day, but slowly.

Madeleine's trips to her summer home in the south came to an abrupt end not only because the free zone was now occupied, but because Netch's generous offer to help smuggle her gowns out of France was not as altruistic as it first appeared. His frequent innuendos about sharing a bed during her visits turned serious one night when he entered her bedroom uninvited. She fought him off and called the gendarmes, who drove her to the train station where she waited during the night for the morning train back to Paris.

When she arrived home her first call was to her attorney asking him to file divorce papers and to stop the transfer of her voluntary monthly check to Netch. "It's about time," was his only remark. Her second call was to Netch notifying him of the divorce and cessation of the monthly check, and giving him forty-eight hours to vacate her house.

"Oh, come on baby, it's just that . . . well, you're still my wife and well, you know, you still have some obligations. Look, I'm sorry things got a little rough . . ."

"You have forty-eight hours, Netch. If you're not out by then I'll have you arrested." She hung up.

She ached to tell Therese. Someday, she thought. She felt good about her decision, but wishing she would have made it sooner. *Therese never asked about their arrangement but she must have wondered. I should have been more candid with her; that I had used him to take care of business arrangements and felt guilty so I let him stay at the house and sent a monthly check. My real mistake was marrying him in the first place and without telling her. Trust becomes a fragile illusion after such a betrayal.*

Ironically another of her nemeses, Thèophile Bader, was no longer an antagonist. She received word that he died after a long illness. She sent condolences to his family and attended his funeral as a courtesy. With Bader and Netch out of her life she should be happy but she wasn't. *I wonder if Therese will even return to France after the war. She may settle in New York; she has connections there, people think well of her.*

On the other side of the Atlantic, Therese was restless in New York, normally a stimulating place for her. She translated for the government and occasionally worked with a few budding theater companies still struggling on the upper west side of Manhattan. Louise had married and moved upstate so Therese took the train to visit, and when Louise came to the city they'd have lunch and visit their mother's gravesite. But her usual optimism for life had waned and her enthusiasm for work had all but disappeared.

She missed Paris, realizing it was truly her home and that Madeleine was a necessary - even though at times complicated - part of her life. Yet she was away from both and there was nothing she could do about. Time moved like a broken clock.

Her listlessness turned into depression. She started projects but didn't finish. She was asked to write the script for a film based on her book *Europe's Children* and told the producer she would, but only when the war was over. She didn't admit that she lacked the concentration for such a project at the time. When asked in an interview if she would be taking photographs in America, she said,

"I've lived the emotions of the war through the lens. How can I possibly return to commercial photography? There's nothing left to take that wouldn't seem trivial."

Most of her time was spent following the Allied forces in Europe, meticulously mapping the progress on large sheets of paper on her desk. When North Africa was secured by the Allies and the U.S. and Great

Britain launched the strategic invasion of Italy in 1943, she became more optimistic. Maybe we're getting close, she thought to herself. She called Bill Donovan.

"My bags are packed, Bill. Any chance getting to Paris with one of the infantry divisions?"

"Not yet, Therese, we don't have a strong-enough foothold right now. I'll get you there sooner or later, so check back with me."

"Can you at least get a message to someone in Paris for me, Bill?"

"Therese, all of our communication lines are used for war-related correspondence only, you know that. Paris is closed off tighter than a drum since Hitler's digging in his heels there. I'm sorry my dear. Be patient, this can't last forever."

In the months to come, the Allied push into Italy moved steadily and the Italian government finally signed an armistice after ousting Prime Minister Benito Mussolini. The Italians danced in the street, but the German forces fighting there stood firm and it took several major offensives until the Allies finally broke through and captured Rome. Therese put a large circle on her map with an arrow pointing to France.

Soon! I know I'll be home soon! That was late spring of 1944.

The telephone rang during the night. She turned the light on next to the bed and glanced at the clock. Three a.m.

"If you're still interested, the closest I can get you to Paris is a town in northeast France called Ammerschwihr near Colmar." She recognized Bill Donovan's voice. "We think it will be a German stronghold once they're forced to retreat from Russia. Our forces will probably need to push them back across the Rhine and behind their own borders at some point. I can make a case for sending someone to take preliminary photos of the landscape, roads, and anything else of interest to our armies. Are you interested? You'll be on your own in terms of transportation while you're there but I'm sure you can find a way to Paris when you finish the assignment."

"Yes! Yes, of course! Yes! I'm ready, just tell me when. I'm packed and have been for a long time. Thank you, Bill. Thank you!"

"Alright, alright. You may encounter some action, so keep your head down. I can get you out of New York on a military plane. Someone will be there to brief you. And by the way, my dear, now you owe me," he said chuckling. "Someday you'll have to tell me what's so important in Paris."

The French village of Ammerschwihr known for its vineyards and rock quarries was indeed a strategic location. The scenic town across the Rhine from Germany became Therese's home during the next several weeks as she photographed the terrain and roads surrounding the tranquil little hamlet. Weary but helmeted German troops were already gathering but paid scant attention to her or anyone else and posed little threat. Clearly, they were exhausted from war and knew they were close to going home. She could see it in their eyes and knew the feeling herself.

As soon as she found a small room at the inn she bought a bicycle and pedaled once a week to the larger town of Colmar to meet with her contact who passed her film on to the OSS and Bill Donovan. Her contact, a simple man who wore a bow tie and tortoise-rimmed glasses had no name; at least not one he could divulge. He explained that was the rule in the Resistance: no names so they can't be traced. She met him in a café on the square where he sipped an espresso every Tuesday morning at eleven o'clock and waited for her to deliver the film. One morning she asked him if anyone made regular trips to Paris, that she had an important message that had to be delivered.

"Hmm, no, the fighting is still intense between here and Paris. It's not safe to travel and the lines are either down or commandeered by the Germans. We're using secured wires and even they're unstable. Are you in any danger from the Germans in Ammerschwihr?"

"No, not really. I think after their defeat in Russia they've given up hope. They don't even notice me, probably thinking I'm just a local resident," she said before getting back on her bicycle.

The townspeople in Ammerschwihr however, knew differently. They weren't sure who she was but assumed she was there for an important reason. At her request they quietly passed on war news almost daily from their hidden radios. It wasn't unusual for someone to stop by the inn with a bottle of local Gewurztraminer or Riesling from their cellar and casually report the latest war news. She liked the cordial collaboration with the townspeople and integrated with them eagerly, tasting their wines, walking with the elders, playing with the children and teaching them to make kites from twigs and old newspapers. She bought string for the kites on the black market in Colmar much to the children's delight.

One quiet afternoon in June when a light rain dampened the cobblestone streets and Therese was leaning her bicycle against the stone wall outside the inn, Jacques Pitou, the local baker, ran from the Patisserie across the road. His eyes were wide and flour dusted his beard as he stood there in his while smock out of breath.

"Miss Bonney," he said quietly, "they've landed. The Allies have landed at Normandy!"

Therese let out a loud shout of joy and they hugged and laughed nervously hoping the Germans wouldn't notice. They both knew what that meant. The Americans were finally on French soil!

Fifty-Five

MADELEINE WOKE to noise in the street and sat up quickly before falling back on the pillow with a slight groan. Reaching for her calendar near the nightstand she checked for appointments. *June 7, 1944, no appointments. Thank goodness!* She stretched and sank into the bed covers. *Therese was sent back to America over two years ago.* It was a thought she repeated almost every day. She pulled the pillow over her head then tossed it off and got out of bed. The floor was cool so she stepped into her slippers and turned on the radio as she was accustomed to doing every morning after Therese left. She turned the dial searching for news.

. . . the largest amphibious invasion in history is taking place in France as nearly 200,000 Allied troops, 7,000 ships, and more than 3,000 planes are heading toward Normandy . . .

She stumbled while reaching for another station and pulled on an errant slipper that had fallen off.

Some 156,000 troops have landed on French beaches, 24,000 by air and the rest by sea where they were met by stiff resistance from well- defended German positions across fifty-some miles of the coast. In spite of the German defense, the Allies have landed on French soil and the French have taken to the streets of Paris!

Stunned, she sat on the edge of the bed, her eyes filling with tears. *My god, will this really be over soon?* She put her hands to her face in disbelief. *I wonder if Therese knows, wherever she is.*

The noise in the street caught her attention again and she went to the window, throwing it open. In the distance she heard cheering even though several ominous German trucks moved slowly through the streets. She wondered where Therese was at that very moment and hoped she'd heard the news.

In Ammerschwihr Therese pedaled faster that morning, her thighs burning and her chest heaving as she reached Colmar on her bicycle in just under thirty minutes, her fastest time yet. She and her OSS contact found a quiet table.

"Is Donovan pleased with the photographs and notes?"

He wore his usual bow tie and his glasses were perched high on his nose. "Yes. He said you'd be asking when you can leave now that Paris might soon be liberated. Your work is helping us a great deal, Miss Bonney, so we hope you're not in a rush to move on."

She said to him in earnest, "I need to get to Paris when my assignment is finished here. Do you know when that will be?"

"No, but Donovan said you'd be asking that too. He said to wait a little longer; that is, if you asked."

"Why is that?"

"For your own safety. There's no telling what will happen in Paris when the Allied forces arrive and if the Germans hold a firm line."

"That's all the more reason I need to get there. Is it possible to get a message to someone there? I might not be in such a rush to leave if that's a possibility. Just a brief message?"

He drummed his fingers on the table and looked around the square. "It's very difficult; there are risks."

"And you don't think I'm taking risks?"

He drummed his fingers harder on the table and looked at her. His eyes softened. "I can see your point. Write an address and your brief message," he said pushing a piece of paper toward her. "The Resistance is everywhere. Maybe we can get a message through but I can't be sure."

She scribbled Madeleine's address and: *I'm trying to get there, hopefully soon. Therese.* "Thank you," she said sliding the note back to him."

"We'll hope for the best," he said, putting the note in his shirt pocket.

"On another matter," she said. "What will happen to these people in Ammerschwihr when the Allies chase the Germans back across the Rhine? Do you expect there will be casualties?"

He massaged his chin and glanced at her. "Ah, we all wish we knew the answer to that in war. My guess is that the Germans won't just up and leave. There could be heavy bombing if they stay and resist."

Therese was silent.

"Miss Bonney if you want to help these people, urge them to go into the forest at the first sign of battle. Their stone houses will fall like playing cards if they're bombed. Their wine cellars might be safe but then they'd have rubble on top of them."

She nodded slowly. "Is the information I'm giving Donovan going to work against these people?"

"No, quite the opposite we hope. It should help us to pinpoint the targets. But again, that depends on how much bombing is needed. This isn't like baking a cake where you follow a recipe and the outcome is assured."

She peddled more slowly back to Ammerschwihr.

The following day she went to see the mayor who was actually the owner of the local pub, *The Wild Boar*. She asked him if the village residents had an evacuation plan if the area was attacked or bombed. He responded that they did. It was the same plan they had for landslides, avalanches, earthquakes, fires, or a measles outbreak.

"And what would that be?"

"Escape into the forest or hide in your wine cellar. We know what to do," he said winking.

The following week she met with her contact at the café, anxious for any news about her message to Madeleine. She knew by the look on his face that he didn't have good news.

He ran his hand across his chin. "We were able to send someone with your message but unfortunately no one was living at that address. In asking neighbors, it seems no one had been living there for some time. Sorry, Miss Bonney, at least we were able to try."

"Yes, well thank you, thank you very much. I'll see you next week."

She walked her bicycle around the square and down a side street near the old church. *No one at that address?* She wandered down by a small stream where some children were fishing on a ramp. Their laughter was not very comforting.

A few weeks later while she was pouring another cup of tea she heard banging at the door.

"Therese! Therese, open up!"

She put her cup down and reached for the latch.

"Get out! We've got to get out of here!" Her bespectacled contact from Colmar stood there out of breath, his tie loosened and his hair drenched with perspiration. A waiting jeep revved the engine, the driver looking at them intently.

"My camera!" She nodded to the bag near the door. He grabbed her sleeve but she broke loose long enough to pick up the bag and run behind him to the jeep. They left mounds of dust as they raced down the road, the contact shouting directions to the driver while Therese sat numb clinging to her bag.

"What's happening? Therese yelled.

"It's time," her contact said.

Fifty-Six

THE LAST BATTLES of World War II left a string of bombed-out French villages especially near the Rhine where the retreating German army settled in for a fight. The five-hundred year old stone architecture in the villages was no match for the massive artillery and bombing it took to force the German soldiers out of France and back into Germany. Therese and her contact, under orders from Donovan, were driven three hundred miles away - far enough to avoid the devastation. When it was over, she was driven back to Ammerschwihr at her request. Donovan tried to talk her out of it, saying nothing is left of the region.

"Dammit, Donovan, you owe me this much. I knew these people. I ate with them, listened to their radios, played with their children."

"Okay, okay. We'll get you back there. But look, Therese, this is war. You of all people should know that. Don't expect to find much."

As she feared, the town of Ammerschwihr had become a stronghold for the retreating Germans and was leveled. According to reports, the buildings and much of the population were all but decimated. When she arrived, some of the fires were still burning and the French 1st Army was there with some of the allied troops filtering in.

"Are we doing anything to help here like moving rubble and looking for people?" she asked a commanding officer in the field.

"Take a look for yourself, there's no life here." He shrugged before getting into a jeep.

She stood in an empty street where only stones and wood beams remained. She wasn't even sure which street it was since the town had crumbled from the bombs. She turned to walk back to a makeshift base but at the far end of the street she thought she saw something move. Squinting, she walked slowly in that direction over rubble and debris. *A sniper? I should get out of here.* She turned back to follow the jeep but all she saw was dust from its tracks. She shifted her camera bag to the other shoulder and got ready to walk. When she looked back toward the street she narrowed her eyes again and stood staring.

What . . .? A dog? An old black dog came ambling down the street and stopped for a long stretch and then spotting her, came wagging its tail.

She ran as fast as she could chasing the commander's jeep, catching up and banging on the fender. Within minutes scores of soldiers uncovered the rubble from wine cellar doors while those inside pushed from below. The townspeople emerged, first the Rousseau family, then old Jacques Droite, the baker and his wife, and others as they told how they could hear the bombs and see the fires raging from cracks in the cellar doors. They used Rieslings, Gewürztraminers, and Pinot Blancs to soak the cellar doors from the inside out to keep them from burning - evidently an old survival technique passed down through generations. While the rubble was still being moved, scores of people came out of the forest where they'd been hiding in 17th century caves.

In the meantime, the allied forces continued to march on Paris. She received a hand-delivered note from Donovan.

Well done, my dear Therese. A Red Cross truck will pick you up Friday evening at dusk. Now go, get yourself to Paris. Keep your head down and stay in touch. BD

She sat in the back with four men. A driver and army nurse sat up front but no one spoke, no one wanted to. She wondered who they were and what their story was, but she kept her eyes forward, thankful to be heading toward Paris even in the midst of isolated battles still raging in parts of northern France.

The aerial explosions lit the sky like bursting stars, illuminating scenes from the landscape like flickering news reels in an old theater. She choked more than once on the unmistakable smell of bombs and burning debris as she gripped the hand rail in the Red Cross truck as it sped along the darkened road, swerving back and forth to miss the flying shrapnel. Finally, she wrapped her face in her purple scarf. *I've had enough of this. I just want to be done with war, to get my life back and be safe again.* She pushed her palms against her ears and squeezed her eyes tight.

Shortly after midnight everything stopped, no noise, no shelling, just a peaceful silence like the lull before dawn on an ordinary day. After blinking several times she stared at the unbelievable sight straight ahead: the dim outline of the Eiffel Tower! *Oh my god!*

She clutched her scarf and squeezed tight and an overwhelming gush of emotion took her breath away. *Am I home? After two years, am I finally home?* She repeated that over and over as the truck slowed to join a caravan of others at the entrance to the city.

Hundreds of barricades were pushed aside as French and Allied trucks drove into Paris in the dark slowing to a crawl as thousands of people spilled onto the road and roamed aimlessly, some with candles or small French or American flags. A cacophony of sounds, joyous shouts, gunshots from renegade German snipers, airplanes overhead, and the distant roar of Allied tanks were heard from all directions.

When the streets looked familiar, Therese signaled the driver to stop and yelled, "thanks," before jumping out. When her feet hit the ground the tears rolled down her face and she brushed them aside with her gritty hand and sleeve. She allowed herself the words that had been waiting. *Where is Madeleine? Who's she with . . . where did she go? Is she alive?*

Without a plan she walked through neighborhoods seeing shattered windows, empty shops, broken bicycles and old car parts weary with rust and propped against buildings in sad repair. *So much more devastation than before!* Nazi flags torn and shredded littered the streets, and occasional bullets from lone German snipers pierced the air or ricocheted off lamp posts sending people to huddle together until it was quiet. She tried to get to Madeleine's street, to see for herself, but barricades and Allied tanks sealed off much of the city.

She found herself at her old apartment and wondered if someone else might be living there. The streets were still dark and she climbed the stairs to see that the door was closed so she knocked lightly before pushing it open. Inside it was just as she remembered. Papers littered the floor and a few clothes on the bed, and dishes in the sink. A flood of memories of that fateful day sprinted through her mind - being dragged off after stuffing a few items in her bag and flown to America. She walked around the apartment, glancing in every room and turning on the water. The pipes moaned at first but water flowed so she took a cold shower, washed her clothes, and collapsed on the bed in a cloud of dust while cockroaches scrambled to the floor and disappeared under the debris.

The hot August sun burned through the east window and onto the bed waking her. She sneezed from the dust and looked around to get her bearings. *Oh, I can hardly believe it! In my own apartment, and in Paris!* She squinted at the pictures on the walls now askew, and ran her hand over the bedspread she remembered but now covered with dust. An old baggy sweater hung lopsided from a hanger in the closet and some favorite hats were miraculously still piled on a shelf above some hanging peasant skirts and sloppy trousers in the closet. She laughed and cried at the same time, pounding her hand on the bed in a joyous gesture until she sneezed again from yet another cloud of dust.

She leaped out of bed, feeling the wooden floor warm her feet where the sun had settled. The floor looked like spice in the grainy ray of light. At the window, a sultry breeze brought with it a hint of jasmine from the tangled vine below and she wiped her eyes making no effort to stop the tears of joy. When she focused again, she straightened and stared at the sight. For miles in every direction the streets were swarming with people! All she could hear was one loud continuous roar and she covered her ears with her hands but then let go, feeling the urge to roar with them. Quickly, she doused her face and found some tooth powder and a toothbrush, then grabbed some clothes, throwing them on before running downstairs.

"I've been away. Have the Allies taken the city yet?" she yelled at a passerby.

"Today is the big day, August 25th 1944, a day we'll always remember." He waved his small French flag playfully. "The Resistance has taken the Hotel de Ville, or the city hall, and the Germans have all

Madeleine and Therese

but retreated except for a few remaining snipers. General De Gaulle is giving an official Paris liberation speech at noon today in the square." He hugged her before running off down the street. Everyone embraced for as far as she could see. Several strangers stopped to throw their arms around her and she hugged back not knowing what else to do. Half-lives were becoming whole again and Paris was on the brink of finding itself once more. Her skin tingled at the thought and the tears stained her face once more.

Light-headed with excitement, she walked among the people and through the streets of Paris with its carnival-like atmosphere. *Unbelievable, just unbelievable.* She'd never seen anything like it. As she got closer to the square, horns honked, confetti filled the air, and the steady din of cheers and song took command on every street as Parisians reclaimed their city, spilling onto the streets to celebrate, stomping on German flags, and tearing Swastika posters from the walls ripping then into tiny pieces.

Therese tried desperately to reach Madeleine's street but the thick tide of people kept pushing her back toward the square. She finally secured a place to stand on a nearby hill where she and Madeleine used to walk, and where she could hear the speech. When De Gaulle shouted, "Paris! Paris outraged! Paris broken! Paris martyred! But Paris liberated!" the roar was so deafening she covered her ears and could almost feel the ground shake beneath her feet.

She watched the people, some ill, some hungry, some weary, but all jubilant in their own way. Mothers carried babies holding them high in the air to witness history, and others leaned together in a reunion and re-creation of spirit. It was at that moment she saw her near a stand of trees, disbelieving at first and then squinting hard. On a knoll about forty feet away Madeleine stood alone under a flowering dogwood tree watching the square from a distance. Breathing hard and her heart pounding, Therese pushed in that directions never averting her gaze for fear of losing sight of her in the maze of people. She stumbled through the high grass and wove her way through crowds and children playing on the grassy hill, and through the deafening noise, the chaos, through the warm August air, her feet barely touching the ground. Madeleine was wearing a summer dress and her sage-colored straw hat, shielding her eyes from the glaring sun. Therese kept pushing toward her. Madeleine was thinner, her hair more gray, and as she got closer, her face, weary and drawn.

At that moment Madeleine turned, looking directly at her with a deep, penetrating and disbelieving gaze. Therese was wearing old military trousers and a taupe-colored sweater. Her purple scarf was wrapped twice and her hair, long and unruly, blew about in the warm breeze. She wasn't sure if Madeleine saw her. She stopped for the longest moment and held her breath. They both stared at each other and then Madeleine put her hand to her mouth. The only thing Therese remembered after that was her face buried into Madeleine's shoulder as they clutched each other. Therese squeezed her eyes shut to stop the tears. Madeleine pulled her face close, her hands trembling. "Open, open your eyes so I can really see it's you." When Therese finally did the world was an ocean with only bits and pieces bobbing to the surface becoming clear momentarily. She couldn't stop the flow of tears. Nor could she hear the roar of the crowd at the end of De Gaulle's speech - only Madeleine's soft whispers, tender and healing, and only intermittent memories of the bewilderment of separation.

Fifty-Seven

AFTER THE reporters left, Solange brought Madeleine a cool glass of water and put it by her bedside. Therese had insisted that Madeleine have a full-time nurse now that she was ninety-eight. Therese offered but Madeleine said what she'd always said. "We need to be free to be creative individuals." Therese thought that amusing since at ninety-eight Madeleine had all but given up her work. Therese surmised that her comment was really meant for her, though at eighty she was slowing down a bit as well.

Solange straightened Madeleine's pillow. "Why didn't you talk to the reporters about your involvement during the war? You know, settle the thing about the Nazis. The reporters . . ."

Therese interrupted. "There's no need for her to talk about that to anyone. It's 1975 and that happened over thirty years ago."

"I know, but she said she wanted to put it to rest. Isn't that why she agreed to the interview?"

"You two stop quibbling." Madeleine said, taking a sip of water. "There's always gossip. People don't always remember things the way they were. Some still confuse me with Coco Chanel who lived with her Nazi lover at the Ritz. It's not my place to constantly be correcting them." She waved her hand impatiently.

"What I wanted to talk about was how I continued making dresses during the war and snubbed the Nazis." She moved a bit and pulled herself up straight. "Some thought I collaborated with the Nazis in order to get the fabric, which of course I didn't."

"Why didn't you tell them that?" Solange said still prying.

"I didn't like the way the question was asked, as if I owed them an explanation. I don't have to tell them anything." She took a labored breath. "I bought the fabric before the war and we stored it under the floorboards of my villa. And I was harassed by the Gestapo continually because I was making dresses. It really irked Hitler. Remember Therese, remember the floorboards?"

"I remember them well."

"It doesn't matter," Solange said. "I think the reporters were pleased with your comments." She glanced at Therese and then left the room to answer the door. She reappeared a few minutes later.

"A young woman said she left her gloves." They all glanced around the room. Therese got up and moved some chairs and Solange looked behind the chairs pushed against the wall. "Ah," she said picking up a pair of beige leather gloves and leaving the room. In a minute she was back. "The young woman wonders if she could have a word with you."

Therese started to say something but Madeleine waved for her to come in. The young woman stood at the door. She straightened her shoulders while clutching her new-found gloves. "Madame Vionnet, I just wanted to apologize for some of my colleagues and their prying questions. We're curious about you and, well . . . as reporters it's hard for us to balance respect for privacy and what we do; that is, uncovering stories. I just wanted to say that." She fidgeted with her gloves and held them up. "Well, thank you for finding these," she added before turning to leave.

"My dear, you know we live in our own times. That's all that's given us. We do our best to leave some notion of our lives for the future so I can understand the interest in our personal lives." The young woman listened and nodded, and Madeleine continued haltingly. "But you must live in your time too, not ours."

"Yes, but great histories do not go out of date," the young woman said timidly.

Madeleine smiled and reached for her water. "I can only say that I cherish the experiences in my life. How marvelous to have been alive in such excitement and glamour - and to have loved so deeply." The young woman glanced quickly at Therese and then back to Madeleine. She stood quietly for a moment and nodded slightly before leaving.

"That was nice," Solange said. "You should write that down and include it in the press packet Therese put together. Sensing the silence she gathered some empty glasses and left the room. Therese moved her chair closer to Madeleine and took her hand bringing it to her face.

"That's the first time you've ever said that."

Madeleine studied her face. "Were words necessary?"

"No, not really."

"Therese, will you be alright when I'm gone? Madeleine whispered.

Therese was silent.

The reporters who visited Madeleine had been kind. Therese read the newspaper tributes: one of the most powerful and wealthiest women in France is fading . . . true original of her time . . . valued personal privacy . . . greatest dressmaker of the twentieth century . . . her dresses clung sensuously to the curves of their often-famous wearers . . . and the list went on.

Spring arrived that year with the promise of clear skies and the budding of all that lie dormant but instead, a thick fog hung limp on the trees, in the doorways, and shrouded street lights with halos. She knew her way even though she could barely see through the fog. The call during the night was from Solange. The doctor was there, the ambulance was on its way. When Therese rushed in and saw Madeleine she asked everyone to leave the room. She sat quietly on the edge of the bed.

Madeleine raised her hand to Therese's face, feeling it like blind fingers. "My life seems so far away, Therese," she whispered.

Therese caressed her hand until it dropped softly on the bedclothes. She touched Madeleine's forehead and stroked her hair, now completely white. "Go with it, then. It's alright." She watched each breath taken, first with effort like being pushed heroically from within only to fall again, then more softly. "I'm here," Therese whispered. When she saw Madeleine weaken, saw her shorter breaths, felt her calmness, she knew Madeleine was aware of her presence. Madeleine's hand found Therese's and then fumbling she gripped Therese's wrist, their rhythm, their pulses beating together . . . until just one.

After losing Madeleine, Therese was diagnosed with heart trouble and was heard mumbling, "Heart trouble! Of course I have heart trouble. The doctors think they are so smart." She was in and out of the hospital but carried on with her work, her projects and volunteering until early January in 1978. At her request she was given a private room in the American Hospital in Paris.

On a late Monday afternoon she sat looking outside. The window glass, old and wavy, distorted the rain as it trickled from the roof onto the pane, hesitating before reaching the bottom. She clutched her shawl, the tea untouched sat cool. *The cup is heavy, too heavy.* She sighed and stretched her arm toward the picture on the table letting her hand rest there. Through the haze, the dimness of her vision, the clouds that lay before her, sat her favorite photograph of Madeleine. Her eyes settled there until her hand slid from the table and rested in her lap. She felt a slight shiver before her shoulders dropped and the shawl slid to the floor. *You understood, Madeleine. You knew.* Therese leaned her head against the window but it slid to rest on her shoulder. Her strength faded and merged with the elements like an ocean mixing with sand at the shore, as nature would have it. A cloud draped the window taking the light, and in the distance she heard her mother's voice, and her sister's playing in the yard. She heard the rain dripping from the metal roof and soon, the fresh smell of lilacs and the fine whisper of birds.

While Paris was reborn after the war - as are all great cities - the mood was different, the people not the same, and the nuance of Paris between the wars was lost to new generations, to new ways of being. One thing didn't change however during those years after the war - or for many years after. Every evening at dusk two women, friends, would be seen walking along the river Seine arm in arm, shoulders brushing.

Fin

AFTERWORD

Madeleine and Therese is a work of fiction imagined from the published and archival research available on the lives of Madeleine Vionnet (1876-1975) and Therese Bonney (1894-1978) both living in Paris between the wars. Other characters and events in the book are either based on real people or imagined. The historical information in the novel draws from numerous sources: newspapers, magazine articles, books, interviews, and personal archives documenting Paris between the wars and the unparalleled accomplishments of these two iconic women in history. I've tried to stay close to the historical events and report them accurately. A lack of personal correspondence however, hinders any attempt at a biography of either Madeleine Vionnet or Therese Bonney - but enough exists to imagine their friendship. Both were enormously guarded about their private lives but their friendship was mentioned throughout the decades in ancillary accounts suggesting a closeness over the years. We know they met around 1919 when Therese Bonney photographed Madeleine Vionnet in her salon. We also know that Therese Bonney guarded Vionnet closely in the last years of Vionnet's life fifty-five years later. A timeline of their lives during these decades puts them in close proximity in Paris as do anecdotal accounts.

This project sat on my desk for several years because my forte was writing fiction and non-fiction - and I had concerns about the historical fiction genre: is it fair, is it close enough to seem real, would I get it right? But the storyline never left my thoughts. It was only later when I had an opportunity to visit the many archives and felt I knew these women, their voice, their values, and their strength and courage, that the story came alive for me and poured forth with the passion I imagined they had for Paris, their lives, their work, and each other.

I'm indebted to the helpful archivists, especially those at the Bonney Archives in the Bancroft Library, University of California at Berkeley; the History of Women in America Collection at Radcliffe; the Stein and Toklas Archives at the Beinecke Rare Book and Manuscripts Library, Yale University; the Fashion Institute of Technology, New York, Special Collections, Madeleine Vionnet files; the Cooper-Hewitt National Design Museum, Smithsonian Library, New York; and the National Archives,

Washington, DC (College Park), Department of Defense correspondence regarding Therese Bonney. In addition, a number of other sources were helpful in this research, especially Betty Kirk's pictorial book, *Madeleine Vionnet,* and Pamela Golbin's pictorial book by the same title; also, *The French Century* by Brian Moynahan, and *Americans in Paris: Life and Death Under Nazi Occupation* by Charles Glass - in addition to all of Therese Bonney's articles and works in numerous magazines and newspapers. I am particularly grateful to a small cadre of early readers including Dallas Huth, Joan Putman, Diana Fink, and Sydnee Elliot, along with those on busses, trains, in restaurants and over coffee who eagerly lent an ear and offered suggestions.

ABOUT THE AUTHOR

Hazel Warlaumont is the author of *The Second Translator: A Novel;* and *Advertising in the 60s: Turncoats, Traditionalists and Waste Makers in America's Turbulent Decade;* along with other works examining history and social institutions. She lives and writes on Whidbey Island, Washington.